A Meeting About Laughter

Russian Theatre Archive

A series of books edited by John Freedman (Moscow), Leon Gitelman (St Petersburg) and Anatoly Smeliansky (Moscow)

This book is part of a series. The publisher will accept continuation orders which may be cancelled at any time and which provide for automatic billing and shipping of each title in the series upon publication. Please write for details.

A Meeting About Laughter

Sketches, Interludes and
Theatrical Parodies
by Nikolai Erdman
with Vladimir Mass and Others

translated and edited by

John Freedman

harwood academic publishers
Australia • Austria • China • France • Germany • India • Japan
Luxembourg • Malaysia • Netherlands • Russia • Singapore
Switzerland • Thailand • United Kingdom • United States

Applications for licences to perform the plays should be addressed to the translator, c/o Harwood Academic Publishers GmbH, 3 Boulevard Royal, L-2449 Luxembourg.

Cover illustration: Boris Erdman's caricature of Kasyan Goleizovsky, 1922.

British Library Cataloguing in Publication Data

Erdman, Nikolai
 A Meeting About Laughter: Sketches,
 Interludes and Theatrical Parodies by
 Nikolai Erdman with Vladimir Mass and
 Others.—(Russian Theatre Archive,
 ISSN 1068-8161; Vol. 2)
 I. Title II. Freedman, John III. Series
 891.7242

 ISBN 3-7186-5580-2 (hardback)
 ISBN 3-7186-5581-0 (paperback)

CONTENTS

PLATES
(Between pp. 112 and 113)

1. Nikolai Erdman as a boy.
2. Nikolai Erdman as a boy.
3. Boris and Nikolai Erdman, late 1910s.
4. Nikolai Erdman as a Red Army soldier, 1919.
5. Nikolai Erdman, early 1920s.
6. Portrait of Nikolai and Boris Erdman by P. Galadzhev, 1922.
7. Boris Erdman as an actor in the role of the Nubian in Oscar Wilde's *Salomé* at Alexander Tairov's Kamerny Theater, 1917.
8. Boris Erdman, set designer for the Experimental-Heroic Theater, 1922.
9. A scene from Nikolai Erdman's adaptation of Eugène Labiche's *The Piggy Bank* at the Experimental-Heroic Theater, 1922. Stage design by Boris Erdman.
10. A costume design by Boris Erdman for Kasyan Goleizovsky's *Spanish Dances* at the Kamerny Ballet, 1923.
11. Boris Erdman's costume designs for Kasyan Goleizovsky's *Spanish Dances* at the Kamerny Ballet, 1923.
12. Boris Erdman's caricature of Kasyan Goleizovsky, 1922.
13. Boris Erdman's costume designs for a program of foxtrots, 1923.
14. Boris Erdman's costume design for the clown Vitaly Lazarenko, 1922.
15. (i) Boris Erdman's drawing of the singer Yury Milyutin; (ii) A self caricature of Boris Erdman, 1922.
16. The first page of Nikolai Erdman's manuscript of the circus sketch "The Comradely Court Case at Housing Cooperative No. 1519", 1928.
17. Vladimir Mass, 1926.
18. Caricature of Vladimir Mass by L. Murzen, 1922.
19. Caricature of Vladimir Mass by the famous Kukryniksy brothers, 1933.
20. Caricature of Nikolai Erdman by the famous Kukryniksy brothers, 1933.
21. Vladimir Mass, Nikolai Erdman and Arnold Barsky with two unidentified women, Gagra 1933.
22. Vladimir Mass and Mikhail Volpin, 1950s.
23. Nikolai Erdman and Mikhail Volpin, late 1950s.
24. Drawing of Nikolai Erdman in his later years. Artist: V. Korenin (?).
25. Nikolai Erdman, 1970.

INTRODUCTION TO THE SERIES

The Russian Theatre Archive makes available in English the best avant-garde plays, from the pre-Revolutionary period to the present day. It features monographs on major playwrights and theatre directors, introductions to previously unknown works, and studies of the main artistic groups and periods.

Plays are presented in performing edition translations, including (where appropriate) musical scores, and instructions for music and dance. Whenever possible the translated texts will be accompanied by videotapes of performances of plays in the original language.

INTRODUCTION

Nikolai Erdman spent the evening of December 1, 1938 in the company of Mikhail Bulgakov. According to Bulgakov's wife, the two writers-in-disgrace "racked their brains" in an effort to come up with a plan that might counteract Erdman's reputation as a writer of unreliable tendencies.[1] Earlier in the year, Bulgakov had addressed a letter to Stalin on Erdman's behalf, but it was ignored. Although the author of *The Warrant* and *The Suicide* had completed three years of Siberian exile in October 1936, he still was not allowed to live in Moscow. More importantly, as the notorious author of numerous plays, sketches, librettos and fables which had been banned for their "seditious, counter-revolutionary" nature, Erdman was essentially barred from joining the Writers' Union. That made it virtually impossible for him to make a living as a writer.

Shortly after the nocturnal tête-à-tête at Bulgakov's home, Erdman composed a blatantly obsequious and uncharacteristically bathetic letter which he sent to Alexander Fadeyev, the new chairman of the Writers' Union. The gist of his message was that he was perishing in isolation and that, cognizant of his "guilt" before the authorities, he was ready to put all of his powers "in the service of the great tasks set before art by the Party and the Government."[2] One of the projects he had in mind was his new play, *The Hypnotist,* which he had begun writing in Siberia. However, his plea was no more effective than Bulgakov's letter to Stalin. Erdman was admitted to the Writers' Union only in 1954, a year after Stalin's death and two years before Fadeyev committed suicide.

Erdman's appeal offers a chilling glimpse at the desperate situation of a writer who had run afoul of a hostile, cynical, and manipulative bureaucratic machine. However, it is another document, probably a rough draft of the Fadeyev letter, which reveals with laconic precision the no man's land in which Erdman existed not only after his arrest and exile, but for long before that as well.

"A few years ago," he wrote, "I applied for Latvian citizenship. I did it for reasons of an artistic character. At that time, being a young poet and

---

[1] Yelena Bulgakova, *Dnevnik Yeleny Bulgakovoi* [The Diary of Yelena Bulgakova] (Moscow: Knizhnaya palata, 1990), 227.

[2] Quoted in John Freedman, *Silence's Roar: The Life and Drama of Nikolai Erdman* (Oakville, Canada: Mosaic Press, 1992), 179.

playwright engaged in an extremely difficult technical and formal task, I felt that the contemporary political situation left me no opportunity to develop my experiments. As a result of all my doubts and hesitations, I had come to the painful conclusion that I wasn't needed. However, in the last two years . . . I have come to see that it is impossible to realize any of my ideas without contact with the Soviet Republic."[3]

Erdman well understood that the social, cultural and political milieu surrounding him was hostile to his artistic vision. Yet he also knew that the conflicts, paradoxes, incongruities and—not least of all—the language and skewed logic of that milieu provided the external impulses necessary to giving his vision form. The insurmountable catch was that if *The Warrant, The Suicide* and everything else Erdman created could only be written in "contact with the Soviet Republic," it was their very existence which dictated that *The Hypnotist* would never see the light of day, nor would he ever begin work on another major play. Indeed, as Erdman had foreseen, no one "needed" him or his talent.

A myth has formed that Erdman was a mere two-shot playwright. But, in fact, *The Warrant* and *The Suicide* were the natural outgrowth—and the crowning achievements—of a decade of extremely intense activity. Between 1922 and 1933, Erdman authored or co-authored no less than fifty works for the theater, cabaret, music hall or circus. In 1923, he wrote the scenario for a ballet staged by the legendary choreographer Kasyan Goleizovsky. Some of his song lyrics, written for Moscow's most popular singers in the early 1920s, are still performed today. Between 1926 and 1933, he participated in the creation of six film scripts. The last of them, *Jolly Fellows*, was written with Vladimir Mass, Erdman's friend and frequent collaborator. Under the direction of Grigory Alexandrov, *Jolly Fellows* went down in history as the first great Soviet musical film comedy. Before he turned to the theater, Erdman had made his debut as a poet in 1919 at the tender age of 19, publishing a handful of poems in journals affiliated with the constellation of poets who called themselves Imagists. And even if Sergei Yesenin, the group's leader, was being typically rash when he called Erdman the most promising contemporary poet, there is no denying that these early poetic works bear the distinct mark of talent.

It was the young poet's extraordinary feel for language which first brought an invitation from his fellow-Imagist Vadim Shershenevich to join the Experimental-Heroic Theater in March 1922. There, the director Boris

---

[3] Quoted in Yury Zayats, "Ya prishyol k tyagostnomu ubezhdeniyu, chto ne nuzhen. . . " [I Had Come to the Painful Conclusion that I Wasn't Needed], *Meierkhol'dovsky sbornik*, issue 1, vol. II (Moscow: Tvorchesky tsentr imeni Vs. Meierkhol'da, 1992), 125. Zayats reconstructed this undated text from a manuscript written in such haste (or with such vigilance?) that many of the words were merely signified by abbreviations. I place it as a draft of the Fadeyev letter, based on both style and content.

Ferdinandov was engaged in an ambitious search for new relationships among the key theatrical elements: actor, movement and text. According to a note in the press, Erdman was "assigned to work on the word."[4] He started by composing experimental rehearsal texts, although he soon began writing performance scripts as well.

Virtually all of Erdman's early dramatic texts, most of which have not survived, were topical satires or theatrical parodies. They poked fun at everything from humorless politicians and the moribund style of the realistic theater, to resourceful wheeler-dealers struggling to survive in the burgeoning socialist state and the spectacular innovations of Vsevolod Meyerhold. Besides the Experimental-Heroic Theater, they were performed in venues with such intriguing names as the Buffonade Theater, the No Tears! Cabaret, the Stand-Up Vanka and the Crooked Jimmy, most of which were bastions of daring irreverence frequented by the intellectual elite. Hot on the heels of Meyerhold's controversial première of Fernand Crommelynck's *The Magnanimous Cuckold* in 1922, Erdman wrote a parodical response called "The Nose-Horned Suitor" for the Nikolai Foregger Workshop. In 1923, when Anatoly Lunacharsky called for a return to traditional artistic values with his famous slogan, "Back to Ostrovsky!," Erdman followed with a comical spoof of the same name for the Crooked Jimmy. As soon as the authorities began forcing all performers to appear before special qualification boards in order to cut down on the flood of non-ideological, unprofessional entertainers filling the stages of Moscow's nightclubs, Erdman rejoindered with a two-pronged attack, writing a sketch called "Theatrical Examinations" for the Crooked Jimmy and "The Qualification Exams" for the Palace Theater. The social, political and artistic worlds of Moscow in the early 1920s were caught up in a mad roar of chaotic change, and there could not possibly have been an environment more suited to a young comic writer whose quirky view of the world thrived on dissonance.

The productions of Erdman's early sketches were often performed with sets and costumes designed by his brother. Boris Erdman, who was born in 1899, started out as an actor in Alexander Tairov's Kamerny Theater. But his true calling was as an artist, and he soon became one of the best-known designers in Moscow. Aside from creating numerous sets for the Crooked Jimmy and the Experimental-Heroic Theater, he was the author of what might be called the "Goleizovsky look," a dynamic, highly theatrical and often erotic style of costume. He also created the costume for the Soviet Union's first great circus performer, the clown Vitaly Lazarenko, molding an image that went down in history as a model for modern circus design. During a career that lasted until his death in 1960, Boris worked in nearly all of Moscow's prestigious venues, including the Vakhtangov Theater (where

---

[4] Quoted in *Silence's Roar: The Life and Drama of Nikolai Erdman*, 32.

he designed the set for Nikolai's adaptation of *Lev Gurych Sinichkin* in 1924), The Moscow Art Theater (Yury Olesha's *The Three Fat Men* in 1930), the Maly Theater, the Mayakovsky Theater, the Stanislavsky Theater and many others. Throughout the 1920s, Boris published his drawings and portraits in theater journals, doing much to define the contemporary state of design.

Boris was not only his brother's frequent collaborator, but was also often the indirect object of Nikolai's poisoned barbs. Two works contained in this volume, *The Destruction of Europe on Holy Square* and "The Qualification Exams," take swipes at the various states of undress which became the rage in modern dance due, in large part, to the Kasyan Goleizovsky–Boris Erdman partnership.

Nikolai Erdman epitomized the truth that theater is a collaborative art. He almost never wrote in isolation, either from the directors who would stage his works or from the actors who would perform them. Once he had completed a draft of *The Warrant*, Erdman worked with Meyerhold to bring it to a final version that suited Meyerhold's specific needs. When Erast Garin mounted a short-lived revival of the play in 1956, Erdman altered the original to suit the new circumstances. The same was true of *The Suicide*, which Erdman prepared in different forms to suit the productions planned by Meyerhold, Stanislavsky and others. This does not mean that the play-wright merely fulfilled the orders of others. He was stubbornly true to his own vision, and always insisted that the key elements of his works be left untouched. However, he was willing to mold them into a context that would best serve those artists who would bring them to life on stage.

Erdman's sketches have retained so much of their liveliness because most were written with specific performers in mind. *The Destruction of Europe* and "The Qualification Exams" were composed for the company at the short-lived Palace Theater, led by the popular comic actor, Vladimir Khenkin. The scenes from *Moscow From a Point of View* were constructed around the capabilities of the troupe of the new Theater of Satire, which was formed in 1924 on the basis of the Crooked Jimmy cabaret. Together with Vladimir Mass, Erdman wrote several sketches for Leonid Utyosov, a popular jazz musician, and Alexander Gril, the emcee at Moscow's Music Hall. When composing his circus sketches for Vitaly Lazarenko, Erdman sent a draft of his work to the performer, imploring him to make suggestions for changes: "I'll do everything you consider necessary," he wrote.[5]

When composing topical works, Erdman often worked with a co-author. "Theatrical Examinations," the text of which is unknown, was written for and with the variety actor and director Alexei Alexeyev. In 1924, when the playwright Nikolai Lvov was working at the Theater of Expressionism, he

---

[5] The undated letter is held in the Russian State Archive of Literature and Art (RGALI), fond 2087, opis' 1, delo 132.

engaged Erdman to write a short, verse play spoofing the domestic rituals of pre- and post-revolutionary Russia. The result was a two-act play called *Housekeeping Bondage,* the authorship of which is shared by both writers. When the director David Gutman began making plans to found the new Theater of Satire, he enlisted several authors to help him compose a satirical play about the misadventures of a family of country bumpkins who are overwhelmed by the mayhem of life in Moscow. Thus came about the legendary *Moscow From a Point of View,* written by Gutman, Viktor Tipot, Vladimir Mass and Erdman. Even Erdman's adaptation of Dmitry Lensky's 19th-century vaudeville, *Lev Gurych Sinichkin,* can be viewed, in a sense, as a collaborative work. Using the original as a springboard, he refocused the play for a modern audience, outfitting it with satirical songs and inserting an original sketch on topical themes.

Erdman wrote several redactions of the interlude for *Sinichkin.* The most detailed account of the original version from 1924, which apparently has been lost, can be found in the memoirs of the actor Leonid Shikhmatov.[6] Updated versions followed at least in 1928, 1929 and 1932, the latter of which was largely a melange of the Erdman–Mass sketches, "The Tragedy of Hamlet, Prince of the Danes" and "The Work Whistle, or the Stomach Incision."[7] There may have been more, since *Sinichkin* was performed every season at the Vakhtangov Theater from 1924 to 1934. The version translated in this volume can be dated to 1929, based on, among other things, a reference to "the twelfth year of the revolution" in the opening monologue. Echoing a "genre" which was in vogue—and mandatory—at that time, it is an anti-religious broadside. However, as is typical of an Erdman text, it is virtually impossible to tell what comes in for more ridicule; religion or the concerted efforts to discredit it.

Although Nikolai Erdman and Vladimir Mass first joined forces in 1924 with *Moscow From a Point of View,* it was not until 1929 that they would come to be known as a team. The première at the Leningrad Music Hall of their satirical revue, *The Odyssey,*[8] a wild burlesque of Homer's poem, signalled the start of a partnership that was as fruitful as it was short and, ultimately, scandalous. During the next four years, they penned six full-length revues for the music hall, numerous short sketches and interludes, and wrote dozens of wickedly satirical fables which ultimately served as a pretext for their arrest in 1933. All of the revues, which were modernized burlesques of classical literary or operatic works, and many of the sketches were subjected

---

[6] *Ot studii k teatru* [From Studio to Theater] (Moscow: VTO, 1970), 144-151.

[7] This is the version which is published in the collection, Nikolai Erdman, *P'esy, intermedii, pis'ma, dokumenty, vospominaniya sovremennikov* [Plays, Interludes, Letters, Documents, Memoirs of Contemporaries] (Moscow: Iskusstvo, 1990). However, the editors erroneously dated it to 1924 instead of 1932.

[8] Also known as *Odysseus.*

to withering attacks from the censor. Despite constant rewrites, few of them were performed more than a handful of times. After returning from exile, they never again wrote together, although from time to time some of their old, short works were performed in the circus or variety theaters.

Born in 1896, Mass was four years Erdman's senior and already had something of a reputation by the time the two first met in 1922 while writing for the Foregger Workshop. His "buffonade," based on Vladimir Mayakovsky's poem, *A Good Attitude to Horses,* had been a critical and popular success when it premiered at the Workshop on New Year's Eve 1921–22. Throughout the 1920s, he produced a large number of short, agit-prop and/or satirical plays, while also working as the literary director in various theaters and as the co-editor-in-chief of the magazine, *The New Spectator.* For a short while, he was Meyerhold's literary director when the latter was artistic director at the Realistic Theater. From the 1940s to the mid-1960s, Mass most often wrote in tandem with Mikhail Chervinsky. This duo created many of the Soviet Union's most popular light comedies. Following Chervinsky's death in 1965, Mass devoted most of his energies to poetry and painting. He died in 1979.

Without slighting Mass's contribution to the Erdman–Mass works, we can state with authority that Erdman was the moving artistic force in the partnership. When asked in the 1970s about the collective work on *Moscow From a Point of View,* Mass himself noted that the other authors "couldn't keep up" with Erdman.[9] Of the seven scenes in *Moscow From a Point of View,* it has been established that the second, "The Room in Which They Rented an Apartment," was written by Erdman alone. He clearly made major contributions to most of the other scenes. Erdman is also the sole author of another scene, "The Self-Taught Communist," which was not part of the original play. Based on several of its references to current events, it can be dated approximately to 1925.

The notion that Erdman took the lead in his co-authored works is further supported by a study of the surviving Erdman–Mass manuscripts. They reveal that Erdman composed most of the texts himself in his unique, calligraphic handwriting and that Mass essentially worked as an editor, adding introductions and conclusions, and occasionally deleting segments of the text or rearranging it in regards to the characters. Most convincing of all is the picture which arises from a comparison of the texts written jointly with those which each of the authors wrote on his own. Mass clearly had a flair for breezy humor and lively dialogue, but none of his works contain the spectacular structural convolutions that distinguish an Erdman text.

---

[9] Quoted in Yelizaveta Uvarova, "Nikolai Erdman, Vladimir Mass, Mikhail Chervinsky," an article in *Moskva s tochki zreniya: Estradnaya dramaturgiya 20–60-kh godov* [Moscow From a Point of View: Variety Drama from the '20s to the '60s] (Moscow: Iskusstvo, 1991), 70.

It is conceivable that Mass, who was a highly respected figure, suggested the idea of teamwork to help shield a writer for whom he had a great respect. By 1929, *The Warrant* had begun attracting serious criticism, and rumor already had it that the working edition of *The Suicide* was a potential bombshell. The irony is that when the authorities resolved to put an end to Erdman's career, Mass was arrested along with him.

The year before their arrest, 1932, was a very productive period for the pair. In addition to working on the script for *Jolly Fellows,* they wrote two sets of interludes for productions at the Vakhtangov Theater, and numerous sketches for the Satire Theater.

The interludes for Carlo Gozzi's *Princess Turandot* were intended to update a production that had been running since 1922. Announcements in the press indicate that Erdman wrote the first interludes to *Turandot* on his own in 1928, although the only surviving texts, of which there are three, date to the 1932 Erdman–Mass collaborations. The present volume includes one which can be identified only tentatively as the first scene of Act II. The others were omitted because one is so steeped in now-arcane topical references, while the other is incomplete.[10] But the interlude translated here, brimming with a mix of bold political satire and acidic theatrical parody, is an excellent example of the way the authors modernized the text while retaining the sparkling spirit of the original.

The interludes for *Hamlet,* of which there were at least three, accompanied a controversial new staging by the then-unknown Nikolai Akimov.[11] He would subsequently become one of the Soviet Union's leading directors and designers. Akimov sought to provide a contemporary reading of Shakespeare's classic by turning the contemplative Hamlet into an engaged man of action. The interludes by Erdman and Mass preserved the traditional image of a doubting Hamlet, while also making of him something of an astute, comic observer of modern Soviet life. These scenes are especially interesting when considered in light of the controversy which was raging around *The Suicide* at that time. It does not require a leap of imagination to espy the subterranean link between Aristarkh's claim in *The Suicide* that "only a dead man can say what a live man thinks," and Rosencrantz's musings on the literary topic of the living and the dead. Furthermore, Rosencrantz's observation that modern playwrights prefer to avoid writing

---

[10] See point 18 in A Note on Translation and Texts.

[11] Fragments of a fourth interlude, intended for the middle of Act II, scene two, exist in typescript, although there is no way of knowing whether it was ever completed or used. The editors of Nikolai Erdman, *Plays, Interludes, etc.* omit the third interlude included in the present volume. One recent scholar has suggested that these interludes were never performed. See V. Mironova, "'Gamlet' po-akimovski" ["Hamlet" à la Akimov], in *V sporakh o teatre*, ed. David Zolotnitsky (St. Petersburg, Rossiiskii institut istorii iskusstv, 1992), 19.

new plays in favor of reworking old ones (echoing a theme Erdman and Mass had already treated in one of their music hall sketches in 1931), was much more than a mere sideswipe at those contemporary writers who were lying low in turbulent political times by churning out dramatizations of the classics. As early as 1930, Erdman had written to a friend about his own fears that he had already said his "farewells to Soviet Theater."[12] In a few brief strokes, the interludes for *Hamlet* dramatically fix the state of cultural affairs in the Soviet Union in 1932.

Meanwhile, Akimov's *Hamlet* was ridiculed so vociferously for its unorthodox approach, that Erdman and Mass could not resist writing their own parody of it. "The Tragedy of Hamlet, Prince of the Danes" was intended to top the bill of an evening of theatrical parodies at the Satire Theater just months after the première of *Hamlet.* But if this merciless lampoon of a friend and colleague was a pure theatrical spoof, the thematics of the three other segments in the program once again tipped the scales into the realm of social commentary. "The Work Whistle, or the Stomach Incision," "A Meeting About Laughter," and "New People, New Songs" paint a cutting picture of the convulsions wracking Soviet society in the early 1930s. Probably because of troubles with the censor, these parodies were never performed. And, while Erdman had no qualms about reusing his favorite segments in various works, the failure of these sketches to make it to the stage may explain why the 1932 version of the interlude for *Lev Gurych Sinichkin* is essentially a mix of the beginning of "The Tragedy of Hamlet" and "The Work Whistle."

"A Meeting About Laughter" occupies a special place in Erdman's œuvre. It was the first of his dramatic works to be published with only minor cuts, appearing in the miscellany *The Sixteenth Year* almost simultaneously with the arrest of Erdman and Mass in October 1933. Not surprisingly, it was subsequently excised from future editions. More importantly, the sketch is clearly a farcical—and bitter—response to the attacks on *The Suicide,* which, by that time, had been banned twice. A comparison of "Meeting" with the extraordinary transcript of the discussion of *The Suicide* at the Vakhtangov Theater in 1930 (included in the appendix of this volume) reveals that Erdman gleefully parodied the tortured attempts of the theater's semi-literate ideologues to couch their criticism in a logical, "educated" form. Certainly, there is nothing coincidental about the similarities between the speaker in "A Meeting About Laughter," who refuses to laugh without the sanction of an official resolution, and the numerous speakers at the Vakhtangov Theater who praised the comic talent of *The Suicide* while haranguing its author for being everything from unprincipled to seditious. Moreover, the absurd list of banned types of laughter which concludes "A

---

[12] Quoted in *Silence's Roar: The Life and Drama of Nikolai Erdman,* 3.

Meeting" reads more than suspiciously like the lists of offending lines in *The Suicide* which were trotted out by several of the speakers at the Vakhtangov.

The Suicide and "A Meeting About Laughter" are further bound together by the fact that, at the behest of Maxim Gorky, it was the former of them which was originally slated to be published in *The Sixteenth Year*. In retrospect, Gorky's belief in that possibility can only be considered a mild form of madness. The discussion at the Vakhtangov Theater, the likes of which Erdman termed a "glorious literary debate" in the first interlude for *Hamlet*, was, itself, a sinister and humorless "meeting about laughter." It could not have left any doubt that, by the 1930s, comedy in the Soviet Union was a doomed enterprise. Erdman's "affection" for this shocking document is borne out by the fact that it is one of only a handful of official documents he preserved in his personal archive. He frequently returned to it as a source for parody in his sketches and in what was to have been his third full-length play, *The Hypnotist*.

Erdman worked sporadically on *The Hypnotist* throughout his years of exile, finally abandoning it only in the early 1940s. The few remaining letters which he wrote to family and friends indicate that he had high hopes for the play, while instinctively realizing that the chances of anything coming of it were slim indeed. Still, it would appear that he completed at least a working draft, because, at one point, he informed Meyerhold that he had written a new play for him. When he happened upon a group of actors from the Moscow Art Theater in Saratov in 1941, he reportedly read them the entire work. He even signed contracts with the Vakhtangov and Moscow Art Theaters for productions of the play in 1940 and 1941, respectively. But, be that as it may, *The Hypnotist* was never performed, and all that survives of it now are two variants of the first three scenes. When he abandoned *The Hypnotist*, Erdman essentially abandoned the theater for good. From that time until his death in 1970 he found a safe haven writing scripts for animated and feature films, often with his new co-author, Mikhail Volpin. It is worth noting that the vast majority of these films (over 45 of them) were of an extremely high quality and several of them are now recognized as classics. However, the fact remains: a born playwright was forcibly and incontrovertibly driven out of the theater.

During most of the Second World War Erdman and Volpin were employed in a curious organization called the Song and Dance Ensemble of the NKVD (that is, the Soviet secret police). The Ensemble's primary purpose was to put on theatrical extravaganzas to boost the morale of Soviet troops. In addition to constructing the overall scenarios of the programs, Erdman and Volpin also wrote short sketches and interludes which tied the various segments together. One of the sketches, "Private Schultz," was widely performed throughout the Soviet Union by amateur theatrical groups. Despite its heavily jingoistic flavor—natural enough under the circumstances—

"Private Schultz" is notable both for its display of Erdman's typical stylistics and for some thinly-veiled references to the author's own biography. In it the hapless private tells of an unfortunate lance corporal who, similar to Erdman, was arrested for writing riddles, while the running jokes about the calming effects of cognac and vodka hint at Erdman's own favorite method of distancing himself from the grim reality of his life.

Two works from the early 1950s stand as minor monuments to what the Soviet ideologists wrought in crushing Erdman's career as it was only beginning, and to what Soviet theater lost as a result. In 1954, Erdman teamed up with Yakov Ziskind to write "On Laughter," a tiny sketch intended for inclusion in variety shows. While its title begs comparison to the biting "A Meeting About Laughter," and the text's structure bears the inimitable Erdman stamp, the piece is little more than a toothless humorous gag. It was as though a great painter had been reduced to whitewashing garden fences for a living. And yet there could be no doubt that the playwright had lost none of his powers. His interludes for a production of *The Two Gentlemen of Verona* at the Vakhtangov Theater in 1952 were a spectacular miniature display of all the Erdmanesque devices; an ultra-smooth blend of lyricism, farce, compound word play and the paradoxical development of action. But, as was fitting for a masterful artist who had been turned forcibly into an anonymous fence-painter, the interludes were only allowed to be performed once it was agreed that Erdman's name would not appear in the posters or programs for the production.

Erdman spent his final years in close contact with Yury Lyubimov, acting as a kind of spiritual advisor for the Taganka Theater which was formed in 1964. The theater's second production, a dramatization of Mikhail Lermontov's *A Hero of Our Time,* was written by Lyubimov and Erdman together. In 1968, Lyubimov asked Erdman to write interludes for a production he was preparing of Sergei Yesenin's dramatic poem, *Pugachyov,* about the notorious cossack who led a rebellion against Catherine the Great. Erdman tackled the task with the same dedication and fine attention to detail that marked everything he did. His notebooks reveal that he read extensively in the literature of the 18th century, collecting obscure names, facts and figures which gave him the opportunity to create a context of authenticity. Meanwhile, he reshaped that information into two brilliant scenes whose portrayal of Russian life was as universal as it was comic and "historically correct." In a sense, this project reunited Erdman with two of his earliest colleagues: Yesenin, who had been among the first to discern talent in the nineteen-year-old poet, and Meyerhold, who had hoped at one time to stage *Pugachyov* himself. It also could not have helped but remind him of the scandal *The Suicide* caused at the Meyerhold Theater. Under the pretext that they were "unworthy" literary creations, the Soviet Ministry of Culture banned the performance of the last dramatic works Erdman was to write.

* * *

Theatrical performances are the most fragile and intangible of all the art forms. We can listen to the music of the great composers, we can read the prose and poetry of the great writers, we can peruse the paintings of the great artists and we can watch the great films. But, once the great theatrical productions close, they are gone forever. Nikolai Erdman's early sketches and parodies are important for drawing back, ever so slightly, the curtain on a lost era. They are saturated with minute details that brilliantly reflect the colorful and contradictory collage of Moscow theater in the 1920s and early 1930s. Perhaps nothing can recreate with such flavor the rollicking atmosphere of the cabarets as *The Destruction of Europe* or "The Qualification Exams." Meanwhile, "The Self-Taught Communist," "A Meeting About Laughter" and the interludes for *Lev Gurych Sinichkin, Hamlet* and *Princess Turandot* portray the killing influence which politics began exerting on art after 1925 with an immediacy no history book of Soviet theater can duplicate.

But, beyond the historical interest they provide, Erdman's short texts are valuable for the considerable light they shed on his thematic interests and his unique compositional style, or, as he put it, the "extremely difficult technical and formal task" he had set himself. Even a cursory comparison of *The Warrant, The Suicide* and the sketches reveals a good deal of cross-pollination among them. Names, situations and even individual textual blocks recur from one work to the next. This is hardly surprising, since such works as "The Qualification Exams," *The Destruction of Europe* and *The Warrant* were not only written simultaneously, they were occasionally written on the same pieces of paper. As Erdman was neatly composing scenes for his first film script, *Mitya,* on one side of the paper, he was laying out scenes for *The Suicide* on the other. Note also, for example, the striking similarity between Act III, scene four of *The Destruction of Europe,* where a group of people barge into Georges Krasikov's apartment making demands, and Act II, scene three of *The Suicide*, where Aristarkh rudely intrudes on Podsekalnikov at an awkward moment. Such echoes abound throughout all of Erdman's compositions. It is evident that, regardless of whether he was working on a topical sketch which was intended to have localized resonance, or whether he was writing a full-length play which was intended to treat timeless and universal themes, the writer was invariably grappling with a specific set of structural problems.

On one level, Erdman created fine-tuned imitations of the clumsy speech patterns which entered the Russian language when, after the revolution, semi-literate workers and peasants were raised to the status of cultural models. But, within this context, he was also working toward a more fundamental problem: the way language itself is capable of dictating the flow of discourse. He took the traditional assumption—that a person generates a thought and then selects the proper linguistic form in which to express it—and he turned it around. This was not merely a clever literary device, but was a fundamentally new, essentially philosophical, approach to the laws that determine or, at least, help explain human behavior. In "The Qualification Exams," one can almost hear the echoes of Erdman's own voice in that of the Balladeer, who states: "If you say, 'Who in the hell needs it?' any conscious citizen will tell you right off: 'Absolutely no one'." The Balladeer understands "instinctively" what Erdman understood intellectually: in order to cause a specific response, one needs only to program the question properly. Once that is done, any subsequent progression of ideas or actions is predictable, at least within a certain range.

More than anything else, Erdman's dramaturgical forays into the realm of behavior are probably what caused such a hostile reaction to his plays. He had touched on something that presented a threat to those who increasingly were taking control of the arts in the 1920s. After all, their purpose was to hasten the appearance of a new kind of human being who would abandon the "old-fashioned habit" of self-preservation and would put him or herself in the service of a state which, itself, would now take responsibility for the welfare of the individual. In other words, at a time when what amounted to a mass experiment in behavior control was just getting under way, Erdman appeared with a profusion of dramatic works, one of whose purposes was to chip away at the mysteries of why people behave as they do. Naturally, no one took the time—or had the sentience—actually to analyze what was so objectionable in his work. It was more than enough simply to focus on lines such as "I read Marx and I didn't like him"—from *The Suicide*—or the satirical swipes at Stalin in "The Qualification Exams." The transcript of the discussion of *The Suicide* at the Vakhtangov Theater makes it clear that the ideologues realized they had seized a tiger by the tail, but they did not know what to make of him. To be safe, they simply forbade the production of his plays.

None of that means, as many continue to believe, that Erdman specifically directed his writings against the Soviet state. There is no doubting that, as any other writer, he created his strange dramatic worlds out of the material provided him by the society in which he lived. But defining him as a dissident or politically oriented writer is akin to defining the shape of one's profile based on the shadow it casts on a crooked wall. Erdman's reputation as a "political writer" was created by politicians, bureaucrats and ideologues who saw politics in everything, whether it be literature or cooking (as in the famous, so-called Stalinist, cookbook, *A Book on Tasty and Healthy Food*). They were the ones who defined his image and then stamped out his career almost before it had begun. And since no one who knew better had the opportunity to counteract this distortion of the truth, it is that false image which, as if in a perverse imitation of one of Erdman's own plays, has come to be accepted as the rule. The truth is that Erdman was involved in an attempt to define the elusive boundaries which lie between experience and our perceptions of it.

That was one of the "whys" of Erdman's drama. But what about the no less ambitious "hows"? Even today, among those who have written about, talked about, or staged Erdman's works, there is little more than a vague suspicion that they contain much more than meets the eye. And yet, the grounds on which to build understanding are there. Two Russian directors who, in the late 1980s, produced very different, but equally boring versions of *The Suicide,* have offered some valuable insights into Erdman's approach.

Speaking of the "philosophy of Erdman's language," Yevgeny Simonov, who also directed *The Two Gentleman of Verona* in 1952, recalled a conversation he once had with the playwright. Said Erdman, "I select every word as though with a pair of tweezers, and I carefully weigh it as if on scales. When I write I try to sense the proportionality of the words, and I weigh each of them as though I were weighing a spider web."[13]

Valentin Pluchek, who began as an actor in Meyerhold's theater and is now the artistic director at the Theater of Satire, expanded on that theme. "If we grant that art is selection," he told me, "then Erdman displays brilliant word selection. . . . Remember that he was a poet before he was a playwright. Erdman displays brilliant musical, rhythmic and thematic word selection. Like any great artist, he has his own unique inner musicality. His monologues for the intellectual and particularly for the writer [respectively, Aristarkh Dominikovich and Viktor Viktorovich in *The Suicide*] are exemplars of perfected musical, rhythmic coordination."[14]

Indeed, everything Erdman wrote—whether it be *The Suicide* or his letters to his mother—abounds in puns, plays on sounds and multi-layered or multi-directional progressions in which the punch lines of his humor crackle in clusters like strings of fireworks. His works are not a mere collection of individual jokes or humorous incidents. They are the sum of a proliferation of interconnected parts, all of which are intended to work towards a common goal, whether that is to elicit laughter or to illuminate one of the works' themes. In this regard Erdman once told Yevgeny Simonov that he understood the ideal of comedy to be "the preparation for one line in which everything would come together."[15] Even as early as 1923 Vadim Shershenevich had already isolated the key characteristics of an Erdman text. In a review of *The Six-Story Adventure,* a five-act play whose text is unknown, he wrote: [Erdman] "has a marvelous (and more so: rare) understanding of *theatricality. . . .* Not a single *trick is wasted.* The tempo

---

[13] Quoted in *Silence's Roar: The Life and Drama of Nikolai Erdman,* 10.

[14] Quoted in *Silence's Roar: The Life and Drama of Nikolai Erdman,* 10.

[15] Quoted in *Silence's Roar: The Life and Drama of Nikolai Erdman,* 11.

of plot development is eccentric. The witticisms are not linguistic, but collisional."[16]

If we are to accept the definition of the theater of the absurd as, in part, "the rigidity of logic, leading to ridiculous conclusions" and "skepticism about the meaning of language,"[17] then it is fair to say that Erdman was a forerunner to that manner of dramatic writing which flourished in the middle of the twentieth century. In fact, both of these attributes can serve as brief definitions of Erdman's drama itself.[18]

One might suggest that Erdman replaced the logic of language with his own peculiar logic of words. His dialogue seldom develops traditionally according to the primary meaning of a given utterance, but rather progresses in unexpected directions as the result of the repercussions which a single word or its derivatives have on the discourse. For example, a gaily wandering exchange in one of the sketches Erdman and Mass wrote for the music hall is loosely tethered to the notions of "writer" and "writing":

WRITER. Allow me to introduce myself. Fyodor Semyonovich Korzhikov, famous Russian writer.

EMCEE. What have you written?

WRITER. That's a strange question. I haven't written anything.

EMCEE. Then why do you say you're a famous Russian writer?

WRITER. You mean you think a writer becomes famous because he writes? A writer becomes famous because others write about him.

EMCEE. Has anyone written about you?

WRITER. Yes.

EMCEE. What did they write about you?

WRITER. That I am the hope of Soviet literature.

EMCEE. How can anyone consider you the hope of Soviet literature if you haven't written anything?

WRITER. Just for that very reason. If I were to write anything, there would be no hope left.

Words in Erdman's texts frequently take on a life of their own, forcing the characters to respond to unwanted or unexpected consequences. In the

---

[16] Quoted in *Silence's Roar: The Life and Drama of Nikolai Erdman,* 35. The italics are Shershenevich's.

[17] Martin Banham, ed., *The Cambridge Guide to Theatre* (Cambridge: University Press, 1992), 989.

[18] Two scholars have recently pointed out that the "eccentric" and "parodical" nature of Erdman's drama links it closely to the Oberiu group of writers, the so-called Russian absurdists of the 1920s. See N. Tarshis and B. Konstriktor, "Istoricheskaya tema u oberiutov" [The Oberiu Writers and the Historical Theme], in *V sporakh o teatre,* ed. David Zolotnitsky (St. Petersburg, Rossiiskii institut istorii iskusstv, 1992), 114.

following excerpt from the interlude to *Lev Gurych Sinichkin,* a character by the name of Pustoslavtsev (Mr Vainglory) is amazed when he is told that "an introductory word isn't such a terrible thing":

> What do you mean a word isn't terrible? A word isn't a sparrow. Let it out and you'll never catch it again. See? You let it out, you don't catch it, and for that they catch you and don't let you out.

Naturally, such an observation was fully intended to strike a political chord. However, it is no less noteworthy for its deft construction in which the original speaker's casual reference to the notions of "word" and "terrible" is suddenly sent careening in an unexpected direction. This brief passage might even be viewed as a distillation of Erdman's own skepticism of and respect for the power of the word. When words are either misunderstood or abused, they can acquire a deeply deceptive, misleading force.

This is evident, in purely farcical form, in *The Destruction of Europe,* where everything that takes place is called into being, as it were, by a single word which is tossed off in unthinking haste. (The same is true of both *The Warrant* and *The Suicide,* although they use the device to a much more complex purpose.) Georges Krasikov wants his beloved Marya to go home with him, but she keeps putting him off " 'til tomorrow." Georges moans that "tomorrow there may be a flood or an earthquake," to which Marya replies she would be happy to go with him in the event of a catastrophe; but an earthquake in Moscow is an impossibility. This flippant response prompts Georges to spread a rumor that a flood is bearing down on Moscow by way of the North Pole and Europe. The rest of the play depicts the improbable adventures of a colorful crew of Muscovites who scramble to avoid perishing in the impending flood.

Similar absurdities take on "real" form in many other sketches. In "The Room in Which They Rented an Apartment"—the reversal of logic is apparent in the very title—people live in spitoons and on other people's feet. In "The Self-Taught Communist" and "The People vs. Vitaly Lazarenko," characters are forced to pay child support on the evidence of a worn-out pair of pants. In "Private Schultz," a simple-minded soldier "proves" that children are born of correspondence. In all of these cases, the word does not so much describe a reality as it actually creates one, at least in so far as the world of the work is concerned.

Finally, there is in Erdman's work a veritable fountain of pure mirth for mirth's sake. He relished a well-turned comic phrase for the joy of the sounds it created or the strange associations it called up. In his constant pursuit for humor in language he often jotted down lists of funny-sounding words and phrases. His fetish for jokes about pants started with his earliest sketches in the 1920s and continued on unabated through *The Suicide* and his interludes for *Pugachyov* in 1968. This was probably a form of self-parody, since he carefully cultivated his image as one of Moscow's most stylish and best-dressed writers.

Naturally, none of the sketches contained in this volume can or should be considered on the same terms as *The Warrant* and *The Suicide.* They were written with a different purpose, for different reasons and for a very different audience. But Erdman's short works served, in the early years, as a kind of workshop for his experimental ideas, while, in the later years, they served as a rare outlet for a playwright who was reduced to letting his best ideas fade away as passing thoughts. And, in addition to being minor gems of dramatic writing, all of them provide various-shaped keys that can help us unlock the many complex mysteries contained in his two major plays.[19]

JOHN FREEDMAN
Moscow, 1994

---

[19] I would like to express my deep gratitude to Anna Vladimirovna Mass, who kindly made available to me her father's archives, from which half of the texts in this volume have been culled.

A NOTE ON TRANSLATION AND TEXTS

Nikolai Erdman's heavy use of compound puns, substandard speech, convoluted "educated" or "bureaucratic" phrases, garbled literary quotes and subtle cultural references make his dramatic compositions some of the most spectacular in the Russian language. Even as topical as most of the texts in the present volume are, they still have an extraordinary power to delight audiences. Performances in 1994 of excerpts from "The Qualification Exams," the interludes for *Turandot* and the interludes for *Pugachyov* by Moscow's Theater "Moderne," were accompanied from beginning to end by what Erdman himself probably would have called "Homeric guffaws."

However, for just those reasons, a translator in moments of despair is justified in wondering whether Erdman wrote expressly in order to confound translation. Literal translations often make nonsense. Mere interpretations of meaning destroy the texture of the original. Ignoring the endless malapropisms ruins the mood and flattens the personalities of the characters. In making these (American) English texts, I have done my best to do what is probably impossible: to be both creative and faithful in equal measure. If the translations do not breathe with the effervescent, poetic and lyrical wit that Erdman commanded with such brilliance, I hope that, at least, they are intriguing, well-defined shadows of some of the funniest and most theatrical dramatic texts ever written in Russian. I cannot help but humbly beg the indulgence of the reader in those instances where I may have sinned against style and/or taste. I am extremely grateful to Julie A. E. Curtis whose careful and knowledgeable readings of the translations steered me clear of some silly errors. Naturally, any infelicities that remain are my sole responsibility.

None of the thirty texts published in this volume has appeared in English; twelve have never been published in Russian or any other language; thirteen have been published in Russian in full, while five have been published in Russian with cuts, or in significantly different versions than those found here. Since many of the Russian publications have been rather carelessly done, I translated from the original manuscripts or typescripts whenever possible. For the interested reader's reference I list below the sources for my translations and the Russian publication information.

1. *The Destruction of Europe on Holy Square.* Translated from a typescript held at the Russian State Archive of Literature and Art (RGALI), fond 2019 (Vladimir Khenkin), opis' 1, delo 53; unpublished.

2. "The Qualification Exams." Translated from Grigory Faiman's publication in Russian in *Teatr*, No. 5 (1989): 114–118. My occasional references in the notes to another version are to an unpublished typescript which was kindly put at my disposal by Yelizaveta Uvarova.

3. "The Room in Which They Rented an Apartment." Translated from a typescript of *Moscow From a Point of View* which was given to me by Galina Poltavskaya of the Satire Theater; published in Russian with large cuts in Yelizaveta Uvarova, ed., *Moskva s tochki zreniya: Estradnaya dramaturgiya 20–60-kh godov* (Moscow: Iskusstvo, 1991): 337–340.

4. "The Self-Taught Communist." Translated from a typescript held at RGALI, fond 2570 (Erdman), opis' 1, delo 12; unpublished.

5. "The Comradely Court Case at Housing Cooperative No. 1519." Translated from a typescript in the personal archive of Anna Mass; unpublished.

6–7. "The People vs. Vitaly Lazarenko" and "The Divorce." Translated from manuscripts held at RGALI, fond 2570 (Erdman), opis' 1, delo 126; unpublished.

8. An Interlude for *Lev Gurych Sinichkin.* Translated from a typescript in the personal archive of Anna Mass; essentially unpublished. An entirely different version (corresponding roughly to the sketches, "The Tragedy of Hamlet, Prince of the Danes" and "The Work Whistle, or the Stomach Incision") is published in Russian under an incorrect date in Nikolai Erdman, *P'esy, intermedii, pis'ma, dokumenty, vospominaniya sovremennikov* (Moscow: Iskusstvo, 1990): 173–185.

9–13. Five interludes for *The Two Gentlemen of Verona.* Translated from manuscripts and typescripts in the personal archive of Anna Mass; published in Russian with incorrect textual placement information in Nikolai Erdman, *P'esy, intermedii, . . . :* 204–216.

14–15. Two interludes for *Pugachyov.* Translated from Grigory Faiman's publication in Russian in *Teatr*, No. 5 (1989): 121–124.

16. First music hall number. Translated from a manuscript in the personal archive of Anna Mass; unpublished.

17. Second music hall number. Translated from a typescript in the personal archive of Anna Mass; published in Russian in a significantly different version in Yelizaveta Uvarova, ed., *Moskva s tochki zreniya, . . . :* 216–218.

18. An interlude for *Princess Turandot.* Translated from a typescript in the personal archive of Anna Mass; published in Russian as the second of three *Turandot* interludes in Nikolai Erdman, *P'esy, intermedii, . . . :* 195–200. For the record, the third interlude published in that volume (but not translated here) is missing an entire page in the middle, a detail which went unnoticed by the editors. The break occurs in the last line on page 201, between the words *blagorodstvu* and *kakoi-to.* The former, which is part of a verse construction, concludes page 8 of the typescript. The latter, which is part of a prose

dialogue, begins page 10 of the typescript. The editors of Nikolai Erdman, *P'esy, etc.* inserted the word *iz-za* and squeezed the two segments into prose in order to make bare sense of gibberish.

19–20. First two interludes for *Hamlet.* Translated from typescripts and manuscripts in the personal archive of Anna Mass; published in Russian in Nikolai Erdman, *P'esy, intermedii, . . . :* 186–191.

21. Third interlude for *Hamlet.* Translated from a typescript and manuscript in the personal archive of Anna Mass; unpublished.

22. "The Tragedy of Hamlet, Prince of the Danes." Translated from a typescript in the personal archive of Anna Mass; published in Russian, with small lacunae, by Anna Mass in *Voprosy literatury,* No. 5 (1989): 249–263. The introduction is very similar to the introduction in the interlude for *Lev Gurych Sinichkin,* published in Nikolai Erdman, *P'esy, intermedii, . . . :* 173–185.

23. "The Work Whistle, or the Stomach Incision." Translated from a manuscript held at RGALI, fond 2019 (Vladimir Khenkin), opis' 1, delo 53; published in Russian, in different form, as part of an interlude for *Lev Gurych Sinichkin* in Nikolai Erdman, *P'esy, intermedii, . . . :* 173–185.

24. "A Meeting About Laughter." Translated from a typescript in the personal archive of Anna Mass; published in Russian, with small lacunae, in the miscellany *God XVI* (1st edition only!), (Moscow: Sovetskaya literatura, 1933). Reprinted by Anna Mass in *Voprosy literatury,* No. 1 (1988): 261–266, and in Yelizaveta Uvarova, ed., *Moskva s tochki zreniya, . . . :* 219–223.

25. "New People, New Songs." Translated from a manuscript held at RGALI, fond 2019 (Vladimir Khenkin), opis' 1, delo 53; unpublished.

26. "Private Schultz." Translated from the Russian publication, N. Erdman and M. Volpin, *Ryadovoy Shul'ts: Sketch.* (Moscow: Otdel rasprostraneniya VUOAP, 1942). The sketch was also published in *Estradny sbornik-kontsert* (Vladivostok: Primorskoe kraevoe upravlenie izdatel'stv i poligrafii, 1942) and *Sbornik stsen i sketchei* (Novosibirsk: OGIZ, 1942).

27. "On Laughter." Translated from the Russian publication in *Repertuarny sbornik,* vyp. 4 (Moscow: Goskul'tprosvetizdat, 1954): 70–72.

28. Transcript of a discussion of *The Suicide* at the Vakhtangov Theater. Translated from a typescript held at RGALI, fond 2570 (Erdman), opis' 1, delo 139; unpublished.

29–30. Two fragments from *The Hypnotist.* Translated from photostatic copies of manuscripts made available to me by Andrea Gotzes; unpublished.

Works by Nikolai Erdman

.

The Destruction of Europe on Holy Square

WITH DANCES AND SONGS

1924

CHARACTERS

GEORGES KRASIKOV
MARYA PETROVNA — also called Marusya
THE FEVERISH GENTLEMAN [1]
SONYA GULYACHKINA — Marya Petrovna's friend
THE INDIAN GUEST
HIS SERVANT
THE CAFÉ OWNER — called Vanyusha and Ivan Grigorych
HIS WIFE — called Glafira Sergeyevna
MISHA — a waiter
FIRST WOMAN
SECOND WOMAN
A YOUNG MAN
PIERRE — Krasikov's friend
THE JEW [2]
SARAH — his wife
ABRASHKA — their young son
FIRST BALLERINA
SECOND BALLERINA

ACT ONE
SCENE ONE

(Georges Krasikov sits on a bench on the boulevard)

GEORGES. She promised to come at four. It is now exactly half-past five. This girl is always so late you'd think she wasn't a girl but a benefit concert. I wouldn't be surprised if she caused me to be made an honorary member in some lunatic asylum. Just imagine, exclusively because of her I bought a splendid little apartment. That cost me 1,095 rubles, not counting the 250 rubles I had to pay to heal my vocal chords. I had to heal my vocal chords

---

[1] The Feverish Gentleman appears nowhere in the text, although some songs he was to have sung are appended to the end of the typescript. It is conceivable, though hardly certain, that the Feverish Gentleman was the same character as the Indian Guest, who sings incomprehensible songs which are "translated" by his servant.

[2] The Jew is not listed in the dramatis personae, although he appears in the text. In his place is listed a certain "Tovazh Kr.," who does not appear in the play.

after my chat with the people at the housing committee. But that's not all. Four times a week I have to accompany her to the theater or the movies. I'm willing to deprive myself of anything for her, but it's all for naught. For four months I've been pleading with her in vain to come home with me after the show. "Dear Georges," she says, "Let's put it off 'til tomorrow." Each tomorrow brings another tomorrow. For four months she's been feeding me breakfasts full of tomorrows as if I were a homeless waif or something. I have a feeling I can't take it any more.

SCENE TWO

(Enter Marya)

MARYA. What? You're already here?

GEORGES. Not "already," Marya Petrovna—"still."

MARYA. Pardon me, but I don't understand.

GEORGES. Marya Petrovna, you are late by exactly one hour and thirty-seven minutes and you still have the nerve to say that I am "already" here?

MARYA. Is it really an hour and a half? Strange, I thought I stopped in to see Sonya Gulyachkina for just a minute.

GEORGES. That's a fine minute that lasts for an hour and a half. What were you doing?

MARYA. Talking.

GEORGES. Talking. You mean you were able to talk calmly while I was perishing here waiting for you? What were you talking about?

MARYA. You.

GEORGES. Me? Hmm. That's a different story. What were you saying about me, Marya Petrovna?

MARYA. Just imagine, Sonya Gulyachkina bet me that you limp on your right leg.

GEORGES. I limp on my right leg. That's a lie! What did you tell her?

MARYA. I said it isn't true.

GEORGES. Oh, thank you, Marya Petrovna!

MARYA. Well, you don't limp on your right leg at all. You limp on your left.

GEORGES. This woman positively will drive me out of my mind.

MARYA. However, it's time to get down to business. Why did you want to see me?

GEORGES. I wanted to see you in order to plead with you to come home with me today.

MARYA. Go home with you?

GEORGES. Well, yes.

MARYA. You know, let's put it off 'til tomorrow.

GEORGES. Again, tomorrow. But don't you understand? I can't wait any longer.

MARYA. In that case, let's go see *The Man Who Killed* [3] at the cinema this evening and I'll give it some thought.

GEORGES. Listen, Marya Petrovna, in the last week we have been to see *The Man with No Name* [4] at the Ars Cinema, the Aquarium Man at the circus and *The Man Who Was Thursday* [5] at the Kamerny Theater. Now you want to go see *The Man Who Killed.* Can't you leave at least this one man in peace? What's he done to you?

MARYA. Well, all right. If that doesn't suit you, we can go to the studio at the Russian Theater. They're performing Lermontov's play, *The Spaniards.*

GEORGES. Marya Petrovna, forget the Spaniards and come home with me.

MARYA. Oh no! I've got to think about it. Let's go to the Third Studio. [6]

GEORGES. Coquette.

MARYA. Well, then, the Maly. [7]

GEORGES. Snake.

MARYA. Well, then, the Hermitage. [8]

GEORGES. Vampire.

MARYA. All right then, the Empire it is, but only after the theater.

GEORGES. I didn't say the "Empire." I said, "You are a vampire!" Will you never stop sucking my blood? *(Begins running back and forth)*

MARYA. You know, I was wrong when I said you limp on your left leg. If only you knew how that distresses me.

GEORGES. Oh, Marya Petrovna, I'm not angry with you.

MARYA. I'm not the point. The point is Sonya Gulyachkina.

GEORGES. What does Sonya Gulyachkina have to do with it? All that's important to me is what you think. You.

MARYA. But the fact is, Sonya Gulyachkina won the bet. In fact, you do limp on your right leg.

GEORGES. Damn it! Tell me frankly, once and for all, will you come home with me or not?

MARYA. I'll go.

GEORGES. When?

MARYA. I don't know. I'll have to think about it. Let's put it off 'til tomorrow.

GEORGES. But don't you understand? For love there is no tomorrow. Tomorrow there may be a flood or an earthquake.

---

[3] This is apparently a fictitious title.

[4] This was a relatively recent German film (1921) then playing in Moscow.

[5] Alexander Tairov staged this play by Sigizmund Krzhizhanovsky (1887-1950), based on the novel by G.K. Chesterton, at the Kamerny Theater in 1923.

[6] Marya is referring to the Vakhtangov Theater. The Moscow Art Theater Third Studio was formed in 1920 and headed up by the great director Yevgeny Vakhtangov (1883-1922). Two years later, it became the Vakhtangov Theater.

[7] The Maly Theater was Russia's oldest and, at that time, most prestigious theater.

[8] The Hermitage was a popular after-hours restaurant.

MARYA. Nonsense.

GEORGES. Well, it may be nonsense, but if it were true, wouldn't you repent after death?

MARYA. If such a thing were believable, I would go home with you today.

GEORGES. Then let's go.

MARYA. Unfortunately, an earthquake is an impossibility.

GEORGES. To hell with the earthquake. Why put off to tomorrow what you can do today?

MARYA. My dear Georges, the longer one holds off dessert, the sweeter it is.

GEORGES. Is that your final word?

MARYA. Yes.

GEORGES. In that case, farewell.

MARYA. Good-bye. See you at *The Man Who Killed*. *(Leaves)*

GEORGES. I don't know whether that man killed anyone or not, but I don't doubt in the least that he's crippled me for life. How can I lure her to my apartment? If only there would be some sort of earthquake. Wait a minute. What a great idea! *(Falls into thought)*

SCENE THREE

(Enter Pierre and the Young Man)

PIERRE. Hello, Georges!

GEORGES. Hello, my dear man, and farewell. Farewell forever.

YOUNG MAN. What do you mean, forever? I didn't know you were leaving.

GEORGES. Alas, unfortunately there's no way to leave.

YOUNG MAN. I don't understand. If you're staying in Moscow, then why are you saying farewell?

GEORGES. I may be staying in Moscow, but nothing of Moscow will remain in Moscow.

YOUNG MAN. You're speaking in riddles. What's going on?

GEORGES. You mean you haven't read the latest radio reports?

PIERRE. No. So what?

GEORGES. Then you don't know what the Gulf Stream is doing even as we speak?

PIERRE. How can I know that when I don't even know who that is? I take it he's one of your friends?

GEORGES. Lord, what an ignoramus. The Gulf Stream is a warm current in the Arctic Ocean.

PIERRE. What does that have to do with me?

GEORGES. What do you mean, what? It's changed its directional course.

PIERRE. I could understand it if the course of the ruble had changed, but what's a directional course?

GEORGES. Listen, you unfortunate soul, it has set course for the North Pole.

PIERRE. In that case, it's not me that's the unfortunate one, because I've got steam heating.

GEORGES. You idiot. It's melting the ice on the North Pole and the snow on the North Pole is now heading for the continent. A flood is in the making and Europe is going to be destroyed under water. And, consequently, you and me with it.

PIERRE. You don't say.

GEORGES. I give you my word. All of Moscow is talking about it.

PIERRE. Listen. What are we going to do?

GEORGES. I think we ought to build an ark.

PIERRE. Do you know when the flood is supposed to begin?

GEORGES. Tomorrow.

PIERRE. Tomorrow? Help! I'm perishing!

GEORGES. There's a good start to things. *(Runs off)*

PIERRE. Help! I'm drowning!

(Enter the Jew)

JEW. How is it that you're drowning on dry land?

PIERRE. Leave me alone. I'm in a hurry!

JEW. In a hurry, indeed. Perhaps I'm in a bigger hurry than you.

PIERRE. Listen, I've got business to attend to.

JEW. Then let's attend to it together.

PIERRE. What do you mean, together?

JEW. You say you've got business to attend to. Well, then, I'll introduce you to Lieberman. He'll buy anything you want to sell, from dog collars to bust enlargement procedures.

PIERRE. You and your Lieberman can go to hell.

JEW. All right, then, I'll introduce you to Arkady Rosen. This guy is as honest as an inflammable safe. I tell you that if you give him money, nobody will ever see it again.

PIERRE. Sorry, but I'm in a hurry.

JEW. I thought you said you have business to attend to.

PIERRE. I don't have any business.

JEW. Then what's your rush?

PIERRE. Do you mean that you don't know about the flood?

JEW. What, a whole flood of goods?

PIERRE. Have you gone out of your mind? I'm telling you, a flood. Understand? A real flood.

JEW. A real one, huh? I see, you're pushing up the price. Well, second of all I'm not bargaining with you and, first of all, I haven't seen your wares yet.

PIERRE. What are you talking about? The fact is, the Gulf Stream is changing its course of direction.

JEW. Changing its course up or down?

PIERRE. Neither up nor down. Its headed for the North Pole.

JEW. If that's the Gulfshtrem from Minsk, then that's not even Gulfshtrem, but Gulfshtrumer and you can rest assured that he's not going to the North Pole, but to Gomel.

PIERRE. You've gone mad. What Gulfshtrumer? Listen, the Gulf Stream is a warm current in the Arctic Ocean. It's changing its course of direction and is melting the North Pole. The North Pole is melting the continent, the continent is melting Europe, Europe is filling up with water and everyone is going to perish.

JEW. Why, that's marvelous!

PIERRE. What's so marvelous about it?

JEW. In that case, I don't have to pay back the 50 rubles I owe Ginzburg.

PIERRE. But you're going to perish, too. Everyone is going to perish.

JEW. You don't say. When is this going to happen?

PIERRE. That's the whole point. The flood starts tomorrow. *(Runs off)*

JEW. Tomorrow! What am I going to do when I don't even have a pair of galoshes? Every time I tell Sarah that we've got to buy galoshes, she says, "What for, is there going to be a flood or something?" I wonder what she'll say now. *(Exits)*

(Enter Gulyachkina)

GULYACHKINA. What, they've already gone? No matter. I'll see Marusya at *The Man Who Killed.* I wonder which one of us won the bet? Still, I'm sure he limps on his right leg. Poor Georges. How she torments him.

(The Servant and the Indian Guest can be heard singing)

What is that?

(Enter the Servant and the Indian Guest)

Lord, what colds they have!

SERVANT. Pardon me, mademoiselle. My master would like to know where one can rent an apartment in this town.

GULYACHKINA. There aren't any.

SERVANT. None at all? The fact is, my master and I have just arrived from India. We need to find a place to stay.

GULYACHKINA. Unfortunately, there isn't a single unoccupied place in Moscow.

SERVANT. Not even one?

GULYACHKINA. Almost. For example, Meyerhold's place is always empty,
  but that's a theater.
SERVANT. What are we going to do?
GULYACHKINA. We'll have to think of something. You say you just arrived
  from India?
SERVANT. Yes.
GULYACHKINA. Well, how does your master like Russia?
SERVANT. Ask him yourself.
GULYACHKINA. Monsieur, how do you like Russia?

(The Indian Guest sings)

GULYACHKINA. What in the world?
SERVANT. Pardon me, I forgot he doesn't speak Russian. Ask him questions
  and I'll translate.
GULYACHKINA. All right. Monsieur, tell me, how do you like our
  Nepmen?[9]

(The Indian Guest sings)

SERVANT. Day and night,
          Here and there,
          The Nepmen sell their wares
          While planning for a springtime
          Rest in Sochi.
          But rest assured,
          They'll never make it to Crimea,
          For there's a pleasant place for each
          Now booked at hotel "Lubyanka."[10]

GULYACHKINA. And how do you like our theaters?

(The Indian Guest sings)

SERVANT. The question that you pose, dear miss,
          Prompts the master to say this.
          Not long ago, he went to the ballet

---

[9] The Nepmen were the petty merchants and wheeler-dealers who proliferated as a re-
    sult of Lenin's New Economic Policy (N.E.P.).

[10] The headquarters of the Soviet secret police was located on Lubyanka Square. As such,
    throughout the Soviet period "The Lubyanka" was the popular name for the various in-
    carnations of that organization. See note 11 to "The Qualification Exams."

To see Lukin's great choreography.[11]
He shot a wad of cash
And, going out the door, he said,
"Too bad I didn't take my soap.
I think I've been to the public baths."

GULYACHKINA. Do you find that our populace has become more cultured?

(The Indian Guest sings)

SERVANT. The master has replied,
　　　In this, his knowledge is true and tried.
　　　He ordered for his spouse
　　　A sleeveless summer blouse.
　　　But someone asked her in a trolley,
　　　Without the slightest hint of folly,
　　　"Tell me, where do you wipe your nose, please?
　　　You haven't any sleeves!"

GULYACHKINA. And what do you think of our contemporary people?

(The Indian Guest sings)

SERVANT. He's got to tell you honestly,
　　　For the past, say, quarter century,
　　　Women always crawled out of their skin
　　　To show off their new dresses.
　　　Now they know no shame nor sin,
　　　And, so as to be fashionable,
　　　Women crawl out of their dresses
　　　To show off their naked skin.

(They dance)

JEW. Hey! What are you doing?
GULYACHKINA. What business is it of yours?
JEW. Indeed. There's a flood coming.
GULYACHKINA. What flood?
JEW. You mean you don't know? Gulfshtrem is gambling on an upturn in the course. He's buying up all the North Pole snows, dunking them in the

---

[11] Lev Lukin (1892-1961) was a popular choreographer who gained scandalous success in the 1920s with his erotic stagings. At his "Evenings of the Undraped Body" dancers frequently performed in brocade swimsuits.

Arctic Ocean and drowning Europe. The whole city is in a panic and everyone's learning to swim. I bought myself a pair of galoshes and Sarah is mending our umbrella.

GULYACHKINA. Listen, why, that's a catastrophe!

JEW. And you thought it was a joke or something? However, don't despair. I'll sell you a trick suit. Not only is it made of tricot, I tell you this suit is as sound as a brick. I'll give you a guarantee for ten years of floods. It'll always look brand new.

GULYACHKINA. This is awful.

SERVANT. Unbelievable.

GULYACHKINA. The only positive side is that now you don't have to look for an apartment any more.

JEW. Oh, the flood has other advantages, too.

GULYACHKINA. Like what?

ACT TWO
SCENE ONE

(Tables at a café. The Owner stands behind the counter)

OWNER. Misha! Misha! Damn it! Misha, am I calling you or not?

SCENE TWO

(Misha enters at a run)

OWNER. What are you, deaf, you mangy bum?

MISHA. Not at all, I simply plugged my ears with corks.

OWNER. What in the world did you do that for?

MISHA. There's a flood coming, and I didn't want water to seep into my ears.

OWNER. That's enough of your foolishness. Unplug your ears immediately, you hear me?

MISHA. Right away. I'll go get a corkscrew.

OWNER. I'll give you a knock on the head so that you'll go spinning like a corkscrew yourself. Have you seen my wife?

MISHA. No sir. I haven't.

SCENE THREE

OWNER'S WIFE. *(With broom and dust pan)* Lord Almighty, I'm plumb tuckered out.

OWNER. Where did you disappear to?

OWNER'S WIFE. I was at the bathhouse, Vanyusha. The bathhouse.

OWNER. The bathhouse? What have you been doing there since morning?

WIFE. I was getting used to water, Vanyusha. Sort of like a rehearsal.

OWNER. Have you lost your senses, mama? Do you think a dry person can get used to water?

WIFE. But there's going to be a flood. And whenever I think about the flood, Vanyusha…

OWNER. Don't think. You're not a fish or something to go thinking about floods.

MISHA. Glafira Sergeyevna, what are you doing with a dust pan?

WIFE. I'm going to shovel water with it.

OWNER. Where?

WIFE. What do you mean, where? It's obvious, where. When the water comes pouring in from Europe, then I'll start shovelling.

OWNER. You'd be better off sweeping the floor than talking nonsense.

WIFE. What should I bother sweeping for?

OWNER. For our clients, and in general.

WIFE. What clients are going to visit us today?

OWNER. Who? Antediluvian people.

WIFE. What antediluvian people?

OWNER. Those who are still alive before the flood.

MISHA. Ivan Grigorych! Look! Three antediluvian people are coming in now.

SCENE FOUR

(Enter two Women and a Young Man)

ALL THREE. Hello!

OWNER. This is my wife and Misha. Hello!

YOUNG MAN. Let's sit a little further from the door.

FIRST WOMAN. Do you think that will help?

YOUNG MAN. Well, at least when the water comes pouring in, we'll be the last to go.

SECOND WOMAN. Oh, is there really any difference? If only you knew how upset I am.

YOUNG MAN. I beg you, please calm down.

SECOND WOMAN. It's easy for you to say calm down. But this will be the first time in my life I've ever drowned. And just look how I'm dressed.

FIRST WOMAN. Please, Anya, that's enough. Your dress is beautiful.

SECOND WOMAN. Oh, you're talking nonsense. I just know that all the drowning people are going to inundate me in laughter.

YOUNG MAN. I assure you, you are wearing a most fashionable dress.

SECOND WOMAN. Oh, stop it. Yesterday at the fashion shop I saw with my own eyes special new designs for the drowning.

FIRST WOMAN. Special new designs for the drowning? What are they made of? How are they sewed?

SECOND WOMAN. It's quite simple. The whole charm of it is that they are made extraordinarily simply. Just imagine, the entire dress is made exclusively of nude.

FIRST WOMAN. That truly is simple. And, most important, it won't ever get wet.

SECOND WOMAN. However, shall we order?

YOUNG MAN. We'll have three cups of coffee, please.

MISHA. Coming right up. (*Serves the coffee*)

YOUNG MAN. Tell me, why are there straws in the coffee?

MISHA. Oh, that gives the drowning something to grasp for.

YOUNG MAN. Ah!

ALL. What was that?

YOUNG MAN. Did you hear that noise?

WIFE. Ladies and gentlemen, it has begun!

FIRST WOMAN. What are you doing?

YOUNG MAN. I'm taking off my shoes.

SECOND WOMAN. What for?

YOUNG MAN. I… I… I want to put on my boater. (*Pulls out a boater*)

FIRST WOMAN. What is that for?

YOUNG MAN. I imagine that in times of floods, it's safer in a boater.

FIRST WOMAN. I never knew you were such a coward.

SECOND WOMAN. You'd be better off attaching sails to your head than putting on a boater.

YOUNG MAN. Don't think that I'm a coward. I am not afraid of anything. On the contrary. (*A noise is heard*) Ah! Help! I'd be happy if there were floods every day.

SECOND WOMAN. What do you mean you're not a coward when your legs are shaking like leaves on a tree?

YOUNG MAN. That has nothing to do with fear.

FIRST WOMAN. Then why are they shaking?

YOUNG MAN. That's, uh… that's, uh… because I want to dance.

FIRST WOMAN. Dance? Well, that's different. I'd be honored. Let's go!

YOUNG MAN. L-l-l-let's go.

(*They dance*)

SCENE FIVE

(*Enter Marya, the Indian Guest, his Servant and Gulyachkina*)

YOUNG MAN. What do you think?

OWNER. Is anything happening?

MARYA. Can it really be that the flood is beginning?
SERVANT. My master will now tell you everything that he has seen.

(The Indian Guest sings)

SERVANT. He said, that, for beginners,
His answer is like this.
Three young stockmarketeers
Were doing dirty business.
They failed to cover their tracks
And barely crawled out of the water
With dry shirts upon their backs.

(Refrain)[12]

OWNER. You mean the water has already begun to appear?

(The Indian Guest sings)

SERVANT. He says to all those here,
There is no reason yet to fear.
But with every passing hour,
Moscow is filling up with water.
It's coming in the rivers
And it's rising in the lakes.
Even at the milkmaid's store
The milk is more watery than before!

FIRST WOMAN. What a nightmare!
SECOND WOMAN. Horrors!
WIFE. It's nothing less than the Apocalypse. It's not for nothing they wrote
about that in the Bible. Have you read the Bible, mademoiselle?
MARYA. The Bible is an awfully indecent book.
OWNER. What do you mean, indecent?
GULYACHKINA. Well, naturally. All the men in it are always giving birth.
Abraham begat Isaac. Isaac begat Jacob. Jacob begat Judas. It's just terrible.
I haven't any idea what their women were up to.
YOUNG MAN. As far as I can tell, they lived a fairly salty life. One of them
even turned into a saline pillar that weighed several lots.
MISHA. No, no, but in the Bible, Noah dreamed up an ark.
SERVANT. Quit your nay-saying.

---

[12] There is no indication in the typescript as to what refrain Erdman had in mind.

MISHA. Not "no"—Noah.
SERVANT. And I say, quit your nay-saying.
MISHA. Not "no"—Noah.
SERVANT. Comrade owner, tell him to quit nay-saying.
WIFE. I don't understand what the police are up to. Europe is drowning and they don't care at all.
OWNER. What are people going to do?
GULYACHKINA. Well, for instance, after *The Flood*,[13] the Moscow Art Theater is planning to stage *The Lower Depths*.[14]

(A loud sound is heard)

ALL. Ah!
MISHA. Ah! Help! Flood!
WIFE. Help! I'm drowning!
FIRST WOMAN. Hold me by the armpits, I can't swim!
WIFE. Lord Almighty! I'm wet! Saints alive! I'm wet!
SERVANT. Sit on a match head, madame. Perhaps that will dry you out.

(Wailing, screaming, oohing and ahing)

SCENE SIX

(Enter two Ballerinas)

ALL. What happened? What's going on? Well? Speak up! Has it begun?
FIRST BALLERINA. Not yet.
OWNER. But you have already drowned.
SECOND BALLERINA. Not yet.
OWNER. Then why are you undressed?
FIRST BALLERINA. We were dancing.
YOUNG MAN. Where were you dancing?
SECOND BALLERINA. At Lukin's.
FIRST WOMAN. What were you dancing?
FIRST BALLERINA. Egyptian, Jewish, Greek, Ryazan and other ante-diluvian dances.
SECOND WOMAN. Oh, how interesting! Show us, won't you, dears?
FIRST BALLERINA. With pleasure. But in that case, we'll have to undress a bit.

---

[13] Yevgeny Vakhtangov had staged Johan Berger's *The Flood* at the Moscow Art Theater's First Studio in 1915.

[14] This refers to the play by Maxim Gorky (1868-1936), originally staged at the Moscow Art Theater in 1902.

SERVANT. You mean you're going to undress even more?

WIFE. Do as you like, but I won't stand for it. Whatever else he may be, my husband is a married man.

SECOND BALLERINA. Have it your way. We'll dance as is. What shall we dance?

YOUNG MAN. Do something Egyptian for us. We'll sit as quietly as mummies.

FIRST BALLERINA. With pleasure.

(They dance)

ALL. Bravo! Bravo! Bravo!

OWNER. Well, those Egyptians are something, aren't they? Always grabbing for each other's behind.

GULYACHKINA. Now do something Greek.

SECOND BALLERINA. With pleasure.

(They dance the same dance)

SERVANT. If I didn't know that was a Greek dance, I would swear it was an Egyptian dance.

OWNER. Those Greeks are sneaky. They stole everything from the Egyptians.

FIRST BALLERINA. It wasn't the Greeks who stole from the Egyptians at all.

OWNER. Well, then, the Egyptians stole from the Greeks.

SECOND BALLERINA. Not that, either.

OWNER. Then who stole from whom?

FIRST BALLERINA. Lukin stole it all from Goleizovsky.[15]

ALL. O-h-h!

SECOND WOMAN. Now show us some Jewish dances.

SECOND BALLERINA. Certainly.

(They do the same dance)

FIRST WOMAN. The same old thing again.

FIRST BALLERINA. Of course.

YOUNG MAN. Well, how do you do Spanish dances?

SECOND BALLERINA. The same way.

YOUNG MAN. How about American dances?

---

[15] Kasyan Goleizovsky (1892-1970), like Lukin, was famed in the 1920s for staging erotic dances at his legendary Kamerny Ballet and other venues. His program of Spanish dances—for which Erdman's brother, Boris, designed the costumes—was particularly popular. Erdman wrote scripts for some of his performances.

FIRST BALLERINA. The same.

GULYACHKINA. You mean to say that Lukin never changes anything at all?

SECOND BALLERINA. No, he makes changes from time to time.

GULYACHKINA. What does he change?

FIRST BALLERINA. The titles.

GULYACHKINA. How convenient. Ladies and gentlemen! In that case, let's dance all the dances of the world simultaneously. It all comes out the same, anyway.

VOICES. It's coming! Let's go! Hit it!

(Everyone dances. Screams are heard: "Hang on! Europe is caving in!")

SCENE SEVEN

(Enter the Jew, Sarah and Abrashka)

JEW. Abrashka, shut the door. Shut the door, I tell you! Sarah, lie down on the floor and start waving your arms and legs. Abrashka, see that you don't burst that bubble.

FIRST WOMAN. Listen, don't hide anything from us. Be frank. Has it already begun?

JEW. You simply amaze me. Has what begun? Has what begun? Everything is already over.

VOICES. Is there really no salvation? What are we going to do?

JEW. What salvation can there be? What are you, submarines or something? With hand on heart, I declare to you that if Sarah let me buy a pair of galoshes, then the flood is inevitable.

YOUNG MAN. We've got to do something.

JEW. I already have.

YOUNG MAN. What did you do?

JEW. I said to Sarah, "Sarah, fix me a bath and give me an alarm clock." So she says to me, "If you want to take a bath so bad, then wait for the flood." So I said to her, "Sarah, you know I hate taking baths. I just want to find out how long I can survive under water." So she fixed me a bath. Then I set the alarm clock at twelve o'clock, and the alarm clock and I got into the bathtub together. So I'm sitting under water and the alarm clock is sitting there with me under water. But I have no idea how much time we both spent there. However, I started to sense that I wouldn't hold out. I crawled back out and water starts pouring out my nose as if I were a fountain at Peter's Palace or something. When everything poured out of me I looked at the alarm clock, and Sarah and Abrashka looked at me. And Abrashka says, "Well, how long did you sit under water?" I didn't say anything and just stared at the alarm clock. So Sarah says to me, "What are you standing there for naked, like some memorial statue. Go get dressed." But I just stood there staring at the alarm clock. Then Sarah says to me again, "What are you, deaf, that you can't go anywhere?" So I answer her, "I can go if I have to, but this alarm clock here is on its last legs." Well, if you can picture this, it turns out that the water didn't have the slightest effect on me, but it ruined my alarm clock. So then I put on my galoshes and started teaching Sarah how to swim. I turned on all the faucets and let them run until there wasn't a dry spot left in the apartment. And suddenly I see that everything around me is starting to swim. The chairs are swimming, the table is swimming, even the trash that I hadn't taken out for four days is swimming. Abrashka is floating on top of the washtub and I'm swimming like a white salmon or something. Meanwhile, Sarah is hanging onto a spider web and screeching like a rusty fan. So I say to her, "Sarah, come over here to me." And she says to me, "I can't!" So I tell her again, "What are you, an alarm clock that you've lost your legs?" And she says, "I can't swim." "Swim on the bubbles," I tell her. And she says, "What good are bubbles when I'm blowing bubbles out my own nose?" And the water kept rising and rising. I started to swim into the kitchen to turn off the faucet but Sarah dug her teeth into my heel and started talking with her hands. Well, I thought then I was a goner for sure, like the Titanic, or something. But suddenly Abrashka, floating on top the washtub, opened the door and we all sailed out into the street.

GULYACHKINA. You mean everything ended all right?

JEW. How can everything be all right when Sarah bit holes in my galoshes?

FIRST WOMAN. What are we going to do now? The flood will begin soon.

JEW. Sarah, lie down on the floor and start waving your arms and legs until you learn how to swim.

YOUNG MAN. Citizens and antediluvian people, perhaps there won't be any flood.

(Abrashka sits on a bubble and the bubble bursts. Everyone starts screaming)

JEW. Sarah, exhale. If there's no air in you, you can't drown.

(Cries: "Grab me by the hair!" "Grab me by the hair!" "Help!" "We're perishing!" "Europe is perishing, turn toward Asia!")

SCENE EIGHT

(Enter Pierre)

PIERRE. Comrade citizens, don't despair! There is yet salvation!

(Cries: "Where?" "How?")

Citizens, my friend Georges Krasikov, who informed me about the impending flood, said he was building an ark. Let's go to his place. He can take us instead of the seven pairs of unclean.[16]

ALL. An ark! An ark! Hurrah! We're saved!

(They all dance)

> People, stand shoulder to shoulder!
> Before the flood we need to be bolder!
> Let's head out straightaway.
> To the ark! Hurray! Hurray!
> To the ark take with you your drums
> And we'll open a rowdy café.
> If you don't have a seat,
> There's no need to weep.
> We're all in the ark.
> We're all in the ark.
> We'll start living again
> And of cares we'll know naught.
> Forget your fears and laugh
> And strike up a raucous fox trot.

ACT THREE
SCENE ONE

(A room in Georges Krasikov's apartment)

GEORGES. Can it really be that she won't come see me tonight? My plan worked beyond my wildest dreams. All Moscow is talking about the flood. Even the state department store hung out a new poster by Mayakovsky: "Seize this life preserver! It's cheap and made by a master's hands."[17] Marusya must have heard about the flood and, consequently, will not try putting off visiting me until tomorrow. Bravo, Georges! You set the bait as though you'd lived your whole life dangling at the end of a fishing rod! Someone's at the door now. Could it really be her? *(Opens the door)*

---

[16] This refers as much to *Mystery Bouffe,* a play by Vladimir Mayakovsky (1893-1930), as to the Biblical story of the Deluge. Mayakovsky's Futurist burlesque of the Noah tale was produced by Meyerhold in 1918 and again in 1921. In it, seven pairs of "clean" characters and seven pairs of "unclean" characters board an ark when the earth is inundated by a flood. After casting the "clean" overboard, the "unclean" return to a paradise-on-earth when the waters recede.

[17] Mayakovsky, in addition to being a poet and playwright, was a talented artist. His satirical drawings, accompanied by his own rhymed texts, often appeared throughout Moscow in poster form in the early 1920s.

SCENE TWO

(Enter Marya)

GEORGES. Marya Petrovna! It's you! What bliss!

MARYA. Don't condemn me for this rash step, but you said yourself that the catastrophe was inevitable.

GEORGES. What catastrophe?

MARYA. What do you mean, what catastrophe? The flood.

GEORGES. Huh? The fl… Oh, yes, yes, yes. The flood. Marya Petrovna, it's terrible, I know, but pay it no mind.

MARYA. My dear boy, I am not some sort of deep-sea diver who can afford to pay it no mind. If only you knew what grief this has caused me.

GEORGES. Are you trying to say that you are repenting for having come to me?

MARYA. Not at all, my dear. What is one girl's demise when all of Europe is perishing?

GEORGES. Marusya… may I call you that? Marusya, will you stop saying "Let's put it off 'til tomorrow?"

MARYA. Alas, tomorrow doesn't exist.

GEORGES. In that case, my beloved, kiss me.

(The door bell rings)

GEORGES. Damn! Marusya, my child, go into the other room. I'll be right with you. Who could that be? *(Opens the door)*

SCENE THREE

(Enter the Owner, his Wife and Misha, carrying wreaths)

GEORGES. Who are you?

OWNER. We are the drowned, so to speak. We are drowning.

GEORGES. What do you mean, the drowned?

WIFE. Just that. Common, ordinary drowned people.

MISHA. Hey, mister, are you Noah?

GEORGES. What?

MISHA. I say, you must be the one they call Noah.

GEORGES. Listen, you've gone mad. I am no Noah. My name is Krasikov. You must be mistaken.

OWNER. Krasikov! It's Krasikov! Just like they said.

WIFE. And you try telling us that we're mistaken.

GEORGES. Pardon me, but what do you want?

OWNER. Tickets, my good citizen. Tickets.

GEORGES. What tickets?

OWNER. Misha and I don't need anything special. We can stand. But I'd be grateful if you'd give my wife a seat. After all, she's a woman, citizen. She's a bit wobbly and is not built to stand for long.

GEORGES. Pardon me?

WIFE. We don't have many belongings, citizen. Just some linens, as per regulations: seven pair clean and seven pair unclean. Don't you worry.

GEORGES. Explain to me, please, once and for all, what is it that you want of me?

OWNER. Don't refuse us, good citizen! Leave us a corner in your ark.

GEORGES. What ark? What corner?

OWNER. And if we don't have enough to cover the expenses now, when we get to Ararat, we'll pay up according to the local rate.

WIFE. Rubles inflate in any climate. Don't you worry.

GEORGES. What kind of idiots are you? Listen, I don't have any ark. I demand that you vacate my apartment immediately.

OWNER. What do you mean, you don't have an ark?

GEORGES. Plain and simple.

OWNER. None? Why didn't you say so earlier? Landlubbers are searching for an ark and you go on talking and talking. You should be ashamed, young man. That's a swinish trick.

WIFE. Incorrigible!

(They leave)

GEORGES. For God's sake! What a crew! I brought a fine one down on my head! Marusya, my child! Come here. I'm sorry I had to leave you alone.

MARYA. There's no need to hide anything from me. Has the flood begun?

GEORGES. No, no, no, Marusya. Of course not.

MARYA. Then why are you all wet?

GEORGES. That's just perspiration.

MARYA. Did you have guests?

GEORGES. Oh, just some idiots.

MARYA. Your relatives, probably.

GEORGES. Yes. I mean, no. But what's the difference? Now, no one will bother us.

MARYA. Other than the flood.

GEORGES. Listen, this flood is starting to drive me out of my mind. Marusya, forget about all that and kiss me!

MARYA. Ah, Georges! I am only a weak, drowning woman!

(They draw near to one another. The door bell rings)

GEORGES. *(Leaps up)* Damn it! Again! Marusya, my child, go wait in the other room. I'll be right back.

(She leaves)

Who in the hell is it now? *(Opens the door)*

SCENE FOUR

(Enter the two Women and the Young Man from the café)

FIRST WOMAN. Pardon me, but are you Krasikov?

SECOND WOMAN. Are you citizen Krasikov?

YOUNG MAN. Comrade Krasikov, is that you?

GEORGES. Yes, but I don't underst…

FIRST WOMAN. I don't know you, but still, I hope you won't refuse me. You have such a kind face.

SECOND WOMAN. If anyone tells you that I'm married, please don't pay them any mind. When travelling, I am a very pleasant woman.

YOUNG MAN. I'm prepared to do the dirtiest, blackest work you want, all the more so since I have good experience. I worked on the black market for two years.

GEORGES. I am sorry, mesdames, but I don't understand. What is it you want?

FIRST WOMAN. Please, save me a space in your ark.

SECOND WOMAN. I would like two places. One for me and one for my daughter. But I beg of you, pay that no mind. My daughter means nothing at all. I am as pristine as a virgin.

YOUNG MAN. I'm a virgin, too! I mean, I also implore you!

GEORGES. There seems to be some mistake, here. I assure you, I do not have an ark.

FIRST WOMAN. How's that? Ah! You're hiding it from us! It's here somewhere!

SECOND WOMAN. Probably in that room there. *(She tries to go into the room where Marya is hiding)*

GEORGES. Stop! You can't go in there.

SECOND WOMAN. Aha! Then it is in there!

GEORGES. I assure you there is no one in there.

SECOND WOMAN. Then why can't I go in? You are deceiving us. Let's go! The ark is in there.

(They try to enter the room. Georges won't let them)

GEORGES. I swear to you, no one is in there. I assure you.

MARYA'S VOICE. What happened?

FIRST WOMAN. Ah! There, you see?

YOUNG MAN. You can't go very far on a vessel like that.

SECOND WOMAN. Oh, pardon us. We apparently got the wrong address. Good-bye.

ALL. Good-bye.

(The three visitors leave)

GEORGES. This all is going to end with me drowning in this flood I dreamed up. My dear Marusya, I am terribly sorry but it's all over now. We're alone now.

MARYA. *(Comes out)* What was happening here?

GEORGES. Does it matter? Time is fleeting.

MARYA. Will the flood begin soon?

GEORGES. Again, the flood. I can't stand it. Calm yourself, Marusya. There will be no flood.

MARYA. No flood? Then I'm going home.

GEORGES. Where are you going? Wait! I meant to say that the flood won't take place right at this moment. Without doubt it will be begin, of course. So it's best not to lose time. Marusya, my love, kiss me!

MARYA. Ah, my darling!

(The door bell rings)

GEORGES. Hang onto me! I'm going to shoot myself! Marusya, pay it no mind. It's just your imagination.

(The door bell rings followed by cries of "Flood! Flood!")

MARYA. Did you hear that? Someone cried, "flood!" Open the door immediately!

GEORGES. Marusya, my child, go into the other room. I'll be right back. *(Opens the door)*

(Enter the Jew, Sarah and Abrashka)

JEW. Sarah, lie down on the floor and start moving your arms and legs. Abrashka, are you breathing again? How many times do I have to tell you not to breathe? I don't understand this child. He's getting ready to live under water and he can't learn not to breathe.

GEORGES. Listen, what is it you want here?

JEW. I have a proposition for you. If you are building an ark, then I'd like to introduce you to Rosen. I tell you, this guy is as honest as an inflammable safe.

21

GEORGES. Leave me alone, please.

JEW. All right. In that case, I'll introduce you to Miller. He'll buy anything you've got, starting with canary seeds and ending with hair-growing potions.

GEORGES. Don't you understand? I'm engaged.

JEW. How can you already be engaged when you and I are partners in a joint-shares stock society?

GEORGES. A what society?

JEW. A society of shares in the construction of the first ark of a Russian national scope. As such, I ask you, what direction will it take for a course?

GEORGES. I don't know! For God's sake, leave me alone!

JEW. You don't know? Well, I do. I say that as a specialist in ark affairs. The ark will run a direct course from Ilyinka Street[18] to the Lubyanka. And, believe me, there will be no shortage of passengers.

GEORGES. I beg you…

JEW. That doesn't suit you? Then let's engage it to transport people of color to the Solovetsky Monastery.[19]

GEORGES. What people of color? Are you mad?

JEW. You mean you don't know? What about the Arabs?[20]

GEORGES. What Arabs?

JEW. You mean you don't know? The ones who spend all their time in the casino.

GEORGES. One more minute will be the end of me.

JEW. Not enough for you, huh? Then we'll charge fares from everybody who'll be jumping on board after we're already underway.

GEORGES. Listen here, you! If you don't clear out of here right now, I'll cave in your head!

JEW. My head? Do you think we're still living in the past, or something?[21] My father used to say, "A Jew doesn't cross himself until thunder strikes." I'll have you know, these aren't the old days. But if you're building an ark on a Russian national scope…

GEORGES. But I'm not building an ark.

JEW. You're not?

---

[18] Ilyinka Street, once one of the most active and colorful trading regions in Moscow, was a hangout for profiteers, black-marketeers and petty thieves. It begins at Red Square and provides a direct route from the Kremlin to the Lubyanka.

[19] In 1918, the famous Solovetsky Monastery was turned into one of the Soviet Union's most notorious prisons for political prisoners.

[20] The writer Nikolai Shakhbazov suggests convincingly that this probably refers to Jews. As the text subsequently shows, these "Arabs" frequent the casinos which, in fact, were a popular meeting place for Jews. According to Shakhbazov, when speaking about Jews, people often referred to them as being French, English, or some other nationality. For a further example of this, see note 8 to "The Qualification Exams."

[21] This is a reference to the Jewish pogroms which took place in tsarist Russia.

GEORGES. No.

JEW. Sarah, start waving your arms and legs faster. Abrashka, you're breathing again! So, our joint-shares stock society has gone under, has it?

GEORGES. Has it ever gone under! And you, get out of here immediately or I'll go under with it out of pure spite. Marusya! I'm coming!

(Enter at a run everyone who had been in the café)

VOICES. There he is! There he is! Let us on the ark! Save us! Help! A woman has been trampled!

PIERRE. Calm down! Georges, I know you are building an ark. You told me so yourself. I beg of you, don't refuse us salvation!

GEORGES. And I beg of you to clear out of my apartment!

VOICES. Ruthless bum! Monster! We won't go. What's the difference, drown here or somewhere else? Citizens, everyone stay here. And don't let him out. Let him drown here for good.

GEORGES. If they all stay, Marusya will leave. Citizens! I admit, there will be no flood. It's something I dreamed up.

ALL. No flood? Hurrah!

JEW. What do you mean, no flood? Then why did I buy a pair of galoshes? Then why did I ruin my alarm clock? And why did I make an aquarium out of my apartment? I expect you to reimburse all my losses. Sarah, quit waving your arms and legs. There won't be any flood. Abrashka, we can breathe again.

GEORGES. Don't worry, please. I will reimburse all your losses. Only, please, just leave me alone.

VOICES. Let's go, citizens! The flood's been called off!

SCENE FIVE

MARYA. Wait a minute! Wait for me!

GEORGES. Marusya, where are you going? I thought you were planning to stay with me today.

MARYA. You know what? Let's put it off 'til tomorrow.

GEORGES. Maybe there won't be any flood, but I'm sunk like a lead sinker.

VOICES. Hurrah! No flood!

(All dance a fox trot)

> People, stand shoulder to shoulder!
> It seems that there won't be any water!
> Let the gloom dissipate,
> We've got business to do. Don't be late!

Friends, strike up the drums!
All make haste for a rowdy café!
There won't be any flood!
Europe, I say,
There won't be any flood!
We can breathe a bit freer
And of cares we'll know naught.
Forget your fears and laugh
And strike up a raucous fox trot.

The Feverish Gentleman's Songs[22]

Bandits have lost all their shame,
Now they are much too smart.
One evening on Domnikov Street,[23]
I was victim to a quick bandit's art.
I asked him about this and that,
And went out of my mind, darn near.
"Citizen, off with your coat,"
The bandit snapped with a sneer.
But suddenly, curling my brow,
I realized what I would do.
Tomorrow will be the flood!
Who cares if I'm in the nude?

*****

Yesterday I had an experience,
I guess it went something like this:
I took my wife to the Jimmy[24]
To gaze at Goleizovsky's high kicks.
My wife, she exclaimed, "For shame!
I've never seen anything like that!
I mean, you're my husband, not Adam.

---

[22] It is uncertain where these songs fitted into the performance of *The Destruction of Europe.* See note 1.

[23] Domnikov Street was something of a red-light district in Moscow in the 1920s. It was razed in mid-century and replaced by what is now called Novokirovsky Prospect.

[24] This is a reference to the popular cabaret, the Crooked Jimmy, which existed in Moscow in 1922 and 1923, and for which Erdman wrote numerous sketches. In 1924, the majority of the troupe moved on to found the Satire Theater.

The Old Testament isn't our habitat!"
But what I didn't know…

*****

Dressed like a real Moscow dandy,
I once went to play some roulette.
I laid down a good deal of money
After hocking my watch, coat and vest.
Then in winter, I left the Casino.
I was drunk, and the game—it was over.
And my kids, my aunt and my wife
Lit into me like one hungry tiger.
But what I didn't know…

The Qualification Exams
1924

CHARACTERS IN ORDER OF APPEARANCE

A BALLADEER
FIRST EXAMINER
SECOND EXAMINER
THIRD EXAMINER
MAESTRO — conductor of the orchestra
FIRST YOUNG WOMAN — a dancer
FIRST YOUNG MAN — a dancer
SECOND YOUNG WOMAN — a dancer
A STORYTELLER
HUSBAND — a songwriter called Georgie
WIFE — a songwriter called Fisochka

SCENE ONE

(The three Examiners of a qualifying committee sit at a table. Enter the Balladeer)

BALLADEER. Good evening, comrades. Or, as they say, bonne soirée.

FIRST EXAMINER. Hello, comrade.

BALLADEER. O.k., comrades, I'm here to get my qualification papers.

SECOND EXAMINER. And who might you be, citizen?

BALLADEER. Me?

SECOND EXAMINER. You.

BALLADEER. First of all, comrade, I'm not one of those intellectuals. And if you think I'm wearing new pants....

THIRD EXAMINER. Pardon me, but your pants don't concern us. Why don't you tell us what you plan to do?

BALLADEER. O.k. Here goes. I intend to inject a healthy note into our national popular entertainment.

FIRST EXAMINER. Is that so? Healthier entertainment is just what we're looking for. I would even go so far as to say that healthy entertainment is the sorest spot of our work. I trust that your repertoire is sufficiently revolutionary?

BALLADEER. Don't you worry about my repertoire, comrades. There isn't an audience anywhere who wouldn't turn red from hearing it. And as for my new pants...

THIRD EXAMINER. There you go about your pants, again, citizen. What is this with you and your pants? Can't you say anything without pants?

BALLADEER. What do you mean, without pants? I'm no "Walpurgisnacht" from the Bolshoi Theater, you know.[1] I'm a balladeer, comrade, and not some old artist's study of a naked body.

SECOND EXAMINER. So, you're a balladeer? What's your name?

BALLADEER. The National Red Satirist Bim-Bom-Smirnov-Sokolsky-Petrov.[2]

SECOND EXAMINER. What?

BALLADEER. Bim-Bom-Smirnov-Sokolsky-Petrov.

SECOND EXAMINER. That is your real name?

BALLADEER. One part of it is real.

THIRD EXAMINER. Which part?

BALLADEER. The tail end—Petrov. Bim-Bom-Smirnov-Sokolsky is a kind of generalizing last name.

FIRST EXAMINER. Look here, citizen, I'm going to have to recommend you take another last name.

BALLADEER. What do you mean, take another last name? I could understand it if I were a woman balladeer or satirist. But, comrades, I'm a man satirist. Men don't change their last names.

FIRST EXAMINER. I'm not talking about your name. I'm talking about your pseudonym—Bim-Bom-Smirnov-Sokolsky. That's not a very successful choice. The fact is, someone might confuse you with the real one.

BALLADEER. That shows how smart you are. That's the whole reason I took it in the first place. I want people to confuse us.

SECOND EXAMINER. You seem to forget that a name like that might arouse objections from a second party.

BALLADEER. That's impossible. There are so many Bims, Boms and Sokolskys these days that you can't even call them names anymore. Properly speaking, they've become a sort of mass market product.

THIRD EXAMINER. In that case, let's get on with the examination.

BALLADEER. I'd be happy to.

SECOND EXAMINER. I hope that you haven't forgotten what you said about healthy entertainment. And I hope that, after you pass your exam and you walk out on stage to start performing at the Aquarium or the Hermitage,[3] you will give us a revolutionary flair of which we all can be proud.

BALLADEER. As far as walking out is concerned, don't you worry. I did a

---

[1] This is probably a reference to the Bolshoi Theater's production of Charles Gounod's *Faust* in 1924.

[2] Bim-Bom was an extremely popular clown duet from the 1890s to the 1940s. Founder Ivan Radunsky (1872-1955) performed the role of Bim, while various circus artists served as his partner. During the first half of the 1920s, scores of young clown acts began imitating Bim-Bom's methods. Nikolai Smirnov-Sokolsky (1898-1962) was a popular cabaret entertainer for whom Erdman himself occasionally wrote material.

[3] The Aquarium and the summer stage at the Hermitage were two of Moscow's most popular venues for escapist comic and musical entertainment in the early 1920s. They were frequently criticized for lacking the proper political orientation.

show in a theater in Samara once, and people started walking out so fast, I barely had a chance to walk in. May I begin?

THIRD EXAMINER. Please do.

BALLADEER. Some very political verses satirizing the day's most topical theme and night. Maestro, bitte, please!

> Mariya's Woods is north of Moscow.
> My wife and I lived there peacefully.
> And then my mother-in-law showed up.
> Who in the hell needs her, pray tell me?

Pretty good, huh?

FIRST EXAMINER. Pardon me, comrade. You promised us a satire on the day's most topical theme and night, and all of a sudden you bring in your mother-in-law. Who in the hell needs that?

BALLADEER. That's just what I said, comrades. Who in the hell needs it? There we were, living like two peas in a pod and—suddenly—there she is. She doesn't like this, she doesn't like that, and then it started. Who in the hell needs it?

FIRST EXAMINER. Absolutely no one, comrade.

BALLADEER. You mean my mother-in-law?

FIRST EXAMINER. That's right.

BALLADEER. That's just what I think, too, comrades. She's worthless. That's why I structured the theme so bluntly. If you say, "Who in the hell needs it?" any conscious citizen will tell you right off: "Absolutely no one." You see, I'm propagandizing a new manner of personal life. We've had enough of the domineering old yoke, comrades.

SECOND EXAMINER. You may have something there. Every mother-in-law is the incarnation of social evil.

THIRD EXAMINER. Well, maybe not every one, but mine sure is.

SECOND EXAMINER. You mean, you think mine's any better?

BALLADEER. It's time we quit standing on ceremony with them, comrades. Let's take 'em out of circulation. Long live the new life. Hurrah!

ALL. Hurrah!

SECOND EXAMINER. Finally, somebody's given us a truly revolutionary repertoire. Please do continue.

BALLADEER. Maestro, Noch ein time.

> In Moscow they wash down the dirt there,
> And say that will keep the air cool there.
> But, when they drenched my brother's new hat,
> I say: Who in the hell needs that?

Quite original, don't you think?

SECOND EXAMINER. The thing is, comrade, you've taken your brother as your topic. But, if you'll pardon me, who could possibly be interested in him?

BALLADEER. Do you know him?

SECOND EXAMINER. No.

BALLADEER. Then how can you say nobody is interested in him? My brother may be a member of the Moscow City Council, for all you know. And there you go suggesting nobody is interested in him.

SECOND EXAMINER. Pardon me. I didn't realize. That's another matter.

THIRD EXAMINER. Tell us, much-respected citizen, don't you have any verses that might expose somebody, so to speak? That might lay open the sore points of our revolutionary experience?

BALLADEER. In other words, something with the sting of satire.

THIRD EXAMINER. Exactly. But it's got to be funny and subtle.

BALLADEER. Funny and subtle? I've got just the thing. Maestro, be so kind. Give me a slow andante.

> You know that you'll always be bored,
> If you go to the theater called Maly.
> *The Bears* [4] in the menagerie roared,
> But who in the hell needs it, pray tell me?

I'd say I hit on a real sore spot, there.

FIRST EXAMINER. But, who are you hinting at, comrade? I don't get it.

BALLADEER. Who else? Him.

SECOND EXAMINER. If you would say clearly whom you're attacking, it would be much more funny.

BALLADEER. You may not think it's funny, but at least it's subtle.

SECOND EXAMINER. Still and all, were I in your place, I'd say who it is I had in mind.

BALLADEER. You would?

SECOND EXAMINER. Of course I would.

BALLADEER. Then say... *(Whispers in the Second Examiner's ear)*

SECOND EXAMINER. You know, comrade, I think you're right. Perhaps it's better to leave it subtle.

THIRD EXAMINER. Listen, I would like to remind you about healthy entertainment. Perhaps for a finale you could recite something extremely revolutionary. Something about the capitalists or the bourgeoisie or something—so that the proletariat can have a good, healthy laugh.

BALLADEER. Something revolutionary? Be so kind, maestro. Prepare your

---

[4] This refers to the play, *The Bears' Wedding,* by Anatoly Lunacharsky (1875-1933). It was staged at the Maly Theater in 1924. Lunacharsky's plays were weak, but as the People's Commissar of Education and a confidant of Lenin, he was protected from the criticism a lesser figure would have encountered. Erdman pokes fun at Lunacharsky in several of his sketches.

big bass drum.

> The whole old world, as it is, is bankrupt
> And has finally reached its finale.
> Long live comrade Stalin
> And the Third Internationale.[5]

THIRD EXAMINER. Comrade, that isn't funny at all.

BALLADEER. Not funny? Who do you think you're trying to laugh at? I recite you some verses about the Third Internationale and all you want to do is laugh?

THIRD EXAMINER. I beg your pardon, citizen. I only meant...

BALLADEER. Comrade, I would beg you. I won't allow anyone to laugh at the Third Internationale. How dare you? Do you think we stirred up a revolution in October for laughs?

THIRD EXAMINER. Pardon me. Allow me to explain...

BALLADEER. What's to explain? You'd be better off just telling me what rank you've qualified me at.

THIRD EXAMINER. The second.

BALLADEER. The second? Why, I'll expose you for who you really are. How dare you sit here in front of me laughing at Stalin and making fun of the Third Internationale? We'll see yet who has the last laugh.

THIRD EXAMINER. I beg your pardon, comrade. We made an error. I should have said the fourth...

BALLADEER. The fourth. Well, now, that's a different story. Maestro, be so kind. Allez the Internationale for my exit.

(Pulls a red banner out of his pocket and leaves)

THIRD EXAMINER. You know, comrade, with entertainment in such a state of health, I don't think its illness will be a very prolonged one.

SECOND EXAMINER. Bring on the next.

---

[5] This verse was banned, ostensibly for its offensive attitude toward the Comintern. It was replaced in performances by the following verse:
> I live on Malaya Bronnaya Street
> And let me say, not skipping a beat:
> Arise! ye starvelings from your slumbers!
> For reason in revolt now thunders!

In connection with the censor's change, the subsequent references to Stalin and the Third Internationale were also cut. There was also a third variant of the quatrain which apparently was not used:
> An aristocrat's son sits in prison,
> Oh, what a sad, sad, sad finale.
> Long live comrade Trotsky
> And the Third Internationale.

SCENE TWO

(Enter two Young Women and a Young Man)

FIRST YOUNG WOMAN. Excuse me, are you the qualifying committee?

FIRST EXAMINER. Yes.

FIRST YOUNG WOMAN. Oh, how nice! Qualify us, will you please?

SECOND EXAMINER. Who are you?

YOUNG MAN. I'm a vampire, comrade.

SECOND EXAMINER. A what?

YOUNG MAN. A vampire. And this lady here is my vamp.

SECOND EXAMINER. I don't understand

FIRST YOUNG WOMAN. That's what our dance is called: "The Vampire, or, In the Den of Terrible Passion."

THIRD EXAMINER. Oh, so you're ballet dancers. I see. And you, young lady—are you a vamp, too?

SECOND YOUNG WOMAN. Oh my, no. On the contrary, I'm a dying swan. But, to tell the truth, there's no point in your qualifying me.

FIRST EXAMINER. Why?

SECOND YOUNG WOMAN. Because my talent has already been discovered by a famous professor with whom I studied.

FIRST EXAMINER. What professor was that?

SECOND YOUNG WOMAN. Lossky.[6]

FIRST EXAMINER. Lossky? But he teaches singing.

SECOND YOUNG WOMAN. That's right. That's just what I studied with him. And just imagine, suddenly, at our fourth lesson he gave me a look, just like this—and then said: "Mademoiselle, with a voice like that, you ought to join the ballet." Say what you will, but he's the authority.

SECOND EXAMINER. Nonetheless, you will have to pass the qualification examination. Please prepare your acts.

ALL. We'll be ready in a moment.

THIRD EXAMINER. Wait a minute.

FIRST YOUNG WOMAN. What's wrong?

THIRD EXAMINER. I would only ask you, citizenesses, not to get undressed. We are married men, after all, and whenever ballet dancers come before us, they have the habit of turning our committee room into a public beach.

FIRST YOUNG WOMAN. Oh my, no! Why would we get undressed? We oppose all those naked costumes ourselves. Only, may we take off our coats?

---

[6] Vladimir Lossky (1874-1946) was a singer, actor and director at the Bolshoi Theater, and a professor at the Moscow Conservatory. He staged the version of *Faust* which was alluded to earlier in this sketch. See note 1.

THIRD EXAMINER. Your coats? Of course.

(They remove their coats, revealing that they are already in ballet costumes)

FIRST YOUNG WOMAN. I'm always amazed how people can dance when they're half-naked. But my costume is quite attractive and very comfortable, wouldn't you say?

FIRST EXAMINER. A-hem. As they say—the naked truth.

SECOND EXAMINER. Comrade dying swan. Begin, if you will.

(Music)

SECOND YOUNG WOMAN. Ah!

SECOND EXAMINER. What's wrong?

SECOND YOUNG WOMAN. I'm nervous. Mister maestro, you launched into your song before I had a chance to get over my nerves. Begin again. *(She dances)* Mister maestro, why are you still playing? I'm already dead.

MAESTRO. What can I do about it if you died four bars ahead of time?

SECOND YOUNG WOMAN. I don't know what bars you've been visiting lately, but I think I did a very nice job.

FIRST EXAMINER. Perhaps, citizeness, with legs like that, you ought to consider going into opera.

SECOND YOUNG WOMAN. You think so?

FIRST EXAMINER. I'm quite certain.

SECOND YOUNG WOMAN. You're the authority, of course. I'll go try the Bolshoi Theater, then. And if worse comes to worst, I'll say you sent me. *(Leaves)*

SECOND EXAMINER. It's your turn now.

FIRST YOUNG WOMAN. The fact is, I forgot to tell you that we were supposed to have a third partner, but he couldn't make it today. He's moonlighting. Basically, he doesn't do anything but sit there like an idiot. Maybe you will take his part?

FIRST EXAMINER. Who? Me?

FIRST YOUNG WOMAN. Yes. *(Takes him by the hand and sits him down)* There. Just sit there and don't do anything.

YOUNG MAN. Pretend you're the proprietor of the den. It's a tavern.

FIRST EXAMINER. I'm sorry, but I can't do that.

YOUNG MAN. Don't be afraid. You don't have to do a thing and you have a very kind face for the part. Maestro, be so kind.

(A dance. The First Young Woman attacks the First Examiner with a knife)

FIRST EXAMINER. Help!

FIRST YOUNG WOMAN. What are you screaming for? You'll ruin my inspiration.

FIRST EXAMINER. What are you doing to me?

FIRST YOUNG WOMAN. I'm stabbing you.

FIRST EXAMINER. What are you stabbing me for?

FIRST YOUNG WOMAN. Because you're the proprietor of the tavern. That's the point of our number.

FIRST EXAMINER. But, if you'll pardon me, I'm not the proprietor of any tavern. I'm a member of the qualification committee.

FIRST YOUNG WOMAN. What's the difference? *(She attacks him again)*

FIRST EXAMINER. Help!

FIRST YOUNG WOMAN. Now you've done it. You ruined my whole dance.

FIRST EXAMINER. I may have ruined your dance, but you and your knife ruined my nose.

FIRST YOUNG WOMAN. I'll have to do the dance again. Comrade, would you please replace this man?

SECOND EXAMINER. Oh, no. Oh, no. Let's just qualify these people in the third rank.

FIRST YOUNG WOMAN. Why, thank you. And should you ever find your-self unemployed, comrade, stop by and see us. Every one of our dances has an extremely easy part where someone just has to sit there and do nothing like an idiot.

FIRST EXAMINER. Careful, there, citizeness. I don't know how to sit like an idiot.

FIRST YOUNG WOMAN. There's nothing to it. All you have to do is sit there like you are now. You're doing a great job.

(They leave)

SCENE THREE

(Enter the Storyteller)

FIRST EXAMINER. Who are you?

STORYTELLER. I'm a storyteller.

FIRST EXAMINER. In that case, there's no point in dallying. Begin please.

STORYTELLER. All right. Two men met at a tiny backwoods station. And so one guy says to the other Jew...

SECOND EXAMINER. Wait a minute. You began by saying that two men met. So what did you mix a Jew in there for?

STORYTELLER. What do you mean? You think a Jew isn't a person?

SECOND EXAMINER. Don't get smart with me. Tell your story without a Jew. There's no point in dragging nationalities into it.

STORYTELLER. Without a Jew? My pleasure. An unbelievable incident took place one Sunday at the local ticket windows at the Kazan station in Moscow. At two o'clock in the afternoon a huge crowd without a Jew gathered.
THIRD EXAMINER. There you go again with the Jew.
STORYTELLER. No, there's no Jew in this one.
THIRD EXAMINER. I would ask you not to tell your story without a Jew in such a manner.
STORYTELLER. I can't tell stories with a Jew. And without a Jew I can't tell stories. So how am I going to tell a story?
FIRST EXAMINER. Tell something about Russians. How come you always have to tell about Jews?
STORYTELLER. About Russians. My pleasure. Two Russians meet. So one Russian says to the other Russian, "Listen Shapshelevich, are you doing business again at Moshelprom?"[7]
SECOND EXAMINER. Sorry. If you're going to tell stories like that, you've got to leave out Russians, too.
STORYTELLER. Who can I tell stories about, then, comrade? How about myself?
THIRD EXAMINER. And who are you?
STORYTELLER. A Jew.[8]
THIRD EXAMINER. That's out, too.
STORYTELLER. Maybe about you?
THIRD EXAMINER. I told you, comrade, no stories about Jews.
STORYTELLER. I can't tell stories about Russians. I can't tell stories about myself. I can't tell stories about you. I can't tell stories about Jews, and you can't possibly tell a story without a Jew. In that case, comrade, can you tell me where one gets qualified for the movies?
FIRST EXAMINER. For the movies? That's not our business. Quit holding things up. Next!

SCENE FOUR[9]

(A Husband and Wife)

HUSBAND. Good day, Your Excellencies.
FIRST EXAMINER. There are no Excellencies here.
WIFE. Forgive him, please. He's near-sighted.
HUSBAND. Isn't this the qualification committee?

[7] The Storyteller confuses the Jewish-sounding name, Moshelprom with the acronym, Mosselprom. Mosselprom, or Moscow Agricultural Industry, was a state agency.
[8] The Storyteller says he is a Tatar in another version of this sketch.
[9] This scene is lacking in another version of this sketch.

FIRST EXAMINER. That's right. Only we aren't Excellencies, we're comrades.

HUSBAND. Oh, well if you're comrades, then that's just what I had in mind.

SECOND EXAMINER. What's that supposed to mean?

HUSBAND. Quite simple. You are excellent choices for the job.

SECOND EXAMINER. Oh. If that's what you mean, that's a different story altogether. Who are you?

HUSBAND. I am none other than a second Glinka,[10] Your Excellency.

THIRD EXAMINER. Glinka? What do you have in common with Glinka?

HUSBAND. Our profession.

FIRST EXAMINER. And what are you by profession?

HUSBAND. By profession, comrades, I am a dead-and-buried talent.

FIRST EXAMINER. First of all, that's not a profession. And second of all, since when is Glinka a dead-and-buried talent?

HUSBAND. Since when? Since 1880. He resides at the Volkovo cemetery.

FIRST EXAMINER. If that's what you mean, that's a different story. What do you want from us?

HUSBAND. Since I'm a dead-and-buried talent, won't you be so kind as to exhume me? Only don't leave my wife behind while you're at it. Allow me to introduce her. (He takes one of the examiners by the hand)

WIFE. Forgive him, please. He's terribly near-sighted. Georgie, that's not me.

HUSBAND. You mean you aren't you?

WIFE. I am me, but that's another man you're introducing.

HUSBAND. Oh, hell. It's terrible to be near-sighted. You're always getting mixed up with some unexpected idiot. Fisochka, where are you? This is my wife, Your Excellencies. She's a very talented dame. Being hereditarily childless, and, having at her disposal two maids and a cook, ever since the early days of our marriage she has devoted all of her free time to the arts.

SECOND EXAMINER. What do you mean, she is hereditarily childless? As I understand it, that means her parents had no children.

HUSBAND. I don't know. Maybe her parents did have children, but she herself never has. Her uncle raised her.

THIRD EXAMINER. Who gave birth to her, then?

WIFE. I wasn't born. I was discovered in a cabbage patch.

HUSBAND. For God's sake, don't destroy her illusions. She's such an innocent little thing.

THIRD EXAMINER. Sorry. But let's get to the point. What do you want from us?

HUSBAND. Allow us to sing you a romance.

THIRD EXAMINER. What romance?

---

[10] The subsequent lines indicate that the Husband is probably confusing the great Russian composer Mikhail Glinka (1804-1857) with the minor poet and author of song lyrics, Fyodor Glinka (1786-1880).

HUSBAND. A very good one.

THIRD EXAMINER. I'm asking you what it's called.

HUSBAND. "Pavel and Hanna." The music is mine.

WIFE. The words are mine.

FIRST EXAMINER. So, you write and sing? What kind of a voice do you have, citizeness?

WIFE. I sing like a bird.

FIRST EXAMINER. I'm asking you what kind of voice it is.

WIFE. A tenor.

SECOND EXAMINER. Pardon me, but only men are tenors.

WIFE. That's discrimination. We have equality of the sexes, these days.

SECOND EXAMINER. As you wish. What kind of voice do you have, comrade?

HUSBAND. I have an alien voice.

SECOND EXAMINER. An alien voice? Whose voice is it, then?

HUSBAND. It's mine, but I have to say what others want me to. May we begin?

THIRD EXAMINER. Please do.

HUSBAND. Ahem. Ahem.

WIFE. Hmm. Hmm.

HUSBAND. "Pavel and Hanna." A duet. The music is mine. *(Begins singing)* "Your name was Hanna..."

WIFE. Georgie, Georgie. Why are you singing with your backside? Turn around in this direction, please. *(Approaches her husband)*

HUSBAND. Fisochka, you know that I'm near-sighted. *(Turns around)* Is that better?

WIFE. Yes.

HUSBAND. Shall we begin?

WIFE. Let's begin.

HUSBAND. From the top?

WIFE. From the top.

HUSBAND. "Pavel and Hanna." A duet. The music is mine.

WIFE. "Pavel and Hanna." A duet. The words are mine.

HUSBAND and WIFE.

> Your name was Hanna. Pavel was mine.
> I remember our innocent days.
> How many times, Oh, how many times
> Did you carve with your knife
> Three letters on the old courtyard tree?
> How, oh, how many could it K.G. be?

(Refrain)

> We flitted and played
> Like butterflies in roses.
> We thought not of love
> But love is what we found.
> We hid in the bushes
> And hearkened the cat's sweet meow.
>
> And then it happened one October.
> The tree bark was stripped away.
> Who could have done it?
> It only could be the K.G.
> Oh, how much joy, how many tears
> Did we learn from that little old tree?[11]

HUSBAND. Wonderful little tune, isn't it?

WIFE. Simply marvelous.

FIRST EXAMINER. Explain yourself, please. What possessed you to write such a thing?

WIFE. Oh, it's autobiographical. I described my romance with Georgie. Georgie was a wonderful suitor. Only, it's too bad that he was so near-sighted.

FIRST EXAMINER. So this is an autobiographical song?

WIFE. Yes.

FIRST EXAMINER. In that case, we can't pass you.

WIFE. What do you mean? Why not?

FIRST EXAMINER. Because there is no place in Soviet entertainment for such criminals.

HUSBAND. What criminals? Which one of us is a criminal? You might say that I'm a second Glinka.

FIRST EXAMINER. You confessed yourself, comrade.

WIFE. Where?

FIRST EXAMINER. In the refrain.

HUSBAND. When?

FIRST EXAMINER. Just now. You said you hid in the bushes and hearkened the CAT's meow.

HUSBAND. But we were in love.

FIRST EXAMINER. That's no excuse. The Criminal Agency Team has only

---

[11] In 1922 and 1923, the Soviet secret police was known by the acronym, G.P.U. (the State Political Directorate), which is the form Erdman uses in this text. From 1923-1934 it was known as the O.G.P.U. (the Joint State Political Directorate). From 1934-1943 it was known as the N.K.V.D. (the National Committee of Internal Affairs). From 1943-1954, it was designated by various acronyms which prefigured the now-famous "K.G.B." The K.G.B. was the official name from 1954-1992. I write "K.G.B." anachronistically for reasons of rhyme and familiarity.

one job: to track down criminals.

HUSBAND. What's the Criminal Agency Team got to do with it?

FIRST EXAMINER. What do you think CAT stands for? You hid in the bushes and hearkened the CAT's meow. It's obvious. You were hiding from the law.

HUSBAND. Fisochka! Look what you did!

WIFE. But, Georgie. These days, no matter what you write, it turns out to be a crime.

HUSBAND. Fisochka, let's get out of here quick before they arrest us. Your Excellencies, next time we'll prepare you something less criminal. For example, a duet about two foreigners: Reva and Lucien.[12]

WIFE. You can kill me if you want, but I'm never writing anything again.

HUSBAND. Fisochka, don't argue with me. You'll keep writing.

WIFE. Georgie, it's final.

HUSBAND. Don't argue with me, Fisochka. Let's go. You'll keep writing.

WIFE. I don't care how pregnant I am with ideas. I'm never writing another word.

HUSBAND. Pregnant! Oh, my God. A cab! Call us a cab!

(They leave)

FIRST EXAMINER. Next! And hurry it up![13]

---

[12] "Reva and Lucien" creates a play on the word, "revolution."

[13] Erdman planned, but apparently did not write, two more scenes: "The Trickster's Trick" and "A Choir of Russian Songsters and Dancers."

Two Scenes from
Moscow From a Point of View

1924

1. The Room in Which They Rented an Apartment[1]

CHARACTERS

The Pupriyak Family

LAVR LAVROVICH — also called Lavrusha
ANNA IVANOVNA — his wife
MISHA — their son
ZOYA — their daughter
ISABELLA PANKRATYEVNA — the children's "auntie"

Tenants of the Apartment

THE SHYSTER — landlord of the apartment
KLAVOCHKA SINICHKINA
SENYECHKA SINICHKIN — her husband
A SHOEMAKER
A COTTON MERCHANT
FIRST CHAIR
SECOND CHAIR
A FEMALE SINGER
A MOTHER
A PHYSICAL EDUCATION INSTRUCTOR
A CHILD — his student
A HUSBAND
HIS WIFE
A BOOKKEEPER
IVAN TARASOVICH — his young son

MISHA. *(Enters)* Papa, don't come in here. Papa, don't come in here. It's dangerous in here.

SHYSTER. Come in, come in, please. Don't be afraid. Don't be afraid, comrades. Come in, come in.

PUPRIYAK. My Lord, what is this?

SHYSTER. This, comrade, is my room where you can rent an apartment.

---

[1] *Moscow From a Point of View, a revue in three acts and seven scenes,* was written in 1924 and first performed October 1 of the same year as the opening production at the new Satire Theater. "The Room in Which They Rented an Apartment" was the second scene.

41

ALL. What?

SHYSTER. I say, this is my room where you can rent an apartment.

ISABELLA. Misha, where's our thermometer? I think I'm dying.

ZOYA. Papa, auntie is dying.

PUPRIYAK. Zoya, go to your mother. Misha, give me the thermometer. Listen here, if you're insane, you're better off admitting it.

SHYSTER. I don't quite understand you, citizen.

PUPRIYAK. Maybe you don't quite understand us, citizen, but I don't understand you at all, citizen. How can we possibly rent an apartment in your room?

SHYSTER. It's quite simple. Just like everyone else does. Take this family here, for instance. It consists of three people. A father and a mother who live on the income of their newborn infant.

ANNA IVANOVNA. What income can their newborn infant have?

SHYSTER. You see, his mother is a homemaker. She doesn't work anywhere. His father was recently laid off. That leaves the infant as the only one with an income.

PUPRIYAK. How can he have an income?

SHYSTER. The fact is that, here in Moscow, the only people allowed in the front door of tram cars are those with infants. So this couple rents out their infant and they live on the income.

ANNA IVANOVNA. Lavrusha, what odd customs. Still an infant, and he already has a family around his neck.

SHYSTER. You see, I rented him a three-room apartment, if I may express it that way. That is, it consists of a three-story, twenty-eight square inch parcel. As the responsible party, he occupies the top floor in his crib. His parents occupy the middle floor and he rents out the lower floor to a shoemaker.

ISABELLA. Lord, let's get out of here. My temperature has hit 100°. Look here, you...

SHYSTER. I wouldn't suggest your leaving, madam. You can't find more comfortable accommodations in Moscow, anyway.

MISHA. But how will we fit in here when we have nineteen pieces of luggage alone, not counting auntie and the canary?

SHYSTER. Don't you worry. We'll squeeze you in.

PUPRIYAK. How can you squeeze us in when you don't have a breath of empty space?

SHYSTER. Because, citizen, we not only squeeze in space, we squeeze in time.

ANNA IVANOVNA. In time?

SHYSTER. It's quite simple. For example, take, *par example,* the dame quartered here who goes to work in the evening and comes home in the morning. A very nice, intelligent dame. One can't help but ask, why shouldn't someone live in her quarters during the night? Say, for instance, you, madam.

ANNA IVANOVNA. Where does she live?

SHYSTER. In the washroom.

ANNA IVANOVNA. Misha, do you happen to have another thermometer? I think I'm dying, too.

SHYSTER. But madam, it's quite convenient to live in the washroom. And most important, it's very hygienic.

PUPRIYAK. If my wife is going to live in a washroom, I'll divorce her. I am an old bookkeeper, comrades, not a deep-sea diver of some kind.

ANNA IVANOVNA. You may think I'm all wet, but...

SHYSTER. So much the better. Still, if that doesn't suit you, we have other places as well.

PUPRIYAK. Where?

SHYSTER. Coming right up. Let's see, one ring for the shoemaker, two for the Sinichkins and three for the rental bureau. *(Rings)*

KLAVOCHKA. Ah!

(The Shyster rings again)

Entrez.

SHYSTER. Good day, comrade.

THE SINICHKINS. Good day, good day.

KLAVOCHKA. Squeeze up to the table. Squeeze up to the table.

SHYSTER. Oh no, thank you. I'm here on business. Allow me to introduce you to comrade Pupriyak. A very cultured comrade.

PUPRIYAK. Pupriyak and his family.

KLAVOCHKA. I imagine you're here to see my infant about the tram car business. Unfortunately, our infant is out right now. He's working the "B" line. You understand, I'm sure. He's all alone and has to service a large number of clients.

ANNA IVANOVNA. Oh, how I sympathize with you. Oh, how I sympathize with you. It must be terrible to tear your child from your breast and send him off to work.

SHOEMAKER. Listen, citizen, lift your foot, will you? Your knee is blocking the light.

SENYECHKA. Sorry.

MISHA. Tell me, do you really live your whole life on your feet? How can you stand it?

SENYECHKA. It's nothing. Here, people even put up with living on other people's feet.

MISHA. But, when do you sleep, if I may be so bold as to ask?

KLAVOCHKA. On Mondays. On Mondays, the shoemaker goes out and gets drunk, so we take turns sleeping in his quarters.

PUPRIYAK. Only on Mondays?

KLAVOCHKA. We have pleaded with him endlessly to go out and get drunk at least one more day a week, but he doesn't want to. He says he's got to increase his productivity.

SHOEMAKER. I'll be transferring soon to cultural work,[2] citizeness. Then you can sleep all week long, except for Mondays.

SHYSTER. While you're transferring to cultural work, let's get down to business, shall we, comrades? When does your landlord come home?

SENYECHKA. On the last tram.

SHYSTER. Then the crib is empty during the day?

SENYECHKA. Yes.

SHYSTER. We'll have to fill it, comrades.

KLAVOCHKA. With whom?

SHYSTER. With this citizeness with the nose, here.

SENYECHKA. We can't allow it.

SHYSTER. But your apartment is unoccupied.

KLAVOCHKA. Comrade, this is not a private apartment. It is "The Rental Bureau for the Allocation of Breast-Fed Passes Guaranteeing the Right of Front-Door Entry." It might be a different story if your citizeness here could pass as an infant. But she doesn't look very infantile to me.

SHYSTER. Redoing the way somebody looks is as easy as spitting. That is to say, it's as easy as spitting into a spitoon. Come here, comrade Pupriyak.

(The Pupriyaks whisper among themselves)

ZOYA. I don't want to, papa.

PUPRIYAK. Zoya, go to your mother.

ANNA IVANOVNA. What do you do if you have to go, you know...

COTTON MERCHANT. Comrades, if you need to go to the washroom, all you have to do is sign up on the waiting list. Once you've done that, go up to the attic. Nobody will see you there.

ANNA IVANOVNA. Come on, Zoya dear, let's go.

(Anna Ivanovna and Zoya leave)

SHYSTER. Now let's try to arrange a place for you. Pardon me, comrade, when do you leave for work?

FIRST CHAIR. What time is it now? Oh my Lord, my watch has stopped. You'll have to talk with my seat about that.

---

[2] In the original, the Shoemaker plans to go to work at Vserabis, an acronym for the All-Union Labor Union of Arts Workers. As he did in many of his sketches, Erdman spoofed the practice of uneducated laborers working in the cultural sphere.

SHYSTER. With who?

FIRST CHAIR. My seat.

SHYSTER. Pardon me, when do you leave work?

SECOND CHAIR. Now.

SHYSTER. Where do you work?

SECOND CHAIR. Here.

SHYSTER. Here?

SECOND CHAIR. Yes.

SHYSTER. What do you work as?

SECOND CHAIR. A chair.

SHYSTER. Then where do you live?

SECOND CHAIR. On this chair.

SHYSTER. Then where does this chair live?

SECOND CHAIR. On me.

SHYSTER. Pardon me, but when do you sleep, then?

SECOND CHAIR. At Lunacharsky's lectures.[3]

ISABELLA. Lavrusha, let's get out of here now or my thermometer is going to pop. Neither it nor I can take this anymore.

SHYSTER. Madam, there's nowhere for you to go, you're better off staying here.

ISABELLA. Are you trying to make a laughingstock of me? Where can I possibly live in this room?

SHYSTER. You?

ISABELLA. Yes.

SHYSTER. On the trapeze.

ISABELLA. The trapeze?

(An explosion is heard)

ALL. What was that?

ISABELLA. My thermometer popped.

SHYSTER. I don't understand what you're worried about, madam. Living on a trapeze is as good as having your own home. The quarters are private, nobody will be passing through, nobody will be stepping on your feet and you'll sleep like a baby. Most important, there won't be any bedbugs.

ISABELLA. What do you think I am? A bird of nature or a society of friends of the Air Force, or something? I don't know how to live in the air.

SHYSTER. Madam, I ask that you not shout in here. You might be subject to a fine. After all, this is a common living area, you know.

FEMALE SINGER. A-a-a-a… A-a-a-a-a… *(Crawls half-way out of the piano)*

---

[3] As the People's Commissar of Education, Anatoly Lunacharsky often delivered speeches and lectures on political and cultural themes. See note 4 to "The Qualification Exams."

PUPRIYAK. What is that?

SHYSTER. A young student at the conservatory lives here in the piano. I imagine she's preparing for exams.

FEMALE SINGER. A-a-a-a-a... A-a-a-a-a-a... A-a-a-a-a-a...

COTTON MERCHANT. Cotton for sale! Good cotton for sale! Five kopecks a plug! Cotton for sale! Good cotton for sale! Five kopecks a plug! (*He hangs out a sign: "Committee for the Struggle against Vocal Elements"*)

SHYSTER. Take your place in line, comrades.

PUPRIYAK. Misha, here's some money. Go stand in line.

COTTON MERCHANT. Cotton for sale! Good cotton for sale! Five kopecks a plug!

SHYSTER. Plug up your ears, madam. Plug 'em up good.

ISABELLA. I've already plugged them up to the tune of eighty kopecks. Do you want me to go bankrupt, or something?

COTTON MERCHANT. I warn you, madam, she has a coloratura soprano. It's a very dangerous voice. You'd better not economize.

PUPRIYAK. Misha, where's the change?

MISHA. What change? Papa, I can't hear anything.

FEMALE SINGER. A-a-a-a-a... A-a-a-a-a... Listen, young man. Give me ten kopecks worth, too. I can't stand it anymore, myself. (*Plugs her ears*) Thank you. (*Begins singing*)

SHYSTER. Comrade! Citizeness! Madam! Milady! Mademoiselle? Idiot.

FEMALE SINGER. Did you want to say something to me?

SHYSTER. Please make note of the place where you stopped. I would like to interrupt you for a minute.

FEMALE SINGER. What's the problem?

SHYSTER. Tell me, do you think we might find some spare living quarters in your piano?

FEMALE SINGER. How shall I put it? Personally, I live on the bass chords, so the trebles are absolutely free. If you were to find a lonely, decent woman, then she could live on the trebles. I have nothing against it.

SHYSTER. Isabella Pankratyevna! Hey, Isabella Pankratyevna!

ISABELLA. What?

SHYSTER. The fact is, this gentlewoman has nothing against a decent lady squeezing in with her. Are you suitable for that or not?

ISABELLA. Huh?

SHYSTER. I say, this gentlewoman here—the cotton, take the cotton out of your ears.

ISABELLA. You mean she quit singing?

SHYSTER. Yes. Yes.

ISABELLA. Honest? It's not dangerous anymore?

SHYSTER. Honest.

ISABELLA. Just a second. You know, I plugged up my right ear so good, I'm afraid I'll never unplug it.

SHOEMAKER. She stuffed up her ears like they stuffed Mooney away in prison.[4] There's a real madam for you, ladies and gentlemen.

ISABELLA. Did you want to say something to me?

SHYSTER. Would you care to live on the right hand?

ISABELLA. On the what?

SHYSTER. The right hand, the trebles. Here in the piano.

ISABELLA. If this keeps up, next you're going to try to find me a home in a clarinet. The piano?! How do you expect me to fit in there?

SHYSTER. What do you want me to do, order you a baby grand to give you more room?

PUPRIYAK. Forget it, Isabella. At your scale, we'll never find an apartment for you in this room.

ISABELLA. Are you suggesting I re-do my figure for the sake of this apartment?

SHYSTER. Perhaps you think someone is going to re-do the laws of living quarters for the sake of your figure?

MISHA. Auntie, you're going to have to slim down.

ISABELLA. How am I going to do that?

SHYSTER. Take up sports, madam.

ISABELLA. Sports? You mean like those people who run around in their underwear? Not on your life.

SHYSTER. You don't have to do it in your underwear, madam. If you prefer, you can do it without underwear.

ISABELLA. Anyway, where would I have room to work out?

SHYSTER. In the kindergarten. We have a kindergarten for all the children on hand, madam. You see? It's called "The Weight Lifter Ivan Poddubny's Industrious Busy-Bee."[5] This kindergarten is equipped with an athletic field and a yacht club in the bathtub.

(Enter Anna Ivanovna and Zoya)

ANNA IVANOVNA. Zoya, suck louder. Suck louder or it won't seem natural.

ZOYA. Papa, I'm afraid. Papa I'm afraid.

PUPRIYAK. Zoya, go to your mother.

ZOYA. Papa dear, don't make me live in a crib. I don't know how.

PUPRIYAK. You should be ashamed, Zoya. Even infants live in cribs. You're a grown woman. You even finished high school, and you tell me you don't

---

[4] This refers to Tom Mooney, an American labor organizer sentenced to 21 years in prison in the United States in 1918. His case was well known in the Soviet Union.

[5] Ivan Poddubny was a world champion wrestler from 1905 to 1908.

know how. You should be ashamed.

SHYSTER. Put her in, put her in.

ZOYA. Careful or you'll smash my pacifier.

SHOEMAKER. Welcome to your new home, mademoiselle.

ZOYA. Merci.

SENYECHKA. I am compelled to remind you, comrade Pupriyak, that, beginning tomorrow, we will begin renting out your daughter.

PUPRIYAK. Rent her out, citizen, rent her out. It's high time she started earning a living.

ANNA IVANOVNA. Are you comfortable, Zoya?

ZOYA. Mama, it's very unstable here. And damp.

KLAVOCHKA. Damp? Spread out a rubber sheet under yourself, citizeness.

ANNA IVANOVNA. Zoya, if you want to get out, don't try it on your own. Ask for help.

(Pupriyak sits in a chair)

FIRST CHAIR. Careful, that's a live person you're sitting on.

SECOND CHAIR. Pardon me, but that's my seat you've occupied.

PUPRIYAK. Finally! We got one of us situated. *(Tosses his cigarette butt in a spitoon)*

ISABELLA. Help! Fire!

MOTHER. What do you think you're doing, citizen? My baby lives in that spitoon, and you go throwing your butts in it.

PUPRIYAK. What baby?

MOTHER. What baby? That's none of your business. My legitimate son, that's who!

MISHA. But madam…

MOTHER. First of all, I'm no madam. I'm a gentlewoman, and second—oh, my God! His entire hair-do has burned to a crisp. There's nothing but ashes left on his bare little skull.

PUPRIYAK. I assure you, my kind woman, it was a coincidence.

MOTHER. Well, it was rather shameless on your part, citizen. I ought to take you to court.

PUPRIYAK. I assure you, milady, I didn't realize. It happened like this: I finished my cigarette and then looked around and saw a spitoon. So I threw my butt in it and suddenly there's fireworks everywhere.

MOTHER. You mean, you think that if you see any old spitoon, you can just toss your butts in it without thinking?

PUPRIYAK. I assumed that the spitoon was put here for people to use it.

MOTHER. If you were a conscious citizen, then you'd know well enough to use the spitoon in a cultured manner. Thank God it was my baby in there. What would have happened if I'd been sleeping in there myself?

MISHA. I gather, then, that we're supposed to throw our butts on the floor?

MOTHER. What makes you think you've got to throw your butts on the floor or on baby's heads? Can't you think of another place to throw them? First, you take the baby out of the spitoon, then you spit or toss your butt in it, then you put the baby back from where you got him. Is that so difficult? What, did you just show up from Africa or something? Or maybe you're some kind of Martian Aelita.[6] You evidently don't know how to behave yourself in a decent home.

PUPRIYAK. But, allow me…

MOTHER. I don't want to talk to you. Don't cry, Petya. Don't cry, my baby. They'll grow back.

WOMAN'S VOICE. Glafira Semyonovna, I'm taking down my Marusya, now. If you want, you can hang your Petya up there.

ANNA IVANOVNA. Oh Lord! They're hanging babies!

SHYSTER. That's right. By the collar. This is our kindergarten, madam. Children need air, madam, so we hang them in the air.

(A whistle is heard)

ALL. Ah! What a racket!

SHYSTER. They're summoning the hanged-baby instructor to the kindergarten. Their lessons are about to begin.

(Enter a physical education instructor in shorts)

ISABELLA. Help! A naked man!

ZOYA. Help! Where? Let me see.

ANNA IVANOVNA. Zoya, turn around.

PUPRIYAK. What do you let people like that in here for?

SHYSTER. What do you mean, Lavr Lavrovich? He is a very educated young man.

ANNA IVANOVNA. Educated?

SHYSTER. He's not merely educated, he's phys-educated. They say he made ten head-butt goals in one game alone.

MISHA. Where?

SHYSTER. Past the goaltender.

MISHA. Whose heads were they?

SHYSTER. Not ten heads, ten goals. You play soccer with your feet, you know.

---

[6] This refers to both the novel *Aelita,* written in 1922 by Alexei Tolstoy (1883-1945), and the 1924 movie made of it by Yakov Protazanov (1881-1945). Often called the first Soviet work of science fiction or the first Soviet utopian novel, *Aelita* told of earth travellers who go to Mars where they discover a decadent society.

MISHA. Then how come you said he played with his head?

SHYSTER. Well, sometimes they play with their heads, too. After all, for a soccer player, what's the difference? Head, feet, they all work the same. Isabella Pankratyevna, it's time for your lesson.

ISABELLA. What lesson?

SHYSTER. What do you mean, what lesson? Your slimming-down lesson.

ISABELLA. But…

PUPRIYAK. Isa, go lose some weight or else you'll wind up without an apartment.

INSTRUCTOR. Children, this is your new comrade. If she can't keep up with you in anything, help her.

CHILD. How old are you?

ISABELLA. Thirty.

CHILD. That means you're older than me. I'm eight.

INSTRUCTOR. Line it up! Even it out! Atten-tion! Begin! One, two, three.
(Puts on a gas mask)

MISHA. Citizen, what are you putting on a gas mask for?

INSTRUCTOR. Because when people engage in sports, a healthy body gives off a healthy odor.

SHYSTER. Isabella Pankratyevna, when you slim down, let me know. I'll arrange your quarters on the trebles.

(Phys-ed lessons)

INSTRUCTOR. One, two, three, four.

(Song :"Oh, the Bird Got Caught.") [7]

INSTRUCTOR. Atten-tion!

SENYECHKA. Klavochka, open your umbrella.

ANNA IVANOVNA. Zoya, you should be ashamed.

ZOYA. Sorry, mama, I broke the baby's milk bottle by accident.

KLAVOCHKA. That's all right, that's all right. We're used to it. We have our own infant. We understand.

(Pupriyak opens the closet. Inside is a bourgeois idyll. The Husband and Wife sing a romance to the accompaniment of a guitar)

HUSBAND AND WIFE.
　　　Oh, how fine, how fine, how fine

---

[7] The first two lines of this once-popular song were: "Oh, the bird got caught. / Now she'll never get out of her cage."

To gaze into your glances,
To love and wilt
And perish in your kisses.
Oh, how fine, how fine, how fine
It is to be with you.
Oh, how hard, how hard, how hard
It is to part with you.
Not to see you, not to hear you,
Not to breathe with you alone.
Oh, how hard, how hard
It is to part with you.

ANNA IVANOVNA. Help! A mouse!
ALL. Where? Where?
ANNA IVANOVNA. Listen. You can hear it gnawing.
SHYSTER. That's probably in the bookkeeper's apartment.
SENYECHKA. Comrade, be so kind, give him a ring. Two long ones and a short one.

(They ring at the closet's side door)

BOOKKEEPER. What's wrong? What's the matter? Nobody will even let you stand quietly for an hour or two.
SHYSTER. Say, do you have a mouse?
BOOKKEEPER. What mouse?
ANNA IVANOVNA. Don't you hear it gnawing?
BOOKKEEPER. That is not a mouse, citizens. That's Ivan Tarasovich gnawing at the rock of science with his young teeth. *(He opens the lower drawer in the closet, revealing Ivan Tarasovich lying on his stomach, memorizing his lessons)*
PUPRIYAK. How can he study in there?
SHYSTER. What's so difficult about it? It's quiet around here.

(The Instructor begins counting, the children begin exercising, the Husband and Wife begin a duet, the Female Singer begins singing, Ivan Tarasovich reads aloud, etc. The lights come down. Silence)

SHYSTER. Comrades, for those who desire it, I propose you get yourselves a good sleep. In an hour, the apartment transforms into a café.

(Conversation in the dark)

SHOEMAKER. Hey, what are you putting your feet on my head for?
SENYECHKA. Comrade, I have the right to expanded living space. I'm a

member of the Bolshevik Central Committee.

SHOEMAKER. My mistake. Make yourself comfortable.

OTHER VOICES. — Citizen, hey citizen!

      — Now what? Every time I try to sleep, you start pestering me.

      — I just wanted to ask…

      — Ask what?

      — Is that your wife or mine?

      — How should I know? We'll straighten it out in the morning.

2. The Self-Taught Communist[8]

CHARACTERS IN ORDER OF APPEARANCE

CHAIRMAN — Mikhailov
SECRETARY
VARIOUS VOICES
A WOMAN
COMRADE UKHOV — a deaf-mute
ORATOR AGAINST
ORATOR FOR
A POET — Comrade Aslyonov
OKURKIN — a poet and store manager

A Poster Text: "A sudden meeting of the circle of the Centroproduct Clerical Bureaucrats will be convened today. It will be devoted to the memory of the circle's honorary secretary, comrade Pushkin, who was viciously murdered by the White Army soldier, D'Anthès, two days before he (that is, Pushkin) died.[9] Synopses, reports, speeches, discussions, poetry, charades, candy, streamers, bons figures and dances 'til morning.

All honorary members, members, candidate members, their families and much respected personages are invited.

Entrance fees:

    Members — free

    Personages — 24 kopecks."

---

[8] "The Self-Taught Communist" was written to replace the original third scene, "Café. 1924." Reports in the press indicate that it first appeared in 1927. However, several elements in the text imply that this version, at least, was written in 1924 or 1925. Among them are references to the revolution having taken place seven years earlier and Pushkin's death having occurred eighty-eight years earlier. The literal translation of the scene's title is "The Red Self-Taught Person."

[9] The great Russian poet, Alexander Pushkin (1799-1837), died of wounds suffered in a duel with Georges D'Anthès, a Frenchman living in Russia.

(On stage are clerical bureaucrats and other members of the public)

CHAIRMAN. Dear full members, members, candidate members and much respected personages! I now declare the meeting open. For seven years now...

SECRETARY. Excuse me, I have a procedural question. Comrade clerical bureaucrats of Centroproduct, have you all registered?

CHAIRMAN. Comrades, don't get ahead of yourselves. I suggest electing the below-mentioned list as honorary members of the presidium.

VOICE. I request it be made public.

CHAIRMAN. I hereby make it public. One: comrade Homer. Two: comrade Shakespeare. Three: comrade Schiller and Goethe. Four: comrade Lord Byron. Five: comrade Mikhailov.

ANOTHER VOICE. What Mikhailov?

CHAIRMAN. Comrade, don't get ahead of yourself. I am comrade Mikhailov. And so; Five: comrade Mikhailov. Six: comrade Sophocles. Seven: comrade Dumas and his sons. Eight: comrade George Sand. Nine: the much-respected comrade Demyan Bedny.[10] Ten: comrade Chateaubriand.

VOICE. Comrades, I reject the candidacy of Chateaubriand.

CHAIRMAN. On what grounds?

VOICE. On the grounds of his rear end.

CHAIRMAN. Comrade, don't get ahead of yourself.

VOICE. Excuse me. I have nothing against Chateau, but I categorically cast my vote against Briand, who is a member of the French parliament.[11]

ANOTHER VOICE. I suggest leaving Chateaubriand in the list with the exception of his rear end.

CHAIRMAN. I put it to a vote. Who's for, who's against, who abstains? It's passed unanimously.

WOMAN. Comrades, my personage's sex protests.

CHAIRMAN. What?

WOMAN. I said, my personage's sex protests.

CHAIRMAN. Uh, just what do you mean by your personage's sex?

WOMAN. Comrades, I am not a member, I am a woman. And I am speaking on behalf of the sex of my personage, that is, on behalf of the personage of my sex. Comrades, I will pose a merciless question. Why, in spite of the October Revolution, is there not a single woman included in the list of the presidium?

CHAIRMAN. Comrades, that is not true. There is a woman in the list and I read her name.

---

[10] Demyan Bedny (1883-1945) was a popular political poet in the early years of Soviet power.

[11] Aristide Briand served as the Prime Minister of France several times between 1909 and 1931. He was an outspoken opponent of the Soviet Union in the 1920s.

WOMAN. What woman?

CHAIRMAN. Sand.

WOMAN. What Sand?

CHAIRMAN. George.

WOMAN. Who's George?

CHAIRMAN. George is her name.

WOMAN. Whose her?

CHAIRMAN. Hers, Sand's. George Sand is a woman.

WOMAN. George is a woman. Merci. Comrades, he is attempting to slip some George into the membership of the presidium in the guise of a woman. Comrades, as a person, I categorically protest.

CHAIRMAN. I assure you that this George is woman.

WOMAN. Please don't harass me. There is no such thing as a woman George. My husband is a George, if you'd like to know.

VOICE. Comrades, in the aversion of confusion I put George Sand's sex to a vote. Who is for sex, please raise your hand. One, two, three, four, five, six. Who is against? One, two, three, four, five, six.

CHAIRMAN. I request the advice of the protocol committee. In the vote on the sex of George Sand, six voted for sex, and six voted against sex. Two remained in sexual abstention. I declare that comrade George Sand departs from the list of the presidium for reasons of indiscriminate sex. Dear members and personages, let's now get on with what comes later. For seven years now…

SECRETARY. Excuse me. Comrade clerical bureaucrats of Centroproduct, at the current moment, in the aversion of hygiene, please don't smoke or spit.

CHAIRMAN. Comrade, don't get ahead of yourself. Dear members and personages, I suggest electing an honorary chairman at today's meeting. I enter the candidacy of comrade Ukhov. The given comrade Ukhov has absolutely officially recommended himself as an author. Furthermore, every Sunday the given comrade Ukhov stands face-forward to the countryside, ten versts from Moscow on the Yaroslavl rail lines, both as a weekend country gentleman and as a revolutionary. Who's for, who's against, who abstains? It's accepted unanimously.

SECRETARY. Please take the floor, comrade Ukhov.

CHAIRMAN. Speak with your hands.

SECRETARY. What?

CHAIRMAN. Speak with your hands, he doesn't understand language.

SECRETARY. How's that?

CHAIRMAN. Comrades, I forgot to tell you that the given comrade Ukhov is a deaf-mute. Nevertheless, he has always related sympathetically to the proletariat. Dear members and personages, the given comrade Ukhov will now stand before you and deliver his introductory word which is entitled "Pushkin as the Oak of Russian Poetry."

(The speech of the deaf-mute, after which the Chairman continues)

Comrade honorary chairman, allow me the floor. May I? Thank you. Dear members and personages, it's been seven years since, just as eighty-eight years ago, a traitorous bullet of a White Army soldier has killed one of us. Comrades, I will not hide from you that this was Pushkin. Pushkin was a real genius. Moreover, from earliest childhood I myself wanted to be a real genius, but my parents were against it. What kind of people were Pushkin's parents? I won't say anything for his mother, because a mother is no theme for a topic. But as for his father, elements entirely alien to us absolutely openly wrote that he was a Blackamoor and that, consequently, the unforgettable comrade Pushkin himself was also some sort of shady figure.[12] However, comrades, the fact that Pushkin was a shady figure does not prove that he was a Blackamoor. Comrades, let's get to the bottom of what makes a Blackamoor from a scientific point of view. For brevity's sake, we will operate using scientific terminology. Attention, I hereby operate. That is, let's begin at the heart of it all. In the apartment living next to me there resides a certain Gnovikov family which, in aversion of unnecessary fermentation and agitation, I shall refer to as NN. Let's approach them point by point. Point a) Gnovikov Ferapont is a bookkeeper of the first rank. Point b) Gnovikova Claudia is a housekeeper. Footnote to point b: Their boy Syomka is four years old and their girl Antenna is five months old.[13] Thesis: A and B are officially registered as brother and sister, but, in fact, they are engaged in secret legal matrimony. Antithesis: They maintain their production (that is, Antenna and Syomka, see footnote) by means of the neighboring masses in the below-mentioned manner. Synthesis: I was once standing in my room, looking at my pants. The more I looked at them the more depressed I got. As for the front half, I had no complaints at all: No matter where I looked, there were pants everywhere. And there were pants at the top, too, but, no matter where you looked in the middle of the back, you couldn't see any pants at all. I was amazed. Wasn't it only yesterday that there were still pants on this spot? And now, today, there's nothing on that spot but a naked spot. Naturally, as a man of intellectual labor, holes to me are no surprise. Because even the best pants wear out from intellectual labor. Be that as it may, I stood there looking at my pants and the more I looked, the more depressed I got.

---

[12] Pushkin was the descendant of an Abyssinian officer who enjoyed the patronage of Peter the Great. He wrote about this forebear, Ibragim, in the unfinished work, *The Blackamoor of Peter the Great.*

[13] Erdman here spoofs the custom that arose a few years after the revolution of naming children with "futuristic" names taken from technological advances. The Gnovikovs' older child, born before the custom had caught on, has a relatively common name, while the newborn girl bears a "modern," technological name.

VOICE. What do you keep going on about pants for? Can't you say anything without pants?

CHAIRMAN. Comrade, don't get ahead of yourself. And so... Where was I? Oh, yes. Comrades, it's been seven years since... Pardon me. A slight slip, there. Seven years... Well, to make a long story short, let's move on to my pants. At that very place where I was interrupted, citizeness Gnovikova, or, for brevity, point B, comes bursting into my room. The aforesaid herself asked me in total cold blood: "Do you, comrade Mikhailov, adore coffee?" "Yes, approximately," I responded. "Ah," she says, "that's charming. Why don't you come to my room for a cup of coffee?" Well, I started to think, there's a good one for you. How am I going to drink coffee when, instead of this spot here on my pants, I have a naked spot? And then I think, no big deal, I'll just sit on it. So off we went. And then we arrived. Well, their room is nothing to speak of: They've got a window and a clock. As soon as I entered, I sat down. She sits down across from me, and at my side, under the guise of her brother, her spouse also takes a seat. And that he is her husband, I know absolutely full well by means of the partition between our rooms. There's no wall between our rooms, just a thin partition. As such, it's true that you can't see anything, but I can hear just fine that he's her husband. Enough of that. We sit there. I'm drinking my third cup of coffee. "Eat something," she says. "We're not greedy about this slop." I drink a fourth cup and suddenly I see there's no husband. Where he cleared out to, I have no idea, but clear out, he did. In this manner, I remained one on one with B. So, she's sitting across from me vis à vis. She's wearing a capote, she's got a brooch on her capote and she says, "Ah!" "Ah!" she says, "comrade Mikhailov, open the window. I'm perspiring terribly." Yeah, I think to myself, here we go. Because how am I going to stand up when that which I use to stand on is covered by nothing at all? "Go ahead and sweat," I tell her, "it's good for you." "No," she says, "I'll ruin my capote." What else could I do? I got up, holding my chair to my backside and started hopping towards the window. She says, "What's the matter, comrade Mikhailov?" "Pardon me," I say, "It's just nerves." I hop over to the window and sense that a memento mori has dawned. I can only do one of two things: Either I hold the chair or I open the window. "Pardon me," I say, "but instead of this spot here, I've got a naked spot." As soon as I said it, I had the feeling I was going to sink through the floor. And then she does this little pas with her eye and says, "What a terrible coquette you are." "Nothing of the sort," I tell her. "It's the result of intellectual labor." So she says, "Give me your pants and I'll patch them." Well, at first I started hemming and hawing, and then I said, go ahead and patch them. She starts patching them. At first, I kept silent. I figured I could hold out. But then I realized I couldn't stand it anymore. She was patching my pants to my body. "I give up," I say. "Quit it, I don't have the courage." "Comrade Mikhailov," she says, "I sympathize with your bachelorhood existence. Why don't you leave me your pants? I'll patch them in my spare time and send them to you when they're done." And then she disappeared behind a screen. Very splendid. I take off my pants. And while I'm taking them off, I think, what a saint of a woman is this B. I took them off and went back to my room. I wait. I waited one day, two days, three days. On the fourth day, I said, to hell with this. You bums, I think, go ahead and live off my pants. I went out and bought a new pair. When the statute of limitations expired, I got a court summons. "Are you comrade Mikhailov?" "Yes." "Are these your pants?" "Yes." "Pay for the kid." Well, of course my mouth went dry instantly and my eyes went black. "What do you mean, pay?" I ask. "For what kid?" "For your own." "Citizen judge," I say, "What am I, a goat or something to go having kids?" "Do you mean to say that you refuse?" "I refuse." "And have you ever visited comrade Gnovikova?" "Yes." "Did you drink coffee?" "Yes." "Pay for the kid." "Comrade judge, call any luminary of science to witness and he'll prove to you that children don't come from coffee. Coffee is no symptom of children." "That may be," he says, "but what about the pants?" "Well, there I have nothing to cover myself with—pants are!" "They are?" "They are." "Are these yours?" "They are." "Pay for the kid." In such a manner, not having had any joint relations with the aforementioned B, I was compelled to take on her sponsorship. Even though that kid of hers is from her husband, comrade Gnovikov, who hides under the guise of her brother in order to support his offspring out of the purses of unsuspecting laborers. This comrade Gnovikov is definitely a Blackamoor, because a respectable person would never pass off his own personal children as illegitimate nephews. Therefore, comrades, the future proved that Pushkin was not a Blackamoor and that Blackamoors like Gnovikov should be booted out in the open with an iron heel. Moreover, I have proof of the aforementioned. Let's take, for instance, a collection of his complete works. I consider it folly to read out the entire collection, because if we were to do that, when would we have time left to dance?

VOICES. That's right!

CHAIRMAN. Comrades, don't get ahead of yourselves. And thus, let's limit ourselves to a few selected passages and quotes. Let's take, for instance, this pearl of Pushkin's oeuvre:

> Autumn filled the courtyard,
> It already was October.[14]

---

[14] This is an imperfect quote from Chapter Four, stanza forty of Pushkin's verse novel, *Eugene Onegin,* the stylistic details of which are lost in translation. Worthy of note is that Pushkin wrote not "October," but "November." Shortly after the Russian Revolution, the word "October" came to stand as a replacement for "the Revolution."

One hundred years ago, Pushkin already knew that, sooner or later, the October Revolution would come to the tsar's court. And you call him a Blackamoor. The next pearl: His relationship to the October Revolution:

> Winter! The peasant is triumphant.
> Magicians fear not the powerful masters.[15]

Who are these magicians? Obviously, it's the workers at our fabulous new electromagnetic plant. Of course, one must admit that Pushkin didn't sing the praises of our leaders. He sang the praises of the little laborers of our revolution. For example: He didn't sing the praises of Kamenev,[16] but he did sing the praises of his secretary, comrade Musique,[17] and he did so quite nicely in the following quatrain:

> Cutting fluffy furrows in the road,
> The battle music thunders.[18]

I believe there is no need for further comment. Whenever speaking with his nanny, Alexander Ivanovich[19] always said...
VOICES. Sergeich.
CHAIRMAN. Comrades, don't get ahead of yourselves. And thus. And thus, what is it I wanted to say? Oh, yes. Comrades, it's been seven years since—I mean to say, even when he was still a toddler, little Sasha once wrote, when addressing his popular nanny:

> Kiss me. Your kisses
> Give me peace sublime.[20]

Obviously, his theme here was the Versailles Peace Treaty, the sole blame for which rests entirely on the international scoundrels of world imperialism, to say nothing of the fact that he also addressed the Soviet government by placing the following exclamation on the lips of Boris Godunov:

---

[15] The first line is a quote from Chapter Five, stanza two of *Eugene Onegin.* The second line is from Pushkin's poem, "Song about Oleg the Prophet."

[16] Lev Kamenev (1883-1936) was one of Lenin's staunch allies and a member of the Politburo until 1926, when he was stripped of his duties.

[17] One of Kamenev's secretaries was named Ivan Muzyka, pronounced similarly to the French "musique."

[18] The first line is from Chapter Five, stanza two of Pushkin's *Eugene Onegin.* The second line is a bungled quote from Mikhail Lermontov's poem, "Valerik," which contains the line, "The regimental music hums."

[19] Virtually every Russian knows that Pushkin's patronymic was Sergeyevich.

[20] This is from Pushkin's short poem which begins with the line, "The flame of desire burns in the blood."

Comrades, for seven years my reign has been peaceful.[21]

Nor did he—that is, Pushkin—pass over the shards of daily life, which are reflected perfectly—uh, which perfectly reflect, uh, reflect, that is, speaking in terms of perfection... Hmm. In a word, perfection is a wonderful thing, but impressionistic comparisons can get you into all kinds of trouble. Thus, in his collection of complete works, the poet, not without inspiration, refers to the resolution of the Moscow City Council concerning the order of street traffic in the following pearl:

He marches to the left and makes a speech.[22]

Dear members and personages, who among us does not know this speech which exposes—I mean, which the commissariat itself often declares? This all makes it obvious that Pushkin marched in lock step with us, the clerical bureaucrats of Centroproduct. One might also examine his life, but that is nothing but nonsense, since we'd wind up talking about his death right away. In regards to death, I wholeheartedly join in with that Goliath of Soviet verses, Vl. Vl. Mayakovsky, who said quite attractively:

D'Anthès was a son-of-a-bitch!
                A worldly mischief-maker.
We ought to ask him:
              Who were your parents?
What did you do
          before 1917?
We would'a ought'a liked to get our hands on this kid D'Anthès.[23]

Unfortunately, this D'Anthès guy slipped our grasp. Considering everything I have said, I propose that the present collection of members and personages pass the following resolution. In honor of the eighty-eighth anniversary of the date of comrade Pushkin's death: To rename the Complete Collected Works of Pushkin as the Complete Collected Works of

---

[21] This is an imperfect quote from Pushkin's play, *Boris Godunov,* the stylistic details of which are lost in translation. Godunov's more poetic utterance actually indicates that it is the sixth year of his reign. This change is obviously intended to resonate in light of the Chairman's constant repetition of, "It's been seven years since...." The seven years following the Revolution were anything but peaceful, and Erdman draws a parallel between the present and the notorious Time of Troubles in the early 17th century, when the Tsar Boris Godunov reigned. The subsequent lines continue this theme as the Chairman begins clarifying his comparison, and then thinks better of it.

[22] This is a bungled quotation from Pushkin's poem, "Ruslan and Lyudmila." The line actually reads: "He walks to the right and strikes up a song."

[23] This is a quotation from Vladimir Mayakovsky's poem, "Anniversary," the final line of which the Chairman recites ungrammatically.

Demyan Bedny. Who's for, who's against, who abstains. It's passed unanimously. Comrades, before voting, I will provide you my unconditional responses to those notes which have been passed to me from members and candidate members desiring knowledge. In the first note, a comrade asks who was smarter, Pushkin or Gogol. I respond. Officially, Gogol was undoubtedly smarter, since a smart man undoubtedly would never fight a duel because you undoubtedly cannot prove anything by fighting. On the other hand, Pushkin was undoubtedly a greater genius than Gogol because Gogol undoubtedly wrote in humdrum prose, while Pushkin wrote in verse. And that is very hard. You know that by your own experience and example, comrade clerical bureaucrats of Centroproduct. It's true that his marriage may have been unsuccessful, his rhymes a bit weak and his character undoubtedly peevish. Moreover, according to his own admission, he couldn't tell an iamb from a trochee. But so what? We simply aren't justified in refusing him the title of genius. The second note states: "Pushkin says in one of his collected works that he's sick of four-foot iambs. It would be interesting to know why he was sick of them and how much does beer cost in the buffet here?" I will respond officially in order of point: First, I don't know. Second, forty kopecks a bottle. The third note: "You ought to pay up your three rubles, Mikhailov." This is unacceptable. Amazing. Are you insinuating that I'm too cheap to pay up three rubles? I'm not that kind of man. My official response: I'll pay up, but I don't know when. Note four: "Comrade Chairman, it's already one a.m. When do we start dancing?" My official response: Don't get ahead of yourself, comrade. And now, comrades, in light of the late hour, the discussion will be limited to one person in favor and one person against. Speaking against comrade Pushkin is comrade A.

ORATOR AGAINST. Comrades, comrades. Belinsky[24] declares absolutely brazenly that Pushkin uses his compositions to accuse. But comrades, if we ask, as Marxists, who was comrade Belinsky?—we will arrive at a given answer. That is totally unconditional. Comrades, I am not a poet. I am a magazine laborer in a third-rate magazine, and I pose a merciless question. How did Pushkin function? He functioned as a given product. Comrades, for seven years we have been experiencing a single, suspended moment in time. That is absolutely unconditional and there's no point in anyone thinking anything, comrades, because that isn't the point. Comrades, you tell me how that could have come about. But, comrades, you forget the historical situation. If we, together as one person, all think together about this theme, it will become clear for you, comrades, that the given orator is correct. Because the given orator is speaking from a point of view,

---

[24] Vissarion Belinsky (1811-1848) was Russia's first major literary critic. His populist views made him the standard critical model during the Soviet years.

comrades. Comrades, you say "long live Pushkin," but I say long live the power of the workers' labor office. Hurrah. I'm done.

CHAIRMAN. Thank you, comrade. Speaking in favor of comrade Pushkin is comrade B.

ORATOR FOR. It's been seven years, comrades, since the previous orator noted very subtly that Belinsky noted that Pushkin is an accuser. Comrades, that is a gross error, for the facts tell us something else altogether. What do we have at hand? This is definitely quite funny. After all, the question is posed in all superficiality. And it just stands there posing. Am I wrong? So why does the previous orator cave in to its implications? Belinsky. Today Belinsky, tomorrow two. And what is Pushkin, a dog? In passing, comrades, the previous orator tossed off a totally demagogical question: "How could that have come about?" He ought to address his question to the primary source. But, for us, comrades, even without that, the answer is obvious. I, for example, comrades, am not a drinker, but I'm going to say what I have to say anyway. Things can't go on like this, comrades, because the previous orator provided relative illumination. He should be ashamed, comrades. I am for. And incidentally, I have spoken on behalf of those of whom I am proud. I'm done.

CHAIRMAN. And now, comrades, a charade on the theme of Pushkin's death. Comrade Aslyonov, take the floor.

POET.   His first word shoots
             With whatever you load in it.
             His second makes a comedy
             Whenever an actor plays it.
             But altogether, he's only just a poet.
             And—don't tell me I don't know it—he is dead.

VOICE. Lermontov?[25]

POET. No. Pushkin. Pushki-Kin. Pushkikin.

VOICE. You've got one too many "ki"s.

POET. You can throw out the extra "ki."

CHAIRMAN. The poet and store manager Okurkin will now read verses produced by himself on the theme of Pushkin's death.

OKURKIN. Leaning over an early grave,
             A tear slides down my face
             And quietly whispers, "Pushkin, dear,
             Open your eyes and lend me your ear.
             If only you would come to life once more,
             You'd definitely want to work in our great store."

---

[25] This speaker confuses Pushkin with Mikhail Lermontov (1814-1941), presumably because both died as a result of duels.

CHAIRMAN. In conclusion, our honorary chairman, comrade Ukhov, will recite some verses of his own composition on the theme of Pushkin's death to the accompaniment of music.

(Dance number)

  And now, comrades, I vote…
VOICES. Dances! Enough! Dances!
CHAIRMAN. In light of disagreement, I vote. Those voting for dances, please stand. Those voting for voting please sit down. Dances are passed unanimously.

Three Circus Sketches

1927

1. The Comradely Court Case at Housing Cooperative No. 1519[1]

CHARACTERS

THE JUDGE
STEPAN VASILYEVICH TYORKIN [2]
TWO JURYMEN, A SECRETARY and A MAN IN UNIFORM

(A table stands on the arena. On the table stands a pitcher of water, a glass and a packet of papers. The Judge, two Jurymen and a Secretary sit at the table. Above the Judge hangs a poster: "The Comradely Court Case at Housing Cooperative No. 1519." There is a small, elevated platform in front of the table and nearby stands a bench)

JUDGE. *(Leafing through the papers)* We will now hear the case of the defendant, citizen Tyorkin, who is accused of beatings and engaging in drunken rowdiness in apartment number thirteen which belongs to our cooperative. Who has appeared for the present case? Defendant. *(Raising his voice)* Defendant... *(Raising his voice even louder)* Citizen Tyorkin... *(Shouts)* Defendant Tyorkin...
TYORKIN. Yes?

(All heads turn toward the door)

JUDGE. Where are you?
TYORKIN. Here I am. *(Appears with a yoke around his shoulders. On one end of the yoke hangs a bucket full of water, on the other end is a half-full sack with objects protruding from it. Tyorkin approaches the Judge's table and steps onto the elevated platform in such a way that the bucket on the front end of the yoke is*

---

[1] This and the following two sketches were written for Vitaly Lazarenko (1890-1939), who first gained fame as a clown in the first decade of the 20th century. In 1914, he set a world record by doing a somersault over three elephants, a film of which brought him international recognition. Close to Meyerhold (he performed in the latter's production of *Mystery Bouffe* in 1921) and Mayakovsky, whose sketches he also performed, Lazarenko was instrumental in introducing theatrical, cinematic and literary devices into circus performances.

[2] In an incomplete manuscript of this sketch, Erdman wrote "Lazarenko" instead of "Tyorkin". In the complete typescript, "Tyorkin" replaces "Lazarenko" throughout.

situated above the head or the knees of the Judge)   Greetings, citizen judge. *(Bows, the bucket tilts and water pours all over the Judge)*

JUDGE. What are you doing?

TYORKIN. Greeting you, citizen judge.

JUDGE. I'm soaking wet.

TYORKIN. *(Bowing)* Pardon me, citizen judge. *(Water pours all over the Judge again)*

JUDGE. I would ask you not to bow, when you are speaking with me.

TYORKIN. *(Bowing)* Yes, sir, citizen judge. *(Water pours all over the Judge a third time)*

JUDGE. *(Leaps up angrily)* What does this mean? What have you brought with you?

TYORKIN. A bucket, citizen judge.

JUDGE. I see that myself. And what is that?

TYORKIN. Where?

JUDGE. *(Pointing to the sack)* On the other side, behind you.

TYORKIN. Behind me? Just a second, I'll take a look. *(Turns around while holding onto the yoke and looks behind himself)* Another bucket, citizen judge.

JUDGE. I'm not asking you about that. What is this here?

TYORKIN. Where?

JUDGE. *(Points to the sack)* Here on this side. In front of me.

TYORKIN. In front of you? Just a second, I'll take a look. *(Turns around together with the yoke and looks in front of himself)* A third bucket, citizen judge.

JUDGE. Are you trying to make a fool of me? For the last time, I am asking you, what have you brought in here?

TYORKIN. Three buckets, citizen judge.

JUDGE. How can there be three when I plainly see that you have only one?

TYORKIN. You see only one?

JUDGE. Yes.

TYORKIN. Well, since you can see one and I see two, then that makes three. Adds up just right.

JUDGE. Are you trying to deceive the court? Take off that yoke immediately and put that bucket on the floor.

TYORKIN. Yes sir, citizen judge.

(Tyorkin bends over. The bucket hits the Judge on the head, the Judge leaps up, holding his head. Tyorkin descends from the elevated platform, takes off the yoke and puts the bucket and sack on the floor)

JUDGE. Now are you going to try to tell me that you have three buckets?

TYORKIN. Yes.

JUDGE. Three?

TYORKIN. Three.

JUDGE. I request that the defendant's words be entered in the protocol. (*Addresses a man in uniform*) Comrades, I summon you all to witness that before us there is only one bucket, and that, consequently, citizen Tyorkin is lying.

VOICES. That's right. Absolutely. True.

TYORKIN. One moment please. You mean, you insist that I brought only one bucket?

JUDGE. Yes.

TYORKIN. One?

JUDGE. One.

TYORKIN. I request that the judge's words be entered into the protocol. (*Addresses the Jurymen*) Citizens, I challenge you to witness the fact that I brought... (*Unties the sack and pulls out two buckets*) ...three whole buckets and that, consequently, the citizen judge is lying.

JUDGE. What kind of charade is this? Why did you bring these buckets in here?

TYORKIN. These buckets contain direct evidence.

JUDGE. Direct evidence?

TYORKIN. Look here. (*Puts a bucket with water on the table, the water pours all over the papers*)

JUDGE. This is unbearable. I can't work like this. You've ruined the whole case.

TYORKIN. Whose?

JUDGE. (*Shaking out the wet papers*) Yours.

TYORKIN. Well, if it's mine and not yours, what are you worried about? (*Takes the papers from the Judge*) I've had so many of these cases, and there will be so many more, that if one gets ruined, I don't particularly care. (*Throws the papers on the arena floor*) I'm a specialist in bucket and basket cases alike.

JUDGE. That does it. Why did you put this bucket on the table?

TYORKIN. I told you, this bucket contains my direct evidence.

JUDGE. How can it contain direct evidence when there's nothing in there but water?

TYORKIN. That's the point. There's water in the bucket and the evidence is in the water.

JUDGE. Where?

TYORKIN. Here, Let me get it for you. (*Removes one sleeve of his jacket, rolls up the sleeve of his shirt and sticks his still-dressed arm in the bucket*) No. That won't work. It's too deep. (*Pulls his arm out of the bucket, shakes it off, splattering water all over the Judge*)

JUDGE. Then pour out some of the water.

TYORKIN. Yes, sir. (*Picks up the bucket and prepares to pour water all over the Judge*)

JUDGE. *(Jumping up)* You're out of your mind. Go over there and pour it out.

TYORKIN. All right. *(Walks to the first row of the grandstand and prepares to pour water on the spectators)*

(Play with a plant: A person sitting in the front row falls off his chair in terror)

JUDGE. Quit your shenanigans. Come over here.

(Tyorkin leaves the bucket behind and approaches the table)

What is your name?

TYORKIN. Stepan Vasilyevich. But you can call me Styopa. Everybody calls me that. I won't be offended.

JUDGE. I would appreciate your not tacking on unnecessary information during the questioning. How old are you?

TYORKIN. Twenty with a couple of years tacked on. But, since that's unnecessary, you can just write down twenty.

JUDGE. Married?

TYORKIN. No.

JUDGE. Children?

TYORKIN. Yes.

JUDGE. All right. Tell me, citizen Tyorkin, do you admit that you are guilty of striking your neighbor, citizen Rukavishnikov, in a drunken manner?

TYORKIN. Me?

JUDGE. Yes.

TYORKIN. Struck?

JUDGE. Yes.

TYORKIN. It was an error, citizen judge. I'm a modest person. I'm calm and delicate, and I can't bear to hit anyone. You can check that if you'd like. I worked in a factory for three months. And in all those three months, not only did I never raise my hand against a single person, but I never even so much as lifted a finger for any reason at all.

JUDGE. Do you work at the factory now?

TYORKIN. No.

JUDGE. Why?

TYORKIN. I was fired.

JUDGE. Why?

TYORKIN. It was a misunderstanding. They said I was always out gallivanting around somewhere. But how could I have been out gallivanting around somewhere, citizen judge? In the last four weeks, not only haven't I been to a bar or the factory, I haven't even left my home one single time.

JUDGE. Then, at present, you don't work anywhere?

TYORKIN. Why should I work when I don't have any money worries even without a job?

JUDGE. If you don't work anywhere, how come you have no money worries?

TYORKIN. Because, citizen judge, I don't have any money at all. So what's there to worry about?

JUDGE. I see. Now, tell me. I gather you consider yourself innocent.

TYORKIN. Yes.

JUDGE. In that case, tell me more about this affair.

TYORKIN. The affair, citizen judge, took place on a Friday. I woke up at ten o'clock and as soon as I went to get dressed, I was suddenly confronted by one of the most complex problems of the cultural revolution.

JUDGE. What was that?

TYORKIN. I should note, citizen judge, that I am a very fastidious person and I can't stand dirt. But, I suddenly noticed that my feet were terribly dirty. And my socks, too. Naturally, I stood in the middle of the room and began thinking, how can I find a way out of this situation?

JUDGE. What was there to think about?

TYORKIN. What do you mean? I thought to myself, if I wipe my socks off and then put them back on my dirty feet, then my socks will moment-aneously become dirty again. Therefore, there's no point in washing them. On the other hand, if I wash my feet and then put my dirty socks back on my clean feet, then my feet will get dirty again. Therefore there was no point in washing them, either. Well, naturally, while I was solving this problem, suddenly Pelageya Ivanovna stopped in to see me.

JUDGE. Who is that?

TYORKIN. My neighbor. And she says, "It's my husband's birthday. Why don't you come have a bite of whatever God sends us?" Well, naturally, being a progressive citizen, I informed her that there is no God. "What do mean?" she asks. So, I said, "There just isn't, that's all." "Where did he go to?" she asks. Like a conscious citizen, I naturally answered her, "Wherever the omnipotent God wanted to go, that's where he went." "Well, God be with him," she says, "but anyway, come see us." "All right," I tell her. She left. Then, I think, "What am I going to do?" I've got big feet, and if I try washing them, I'll probably be late. I'll wash my ears instead, I think to myself. They're smaller and I don't have to put socks on them. In the end, I washed my hands and set off. I go and go, and while I'm going, I'm looking around and looking around. And then suddenly, there it was. It looked like a table standing there. Like this. *(Positions a stool in front of himself)* On the table was a tablecloth as white as snow. Sort of like this. *(Pulls out a huge, dirty handkerchief and spreads it out on the stool)* Just like snow. Naturally, there were all kinds of unheard-of hors-d'oeuvres. And, naturally, there was more there unheard-of than heard-of. It looked something like this. *(Pulls a dried fish, an onion and a piece of sugar out of a bucket)*

JUDGE. What are you doing?

TYORKIN. This, citizen judge, is my direct evidence. I want to paint you a real pretty picture of all the details. Rukavishnikov was sitting here, his wife here, and over here was Makar Timofeyevich from room seven. And they say, "Take a seat, friend." So, I sat down. I'm sitting there and sitting there, and meanwhile I'm looking around. Suddenly I saw it. Standing right there next to the table was a bucket. *(Puts the bucket in place)* And suddenly Rukavishnikov sticks his hand in the bucket, like this. *(Demonstrates)* He pulls them out. *(Pulls two bottles out of the bucket and puts them on the table)* And he puts them on the table.

JUDGE. What are those?

TYORKIN. Direct evidence.

JUDGE. Listen here, you amaze me.

TYORKIN. You mean, you think I wasn't amazed myself? I was stunned. I even asked him, "Citizen Rukavishnikov, what are you keeping direct evidence in a bucket for?" And he said, "To maintain the proper temperature." Then he poured a glass of wine *(Pours a glass of wine)* and encouraged me to have a drink. I want you to know, citizen judge, that I don't drink. "My dear man," I said, "I haven't touched the stuff since birth." But he says, "In that case, I'll drink for you." That's what he said, and then he downed the glass. *(Drinks the glass)* He finished off that glass and then offered one to Makar Timofeyevich. *(Pours a second glass of wine)*

JUDGE. What are you doing?

TYORKIN. Nothing.

JUDGE. What do you mean—"nothing"—when you just drank an entire glass of wine?

TYORKIN. That wasn't me! That was Rukavishnikov who drank it. If you want to know, I don't drink at all. But Rukavishnikov, he definitely drinks, and, as I already told you, he offered a glass to Makar Timofeyevich. And Makar Timofeyevich made quick work of his glass, too. *(Drinks the glass of wine)* Then he poured out another one. *(Pours a glass)*

JUDGE. What are you doing?

TYORKIN. I'm not doing anything at all. I'm just sitting there watching. But Makar Timofeyevich, he poured himself another glass and downed it, too. *(Drinks the glass of wine)*

JUDGE. Are you crazy? A third?

TYORKIN. The second. Rukavishnikov—he drank one glass. And Makar Timofeyevich—he drank two.

JUDGE. How can it be the second, when it's the third?

TYORKIN. You seem to be a little confused, dear citizen judge. Rukavishnikov—my neighbor, Pelageya Ivanovna's husband—he drank the first glass. And Makar Telyatovich—I mean, Telyat Pegonyalych, that is, Gonyal Timofeyevich—he drank the second. So, he drank the second and Rukavishnikov says, "that's enough," he says. "Now I'll drink one." And he poured a glass and drank it. *(Pours a glass and drinks it)*

JUDGE. Are you drinking again?

TYORKIN. How can I be drinking again when I never had a drink to start with? I'm telling you in plain Russian, it isn't me who's drinking. It's Rukavishnikov who's drinking. So, I start thinking, "I sure hope this doesn't get me in trouble."

JUDGE. This is outrageous.

TYORKIN. Absolutely. That's just what I said to him: "This is outrageous." But what does he do? He pours himself a fourth glass and downs it. *(Demonstrates)*

JUDGE. Will this never end?

TYORKIN. It ends right now. See? There's only a tiny bit left at the bottom of the bottle. *(Drinks)* All gone. At this point, Rukavishnikov stands up. "Let's go get some more direct evidence," he says. But he can hardly stand on his own two feet. And he fell on me in a heap, like I'm going to fall in a heap on you right now.

JUDGE. Have this man removed immediately. He is dead drunk.

TYORKIN. How can I be drunk when I haven't had a single drink? The whole point is that, right now, I'm just as sober as you, for example. And both of them fell on me in a heap, like I'm going to fall in a heap on you, for example. First, Rukavishnikov, and then Tatar Makarych, I mean, Makar Tatarych. I look at them and think, "Lord! What a crew I fell in with!"

JUDGE. You should be ashamed.

TYORKIN. That's what I said, too: "You should be ashamed. Take me, for instance…." And then, suddenly I hear this "boom, boom, boom, boom." "What's that?" I say. "That's Taras Tarasovich's wall clock striking," they say. "That's impossible," I say. "God's truth," they say, "his clock is always striking." "It is?" I ask. "It is," they say. "What are you animals doing?" I ask them. "Your neighbor's clock is striking somebody and you just stand there doing nothing," I say. Well, I look at them and they're so drunk they don't understand a thing. What else could you expect from them? Well, naturally, as the only sober one there, I ran into Taras Tarasovich's room and I say, "Is that your clock striking?" "Yeah," he says. "Aha, so you admit it," I say. "What are you letting it do that for?" "I've got nothing to do with it," he says, "it does it on its own." "Who?" I ask. "What are you talking about?" he says, "no one." Well, in a word, I can see this guy got his self-defense all mixed up. So I exposed him. "You bum," I say. Suddenly Matros Matrosovich turned as red as a flag or something and started coming at me. That's when it all happened.

JUDGE. What?

TYORKIN. I'll give it to you with all the details. Let's say you are me and I'll be, let's say, Makar Makarych. Well, Makar Makarych wound himself up and—wham!—he popped me in the face. *(Strikes the Judge, who falls)* Well, naturally, I got up…

(The Judge gets up)

And he let me have it from the other side.
JUDGE. O-o-o-h. Water, water.
TYORKIN. Water? My pleasure. *(Picks up the bucket and pours water over the Judge)*

(The Judge screams and staggers away)

So then that total idiot, Rukavishnikov, comes barging in, trips and falls. *(Falls)* I tell him, "You see," I tell him, "what vodka does to a man?" And he just lies there grinning like a fool.
JUDGE. Arrest him.
TYORKIN. That's right. All Rukavishnikovs should definitely be arrested.

(They seize Tyorkin and lead him to the exit)

Take him away. Take him away. Next time, he shouldn't oughta drink.

2. The People vs. Vitaly Lazarenko

A CIRCUS SKETCH

———————————————————

CHARACTERS

SPRECH-STAHLMEISTER — the master of ceremonies, playing a judge
LAZARENKO
GNOVIKOVA — Lazarenko's neighbor
A CHILD — belonging to Gnovikova

———————————————————

SPRECH-STAHLMEISTER. Comrade Lazarenko.
LAZARENKO. Yes.
SPRECH-STAHLMEISTER. What do you have to say in your defense?
LAZARENKO. Citizen judge, first of all, I wasn't expressing any opinions at all. I simply went to see one of my lady friends to invite her to a movie. But her father wouldn't let her go. Well, I put up with him as long as I could, but I just couldn't put up with him any more. "Listen, pop," I said, "you're no dad of your own daughter. You're a dirty dog."
SPRECH-STAHLMEISTER. *(Interrupting)* I'm sorry...
LAZARENKO. Sorry? No. I'm the one who's sorry, here, citizen judge. I

mean, what's so offensive here? I myself had a little dog—Poopsie, I called her—and she got a gold medal at a dog show. Well, anybody would be proud to have a dog like that for a parent. I don't see what's so offensive.

SPRECH-STAHLMEISTER. Excuse me, but we aren't talking about dogs. You've been summoned about a different case altogether.

LAZARENKO. A different case? Citizen judge, if that was comrade Gavryushin complaining about me—I want you to know that I didn't beat him up. We just had a little bet between us. I said, "It's like this," and he said, "It's like that." So I said to him, "If you want me to, I'll use Marx to hammer that idea out of your head." And he says, "Oh, no you won't." So I grabbed volume sixteen of Marx's collected works and gave it to him—just like that, in the kisser. Well, naturally, since he's not a Marxist, he was at a loss for a reply. And he just fell there in a motionless heap.

SPRECH-STAHLMEISTER. That's a rather weighty conclusion you've come to, comrade.

LAZARENKO. You're telling me. It must have weighed a good four pounds, considering that it was a hardbound book. And then there was the time I attacked a guy using Engels. He's a good writer, too. But he's not as weighty.

SPRECH-STAHLMEISTER. Wait a minute. You have been summoned here for something else altogether.

LAZARENKO. For what?

SPRECH-STAHLMEISTER. Do you know comrade Gnovikov?

LAZARENKO. I do.

SPRECH-STAHLMEISTER. Are these your pants?

LAZARENKO. They are.

SPRECH-STAHLMEISTER. Pay for the kid.

LAZARENKO. Help! What kid?

SPRECH-STAHLMEISTER. Yours.

LAZARENKO. Comrade judge, what do you think I am? A goat? I don't have any kids.

SPRECH-STAHLMEISTER. You mean you deny it?

LAZARENKO. I deny it.

SPRECH-STAHLMEISTER. Have you ever been to see comrade Gnovikov's wife?

LAZARENKO. I have.

SPRECH-STAHLMEISTER. Did you have a cup of coffee with her?

LAZARENKO. I did.

SPRECH-STAHLMEISTER. Pay for the kid.

LAZARENKO. Comrade judge, call any luminary of science to witness and he'll prove to you that children don't come from coffee. Coffee is no symptom of children.

SPRECH-STAHLMEISTER. What about the pants?

LAZARENKO. Why do you keep going on about pants, comrade judge? Can't you say anything without pants?

SPRECH-STAHLMEISTER. I am asking you how comrade Gnovikov's wife wound up with your pants.

LAZARENKO. Let me tell you about that, citizen judge. One day I noted that, right here on this spot on my pants, there was a naked spot. Suddenly, comrade Gnovikov's wife shows up and says, "I'll patch them for you." So I said, "Go ahead." One day passes, the second day passes, and still there's no pants. And then, when the statute of limitations runs out, I get called into court. They say to me, "Is that you, comrade Lazarenko?" And I say, "It's me." They ask, "Are these your pants?" And I say, "They are." And then they say, "Pay for the kid." But I'm telling you, her kid is her husband's.

SPRECH-STAHLMEISTER. Comrade Gnovikova, I thought you weren't married.

GNOVIKOVA. I'm not. I'm a virgin.

SPRECH-STAHLMEISTER. Do you live alone?

GNOVIKOVA. I live with my brother.

LAZARENKO. Citizen judge, they're just registered as brother and sister. But, in fact, they're joined in secret legal matrimony.

SPRECH-STAHLMEISTER. Why would they want to do that?

LAZARENKO. So as to maintain their own productivity at the expense of the neighboring working masses. They give you a cup of coffee and then it's "Pay-for-the-kid."

SPRECH-STAHLMEISTER. How do you know he's her husband?

LAZARENKO. By means of the paper-thin partition between our rooms. True, you can't see anything, but I can hear that he's her husband.

SPRECH-STAHLMEISTER. What do you have to say about that, citizeness Gnovikova?

GNOVIKOVA. It's impossible to determine a husband by the sounds he makes. All I know is that my baby was born from coffee and this man drank coffee with me. It's his fault.

LAZARENKO. Citizen judge, she's contradicting science. According to Darwin's theory, humans descend from the apes, not from coffee.

SPRECH-STAHLMEISTER. From the apes?

LAZARENKO. From the apes.

SPRECH-STAHLMEISTER. Pay for the kid.

LAZARENKO. *(Picks up the child)* For this one?

SPRECH-STAHLMEISTER. For that one.

LAZARENKO. Therefore, practically not having had joint relations with the aforementioned woman, you insist that I take on her sponsorship? All right, I'll pay for the kid. How much?

SPRECH-STAHLMEISTER. A third of your salary.

LAZARENKO. In that case, she'll never get a kopeck from me.

SPRECH-STAHLMEISTER. What do you mean?

LAZARENKO. Just that. Because I already pay three-thirds of my salary for three other kids and there isn't anyone who can make anyone pay a fourth third even out of the biggest salary you can imagine.

SPRECH-STAHLMEISTER. If you already pay out three-thirds of your salary, what do you live on?

LAZARENKO. I live on the salary of one of my infants, for whom my wife receives a third of our neighbor's salary. He's a guy who stopped in for coffee once.

SPRECH-STAHLMEISTER. In that case, I can't possibly conceive of a resolution to the problem.

(All leave except Lazarenko)

LAZARENKO. You see there, citizeness? He can't conceive, but you can. Comrade women, I propose a new slogan: "Beware the conceivable dangers of coffee." *(He runs out)*

(We hear the strains of the song, "Oh, Why This Night?")

3. The Divorce

A DOMESTIC SKETCH

CHARACTERS IN ORDER OF APPEARANCE

LAZARENKO
SPRECH-STAHLMEISTER — the master of ceremonies
THE JUDGE
NASTYA PUPOCHKINA — Lazarenko's wife

LAZARENKO. Pardon me, but what time is it?

SPRECH-STAHLMEISTER. Eight o'clock.

LAZARENKO. Eight o'clock? Holy Moses! A cab! Call me a cab!

SPRECH-STAHLMEISTER. What do you need a cab for?

LAZARENKO. I'm late for court. I'm having it out in court, today.

SPRECH-STAHLMEISTER. With who?

LAZARENKO. A certain bum.

SPRECH-STAHLMEISTER. What bum?

LAZARENKO. My wife. Cab! Call me a cab! I'll pay one ruble for one passenger with baggage. Holy Moses. I'm late.

SPRECH-STAHLMEISTER. No need to worry, comrade Lazarenko. You'll be tried right here.

LAZARENKO. Here? That's impossible.

SPRECH-STAHLMEISTER. I assure you, it's true. Look. The witnesses have already gathered and the judge will be here any minute. We arranged a show trial for you.

(Enter the Judge, who sits at a table. Following him is a young woman)

JUDGE. The court shall now hear the case of citizen Lazarenko, who is seeking to evict citizeness Pupochkina. Citizen Lazarenko, what do you have to say about this matter?

LAZARENKO. First, allow me to ask you, citizen judge—am I allowed to speak the truth in court?

JUDGE. Not only are you allowed to, but you are bound to tell the truth.

LAZARENKO. I'm bound to? Thank God. In that case, I am bound to tell you, citizen judge, that this woman was my first. And this first woman of mine is the last of the low-down bitches.

JUDGE. How dare you, citizen? Who allowed you to use such language?

LAZARENKO. You.

JUDGE. What do you mean, me?

LAZARENKO. Just that. You. I asked you, can I speak the truth and you said I could.

JUDGE. You can tell the truth, but you can't say "bitch."

LAZARENKO. I can tell the truth, but I can't say "bitch?"

JUDGE. If you are going to use language like that, I will have to fine you. Please state your case.

LAZARENKO. With pleasure. This woman here...

JUDGE. Wait a minute. What is her relation to you?

LAZARENKO. She used to be my wife, but now she is my daughter.

JUDGE. Your wife became your daughter? How could that have happened? What daughter?

LAZARENKO. She's a daughter-of-a-bitch, citizen judge.

JUDGE. Citizen Lazarenko, I am fining you five rubles for those words.

LAZARENKO. Five rubles?

JUDGE. Yes.

LAZARENKO. For those words?

JUDGE. Yes.

LAZARENKO. In that case—here. Ten rubles.

JUDGE. Why ten?

LAZARENKO. Because, citizen judge, I'm going to give her another five-rubles-worth of an earful. Nastya. Nastenka.

PUPOCHKINA. What do you want?

LAZARENKO. You're a bitch. You're a daughter-of-a-bitch.

PUPOCHKINA. Citizen judge, please forbid him...

LAZARENKO. Nobody can forbid me anything, now. I already paid for those words.

JUDGE. Citizen Lazarenko, state your case or I'll have you removed from the court. Come over here and speak.

LAZARENKO. From the beginning?

JUDGE. From the beginning.

LAZARENKO. From the very beginning?

JUDGE. From the very beginning.

LAZARENKO. With pleasure. From the very beginning, it was just like this, citizen judge. You see, I was sitting at home, thinking. And I was wondering, what could I possibly do to kill a few hours in a cultured sort of way? I thought—maybe I'll wash my feet and then head down to the bar. Finally, I realized—hell—my feet aren't going anywhere. I can always wash them tomorrow. And I can go down to the bar tomorrow, too. So what's the big deal? You go to the bar, get drunk as a swine and lose your human face. I pictured it all so vividly that I almost got sick. So, I decided: No, I won't go down to the bar tomorrow, after all. I'll go down there today. So, off I went. And when I got there I ordered me a mug of beer.

JUDGE. I consider this insufficient...

LAZARENKO. I'm very happy to hear that. That's what I thought, too. So, I drank off the first mug and ordered a second. Then I drank off the second mug and ordered a third.

JUDGE. The court is not interested in the least in hearing about your drinking binges.

LAZARENKO. Well, obviously, it's much more interesting to go on a drinking binge than to hear about one. But what can you do, citizen judge? To each his own. Where was I? Oh, yeah. I drank off the third mug, and I was so drunk I began hallucinating that I was stone sober. So I decided to go for a walk. I'm walking along the street and thinking. How is it, I think to myself, that they can't build buildings like they used to? All the buildings are swaying in the wind. And all the fences and people, too. Even the sidewalks are uneven—they either tilt to one side or the other. And I start wondering, how's a sober man supposed to walk in a straight line?

JUDGE. Wait a minute. Are you sober now?

LAZARENKO. Stone sober, citizen judge.

JUDGE. Come over here and breathe in my face. Ah! You smell like a brewery!

LAZARENKO. Don't pay it any mind, citizen judge. That's just because I'm nervous. I've been like that since childhood. But, pardon me, where was I? Oh, yeah. So, I finally came to a tram stop. I'm standing there and standing there, until a tram finally came up to me. And then I got on the tram and off we went. Suddenly a woman gets on the tram with her baby. And she says to me, "Relinquish your seat to a woman." And I say, "We didn't liberate women so that they'd start taking our places." And then somebody else says, "She's got a baby." So, I say, "Let her put the baby on my knees, if she wants." So there we are, tooling down the road. Here, I've got to tell you that my pants didn't have a single spot on them. Just like brand new. When we get to the second stop, I lift the baby off my knees. And my pants are covered in spots—just like an old, worn-out pair of pants. Obviously, I jumped up and started shouting, and the baby started crying. Then I look out the window and I see that I missed my stop. So I jump out on the running boards and leap off the moving tram. And—boom! There's a policeman standing right there. "That'll be a ruble from you," he says. And I say, "A ruble for what?" And he says, "For unloading off the tram where there's no stop." So, I say, "What do you mean? You mean a full-grown adult can only unload at stops, but a baby can unload anytime he wants— right on some stranger's knees? What happened to justice?" Anyway, I paid the fine and set off. Pretty soon, I came to a boulevard. And sitting there on a bench was this... that... Pardon me, citizen judge, but if I say "bitch," are you going to fine me again?

JUDGE. I will.

LAZARENKO. In that case, here's two-and a-half rubles.

JUDGE. For what?

LAZARENKO. For half.

JUDGE. For what half?

LAZARENKO. For the first half.

JUDGE. I don't understand.

LAZARENKO. Let me explain. Sitting there on a bench was this daughter of...

JUDGE. Who?

LAZARENKO. This daughter of...—right here, citizen judge.

JUDGE. I forbid you to speak.

LAZARENKO. What for?

JUDGE. For using forbidden words.

LAZARENKO. You can't do that, citizen judge. There's no end to it.

JUDGE. That's just why I'm forbidding you to speak. Because there's no end to your using that word.

LAZARENKO. I didn't mean that there's no end to my using that word, I mean that there's no end to the word.

JUDGE. What are you talking about?

LAZARENKO. All I said was "daughter of." I understand that if I say that without saying the end, then that's forbidden. But if I say the end, then you can say that.

JUDGE. What are you talking about?

LAZARENKO. What I was trying to say, citizen judge, was that this daughter of mercy was sitting there on this bench. See what I mean?

JUDGE. Oh, so that's it. Go on.

LAZARENKO. So this daughter of... mercy was sitting there on a bench. Her head was thrown back and she was taking a sun bath with her nose. I took a gander at her and think to myself, "Not a bad-looking dame." And I asked her if I could sit down next to her. She says, "Go ahead." In short, we started getting acquainted and fell into conversation. And I started telling her about love. Blah, blah, blah and so on. Then I ask her if she's literate, and she says she is. "Can you write?" I ask her, and she says she can. So I say, "Then, let's go down and sign our marriage papers," and off we went to the marriage palace. After we did that, I suggested we go see my mom and tell her I got married.

JUDGE. How could she have married you if she didn't even know you?

LAZARENKO. That's just why she married me. If she'd known me, she never would have done it. So, where was I? Yeah, we went to see my mom. And mom says, "Let her live with you." And that's how we moved in together. After a week, I tried sending her off to her own mother. But she wouldn't go. Every time I try sending her to her mother, she won't go. Be a sport, citizen judge, evict her out of my quarters.

JUDGE. I can't do that. She has as much right to your quarters as you do.

LAZARENKO. Then evict her to some other quarters.

JUDGE. Such as?

LAZARENKO. I don't know. How about the Chinese quarter? Since we've gone our separate ways, I just can't live with her any more.

JUDGE. Why did you go separate ways?

LAZARENKO. Because we have different paths in life. Every time we get a day off she wants to go for walks on Sparrow Hills.[3] She says the fresh mountain air is incredible there. But I like to go down to the industrial regions. I tell her the air there is three times as incredible.

JUDGE. Is that really grounds for divorce?

LAZARENKO. Well, and she's always accusing me of being uncultured. She says I never even pick up a book. I don't know where she gets an idea like that. I never go anywhere without my book on my days off.

JUDGE. What book?

LAZARENKO. My savings book, citizen judge. How else would I get any money?

JUDGE. Is that really grounds for domestic strife? I suggest that you kiss and make up.

---

[3] The view from the woods at Sparrow Hills offers a panoramic view of Moscow. It was the vantage point from which Napoleon first gazed on Moscow. During most of the Soviet years, this location was called Lenin Hills.

LAZARENKO. Nastya, did you hear what the court says?
PUPOCHKINA. Yeah.
LAZARENKO. Then, give me your hand.

(They kiss)

JUDGE. Have you come to a decision?
LAZARENKO. The fact is, citizen judge... Wait a second.

(They kiss)

JUDGE. Well, have you come to a decision?
LAZARENKO. The fact is, citizen judge... Lips as sweet as sugar! You couldn't buy it any sweeter!

(They kiss. The Judge rings his bell. They continue kissing. The Judge rings more insistently)

Citizen judge, don't bother us, please. We're busy.
JUDGE. The case is closed.
LAZARENKO. Citizens and citizenesses! Comrade Shakespeare once said, "'Tis better seven times to marry than once to divorce." And I join in with the immortal Griboyedov to add:

> If your wits are at an end,
> Don't think about divorce.
> You're better off staying sober
> Than shouting yourself hoarse.[4]

(The orchestra plays "A Splendid Moon Floats Over the River."[5] Singing, Lazarenko and Nastya leave the arena locked in an embrace)

---

[4] Erdman has Lazarenko erroneously attribute this ditty to Alexander Griboyedov (1795-1829) as a joke aimed at Meyerhold's famous 1928 staging of Griboyedov's play *Woe from Wit* under the title of *Woe to Wit*. In addition to numerous passages from Griboyedov's rough drafts, this production included bits and pieces of other writers' works and occasional popular or folk poetry.

[5] This naive and sentimental "boulevard romance," popular in the 1920s, sang the praises of eternal love.

An Interlude for *Lev Gurych Sinichkin*

1929

BORZIKOV. All right, Pyotr Petrovich, let's begin. Where are you going?

PUSTOSLAVTSEV. Oh no! An introductory word!

BORZIKOV. What's wrong with you?

PUSTOSLAVTSEV. It's my heart. I'm terribly nervous.

BORZIKOV. Calm down, won't you, Pyotr Petrovich? An introductory word isn't such a terrible thing.

PUSTOSLAVTSEV. What do you mean a word isn't terrible? A word isn't a sparrow. Let it out and you'll never catch it again. See? You let it out, you don't catch it, and for that they catch you and don't let you out. Just like with Scylla and Charybdis or something.[1] Oh, well. Here goes.

BORZIKOV. God be with you, Pyotr Petrovich.

PUSTOSLAVTSEV. Various spectators and working front! In my personage you meet face to face with those personages in whose name I am speaking. Greetings! Karl Marx was immeasurably correct when he said… uh,… I don't remember exactly what it was he said, but I remember exactly that whatever he may have said, it was immeasurably correct. If I have committed some error here, may the working front correct me…. In that case, I continue. Contemporary theater has entered a dead-end street. For the theater to find a way out of this dead end, it must even up its left leg with Soviet society and march in step. It must march, paying attention to what

---

[1] Scylla and Charybdis are figures from Greek mythology. In *The Odyssey,* Odysseus lost six sailors to the voracious sea-nymph Scylla when steering clear of the monster Charybdis.

society's left leg wants. Above all, society's left leg wants ideology. What is ideology? It is our bread. For if we have no ideology, we will have no bread. And if we have no bread, there will be no ideology. Greetings! Oops, that's not it. Oh, yes. What does our ideology consist of? The repertoire. Repertoires can be sustained and they can be unsustained. A sustained repertoire is impossible to maintain while an unsustained repertoire is impossible to restrain. Basically, it is extremely difficult to work with Soviet society. That's what the capitalist stooges say. However, I say the following: With the equity characteristic to it, Soviet society maintains that, in the twelfth year of the revolution, entertaining plays are harmful for the proletariat. For this reason, we have chosen a play of the revolutionary type, and we are firmly convinced that, in the twelfth year of the revolution, it will be incapable of entertaining anyone. There you have it. You undoubtedly imagine asking yourself the question: Why have we settled on a play by Fyodor Semyonych Borzikov? I will not attempt to hide from you the fact that Fyodor Semyonych Borzikov carries with him enormous revolutionary baggage, immemorial parents and a vast knowledge of contemporary life. I declare that Fyodor Semyonych Borzikov knows more than Anatoly Vasilyevich Lunacharsky![2] Because if you were to ask Anatoly Vasilyevich whether he knows Fyodor Semyonych, I am sure that he doesn't. But if you were to ask Fyodor Semyonych whether he knows Anatoly Vasilyevich— without the slightest doubt he does. Therefore, Fyodor Semyonych knows more than Anatoly Vasilyevich.[3] There you have it. The play is called *Brother and Sister.* [4]

Its action takes place during that chunk of time between the birth of Christ and the civil war within one family. This device allows the theater to show how various ways of life determine one and the same consciousness. In consummation, I would like to inform you that a revolutionary play is not yet a revolutionary performance. For if a revolutionary play is entirely dependent upon its author, a revolutionary performance is entirely dependent on you. For if the public applauds where it wishes rather than where it should, then there will be no ideology left at all. There you have it. Nevertheless, I am firmly convinced that with mutually exerted effort we will be able to create a truly healthy show, because healthy shows these days are the sorest spot in our work as such. I'm done. (*Speaking to Borzikov as he leaves the stage*) Well, how did I do?

---

[2] See note 4 to "The Qualification Exams."

[3] This joke about Lunacharsky is repeated in the first music-hall number included in this volume.

[4] I replaced the ellipses in the typescript with the title *Brother and Sister.* That is what Mitka subsequently calls the play. The original interlude was called *The Broken Bridge,* as was a 1929 rough draft for the text translated here. This latter title is occasionally encountered in the secondary literature.

BORZIKOV. I consider that there were a few weak moments, but several instances were marvelous. Take, for example, that moment when you compared me to Shakespeare.

PUSTOSLAVTSEV. You? And Shakespeare? I compared you to Lunacharsky.

BORZIKOV. Oh yeah. I always confuse them.

PUSTOSLAVTSEV. Nalimov!

NALIMOV. Yes?

PUSTOSLAVTSEV. Put up the Christmas set.

NALIMOV. It's already up.

PUSTOSLAVTSEV. Then let's begin. Everyone to their places.

NALIMOV. Pyotr Petrovich!

PUSTOSLAVTSEV. What do you want?

NALIMOV. The cousin is off shooting a movie.

PUSTOSLAVTSEV. Here we go again. Then who's going to play the cousin? Can't Mitka play the cousin?

NALIMOV. Mitka! Can't you play the cousin?

MITKA. Essentially no, but if you order me to I can.

NALIMOV. He says essentially no, but if you order him to he can.

PUSTOSLAVTSEV. Have him play it. It's not a big role. He can do it. Tell him that when he hears the drum roll, he should say, "Ah! What's that?"

NALIMOV. Mitka! When you hear the drum roll, say, "Ah! What's that?"

MITKA. When I hear the drum roll: "Ah! What's that?" Got it.

PUSTOSLAVTSEV. Once again, everyone to their places! Curtain…

NAPOIKIN. What's on today? What's on today?

MITKA. *Brother and Sister.*

NAPOIKIN. Am I in that one or not? Am I in that one or not?

NALIMOV. Of course. You're in the first episode.

NAPOIKIN. Oh my God! Wigman! My wig!

PUSTOSLAVTSEV. Nalimov!

NALIMOV. Yes?

PUSTOSLAVTSEV. We're beginning!

NALIMOV. Curtain! *(Sinichkin begins a drum roll)*

MITKA. Ah! What's that? What's that?

PUSTOSLAVTSEV. Stop! Stop!

NALIMOV. I'm not going anywhere, Pyotr Petrovich.

PUSTOSLAVTSEV. I didn't say don't go anywhere, I said stop!

SINICHKIN. Well, how do you like that? My prettiest spot, D flat, and you start talking behind my back.

PUSTOSLAVTSEV. What are you doing, my dear man? What are you doing, I ask you?

SINICHKIN. Making music.

PUSTOSLAVTSEV. You call that making music? You mangy devil! Is that the way you're supposed to begin? I ask you, is that the way you're supposed to begin?

SINICHKIN. Well, how then? Your play may be no *Orpheus in the Underworld*,[5] but they both begin with a counterpoint.

PUSTOSLAVTSEV. You, my dear man, have lost your mind! In a word, if you think you can play without a conductor, you have another thing coming! I'll run you out of my theater! Follow the conductor, please.

SINICHKIN. This is awful, Pyotr Petrovich. You have to butt in every time I have a burst of free inspiration.

PUSTOSLAVTSEV. Nalimov!

NALIMOV. Yes?

PUSTOSLAVTSEV. Once again, everyone to their places! Maestro? Let's have the Christmas music. Curtain!

ALL. O Tannenbaum, o Tannenbaum,
  Wie grün sind deine Blätter!

SURMILOVA. Du grünst nicht nur zur Sommerzeit.

BERSENEVA. Wandochka, my child! Don't sing so loud! You might strain your vocal chords.

SURMILOVA. Better I should do it than you, mama. You've been singing at Christmas parties for forty-nine years. You've worn yourself out, my busy little worker bee. Give it a rest. I'll replace you. *(Sings)* Nein, auch im Wiiii…. Ha, ha!

BORZIKOV. What do you mean, "ha, ha?"

SURMILOVA. Just that. "Ha, ha."

BORZIKOV. Pardon me, but what kind of "ha, ha" is that?

SURMILOVA. I wanted to ask you what kind of "ha, ha" it is. I'm not the author. You wrote here, "Wiiin…ha, ha."

BORZIKOV. Oh! You mean, "ha, ha." Right there I explain what this "ha, ha" is: "A coughing fit shakes her breast." "Ha, ha" is the beginning of the coughing fit. Understand? *(Shows her)* Ha, ha. Like that. It is a very effective moment, Raisa Ninishna.

SURMILOVA. Oh, so it's a very effective moment, is it? Why, thank you! Ha, ha! Let's continue!

PUSTOSLAVTSEV. Raisa Ninishna, why haven't you begun your coughing fit?

SURMILOVA. Don't worry, I'll do it during the actual performance. Ha, ha! Let's continue.

BERSENEVA. Wandochka, my doll! What's the matter?

SURMILOVA. Ha, ha. Nothing. It's just a coughing fit. It'll pass. Let daddy sing for now.

---

[5] This is certainly a reference to the satirical adaptation of Jacques Offenbach's operetta which was written by Erdman and Vladimir Mass at approximately the same time as this interlude.

BERSENEVA. Daddy, sing!

NAPOIKIN. Sing, daddy! I refuse to rehearse.

BORZIKOV. What's the matter?

PUSTOSLAVTSEV. What happened?

NAPOIKIN. I can't work like this. This is a dress rehearsal and nobody has learned their lines. Thrice or even four times we've given the cue, "Sing, daddy," but, as you can see—daddy, for some reason, isn't singing.

BORZIKOV. Pardon me, but you are daddy.

NAPOIKIN. Me?

BORZIKOV. Naturally.

NAPOIKIN. Impossible. Are you sure of that, young man?

BORZIKOV. I declare absolutely officially, in the presence of witnesses, that you are daddy. Because I am the author.

NAPOIKIN. Ah, you're the author. Tell me, please. Uh-oh. What am I going to do? What am I going to do? *(Takes off his wig and looks at it)* I'll be damned, the wig is grey! You're right. I recall when Salvini wound up in an analogical situation. When Salvini....[6]

PUSTOSLAVTSEV. My dear man, you are fined.

NAPOIKIN. What am I going to do? What am I going to do?

SURMILOVA. I demand the rehearsal be resumed.

NAPOIKIN. Be so kind. *(To the prompter)* Dear man, won't you give me my lines a bit louder, please?

SURMILOVA. Ha, ha. Daddy, sing.

NAPOIKIN. Come on.

PROMPTER. Nein, auch im Winter, wenn es schneit.

NAPOIKIN. Huh?

PROMPTER. Nein, auch im Winter wenn es schneit.

NAPOIKIN. What the hell?

PROMPTER. Nein, auch im Winter wenn es schneit.

NAPOIKIN. I refuse to rehearse!

PUSTOSLAVTSEV. Why?

NAPOIKIN. I cannot rehearse with a drunken prompter. You ought to hear what he's feeding me.

PUSTOSLAVTSEV. What are you feeding him, you son of a bitch?

PROMPTER. Nein, auch im Winter wenn es schneit.

BORZIKOV. That's just what it should be. It's in German.

NAPOIKIN. In German? I refuse to perform in German. I'm not Chekhov.[7]

BORZIKOV. But my good man, if you are rehearsing a formerly intellectual daddy, you have to speak German.

---

[6] This refers to the great Italian actor Tommaso Salvini, who toured Russia four times between 1880 and 1901.

[7] This refers to the great Russian actor, Mikhail Chekhov (1891-1955), who emigrated to Europe in 1928 and began acting shortly thereafter for Max Reinhardt in Germany.

NAPOIKIN. If I could speak German, I probably wouldn't have to rehearse.

BORZIKOV. In that case, sing in Russian.

NAPOIKIN. Be so kind, maestro. Give me the key. *(Sings)* O, Christmas tree, O Christmas tree! How graceful are thy branches! *(A clock chimes)*

MITKA. Uncle, it's time for you to take your pills. Uncle, it's time for you to take your pills.

NAPOIKIN. Uncle, it's time for you to take your pills. I refuse to rehearse!

BORZIKOV. Now what?

NAPOIKIN. Pyotr Petrovich, I tell you, none of them knows their lines! "Uncle, it's time to take your pills. Take your pills!" How come uncle isn't taking his medicine?

BORZIKOV. But you are the uncle.

NAPOIKIN. Cut the humor, young man. I am daddy. Do you think I don't know the play or something?

BORZIKOV. You are a daddy and an uncle.

NAPOIKIN. I refuse to play two roles!

BORZIKOV. Don't you understand? It's one role. You are their daddy and his uncle.

NAPOIKIN. Ah! I'm their daddy and his uncle. I recall an analogical situation with…. All right. Be so kind.

MITKA. Uncle, it's time for you to take your pills.

NAPOIKIN. Merci, nephew.

SURMILOVA. Nanny! Nanny! Nanny!

NAPOIKIN. A thousand pardons, but perhaps I am the nanny, too?

BORZIKOV. No, you are not.

NAPOIKIN. Thank God, at least I'm not someone.

SURMILOVA. Nanny!

NEKRASOVA. What is it, my little brat?

SURMILOVA. Daddy's pills.

NEKRASOVA. Right away. *(Drum roll)*

MITKA. Ah! What's that?

NALIMOV. Damnation! It's the first shot of the revolution!

SURMILOVA. Hurrah!

MITKA. Ah! What's that?

NALIMOV. Damnation. It's the first…

MITKA. Ah! What's that?

NALIMOV. Damnation!

MITKA. Ah! What's that? Ah! What's that? Ah! What's that? Ah! What's that?

PUSTOSLAVTSEV. What are you doing, you idiot?

SINICHKIN. Making a revolution, can't you tell?

PUSTOSLAVTSEV. You mangy devil, what do you keep making an endless revolution for? One is enough!

SINICHKIN. Sorry. I got carried away, Pyotr Petrovich.

PUSTOSLAVTSEV. Sorry, indeed. He wants an endless revolution.

MITKA. Ah! What's that?

NALIMOV. Damnation. It's the first shot of the revolution.

SURMILOVA. Hurrah. I sense that something is being reborn within me and that callouses are growing on my hands.

NALIMOV. Fie, Wanda, fie. I condemn you.

SURMILOVA. Condemn God. I don't care about your condemnations. Hurrah.

NAPOIKIN. Oh, my old ears. What do they hear? Silence, my daughter.

SURMILOVA. I am not your daughter. I am the daughter of a million workers.

NAPOIKIN. Wanda, don't slander your mother.

NALIMOV. Father, a red swarm has surrounded our own home.

NAPOIKIN. Goga, I see that they are breaking into our rooms like a bunch of filthy bootmakers….

NALIMOV. Wait for me here. (*Drum roll*)

MITKA. Ah! What's that?

NALIMOV. Father, I booby-trapped the bathroom.

NAPOIKIN. How fortunate you're an engineer.

SURMILOVA. Scoundrels! You've signed your own death warrant. (*Flings open the window*) Workers! Come arrest my father, the general.

BERSENEVA. Lord Almighty! Daughter against father.

PROMPTER. "Falls in a faint."

NAPOIKIN. Constables, take my communist daughter to the police station.

BERSENEVA. Lord Almighty! Father against daughter.

PROMPTER. "Falls in a faint."

BERSENEVA. I did, already.

NALIMOV. Daddy, I know a crooked path that leads into the mountains. Let's go out the back entrance and head for the Urals.

NEKRASOVA. You forgot your pills, master.

SURMILOVA. Nanny, forget the pills, it's time for you to run the country.[8]

NEKRASOVA. For pay like that? I'm no fool. Do it yourself.

SURMILOVA. Nanny, you are a lumpen proletariat.

BERSENEVA. Alas. I've gone out of my mind.

> O Tannenbaum, o Tannenbaum,
> Wie grün sind deine Blätter!

SURMILOVA. Where did you come from, boy?

CHAKHOTKIN. From work.

---

[8] This is a reference to Lenin's famous statement that, in the new Soviet state, any cook should be able to run the government.

SURMILOVA. Where do you work?
CHAKHOTKIN. Here. Underground.
SURMILOVA. Who are you, boy?
CHAKHOTKIN. I am a tiny cog in that enormous machine whose name is the Party.

(Love scene)

SURMILOVA. Look at me, little cog. You are the first man who has ever looked at me not as he would at a bitch, but as he would at a comrade.

(They kiss)

Oh, happiness! I sense that callouses are growing on my lips. My little cog, will you love me?
CHAKHOTKIN. Until the grave or even longer. Maybe until the world revolution. Farewell.
SURMILOVA. What is your name?
CHAKHOTKIN. Shh! We're surrounded by enemies.
SURMILOVA. Then tell me the number of your party membership card so I can whisper it at night.
CHAKHOTKIN. 4-71-16.
SURMILOVA. Cousin, you're with us. Go with them. *(Exits)*
MITKA. No. I'm staying with my violin and my insane aunt. Art is above politics.
BERSENEVA. O Tannenbaum, o Tannenbaum,
          Wie grün sind deine Blätter!
PUSTOSLAVTSEV. Masses—circle up! Presidium—in the middle. "Eenie, meenie, minie moe. Pick a lover by the toe." Well, pick the one you want.
SURMILOVA. I choose my cousin the ploughboy.
PUSTOSLAVTSEV. Cousin ploughboy, you're in.
BERSENEVA. The elections are over. Strike up the revolution.

(An accordion is heard)

NAPOIKIN. Don't move. All right, peasants. Give up your communists.
ALL. No way. We won't do it.
NAPOIKIN. Give them up.
ALL. No way. We won't do it.
NAPOIKIN. Where is my right hand, Colonel Starozhinsky? Where is my right hand, Colonel Starozhinsky?
PUSTOSLAVTSEV. Nalimov!
NALIMOV. Yes?
PUSTOSLAVTSEV. Where's his right hand?

NALIMOV. He's off shooting a movie.

PUSTOSLAVTSEV. He's off shooting a movie. The cousin is off shooting a movie. Before you know it, there won't be an actor left in the theater.[9] *(Approaches Sinichkin)* Listen, dear man, couldn't you play his right hand?

SINICHKIN. If you do a good job of makeup, I can.

PUSTOSLAVTSEV. Here's a hat. Go out on stage and get on with the show.

NAPOIKIN. Where is my right hand, Colonel Starozhinsky?

SINICHKIN. Right here.

NAPOIKIN. Defile women.

SINICHKIN. There's a role for you.

NAPOIKIN. Defile women.

SINICHKIN. Pyotr Petrovich, show me what to do.

PUSTOSLAVTSEV. Fyodor Semyonych, perhaps we might replace the word "defile" with "court?"

BORZIKOV. Men only court women in operettas. In revolutionary plays, they defile them.

PUSTOSLAVTSEV. Listen, dear heart, let's give this scene a, uh, rather indefinite tone. Let's create the image of a, uh, stallion-like colonel. Just curl your moustache a bit and stamp your foot threateningly. Or squint one eye something like this—got it?

SINICHKIN. A stallion? I got it. *(Starts whinnying)*

ALL. O shame! O misfortune!

NAPOIKIN. All right, now. Give up your communists.

ALL. Oh, no! There's one.

NAPOIKIN. Daughter mine.

SURMILOVA. Father.

NAPOIKIN. Alas, I have to shoot you.

SURMILOVA. Shoot, you scum. Pray. 4-71-16!

NAPOIKIN. Oh, for Christmas tree's sake, I can't do it.

SURMILOVA. Chicken.

NAPOIKIN. I want to, but I can't. *(Pulls his hair)*

CHAKHOTKIN. Wanda!

SURMILOVA. Cog!

CHAKHOTKIN. Let's run.

SURMILOVA. Wait a second. Let me shoot my father first.

NAPOIKIN. Daughter mine. What's this I hear?

SURMILOVA. Shut up, scum.

NAPOIKIN. I'm your father.

SURMILOVA. No, daddy, you're no father. You're a son of a bitch, daddy. *(Shoots)*

---

[9] This is an obvious reference to the competition for actors' services which theaters were suddenly facing from the new film industry.

NAPOIKIN. Ah! You hit my right hand.

SINICHKIN. His right hand? A-a-a-h! *(Falls)*

PUSTOSLAVTSEV. What are you doing?

SINICHKIN. I'm acting.

PUSTOSLAVTSEV. What are you acting?

SINICHKIN. His right hand, Pyotr Petrovich. She shot his right hand.

PUSTOSLAVTSEV. You mangy devil. Go back to the orchestra.

SINICHKIN. There you have it. Somebody's always trying to rub out a budding career.

SURMILOVA. I shot your hand? Now I'll shoot you in the heart.

NALIMOV. Wait! Sister!

SURMILOVA. Brother!

NALIMOV. What good fortune. Now I'll shoot you.

SURMILOVA. Shoot, you bastard.

NALIMOV. Damnation. My hand won't obey me. It just won't obey me. I can't do it, father. I can shoot anyone, but not my sister. You shoot her.

NAPOIKIN. I can't. I want to, but I can't. You shoot her.

(Chakhotkin wrests the pistol from them)

NALIMOV. Ah.

SURMILOVA. Cog, don't shoot. I'll do it. *(Shoots)* There. One less bastard. *(Shoots)* There. Two less bastards. The past has been eradicated.

BERSENEVA. O Tannenbaum, o Tannenbaum.

SURMILOVA. Oh my God! That's my former mother. *(Shoots)* There. Three less bastards. Cousin. Take that. *(Drum roll)*

MITKA. Ah! What's that? *(Falls)*

SURMILOVA. Four less bastards. Cog, now that we've finished off the past, I'm all yours. Hurrah, peasant women! We've broken free of our chains!

Five Interludes for
The Two Gentlemen of Verona
1952

1. Launce's Monologue before Departure[1]

LAUNCE. I'm going to sit down right here and, for one last time, give it some thought. Should I take my dog with me to Milan or not? Let's try to reason philosophically. How would a philosopher with a dog reason were he in my place? In my opinion, he would reason like this. *(Closes his eyes and counts on his fingers)* If it comes up even, I take him. If it comes up odd, I don't. *(It comes up odd)* I don't take him.

Let's try reasoning philosophically three times. *(Fingers again come up odd)* Again, I don't take him. That means I don't take him twice. How's that possible? I'm only going to Milan once and I don't take my dog with me twice. Total nonsense. A dead end. Let's try to find a way out of the dead end. We will reason in an entirely new fashion. I'll take him if it comes up odd, and I won't take him if it comes up even. *(Counts and the result is even)* Oh, Lord! That means that by resorting to philosophy and proper reasoning, there is no need to take my dog to Milan. On the other hand, if people were to reason properly, who the hell would need philosophy? And, in general, is philosophy applicable to a man and his dog?

Tell me this. Have you ever had occasion to stroll the streets of Verona at six in the morning? Well, let's say seven. On a rainy morning, to boot, when your feet are slopping in mud puddles. You've got some dog-eared rag of a coat draped over your shoulders. Everyone is still sleeping. The shutters are all closed. There's not a man on the street. Only people out walking their dogs. Think about it. Some scruffy little thing is holding a big, imposing, respected person on the end of its leash, dragging him from post to post as if he were a snot-nosed kid. And this person, wearing shoes with untied shoelaces dangling loose, a raincoat tossed on over his nightclothes and acting like he's some big, important person, keeps muttering, "Well, do it! Come on, do it!" And the dog doesn't do anything of the sort, dragging its master from post to junk heap. And his master just keeps tagging along behind. Yeah. But if anybody else—say, his wife—tried leading him around like that, he wouldn't go for the world. He won't even go with her to the theater, let alone a junk heap. What does this dog do, besides the fact that sometimes it "does it?" They say a dog is a guard. But I personally know hundreds of dogs for whom people are specially hired so they won't

---

[1] This interlude followed the end of Act I.

be stolen. Have you ever heard of anyone stealing guards? It's true, guards sometimes steal. I used to be a guard, I know. But the other way around? It's nothing but a doggone lie. And then they also say that a dog is man's best friend. Nonsense. In fact, it's dogs who make people lose friends. I have a friend. I went to see him yesterday to say goodbye. I knocked on his door. I heard a vicious growl and then I heard my friend's voice: "Wait a second, I'll lock the dog in the other room." After a ten-minute struggle, the door opened. I went in. "Lord, how happy I am you came. Sit down, please. No, only not in that chair. That's my dog's favorite chair. No, don't sit on that one either." So I asked him, "That's his favorite chair, too?" And he said: "Just the opposite. For some reason, he can't stand that one. He never sits in it and doesn't like others to sit in it, either. You're better off sitting on that stool, or even better yet, just stand. Only don't make any sudden moves. I'll let him out, now. First, he'll sniff you over and then, maybe, he won't bite you." And so he opened the door and man's best friend came into the room. He's got teeth out to here, his fur is standing on end and he came up to me and started sniffing.

"Launce, don't move!" my friend shouted. "Launce, don't shiver. Launce, stop beating your heart. He hates that sound. Don't forget, he's got lockjaw. If he sinks his teeth in you, we'll have to pry his jaws apart with an iron shovel and we might damage his teeth."

Well, I don't know whether the dog damaged itself or not, but my former friend's neighbors ended up taking me to the doctor. The doctor sewed me up, gave me a shot and said, "If you value your life, don't drink." So I said, "Signor doctor, the only reason I value my life is because I drink." "If you drink," he says, "you'll get rabies." "Soon?" I asked. "In about three months," he said. Can you picture my situation? If I drink, I get rabies in three months. If I don't drink, I won't hold out for a week. And all of that because of who? A dog. And they call a dog man's best friend!

So, I'm sitting here tormenting myself. Should I take my dog with me to Milan or not? Meanwhile, he doesn't so much as twitch an ear. No, there he twitched. Ah, you lucky dog, you. Otherwise, I wouldn't have taken you. Oh, my sweetie. Oh, my poopsie.

2. Launce's Monologue[2]

LAUNCE. *(With his dog)* Yeah. The heart fills with sorrow when he who is supposed to be a faithful servant turns out to be an ungrateful dog. That's

---

[2] This interlude replaced Launce's monologue at the beginning of Act II, scene three. The editors of Nikolai Erdman, *P'esy, intermedii, pis'ma, dokumenty, vospominaniia sovremennikov* (Moscow: Iskusstvo, 1990), erroneously suggest it was performed as a part of Act III, scene two.

right. I'm talking about you. What would you be without me? Just think about the family you were born into. Your father was a shyster and a scoundrel. One day he scampered into the courtyard where your mother lived and then he disappeared forever. I don't know what he promised her, but your mother behaved like an idiot. Your mother had a kind character and beautiful fur. Her character didn't do her the slightest good and her fur was her downfall. She perished at the hands of a poacher. Your two brothers and three sisters were drowned in a washbowl. They were supposed to drown you last. You couldn't see what was coming because you were still blind. But I saw it. And I said, "Let me have this pup. He's got fur like his mother's. When he grows up to be big, I'll sell him to a poacher and get back the money I wasted on feed." So I started to feed you. This finger here replaced your mother. I wet it in milk and you sucked on it until you grew teeth and I grew callouses. When you turned eight months old, I bought you a little rug which I put by the door. Now, if you haven't lost all shame, tell me something. Has there ever been a time, even once, when you have come home and seen me sprawled all over your little rug with a bone in my mouth? Never. But how many times have I found you sprawled in my bed in just such a pose? You weren't even three months old yet, when you constantly started crawling up on that very spot where I always lay my head. That's right. That's right. You crawled all over my pillow. And which of us bit my grandmother's ankle? Me or you? Aha, you hold your silence. And what did you do when a gang of thieves tried stealing our ham from the larder just before Christmas? You sat there like a whipped puppy, waiting for them to break down the door. And when they finally broke it down, you raced in there ahead of them and fended them off until you had eaten the whole thing. But, you see, despite all of that, I scratched you behind the ears and brought you bones. Finally, I brought you to Milan. And what did you go and do yesterday? You started dogging after the duke's dogs and followed them home. And when I started chasing after you, you hid under the table. And when I crawled under the table after you, the duke entered with his courtiers and they sat down to eat. They ate and I sat there under the table listening to them slurp and chomp. Then some frivolous dame started wiggling her legs and stuck her high heel in the back of my head. "Carro, is that you?" she asked. What could I do? I whimpered softly and licked her leg. That's what I did. But what did you do? Not even forty minutes had passed before there came to pass that which I feared most of all. And when that came to pass, the duke leaped up from the table and shouted at the top of his lungs, "Quick! Open all the windows!" One of the courtiers dropped his hand under the table, grabbed you by the scruff and pulled you out in the open. "What kind of a dog is this?" he shouted. Then somebody else shouted, "We ought to whip it!" And the duke said, "We ought to hang it, for what it's done." Then I heard you give out a squeak. And when I thought about the fact that he who was squeaking was the same one who ate my Christmas ham, who bit my grandmother's ankle, who crawls all over that on which I lay my head, whose ears I love to scratch and whom I always bring hot bones, my heart couldn't bear it. I crawled out from beneath the table and said, "Noble signore! It's not the dog's fault. I did it." You can imagine what happened then. Now, I ask you, how many masters would do such a thing for their servants? However, here comes my master, now. If only once in his life he would take on himself even the tiniest bit of blame for my sins, I would be prepared to worship him.

3. A Scene by a Tavern[3]

CHARACTERS

SPEED
LAUNCE

SPEED. Launce! Friend! Who? Why? When? And how long?

LAUNCE. My dog. Because I'm an idiot. Just now. And for about two months.

SPEED. Do you mean to tell me you came to Milan with your dog?

LAUNCE. Absolutely not. I don't want to talk about it at all. But, yes, it's true, I came with my dog.

SPEED. Why?

LAUNCE. I already told you. Because I'm an idiot. Philosophy did me in.

SPEED. That was a dumb move, bringing some courtyard mutt to the duke's court in Milan. Do you know what kind of dogs he has?

LAUNCE. No.

SPEED. They're enough to make your head spin. This morning one courtier led his dog out into the courtyard. He snapped his fingers like that—and the dog started walking on its front legs, then on its back legs.

LAUNCE. For long?

SPEED. Well, I don't know. Five minutes, ten.

LAUNCE. That's nothing.

SPEED. Well, maybe you think it's nothing….

LAUNCE. Wait a minute. Maybe I didn't understand you. How did you say it walked?

---

[3] This interlude replaced, or was appended to, Act II, scene five. The editors of Nikolai Erdman, *P'esy, intermedii,* etc., erroneously suggest it was performed as a part of Act II, scene one.

SPEED. First on its front legs and then on its back legs.

LAUNCE. First... then... That's nothing. My dog, for instance, walks on its back legs and front legs all at one time. There's a dog for you. And not for just ten minutes, but for as long as you want. All you have to do is snap your fingers.

SPEED. You dunderhead. If he walks on his back legs and his front legs together, then he's simply walking on all fours.

LAUNCE. Yeah, well so what?

SPEED. All dogs walk like that.

LAUNCE. Maybe they do, but not everybody snaps their fingers at them. But what about this duke? Does he have any other dogs?

SPEED. All kinds. But his best one is a hunting dog. He's grey with brown spots and an inaccessible intellect. Tell him, "Play dead!"—he lies down. "Shut the door!"—he shuts the door. Tell him, "Speak!"—he barks. Just like a person.

LAUNCE. You mean people bark?

SPEED. But this dog doesn't only bark. Tell him, "Bring my slippers!" and he brings them.

LAUNCE. That's nothing.

SPEED. A dog acts like a person and you say that's nothing.

LAUNCE. I say that's nothing because it isn't true.

SPEED. Prove it.

LAUNCE. All right. Let's say we go to the hotel and you tell Signor Proteus, "Signor Proteus, bring me my slippers!" Even though he's a person, he won't bring them to you.

SPEED. Yeah, but if Signor Proteus shouts at you, "Hey, Launce! My slippers, and fast!"—you'll bring them.

LAUNCE. But that's not because dogs act like people. It's because people act like dogs.

SPEED. You're impossible to argue with, but I love you anyway. What nice thing could I do for you? Do you want me to show you Milan? All of its points of interest?

LAUNCE. I already saw them.

SPEED. What points of interest could you have seen when you just arrived?

LAUNCE. Reasoning philosophically, every person who comes to some town for the first time is interested in only three points of interest.

SPEED. What are those?

LAUNCE. Those points which might be capable of holding him in that town for a prolonged period.

SPEED. Such as?

LAUNCE. The cemetery, the prison and women. Moreover, the cemetery is capable of holding us forever, the prison—for years, and women—for hours. I already had a good close look at the cemetery and the prison. As for the women, I don't want to see them even from a distance.

SPEED. Why?

LAUNCE. Because it's because of women that men most often wind up in prison or a cemetery.

SPEED. How's that?

LAUNCE. Reasoning philosophically, there are two methods. The first method: You arrive in some town, fall in love with a woman, get her to agree to meet with you, her husband finds out, challenges you to a duel, kills you and you wind up in the cemetery. Second method: You arrive in some town, fall in love with a woman, her husband finds out, challenges you to a duel, you kill him and wind up in prison. That's it.

SPEED. Launce, you seem to be rather depressed. Let's go have a drink.

LAUNCE. I'm afraid of getting rabies. You know, I already had a fear-of-drink attack and I attacked a man in a wild fury.

SPEED. Who was that?

LAUNCE. A tavern keeper. He was watering down my wine.

SPEED. They don't do that here. Let's go to that tavern there, have a chat and a drink.

LAUNCE. Unfortunately, a dog bit me and I can't.

SPEED. How come? Aren't you able to sit down?

LAUNCE. I already told you, a dog bit me.

SPEED. You mean you aren't able to drink?

LAUNCE. I can drink, but I can't sit. It's too painful. But I'm prepared to drink standing if you're paying.

SPEED. Let's go.

LAUNCE. I warn you, I can take in more when I'm standing.

4. A Scene from Act Three[4]

CHARACTERS

LAUNCE
SPEED

LAUNCE. For some reason, I'm considered a fool. However, I have enough brains to guess that my master is something of a scoundrel. Meanwhile, my

[4] This interlude is a reworking of the end of Act III, scene one. The editors of Nikolai Erdman, *P'esy, intermedii*, etc., erroneously suggest it was performed as a part of Act II, scene three.

master, who is considered smart, can't figure out that I'm in love. All the same, I'm in love. With whom? Six horses bound in tandem wouldn't be able to drag that secret out of my heart. The only thing I'll say is that it's a woman. In the fullest sense of the word. She weighs two-hundred and thirty-four pounds. Nevertheless, she's as easy to lift as a bird and makes fabulous sour milk. Her name is Jen. She's a milkmaid. When she was sixteen, she set out from her village to learn how to be a milkmaid in the city. And it didn't take her long to learn. Many years have passed since then, but milking is still her specialty. I fell in love with her like a poet—at first glance. And now, for three days I've been composing a list. *(Pulls out a sheet of paper)* It is a list of her good qualities and her bad qualities. If it turns out she has more bad qualities than good, then I probably won't marry her. And if it turns out she has more good qualities than bad, then she probably won't marry me. That means no one gains anything or loses anything from our love. What could possibly be better and purer than a relationship like that? *(Looks over the list)*

(Enter Speed)

SPEED. Launce, what are you reading?
LAUNCE. Words written in ink.
SPEED. Let me read them.
LAUNCE. You don't know how to read.
SPEED. That's not true. I actually read pretty good. Come on, give it here, Launce. After all, I'm your best friend.
LAUNCE. I had one friend like that who stole my pants when I was sleeping.
SPEED. That's unfair, Launce. If all I had was one pair of pants and you needed pants, I'd give them to you.
LAUNCE. Give them to me, then.
SPEED. Unfortunately, right now, I don't have only one pair of pants. I have three other pairs besides. So right now, I have nothing to give you. But you give me that there to read. Come on, give it to me, give it to me. *(Tickles him and grabs the sheet of paper)* "A list of good and bad qua-li-ties." Whose are these?
LAUNCE. Six horses bound in tandem wouldn't be able to drag that secret out of my heart. I can't stand men who tell about their romances and compromise women.
SPEED. Launce, you're a prince. *(Reads)* "She rea-l-ly knows how to milk." Ah, so it's some sort of milkmaid.
LAUNCE. See? You didn't guess.
SPEED. She's not a milkmaid?
LAUNCE. She's a milkmaid, but she's not just any sort of milkmaid. It's the milkmaid Jen who lives across from the butcher's house.
SPEED. She's a fatty.

LAUNCE. Two-hundred and thirty-four pounds.

SPEED. What do you care about her qualities?

LAUNCE. What do you mean, what? I live with her.

SPEED. You're in love?

LAUNCE. I already told you, I can't stand men who tell about their romances and compromise women.

SPEED. *(Reads)* "She rea-l-ly knows how to har-row." What, does she have scary eyes or something?

LAUNCE. Huh? No.

SPEED. Then how come you write that she knows how to harrow?

LAUNCE. And how come you say that you know how to read? It says right here that she knows how to harrow the grassy fields, not with her eyes.

SPEED. The grassy fields? What for?

LAUNCE. To feed the cows.

SPEED. What's in it for you?

LAUNCE. Sour milk.

SPEED. Launce, you found yourself a bed of roses. *(Reads)* "The gru-el...." Who's cruel?

LAUNCE. Nobody's cruel.

SPEED. Then, how come you write here, "cruel?"

LAUNCE. That doesn't say "cruel," it says "gruel." "The gruel she fixes is good."

SPEED. How can you write like that, Launce? "Gruel," "cruel," what's the difference?

LAUNCE. Are you kidding? Your master may feed you gruel so cruel you can't eat it, but haven't you ever eaten good gruel?

SPEED. Well, yes.

LAUNCE. Then you ought to know that not all gruel is cruel gruel.

SPEED. I suppose you're right. *(Reads)* "She ver-y much loves men." Oh, that's bad.

LAUNCE. Why?

SPEED. Because if she loves men, she'll cheat on you with them.

LAUNCE. What makes you think she'll cheat on me with them? Maybe she'll cheat on them with me. Remember, Speed, we always get tired of whatever we have a lot of and we always value what we have too little of. So, since she has a lot of men, that means she'll cheat on them with me.

SPEED. But you're a man, too.

LAUNCE. But there's only one of me, which means there's not enough of me.

SPEED. You know, Launce, arguing with you is nothing but a waste of time.

LAUNCE. In that case, it's your master who's wasting time, not you.

SPEED. My master? Why?

LAUNCE. Because he's waiting for you at the North Gates while you're just lollygagging around here.

SPEED. Why didn't you say so before? So I'm supposed to go to him, is that it?

LAUNCE. I wouldn't just go, if I were in your shoes. I'd run. And quick. Although, on the other hand, maybe it's best you not run too hard. Otherwise, I won't be able to keep up.

SPEED. Why? Are you going with me?

LAUNCE. Yes. I want to see you catch it from your master.

5. A Scene in the Forest[5]

CHARACTERS IN ORDER OF APPEARANCE

LAUNCE
SPEED
FIRST OUTLAW
SECOND OUTLAW

LAUNCE. Signor Proteus! Signor Proteus! Hey! Halloo! How he lost me, I'll never be able to figure out. Hey! Halloo!

SPEED. It's Launce. I'll give him a good scare, the dear heart. Listen, men, you approach him from the other side. Shhh. *(He dons a mask. Leaping out of the bushes, shouts in a loud voice)* Halt! Don't move! Your money or your life!

LAUNCE. Pardon me, I didn't hear you. What's that you said?

SPEED. I said, your money or your life. Rat-a-tat-tat-tat-tat! Now did you hear me?

LAUNCE. This time I heard you, but other than rat-a-tat-tat-tat-tat, I didn't understand a thing you said. My money or my life? Are you suggesting I choose between them?

SPEED. That's right, and be quick about it!

LAUNCE. Just a second. *(Moves off to the side and counts on his fingers)* If it comes up even, I'll give him my life. If it comes up odd, I'll give him my money. *(It comes up odd)* My money. However, that's what I thought myself. *(Approaches Speed)* Philosophically speaking, it comes up my money.

SPEED. You see? Well? What are you waiting for?

LAUNCE. One more second, please. You are suggesting I choose between life and money. Whose life, exactly, did you have in mind?

SPEED. Yours, you dunce!

---

[5] This interlude is a substantial reworking of Act IV, scene one. Valentine was replaced by Launce.

LAUNCE. I see. Mine. So that's how it is? And whose money did you have in mind?

SPEED. Yours, yours, damn you!

LAUNCE. Also mine? So, it's my life and my money. Then the deal is off, because I can't choose between my life and my money.

SPEED. Why?

LAUNCE. Because I have no money. I still have something of a life left me, but as for money—none whatsoever.

SPEED. None?

LAUNCE. None.

SPEED. Excellent, then we'll hang you.

LAUNCE. Are you saying that if you hang me, I'll suddenly have money? Lord Almighty, if that was the case, everyone would hang themselves.

SPEED. Don't try pulling the wool over my eyes. Pick a branch. Make your choice, you mongrel.

LAUNCE. Make what choice?

SPEED. Choose any branch, mongrel.

LAUNCE. I see. Why, thank you. I just recently lost my dog. Are your mongrels purebreds?

SPEED. What do you think I'm talking about, you idiot? Pick a branch, mongrel, in this tree.

LAUNCE. In this tree? What branch of the mongrel family lives in trees?

SPEED. Listen, bud, don't tempt my patience. Get it into your thick-as-an-oak head that I'm telling you to pick the branch on which you want to be hung.

LAUNCE. But I don't want to be hung.

SPEED. Choose, I'm telling you.

LAUNCE. One second, please. Are you really going to hang me?

SPEED. There's no need to doubt it.

LAUNCE. Then I choose this one. *(Points out a puny little branch near the base of the tree)*

SPEED. Listen, bud, we're not making jokes, here. All right, gang. Search him and I'll go get a rope. *(Whispers)* I've got to warn the chief that there are unexpected visitors in the forest. *(Leaves)*

FIRST OUTLAW. Open up your basket, bum!

SECOND OUTLAW. Wine!

FIRST OUTLAW. Four bottles.

SECOND OUTLAW. This is great!

LAUNCE. This wine belongs to my master, Signor Proteus.

FIRST OUTLAW. Well, right now we are going to drink to his health, and until we've hung you, you can watch how we do it.

LAUNCE. You are going to drink and I am going to watch?

SECOND OUTLAW. That's right.

LAUNCE. Then you'll never be able to hang me.

FIRST OUTLAW. Why?

LAUNCE. Because I have a weak heart. If I have to stand by idly watching other people drink, it might give out.

SECOND OUTLAW. All right, then we'll test whether it can hold out or not.

LAUNCE. Wait! Come to your senses! For God's sake! You'll die! Do you know what's in that wine?

FIRST OUTLAW. What?

LAUNCE. It's poisoned. There's poison in that wine.

SECOND OUTLAW. Poison?

LAUNCE. Poison. One gulp and…. Say, do you have any relatives?

FIRST OUTLAW. Yes. An uncle.

LAUNCE. How about an aunt?

FIRST OUTLAW. My aunt died.

LAUNCE. Well, you take one gulp, there, and no sooner will you say farewell to your uncle, than your auntie will be greeting you.

FIRST OUTLAW. How will she greet me?

LAUNCE. How? Well, I don't know how they greet one another in the other world. Probably something like, "Hi there. I'm your aunt."

SECOND OUTLAW. What a bunch of nonsense. Who poisoned the wine?

LAUNCE. Signor Proteus.

SECOND OUTLAW. Why?

LAUNCE. Signor Proteus is in love with miss Silvia. Miss Silvia loves someone else. She is getting married to still another, so she ran off with a third. So, even if they catch her, Signor Proteus won't get her anyway. Therefore, he decided to poison all his rivals and he poured poison into one of these bottles.

SECOND OUTLAW. In one?

LAUNCE. In one.

SECOND OUTLAW. Then we can drink three of them, since there's poison only in one.

LAUNCE. But I don't know which one the poison is in. What if you start out with the wrong bottle? Imagine the consequences. You pick up the bottle, take a swig and…

FIRST OUTLAW. Hi, there. I'm your aunt.

LAUNCE. You got that right.

FIRST OUTLAW. Damn. But, that would be a crime to deprive ourselves of four perfectly good bottles just because of one of them is poisoned.

SECOND OUTLAW. To say nothing of the fact that, obviously, none of them has been opened.

FIRST OUTLAW. What do we do?

SECOND OUTLAW. Where's the solution?

LAUNCE. The solution is quite simple.

FIRST OUTLAW. How's that?

LAUNCE. First, answer one question for me.

SECOND OUTLAW. Well?

LAUNCE. Who are you?

FIRST OUTLAW. You mean you haven't figured that out yet, you idiot?

LAUNCE. No.

FIRST OUTLAW. We're outlaws.

LAUNCE. Outlaws! Help! I'm being robbed!

FIRST OUTLAW. Shut up, you bum! You think you can shout like that?

LAUNCE. Are you trying to say that you can rob, but I can't shout? Those are some pretty strange rules. Who is your leader?

SECOND OUTLAW. Other than our chief, we have no leaders. With us, it's all for one and one for all. Each of us is ready to give his life for another.

LAUNCE. You're ready to give your life for another? Why didn't you tell me that from the start? Line 'em up. That's right, that's right. Excellent. All right, here's the method. You take… no, let's say you take one swig of wine out of each bottle. Meanwhile, you watch carefully to see which bottle kills him. For example, let's say the third bottle kills him. Then you take the third bottle and throw it away. Then you can drink up all the rest.

FIRST OUTLAW. Uh-huh. He gets to drink up the rest, but what about me?

LAUNCE. What's it to you? You'll be dead, anyway. And since you'll be dead, what's the difference? Plus, it all comes out according to your rules. You give your life for him. What are you waiting for? Try it.

FIRST OUTLAW. I refuse.

LAUNCE. Well, all right, then let him test them and die. And then you can drink all the rest. Isn't it all the same?

SECOND OUTLAW. I'm going to take this bottle here and give you a good knock on the head.

LAUNCE. Then, insofar as I understood what you have said, you also refuse. All right, then I'll test them.

SECOND OUTLAW. You?

LAUNCE. Me.

FIRST OUTLAW. Are you saying that you will sacrifice your life for us?

LAUNCE. What's so surprising about that? You shouldn't think that only outlaws are good people. Even among honest people there are a few who aren't so bad themselves. Moreover, I'm going to die anyway. In general, don't try to stop me. I have decided. (Seizes a bottle and drinks from it) Ah!

SECOND OUTLAW. What?

LAUNCE. Oh!

FIRST OUTLAW. What? What?

LAUNCE. I'm dying! No, wait a minute. Maybe it just seemed that way. Let me verify that. (Finishes off the bottle) Uh-huh. It just seemed that way. That means the poison is in one of the other bottles. (Picks up another bottle) Oh,

Lord! If you are ever in Milan and should see the milkmaid Jen, tell her that I died with her name on my smacking lips. Jen! Jen! *(Drinks)* Jen! Jen! *(Drinks)*

FIRST OUTLAW. Wait, you scoundrel! That's enough, you've already tested it.

SECOND OUTLAW. It's already obvious there's no poison in this one.

LAUNCE. And what if it settled to the bottom? No, no. If I'm going to sacrifice myself, I'm going to do it to the bitter end. *(Finishes off the bottle)* No. Nothing on the bottom. That means the poison is in this one. *(Picks up the third bottle and drinks it down)* Now everything is clear, gentleman. Since there was no poison in these bottles, that means it's in this last one here. There's no need even to test it. I'll pour it out. I'll dig a hole, pour it out and cover it up. Otherwise, some animal might come up, lick it and…. It's terrible even to think about it. *(Goes behind the tree and drinks down the last bottle)* There. I buried it good.

(Enter Speed at a run)

SPEED. *(In a thundering voice)* Shudder, scoundrel! Now we're going to hang you!

LAUNCE. Yeah, yeah. Please do. Either hang me or, at least, lean me up against somebody, because I can't stand on my own two feet.

SPEED. What the hell? Are you drunk? You're drunk. Well, if you're drunk, it's too late to scare you. The joke didn't work. To hell with it. *(Removes his mask)* Look, Launce, it's me. Friend, come to my embraces.

LAUNCE. *(Slurring his speech)* I won't make it that far.

SPEED. Launce, old pal, it's me. I was just playing a joke on you.

FIRST OUTLAW. It's him that played a joke on us. Admit it, deceiver, there wasn't any poison in those bottles, was there?

LAUNCE. Children mine, wine is poison. And never have I understood that quite as acutely as I do right now. *(To Speed)* Hey, buddy, you don't happen to know my way home, do you?

SPEED. Launce! You still don't recognize me? It's me.

LAUNCE. Me? And who am I?

SPEED. Your friend Speed.

LAUNCE. Well, if my friend's so speedy, I'm out of here, too. *(Closes his eyes and collapses)*

(They grab hold of him)

SPEED. Hey, gang, do you hear voices? Somebody's coming. Carry him out of here on the double.

(They carry Launce away)

Two Interludes for *Pugachyov*

1968

1.

CHARACTERS IN ORDER OF APPEARANCE

CATHERINE — *Catherine the Great, Empress of Russia*
ALEXANDER VASILYEVICH KHRAPOVITSKY — *Catherine's State Secretary* [1]
A DEPUTY
SÉGUR — *the French Ambassador* [2]
WANZHURA — *a flautist* [3]
MARTINI — *a violinist* [4]
VARIOUS DEPUTIES

(Catherine and her state secretary, Alexander Vasilyevich Khrapovitsky. He holds a folder of papers bound in Moroccan leather. He opens it and hands the first sheet to the Empress)

CATHERINE.[5] What is that?

KHRAPOVITSKY. A list of your great deeds, Your Highness.

CATHERINE. Read it.

KHRAPOVITSKY. Registered counties—twenty-nine. Towns built—one hundred and forty. Executed...

CATHERINE. Are you mad? What are executions doing in this list?

KHRAPOVITSKY. Executed treaties and pacts, Your Highness...

CATHERINE. Oh, so that's...

KHRAPOVITSKY. Thirty. Conclusive victories—seventy-eight. Decrees about laws—eighty-seven. Decrees, easing the plight of the people—one

---

[1] Alexander Khrapovitsky (1749-1801) was one of Catherine's literary secretaries and a minor playwright.

[2] Louis Phillippe Ségur (1753-1830) was a historian, poet and memoirist who served as the French ambassador to Russia during the reign of Catherine II.

[3] Ernest Wanzhura (also spelled Vanchura, 1750?-1802) was a composer and musician who worked in, and wrote for, Petersburg theaters from 1783 to his death.

[4] The model for this character may be Giovanni Battista Martini (1706-1784), the Italian composer and theorist whose students included Carl Bach and Wolfgang Mozart, or it may be Giovanni Paolo Martini (1741-1816), a German composer who settled in France. Erdman's inclusion of him in Catherine's court would appear to be a joke.

[5] It is uncertain where these two interludes were to have fitted into the production at the Taganka.

hundred and twenty-three. In all—four hundred and ninety-one deeds.[6]

CATHERINE. When it reaches five hundred, write it out again on a clean piece of paper and I'll send it to Voltaire.[7] What else have you?

KHRAPOVITSKY. A report from the chief of police about the fire on Vasilyevsky Island.

CATHERINE. Is it bad?

KHRAPOVITSKY. Fairly so, Your Highness. So far, one hundred and twenty-four buildings have burned.

CATHERINE. We'll rebuild them. There was a worse fire in 1762 and we rebuilt then. Alexander Vasilyevich, I would like to state it categorically: We may burn more often than all of the other European states, but, of all the European states, we rebuild more quickly. What else?

KHRAPOVITSKY. A report from Count Vyazemsky[8] on the small-pox inoculations he gave his offspring.

CATHERINE. Who dares say we are lagging behind, now? I would hazard to say that if we keep making this kind of progress, we will soon surpass everyone in inoculations. The Spanish Infanta didn't give herself an inoculation and she died. But Kostya and Sasha inoculated themselves and they are still alive. Doesn't it follow that we have already surpassed Spain? Is that all?

KHRAPOVITSKY. There are a few more reports, Your Highness.

CATHERINE. Read them. Only do it quickly.

KHRAPOVITSKY. *(Reads quickly)* A report about the flood in Tver, a report about the flood in Riga, a report about the plague in Tula, a report about the plague in Serpukhov, a report about a prison break in Kazan by the merchant Druzhinin and the cossack Pugachyov.[9] *(He holds out the last piece of paper and falls into an awkward silence)*

CATHERINE. What is that?

KHRAPOVITSKY. Verses, Your Highness.

CATHERINE. What verses?

KHRAPOVITSKY. For your comic opera, Your Highness.[10]

---

[6] An audience in the late 1960s certainly would have perceived this list of numbers as a reference to contemporary official Soviet reports, which were often filled with long lists of "great deeds."

[7] When Catherine was still considered by Europeans to be a progressive in the early years of her reign, she actually did correspond with Voltaire.

[8] Alexander Vyazemsky (1727-1793) was a major political figure and trusted member of Catherine's inner circle.

[9] Emilyan Pugachyov (1740 or 1742-1775) was the leader of a cossack rebellion, for which Catherine had him executed.

[10] Catherine is listed officially as the author of some 30 tragedies, comedies and comic operas, written in Russian. Since she was German and had an imperfect command of Russian, it is often speculated that others actually wrote them, while she published them under her own name. She also wrote six short dramatic "proverbs" in French.

CATHERINE. Alexander Vasilyevich, you have a terribly strange habit of keeping the most interesting things for last. Give me the verses.

KHRAPOVITSKY. Verses without music, Your Highness, are like a flower without scent. Be so kind, Your Highness, as to listen to these verses in tandem with music.

CATHERINE. Well, where is it?

KHRAPOVITSKY. Wanzhura and Martini are waiting at the doors, Your Highness.

CATHERINE. Who else is there?

KHRAPOVITSKY. A mixed choir, Your Highness. And the French ambassador.

CATHERINE. Let them all in. The French ambassador can listen, too. At least he won't be able to muddle my head with stories about the Turks. I presume that he, being a Frenchman, has a better understanding of verses than of Turks.

(*Khrapovitsky lets Wanzhura and Martini enter. The former is holding a flute, the other—a violin. They are followed in by the choir and count Ségur. All bow*)

CATHERINE. Good day, gentlemen. Good day, count. To what do I owe this early visit?

SÉGUR. Your Highness, concerned about recent events on the Russo-Turkish border, my minister has addressed me with an urgent request.

CATHERINE. Well, now, count. Isn't that a coincidence? I also have a request for you.

SÉGUR. Your wish is my command, Your Highness.

CATHERINE. Let's both of us have a listen to the verses which Alexander Vasilyevich has written for my new opera. As strange as it may seem, I myself can't write verses at all.

SÉGUR. But, Your Highness, why would you need to know how to write verses, when you already know how to run a state like no one knows how?

CATHERINE. Yes, but the Chinese emperor knows how to write verses.

KHRAPOVITSKY. He may know how to write verses, Your Excellency, but he's not very good at running state affairs.

CATHERINE. I can't agree with you, Alexander Vasilyevich. I don't think his verses are all that good.

KHRAPOVITSKY. May we begin, Your Highness?

CATHERINE. (*To Ségur*) I beg your indulgence of my artists in advance. Naturally, they have a long way to go to match yours. Voltaire just wrote me a few days ago that your French ballet dancers have so turned the heads of your Parisians, that no one even noticed that you instituted new taxes.

SÉGUR. I will not feign false modesty, Your Highness. In truth, France is a land of impressive artists.

CATHERINE. And very impressive taxes. However, give us a little time, count. We will catch up with you, yet. You may begin, gentlemen.

(The choirmaster gathers the choir. One of the singers walks to one side and lies on the floor)

Alexander Vasilyevich, take my manuscript and read my first author's direction to the count.

KHRAPOVITSKY. *(Reading from the manuscript)* "Act One. Scene One. The theater represents a courtyard or a meadow alongside Lokmeta's house. There are games and dances in the courtyard. *(He points to the singer lying on the floor)* A woeful knight, who has become bored with the game-playing, is lying in the grass. Then, having stuck a pin on the end of a stick, he begins plucking raisins out of the cellar through a window. Then he begins playing a game of pitching nails."[11]

CATHERINE. The Russian loves no other game so much as pitching nails. It is played with the aid of nails and a rope.

SÉGUR. Indeed, Your Highness! One is amazed. I don't know what astounds me more—your subtle knowledge of the theater's laws or your profound knowledge of Russian life?[12]

CATHERINE. Say what you will, but I know my people. *(Gestures to the musicians)*

(Martini waves his bowstring. Music, games and dances)

CHOIR. *(Sings)*
> Leaving behind our toil and labor,
> We shall forget our tears, perchance.
> Come, let us lose ourselves happily
> In joyous games of song and dance.

KHRAPOVITSKY. *(Approaches Catherine)* I await your sage artistic advice with bated breath, Your Highness.

CATHERINE. Let me tell you categorically, Alexander Vasilyevich. If I knew how to write verses, I would have done it better. Tell me once again—how does it start?

KHRAPOVITSKY. "Leaving behind our toil and labor, we shall forget our tears, perchance."

CATHERINE. You see there? Tears. Don't tell me that a word like that doesn't grate even on your own ear. Day and night I toil for the happiness

---

[11] Erdman merely repeated the actual stage directions from the beginning of Catherine's comic opera, *The Woeful Knight Kosometovich* (1789).

[12] Ségur's surprise at Catherine's knowledge of the theater's laws refers not only to the awkward action described in the Empress's stage directions. Several of her plays bear the disclaimer that they were written "without maintaining the usual theatrical rules."

of my people. In fact, I don't only toil, I have even instituted a happiness medal.[13] *(Takes a medal out of a small box)* Look here, count. With this medal, I will honor my deputies today. *(Reads)* "Happiness and virtuous deeds are the destiny of every Russian." That's what it says on this side. It's even better on the other: "Let there be joy and merriment in Russia." And you write about tears. Where have you ever seen such a thing? *(Indicates the weeping choir)* I am asking you, Alexander Vasilyevich. Where have you ever seen such a thing?

(The Empress's deputies are announced. They enter. They line up and she hangs medals on several of them. She stops before the last of them)

Whence come you, my friend?
DEPUTY. From Kazan, Your Royal Highness.
CATHERINE. I am dissatisfied with your city.
DEPUTY. In what have we angered you, Your Royal Highness?
CATHERINE. You keep a bad prison. Who was it that escaped recently?
KHRAPOVITSKY. The merchant Druzhinin and the cossack—pardon me, Your Highness, but it seems to have slipped my memory. *(He pulls out a piece of paper)* And the cossack Pugachyov.
DEPUTY. We'll capture him, Your Royal Highness.
CATHERINE. *(Removing the medal from him)* When you catch him, then you'll get it.

---

[13] Erdman here spoofs the Russian custom of awarding medals and honors for all kinds of minor occasions. This practice was especially widespread in Soviet times and would have been perceived by an audience in the 1960s as an Aesopian reference to contemporary life.

2. The General and the Nobility

CHARACTERS IN ORDER OF APPEARANCE

THE GENERAL [14]
FIRST NOBLEMAN
AN OFFICIAL
SECOND NOBLEMAN
THIRD NOBLEMAN
FOURTH NOBLEMAN
A PEASANT MAN
A MAN WITH WREATHS
VARIOUS PEASANT MEN, WOMEN AND CHILDREN

GENERAL. Gentlemen, Her Highness has issued an order: In order that our most virtuous Empress and her retinue may travel as befits her, we are to construct seventy-six way stations from Petersburg to Kiev. There must be a minimum of five hundred and fifty horses at every station.
FIRST NOBLEMAN. How many will that be all the way to Kiev?
GENERAL. Horses? Let's see. (*To an official with an abacus*) Count!
OFFICIAL. (*After calculating*) Forty-one thousand and eighty.
SECOND NOBLEMAN. Is that in one direction, Your Excellency?
GENERAL. Yes.
SECOND NOBLEMAN. How many will that be in two directions?
GENERAL. Let's see. (*To the official*) Count.
OFFICIAL. (*After calculating*) That would be exactly one hundred and ten thousand horses.
THIRD NOBLEMAN. One hundred and ten thousand! Isn't that too many, Your Excellency?
GENERAL. Well, they have to get there and back, you know.
THIRD NOBLEMAN. Oh, my! Will we be able to do it?
GENERAL. He who can't, himself will take a little journey.
THIRD NOBLEMAN. Whereto, Your Excellency?
GENERAL. Whereto? Wherever they send him. And you can rest assured, my respected man, it will be a one-way journey with no return ticket. Let's move on to what comes next. Each station shall be outfitted with palaces, service personnel, dining rooms, offices, buffets, reception rooms, pre-

---

[14] Although Erdman does not indicate it anywhere, this character clearly is the famous Grigory Potyomkin (1739-1791), the Russian general and one of Catherine's lovers.

reception rooms, and comfort stations.[15]

FOURTH NOBLEMAN. What does that mean, Your Excellency?

GENERAL. Pardon me, but who are you?

FOURTH NOBLEMAN. A marshal of the nobility, Your Excellency.

GENERAL. There, you see? You may marshal around the nobility, but you don't even know that a comfort station is a well-outfitted outhouse. It's time you learned that courtiers don't court their necessities in courtyards. Ha, ha, ha!

ALL. Ha, ha, ha!

FIRST NOBLEMAN. *(To the Second Nobleman)* Subtle little joke!

SECOND NOBLEMAN. It's his high-class education.

GENERAL. Chandeliers, mirrors, curtains, carpets, chairs, sofas, vinegar for fumigation, as well as brooms and feather brushes will be brought from Moscow to clean up the dust. Sulphur and saltpeter have been ordered from Kharkov and Kremenchug for fireworks.

THIRD NOBLEMAN. For fireworks we also need shingles, Your Excellency.

GENERAL. You can strip the peasant huts of shingles, gentlemen. And do it today.

THIRD NOBLEMAN. What if it should rain, Your Excellency?

GENERAL. Then see to it the shingles are stored in a dry place.

THIRD NOBLEMAN. What I meant to say, Your Excellency, was that, if we strip all the roofs ahead of time and it should begin to rain, then all the peasants' belongings are liable to get wet.

GENERAL. What belongings could peasants possibly have? And anyway, rain isn't eternal. If things get a bit wet, they'll eventually dry out. Fill all the granaries and barns with sacks of wheat. If there isn't enough grain to go around, fill sacks with sand.

THIRD NOBLEMAN. With sand?

GENERAL. What do you care? It's not to be eaten, it's to make an impression.

FIRST NOBLEMAN. *(To the Second Nobleman)* What a genius!

SECOND NOBLEMAN. It's his high-class education.

GENERAL. Construct triumphal arcs and gates along the entire road which the august caravan will travel. Either whitewash or paint the walls of every house which will be visible from the road. And wherever there are walls that can't be improved either by whitewashing or painting—tear them down. In their place, line up rows of young girls with flowers bound in red

---

[15] Here, and throughout the remainder of the interlude, Erdman spoofs the building of what are now known as "Potyomkin villages." A probably apocryphal legend has it that Grigory Potyomkin often preceded Catherine on trips about Russia, "cleaning up" the run-down sights of the countryside for the benefit of the Empress, and to the detriment of the populace. Apocryphal or not as regards Catherine, the whitewashing of local "color" for the benefit of visiting Soviet dignitaries was a common practice, and no audience in the late 1960s would have missed the hint.

ribbons. Herd peasants into all the empty stretches along the village roads. Hey, peasants!

(The peasants approach. The General looks them over)

Is this really all you've got?

FOURTH NOBLEMAN. That's all we've got, Your Excellency.

GENERAL. You should have extras for the occasional emergency. This is the Empress who'll be passing through here, you know. *(To a Peasant)* Aren't you ashamed to be going around in a shirt like that?

PEASANT. Yes, sir. Of course I am.

GENERAL. Don't you have another?

PEASANT. Of course I do, sir.

GENERAL. So, then why are you going around in this ragged old thing? You ought to put on your other.

PEASANT. If you say so. Only it's more ragged than this one, Your Excellency.

GENERAL. Listen here, gentlemen. Didn't you read my instructions?

FOURTH NOBLEMAN. How can you possibly doubt us, Your Excellency? Bring in the wreaths!

(A man runs in with wreaths made of wild flowers)

Put them on!

(The man dons a wreath)

Not on yourself, you idiot. On them.

(The man puts a wreath on the peasant nearest to him)

Not on the men. On the girls.

OFFICIAL. *(Whispers to the General)* Allow me to remind Your Excellency of Her Highness's own authentic words: "Catherine's route must be as a Roman road." You know, Roman men used to go around in wreaths, too.

GENERAL. Do you know that for certain?

OFFICIAL. Like this... *(He draws his hand across his neck, as if cutting his throat)*

GENERAL. Put 'em on the men, too.

(They put wreaths on the men)

FOURTH NOBLEMAN. Give ribbons, beads and leaves to the girls and old women. Everyone gets ribbons and leaves. Every other person gets beads.

GENERAL. *(Looks over the women)* The girls'll do, but these old women are a fright.

FOURTH NOBLEMAN. Girls! Stand in front of the women. How's that?

GENERAL. They look a lot better when you can't see them, of course. Only, all of these girls are barefooted.
FOURTH NOBLEMAN. We can cover up their bare feet, too.
GENERAL. How?
FOURTH NOBLEMAN. With children, Your Excellency. Bring in the kids!

(Children are seated at the feet of the girls)

GENERAL. Where in the hell did you get... Oh, well. You covered up the old women with girls. And you covered up the girls with kids. What are you going to cover up the kids with?
FOURTH NOBLEMAN. Bouquets, Your Excellency! Hand out the bouquets! What do you think, Your Excellency? If the caravan's going fast enough, don't you think it ought to work?
GENERAL. Only if it's going very fast. Now what do we do with the men?
FOURTH. No problem. *(To the men)* Off with your shirts!

(The men take off their shirts)

Put on these.

(The men are given long red shirts)

Off with your pants!

(The men put on new ones)

OFFICIAL. *(Whispers)* By the way, Your Excellency, Roman men didn't wear pants.

GENERAL. *(Thinks a moment)* Do you think that the Empress might like that?
OFFICIAL. Well, I doubt Count Mamonov will.[16]
GENERAL. You think he'll be travelling with her?

(The Official draws his hand across his neck, as if cutting his throat)

FOURTH NOBLEMAN. *(To the assembled peasants)* Now, listen to me carefully. I will pass in front of you as if I were a horse, and then as if I were the Empress. The Empress's carriage will be pulled by thirty horses. As soon as you see the first horse, shout: "Hurrah!" There, you just saw the first horse. *(He runs past the line of peasants, jumping up and down like a horse)*
PEASANTS. Hurrah!
FOURTH NOBLEMAN. Now, the horses have gone past and you just saw

---

[16] Alexander Dmitriev-Mamonov (1758-1803) was an officer, a minor playwright and, as one of Catherine's lovers, a rival to Potyomkin. In 1787, he made his first journey with Catherine to the south of Russia.

the Empress's carriage. You've got to shout louder than you did for the horses. Wave your ribbons and throw flowers. *(To the first peasant in line)* As soon as I go past you, take off your new pants and your new shirt and put on your old ones.

(The peasant starts getting undressed)

How come you're not saying anything? While you're getting undressed, you've got to shout, you know. Even if the Empress can't see you anymore, she'll still be able to hear you pouring out your ecstatic admiration. *(To the next peasant in line)* Now, I've gone past you. Take off your clothes. You blockhead! Quicker! Time is of the essence.

GENERAL. What's the hurry?

FOURTH NOBLEMAN. Are you kidding? It's only twenty versts to Ilyinsky, and we've got to have something to dress the peasants in there, too. These peasants have to get out of their new clothes, so that those peasants can get out of their old clothes and into their new clothes.

GENERAL. You know what? In order to speed things up, just see to it that the peasants down the road are already waiting there naked.

FOURTH NOBLEMAN. What a great idea. Thank you. And so, Your Excellency, we will undress—or, that is to say, we will dress—every man, woman and child from here all the way to Rotten Gully. Everything beyond Rotten Gully belongs to another province. Whatever happens there is somebody else's problem.

1. Nikolai Erdman as a boy.

2. Nikolai Erdman as a boy.

3. Boris and Nikolai Erdman, late 1910s.

4. Nikolai Erdman as a Red Army soldier, 1919.

5. Nikolai Erdman, early 1920s.

Театр Гитис.

О. Г. Т.

НИКОЛАЙ

БОРИС.

ЭРДМАНЪ.

П. Галаджев.

6. Portrait of Nikolai and Boris Erdman by P. Galadzhev, 1922.

7. Boris Erdman as an actor in the role of the Nubian in Oscar Wilde's *Salomé* at Alexander Tairov's Kamerny Theater, 1917.

Опытный Героический Театр
Худ ожн. Борис Эрдман.

8. Boris Erdman, set designer for the Experimental-Heroic Theater, 1922.

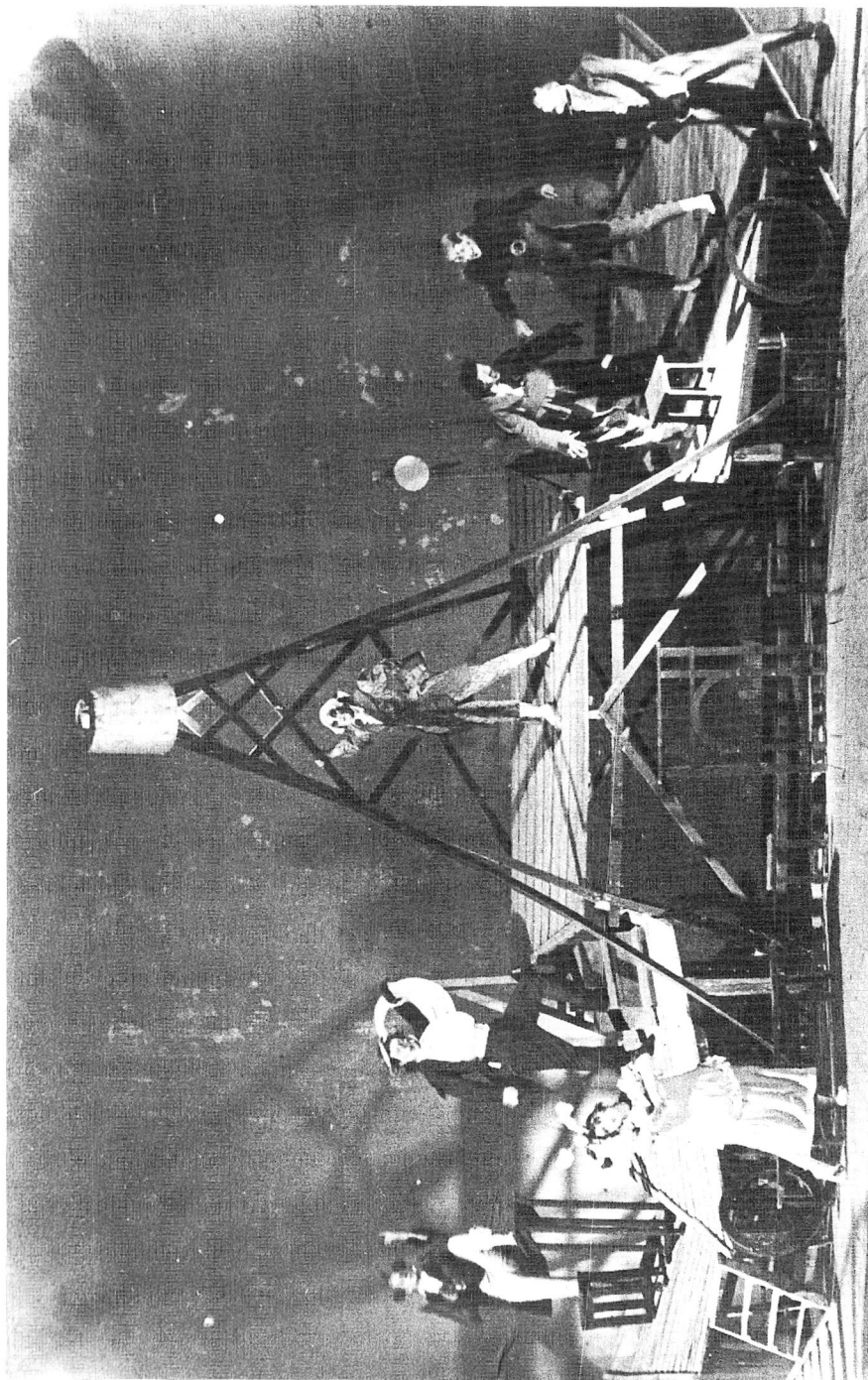

9. A scene from Nikolai Erdman's adaptation of Eugène Labiche's *The Piggy Bank* at the Experimental-Heroic Theater, 1922. Stage design by Boris Erdman.

БОРИС ЭРДМАН.

ПРОЕКТ КОСТЮМА К ИСПАНСКИМ ТАНЦАМ.

10. A costume design by Boris Erdman for Kasyan Goleizovsky's *Spanish Dances* at the Kamerny Ballet, 1923.

М. К. Б.

БОРИС ЭРДМАН.

Проект костюма к испанским танцам.

11. Boris Erdman's costume designs for Kasyan Goleizovsky's *Spanish Dances* at the Kamerny Ballet, 1923.

КАСЬЯН ГОЛЕЙЗОВСКИЙ.

Шарж Б. Эрдмана.

12. Boris Erdman's caricature of Kasyan Goleizovsky, 1922.

13. Boris Erdman's costume designs for a program of foxtrots, 1923.

Борис Эрдман.

Проект костюма клоуна
Виталия Лазаренко.

14. Boris Erdman's costume design for the clown
Vitaly Lazarenko, 1922.

Борис Эрдман.

I. ЮРИЙ МИЛЮТИН. II. АВТОШАРЖ.

15. (i) Boris Erdman's drawing of the singer Yury Milyutin.
(ii) A self-caricature of Boris Erdman, 1922.

На арене стол. На столе графин с водой, стакан и папки с бумагами. За столом судья. (Шпрех.). Над судьей плакат. — „Товарищеский суд ЖАКТА № 1519." — Перед столом небольшое возвышение. Неподалеку скамья. На скамье униформа.

Судья. (перелистывая бумаги.)

„Слушается дело по обвинению гражданина Теркина в нанесении побоев и учинении пьяного дебоширства в квартире номер тринадцать, дома номер четырнадцать принадлежащего нашему ЖАКТу." Кто явился по настоящему делу? Обвиняемый! (Повышая голос.) Обвиняемый!! (Еще более повышая голос.) Гражданин Теркин!!! (Кричит.) Обвиняемый Теркин!!!!

Голос Лазаренко.

Я! (Все головы поворачиваются по направлению к выходу на арену.)

Судья.

Где вы?

Лазаренко.

Вот он я. (Появляется Лазаренко с коромыслом на плече. На одном конце коромысла подвешено ведро полное воды, на другом конце довольно объемистый мешок распираемый изнутри какими-то предметами. Лазаренко подходит к судейскому столу и встает перед ним на возвышении таким образом, что ведро на переднем конце коромысла оказывается над головой или над коленями сидящего за столом судьи.)

Лазаренко.

Здравствуйте, гражданин судья. (Лазаренко кланяется, ведро накреняется и вода льется на судью.)

16. The first page of Nikolai Erdman's manuscript of the circus sketch "The Comradely Court Case at Housing Cooperative No. 1519", 1928.

17. Vladimir Mass, 1926.

18. Caricature of Vladimir Mass by L. Murzen, 1922.

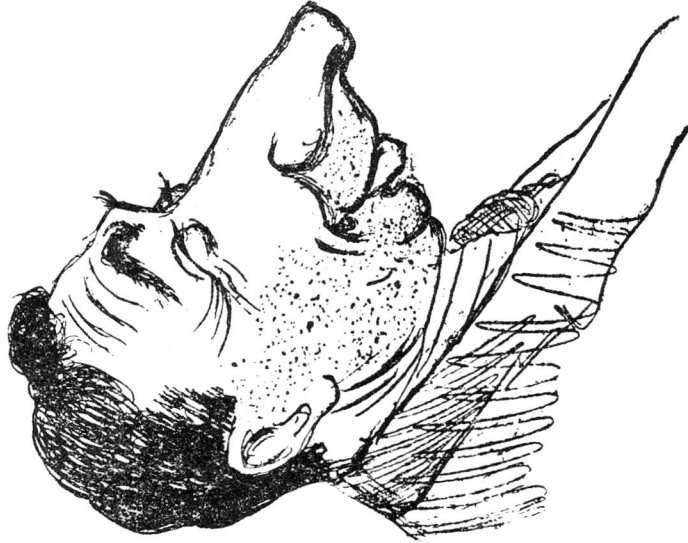

дружеский шарж КУКРЫНИКСЫ

сценарист В. З. Масс

19. Caricature of Vladimir Mass by the famous
Kukryniksy brothers, 1933.

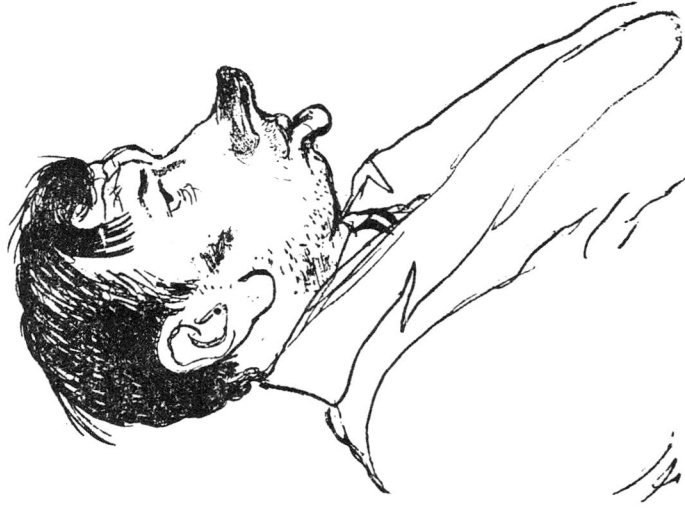

дружеский шарж КУКРЫНИКСЫ

сценарист Н. Р. Эрдман

20. Caricature of Nikolai Erdman by the famous
Kukryniksy brothers, 1933.

21. Vladimir Mass, Nikolai Erdman and Arnold Barsky with two unidentified women, Gagra 1933.

22. Vladimir Mass and Mikhail Volpin, 1950s.

23. Nikolai Erdman and Mikhail Volpin, late 1950s.

24. Drawing of Nikolai Erdman in his later years.
Artist: V. Korenin (?).

25. Nikolai Erdman, 1970.

Works by Nikolai Erdman
with Vladimir Mass and Others
1931–1954

Two Music Hall Numbers

WRITTEN WITH VLADIMIR MASS

1931

1.

CHARACTERS

EMCEE — *Comrade Gril* [1]
WRITER — *Fyodor Semyonovich Korzhikov*
CRITIC — *Pyotr Semyonovich Morzhikov*

EMCEE. Comrades, for the first number of our program...

WRITER. Say, are you an administrator here at this theater?

EMCEE. What do you want?

WRITER. I want to get a pass for tonight's performance.

EMCEE. And who might you be?

WRITER. Allow me to introduce myself. Fyodor Semyonovich Korzhikov, famous Russian writer.

EMCEE. What have you written?

WRITER. That's a strange question. I haven't written anything.

EMCEE. Then why do you say you're a famous Russian writer?

WRITER. You mean you think a writer becomes famous because he writes? A writer becomes famous because others write about him.

EMCEE. Has anyone written about you?

WRITER. Yes.

EMCEE. What did they write about you?

WRITER. That I am the hope of Soviet literature.

EMCEE. How can anyone consider you the hope of Soviet literature if you haven't written anything?

WRITER. Just for that very reason. If I were to write anything, there would be no hope left.

EMCEE. Who wrote that about you?

WRITER. Pyotr Semyonovich Morzhikov. Pyotr Semyonovich, won't you come over here?

---

[1] Alexander Gril (also spelled Grill, ?-1946) was a popular music hall and variety emcee in the 1920s and 1930s. Both sketches published here were written for him.

(Enter Pyotr Semyonovich Morzhikov)

Allow me to introduce you. This is Pyotr Semyonovich Morzhikov, the best Soviet critic.

EMCEE. What have you written?

CRITIC. I wrote that Fyodor Semyonovich Korzhikov is the best Soviet writer.

EMCEE. Is he really the best?

CRITIC. Without a doubt. Fyodor Semyonovich Korzhikov is a man with an unsullied name, enormous revolutionary baggage, and great erudition. I consider that Fyodor Semyonovich Korzhikov knows more than Anatoly Vasilyevich Lunacharsky. Because if you were to ask Anatoly Vasilyevich whether he knows Fyodor Semyonovich, I am sure that he doesn't. But if you were to ask Fyodor Semyonovich whether he knows Anatoly Vasilyevich—without the slightest doubt he does. Therefore, Fyodor Semyonovich knows more than Anatoly Vasilyevich.

EMCEE. Indeed, you have convinced me that Fyodor Semyonovich is a great writer. I am only slightly disturbed by the fact that he hasn't written anything. And, I gather, he isn't writing anything at present.

CRITIC. One doesn't say that a writer "isn't writing." One says that a writer is "holding his silence." I won't argue that comrade Korzhikov is holding his silence, but he is holding his silence on the right road.

EMCEE. How is that?

CRITIC. You see, we recently had a heated discussion about what comprises the main road of Soviet literature: the living or the unliving man.[2]

EMCEE. And what conclusion did you come to?

CRITIC. We concluded that, at present, a living man is a dead affair, and that the correct road for literature is the unliving man.

EMCEE. Why is that?

CRITIC. Because an unliving man is a dead man. And it is customary either to speak well about the dead or not to speak at all. So, Fyodor Semyonovich decided to say nothing. He may be silent, but he is silent on the right road. And nobody can accuse him of anything in that.

EMCEE. Well, that depends. It isn't important that a writer is holding his silence. What is important is what he is holding his silence about. Is he holding his silence about our faults or about our achievements?

CRITIC. You can't trick me with that one. I consider that we have no faults.

EMCEE. If we have no faults and you are holding your silence, that means that you are holding your silence about our achievements. And that is

---

[2] The following section about the "living and the unliving" formulates one of Erdman's and Mass's favorite topics and they often reused it in other sketches, as in the first interlude for *Hamlet*. It may well be a parody of comments contained in the discussion of *The Suicide* at the Vakhtangov Theater. See note 17 to the transcript of that discussion.

already a fault.

WRITER. Yes, that is a bit awkward. You know, perhaps I'll write something.

EMCEE. Such as?

WRITER. Something classical.

EMCEE. For example?

WRITER. It's difficult to say right now. For example, comrade Raskolnikov[3] just wrote Leo Nikolayevich Tolstoy's *Resurrection.* And, at present, Smolin[4] is writing Gogol's *Dead Souls* for the Art Theater. Still, I think there will be something left for me. It seems to me that no one has written Dostoevsky's *The Brothers Karamazov* for a long time. I suppose that's what I'll write.

EMCEE. I imagine it's difficult to write *The Brothers Karamazov.*

WRITER. I wouldn't say it's so difficult. After all, it's almost already written. But you're right that it's difficult to read. What a big book! I've been planning to read it for years, but I never quite got around to it. But now I guess I'll have to, to say nothing of rewriting it.

EMCEE. Why rewrite it if it's already written?

WRITER. If I don't rewrite it, I don't get paid. Basically, there's all kinds of irritating details connected with a writer's job. But maybe I'll skip all these brothers and just write something about our achievements.

EMCEE. Which ones in particular?

WRITER. It depends on the advance I get. Some achievements bring in a hundred rubles, and some bring in even more.

EMCEE. Why do you have to write only about achievements? A writer should also write about faults.

WRITER. No he shouldn't.

EMCEE. Yes he should.

CRITIC. No he shouldn't.

WRITER. Comrade Gril, you're just the man to settle this argument.

EMCEE. With pleasure.

WRITER. What do you think a writer should write about, achievements or faults?

EMCEE. That's a very complex question. I consider that sometimes it's better if a writer writes about our faults than if he writes about our achievements.

WRITER. Why's that?

EMCEE. I'll tell you why. Let's say a writer writes something like this: "For the first time in thirteen years there has appeared in our town a man who takes bribes." That concerns our faults, but I consider that you can write about that. But what if a writer writes something like this: "For the first

---

[3] Fyodor Raskolnikov (1892-1939) was a minor playwright and ideologue. His dramatization of *Resurrection* premiered at the Moscow Art Theater in 1930.

[4] Dmitry Smolin (1891-1955) was a playwright active in the 1920s. His dramatization of *Dead Souls* for the Moscow Art Theater eventually premiered in 1932.

time in thirteen years there has appeared in our town a man who doesn't take bribes?" That concerns our achievements and I think we're better off not writing about that. However, why don't you step along to the box-office and I'll see to it that you are issued a pass. And now, we can begin our program.

2.

CHARACTERS

EMCEE
A YOUNG WOMAN

EMCEE. For the next number in our program...

(A young woman enters at a run)

WOMAN. Here I am, comrade Meyerhold.
EMCEE. Where's Meyerhold?
WOMAN. You mean you're not comrade Meyerhold?
EMCEE. No.
WOMAN. That's impossible.
EMCEE. I assure you that I am not Meyerhold.
WOMAN. Surely, you're joking.
EMCEE. Cross my heart.
WOMAN. Are you prepared to swear to God about that?
EMCEE. I will not swear to God, because there is no God.
WOMAN. What?
EMCEE. There is no God.
WOMAN. That's impossible.
EMCEE. I assure you.
WOMAN. Surely, you're joking.
EMCEE. I will repeat it again: There is no God.
WOMAN. How is that possible? Where did he disappear to?
EMCEE. Where did he disappear to? God is omnipotent—wherever he wanted to go, that's where he went.
WOMAN. Well, to hell with God, if there is no God. But where is comrade Meyerhold?
EMCEE. I don't know. He's probably in his theater.
WOMAN. You mean this isn't comrade Meyerhold's theater?
EMCEE. No.
WOMAN. Surely, you're joking.

EMCEE. I assure you I'm not. The Meyerhold Theater is next door. You are welcome to go there, if you like, but I am busy. I have to begin our program.

WOMAN. I'm busy too, and I don't have time to go next door. I didn't come here to see the show, I came on business.

EMCEE. What business is that?

WOMAN. Tell me, comrade, are you a good man?

EMCEE. I think I am a very good man. Otherwise, I am seriously mistaken in my evaluation of people. Why do you ask?

WOMAN. Because all actors are so rude. And it seemed to me that you might be rude.

EMCEE. So that's it. But what is it you want, if you don't mind my asking?

WOMAN. You see, I want to work in the theater.

EMCEE. Which one?

WOMAN. What's the difference?

EMCEE. What can you do?

WOMAN. I can't do anything. That's why I want to work in the theater.

EMCEE. I see. Tell me, do you have any particular characteristics which might justify your becoming an actress?

WOMAN. What kind of characteristics?

EMCEE. Well, for example, do you have a sense of rhythm, a refined temperament or a nice voice? Or are you deprived in those departments?

WOMAN. I can't vouch for my temperament, but I'd say my voice is quite influential. My daddy works for the government.

EMCEE. Where exactly?

WOMAN. In store No. 13.

EMCEE. Tell me, do you think your father might be able to get me, say, twenty pounds of butter for my sick mother?

WOMAN. He probably can.

EMCEE. I see. I would say that some of your characteristics are definitely quite promising.

WOMAN. Then again, maybe he can't.

EMCEE. I see. Perhaps you should try joining the Bolshoi Theater.

WOMAN. The Bolshoi Theater is too big. I would rather work here with you.

EMCEE. I see. In that case, we shall have to examine your possibilities. Let's begin with theory—in the field of theater history. Tell me, sweetheart, who did Mochalov live with?

WOMAN. Mochalov?

EMCEE. Yes.

WOMAN. His mother.[5]

---

[5] Pavel Mochalov (1800-1848) was one of the great Russian actors. His scandalous decision to abandon his wife and live with his mistress caused serious problems with the government authorities. He and his mistress were threatened with exile if they didn't break off their liaison, and eventually, under that pressure, he did return to his wife.

EMCEE. Well, all right. Now let's move on to practice. Perhaps you might read us something?

WOMAN. All right.

EMCEE. What have you prepared?

WOMAN. Tolstoy.

EMCEE. Which Tolstoy?

WOMAN. The vegetarian.

EMCEE. What will you read?

WOMAN. One of his works.

EMCEE. Which one?

WOMAN. *War and Peace.*

EMCEE. What part?

WOMAN. The whole thing.

(The emcee falls off his chair)

"*War and Peace,* a composition by Tolstoy. As published by *Flame Magazine.*[6] Volume One, Part One, Chapter One. Eh bien, mon prince." That's French. Asterisk, footnote. "So, prince. Genoa and Lucca have become nothing more than estates of the Buonaparte family. No, I warn you, if you allow yourself again to defend the evils and terrors of this Antichrist," open parentheses, "believe me, that's what he is," close parentheses, "then I no longer recognize you."

EMCEE. Are you going to read all of it?

WOMAN. Of course I am. The end is the best part. "Vous n'êtes plus my loyal servant, comme vous dites. Well, hello, hello. Je vois que je vous fais peur, do sit down and tell us all." *(Pins on a long white beard)*

EMCEE. Who is that?

WOMAN. Tolstoy. Whenever I read the author's narrative, I put on a beard. "Thus, in July of 1805, spoke the well-known Anna Pavlovna Scherrer, the maid-of-honor and confidante of Empress..."

EMCEE. Hold it! Stop it! Quit it!

WOMAN. How can I do that? There's still four more volumes until the end.

EMCEE. Do you think I'd be able to listen to this all the way to the end? Quit reading.

WOMAN. It's always the same old story. No matter who I try reading this book to, nobody can listen to it through to the end. This *War and Peace* is incredibly boring. I wouldn't have picked it up myself, unless one of my girlfriends hadn't suggested it.

EMCEE. Who is your girlfriend?

WOMAN. Lyalya Shishkina. Her husband works in a children's cafeteria.

---

[6] *Flame Magazine—Ogonyok* in Russian—was and still is a popular news and features magazine, roughly similar to the American *Life Magazine.*

EMCEE. Tell me, do you think your friend might be able to get me, say, twenty pounds of butter for my sick mother?

WOMAN. She probably can.

EMCEE. You know, *War and Peace* isn't such a bore, after all. Only we'll have to shorten it a bit for the music hall. For instance, we'll just cross out everything except the title. Then we'll add "Poincaré" to it.[7] That makes "Poincaré—war and peace." It'll be a great number. If you want, we can perform it together.

WOMAN. I don't know how to perform yet.

EMCEE. In the music hall, you don't have to know how to perform. You just have to be adept at adapting.

WOMAN. Adept at adapting what?

EMCEE. At adapting everything so that it comes across in the proper positive light.

WOMAN. How do you do that?

EMCEE. It's easy. Stand right here and say the title.

WOMAN. *"War and Peace. A publication of Flame Magazine. "*

EMCEE. Forget the fires, if you will. This isn't a café chantant here. Try it again.

WOMAN. *"War and Peace..."*

EMCEE. "It's the thirteenth year of the new century. War, war, war. The echelons are marching, telephones are ringing, everyone is groaning: Oh, oh, oh." *(To the young woman)* Now you say: "And meanwhile, in Paris."

WOMAN. "And meanwhile, in Paris."

EMCEE. Maestro, won't you give us a tune? *(He dances)* "It's now the new century's twenty-fifth year. Peace, peace, peace. We're holding firm and we're building fast: Clank, boom, screech."

WOMAN. "And meanwhile, in Paris."

EMCEE. Maestro, strike up the band. *(He dances with the young woman)* Now do you understand the principles of our work?

WOMAN. You know, you are the first person who has made me understand Leo Tolstoy's *War and Peace.* Whenever I read it myself, it always seemed somehow different—so boring and old-fashioned. But this music gives it such a noble grace. How charming! But, tell me, can you really adapt anything like that?

EMCEE. Well, maybe not anything, but most anything. For example, Dostoevsky's *Crime and Punishment* is a killer when done as a tap-dance.

WOMAN. That's impossible.

---

[7] Raymond Poincaré was the French president from 1913-1920, and prime minister in the years 1912-1913, 1922-1924, 1926-1929. In the Soviet Union he was known as a militarist who played a key role in the outbreak of World War I, and as a leader in the anti-Soviet intervention during the Russian Civil War. For those reasons, he was tagged with the nickname, "Poincaré—war."

EMCEE. I assure you.

WOMAN. Surely, you're joking.

EMCEE. Not at all. Stand right here. All right, here we go. "Crime, crime, crime. A French bourgeois and an English sir do nothing but trash the U.S.S.R."

WOMAN. "And meanwhile, in Paris."

EMCEE. All right, that's enough. It's time to get on with our program. The setting is New Zealand. The people, oppressed by colonial imperialism are singing a song of protest against the foul and violent imperialists.

WOMAN. And all the comrades sing: "And meanwhile, in Paris." Maestro, strike up a tune! *(She dances)*

EMCEE. Get this madwoman out of here!

An Interlude for *Princess Turandot*

WRITTEN WITH VLADIMIR MASS

1932

CHARACTERS

TRUFFALDINO
BRIGHELLA

TRUFFALDINO.[1] Listen, Brighellochka, why are you always taking off your hat?

BRIGHELLA. The fact is, Truffaldinchik, it pinches the crown of my head terribly. I am constantly struggling with it.

TRUFFALDINO. In that case, toss out the hat and buy yourself a new one.

BRIGHELLA. Toss out the hat?

TRUFFALDINO. Well, yes.

BRIGHELLA. This one?

TRUFFALDINO. Well, yes.

BRIGHELLA. Like this? *(Throws down the hat)*

TRUFFALDINO. Well, yes.

BRIGHELLA. *(Picking up the hat)* On what grounds?

TRUFFALDINO. On what grounds? If it's too tight, that means the hat is too small for the crown of your head.

BRIGHELLA. The hat?

TRUFFALDINO. Well, yes.

BRIGHELLA. For the crown of my head?

TRUFFALDINO. Well, yes.

BRIGHELLA. For the crown of what head? For this one?

TRUFFALDINO. Well, yes.

BRIGHELLA. Ai, yi, yi, yi, yi, yi. What a fool you are, Truffaldino. You think it's too tight because this hat here is too small for the crown of my head?

TRUFFALDINO. Well, yes.

BRIGHELLA. Nothing of the sort. My hat is just the right size. But the crown of my head, here—it's definitely too big for my hat. That's why it's too tight. But, what can you do? You can't throw out your head and buy a new one.

---

[1] It is uncertain where this interlude fitted into the performance at the Vakhtangov Theater, although it may have replaced Act II, scene one.

There's nothing left to do but suffer.

TRUFFALDINO. You know, Brighella, the situation is much more serious than I thought.

BRIGHELLA. It's a no-exit situation.

TRUFFALDINO. So we haven't crowned off the solution to the problem, after all?

BRIGHELLA. Of course not.

TRUFFALDINO. Then, what next?

BRIGHELLA. The problem is in the crown of my head.

TRUFFALDINO. And what's your head in?

BRIGHELLA. My hat.

TRUFFALDINO. Wait a minute. If the solution is in the crown of your head and your head is in your hat, then it seems to me the whole problem is crowned off wonderfully.

BRIGHELLA. You know, Truffaldinushka, I think we've hit on the right road.

TRUFFALDINO. Of course. All you have to do is buy a slightly bigger hat…

BRIGHELLA. And the crown of my head will shrink a little smaller.

TRUFFALDINO. No.

BRIGHELLA. What?

TRUFFALDINO. The crown of your head will stay the same.

BRIGHELLA. The crown of my head will stay the same? What a misfortune. Then nothing will come of it.

TRUFFALDINO. What's the crown of your head have to do with it? We concluded that the whole problem is crowned off wonderfully.

BRIGHELLA. But what about the crown of my head?

TRUFFALDINO. We crowned off that problem, too.

BRIGHELLA. Well then, if the crown of my head is in my hat and the whole problem has been crowned off wonderfully, that means the whole thing is in my head.

TRUFFALDINO. An enigma.

BRIGHELLA. A dead end.

TRUFFALDINO. Wait a minute, let's try to reason it out dialectically.

BRIGHELLA. Dialectically?

TRUFFALDINO. Yes.

BRIGHELLA. Listen, Truffaldino, maybe it's not worth it?

TRUFFALDINO. (*Leads Brighella off to the side*) There's no other solution, it's all we can do.

BRIGHELLA. Well, if it's all we can do, let's give it a try.[2]

TRUFFALDINO. Thus, reasoning dialectically… What are you shaking for?

_____

[2] This and the preceding two lines are crossed out in the manuscript. (From Brighella's "Listen, Truffaldino…," through Brighella's "…let's give it a try.")

BRIGHELLA. Listen, Truffaldinushka, I have kids. And me, I myself want to live, I'm still young… *(Falls on his knees)* Your Ideologexellency, don't make me reason.

TRUFFALDINO. You eccentric, what are you afraid of?

BRIGHELLA. What am I afraid of? You start reasoning and reasoning about something, and then, when somebody starts figuring out what you're talking about, they start working you over and they give it to you—Averba-boom!—right on the head.[3] Then you'll see what I'm afraid of. It's terrible even to think about it.

TRUFFALDINO. You know, I, by the way, don't know fear.

BRIGHELLA. Shhhh… Speak more quietly.

TRUFFALDINO. Why?

BRIGHELLA. Afinogenov might be here.[4] You wouldn't want to offend him. Maybe you don't know *Fear*. That's your good fortune. But why say so aloud? In general, you should never argue with playwrights. Otherwise they'll start feeding you nothing but bread and water, like the Art Theater.

TRUFFALDINO. I know *Bread* is playing at the Art Theater,[5] but what does water have to do with it?

BRIGHELLA. That's what they're making bread out of these days.

TRUFFALDINO. So there's water in the bread, *Bread* is playing at the Art Theater, and therefore the Art Theater is all washed up? It's a dead end.

BRIGHELLA. A no-exit situation.

TRUFFALDINO. In that case, we'll have to reason dialectically anyway.

BRIGHELLA. But what if they give it to us—Averba-boom?

TRUFFALDINO. You can do it in such a way that they won't Averba-boom us.

BRIGHELLA. How's that?

TRUFFALDINO. You just say some word and then start dissociating yourself from it. Dissociate yourself from every word you say.

BRIGHELLA. What's in it for me?

TRUFFALDINO. They'll praise you for it. They'll say, "He's admitted his mistakes, he's admitted his mistakes." Sort of like a methodological quadrille. Only I advise you to do one thing. When you make a mistake, make a whole bunch of them at once and then dissociate yourself from each

---

[3] This is a reference to the Marxist literary critic Leopold Averbakh (1903-1939). He was a leader in the proletarian movement in Soviet literature from 1926-1932, and his harsh articles stung all who did not share his views.

[4] Alexander Afinogenov (1904-1941) was a popular playwright in the 1920s and early 1930s. His play about the intelligentsia, *Fear,* stirred a controversy when it was staged at the Moscow Art Theater in 1931.

[5] This refers to the Moscow Art Theater's 1931 production of *Bread,* by Vladimir Kirshon (1902-1938). *Bread* provided a plodding view of the so-called class war in the Soviet countryside.

one individually. That way, they'll praise you longer.

BRIGHELLA. All right, Truffaldino, let's try it.

TRUFFALDINO. And so, at present we have the following: a hat, some bread, the crown of a head and some water. The problem of the hat has yet to be crowned off, and there's water in the bread. What do we need to rid ourselves of, in order to settle the problem? The crown of the head and the water, or the hat and the bread? In other words, the question concerns form and content. Take the hat, for instance. Is that form or content?

BRIGHELLA. The hat?

TRUFFALDINO. Yes.

BRIGHELLA. One hat is form. But, if somebody were to give me, say, twenty a month, I'd be more than content.

TRUFFALDINO. What's twenty hats got to do with it?

BRIGHELLA. What do you mean, Truffaldinchik? I'm reasoning material-istically…

TRUFFALDINO. Knock it off. That's a crude error.

BRIGHELLA. An error. I dissociate myself.

TRUFFALDINO. In that case, what do you think, now?

BRIGHELLA. This is what I think: A hat with a uniform is form, but a civilian hat is content.

TRUFFALDINO. That's a mechanical approach.

BRIGHELLA. Mechanical? I dissociate myself.

TRUFFALDINO. Wait a minute. Listen to me…

BRIGHELLA. I dissociate myself.

TRUFFALDINO. But, Bri…

BRIGHELLA. I dissociate myself, I dissociate myself and that's the end of the conversation.

TRUFFALDINO. So then, you now think…

BRIGHELLA. I think that a hat is f-f-f… c-c-c…, I dissociate myself.

TRUFFALDINO. From what?

BRIGHELLA. From everything. I dissociate myself from all hats.

TRUFFALDINO. But such a declaration makes no sense at all.

BRIGHELLA. I dissociate myself from all sense, too.

TRUFFALDINO. You mean to say that you are dissociating yourself formally?

BRIGHELLA. Formally. I dissociate myself.

TRUFFALDINO. From what?

BRIGHELLA. From dissociation.

TRUFFALDINO. You can't do that.

BRIGHELLA. I can't? In that case I dissociate myself from my dissociation from dissociation.

TRUFFALDINO. What?

BRIGHELLA. In that case I dissociate myself from my dissociation from dissociation.

TRUFFALDINO. A dead end.

BRIGHELLA. A no-exit situation. *(Begins dancing)*

TRUFFALDINO. What are you doing?

BRIGHELLA. I admitted my mistakes. I admitted my mistakes.

TRUFFALDINO. Listen, Truffaldinchik, tell me in secret, anyway, what are form and content?

BRIGHELLA. I'll tell you right now.

TRUFFALDINO. Listen Brighella, do you know Hegel?

BRIGHELLA. Is that the guy they stood upside down on his head?[6]

TRUFFALDINO. Yes. Anyway, this Hegel said, "Form conditioned by its content becomes a law of development of its content." Understand?

BRIGHELLA. Listen, Truffaldinchik, shouldn't we dissociate ourselves from that?

TRUFFALDINO. For the time being, no.

BRIGHELLA. In that case, I understand.

TRUFFALDINO. That means that form and content are one.

BRIGHELLA. I've known that for a long time.

TRUFFALDINO. Who told you?

BRIGHELLA. Anyuta.

TRUFFALDINO. What Anyuta?

BRIGHELLA. Shishkina. You know, she and I once had an intimate conversation after which she said to me, "Fie!" She said, "The content for me is in an unacceptable form." That means that content can also be form.

TRUFFALDINO. Well, yes. There must be some mutual attachment.

BRIGHELLA. Yes, yes. That's just what I suggested to her.

TRUFFALDINO. Who?

BRIGHELLA. Anyuta.

TRUFFALDINO. Absolutely true. Form flows into content and content flows into form.[7]

BRIGHELLA. That's true. For example, if you take the water out of the Art Theater and pour it into my hat, then the hat loses its form and the water becomes its content. But if you throw my hat in the water, then the water becomes the form and the hat becomes its content. And if you take it out of the water and put it on your head, then your head loses all its contents and

---

[6] George Wilhelm Friedrich Hegel's theory of dialectic had a major influence on Marxist thought, and, as such, he was highly regarded by Marxist-Leninists. However, his theory of absolute idealism was diametrically opposed to Marxist materialism. In order to maintain him in the pantheon of accepted philosophers, Marxist-Leninist theoreticians had to turn much of his philosophical system "upside down."

[7] The beginning of this and the preceding nine lines are crossed out in the manuscript. (From Brighella's "I've known that for a long time," through Truffaldino's "Absolutely true.")

the hat takes on the form of your head. Only, I don't understand what the point of the bread is here.

TRUFFALDINO. Indeed, what's the point of the bread?

BRIGHELLA. You know, Truffaldinchik, you and I ought to do a little bit of research. We've already learned how to dissociate ourselves, but we still don't know how to reason. Pretty soon, we're going to be lagging behind all the theaters in town. Even the Bolshoi threw out a poster with a slogan on it: "Art to the Workers."

TRUFFALDINO. They really threw out a slogan?

BRIGHELLA. That's right.

TRUFFALDINO. How far away did they throw it?

BRIGHELLA. So far away, that you'll never see it again.

TRUFFALDINO. Brighella, I think you have just elicited improper laughter from the audience.

BRIGHELLA. What do you mean improper?

TRUFFALDINO. You must try to elicit in the audience healthy, positive laughter. But at the present moment, it's laughing with an unhealthy, animal-like laughter.

BRIGHELLA. Indeed, typically animalistic laughter. Respected public, please don't put me in an awkward position. Laugh in some sort of legal laugh, not in that negligent, animalistic laughter. Laugh in such a way that your laughter causes the ventilation or something to start working. Well, maybe not the ventilation, but, let's say, the snack bar. You should laugh in Shakespearean laughter. Listen, Truffaldinchik, what kind of laughter did Shakespeare laugh?

TRUFFALDINO. That hasn't been determined yet. If he was the son of a Lord, then he laughed the belly laugh of the rotting upper crust, but if he was the son of a salt-of-the-earth merchant, then he laughed the healthy and positive laughter of a half-starving commoner.

BRIGHELLA. When they start playing Shakespeare in our theater, what kind of laughter are we going to laugh?

TRUFFALDINO. It depends on the director. If it's some director alien to us, then our laughter will be unhealthy. But if it's our young, Soviet director Akimov,[8] then we will laugh in our young, Soviet, healthy, positive laughter... through our tears.[9]

BRIGHELLA. You know, Truffaldinchik, I think animalistic laughter is the healthiest there is.

---

[8] This is a reference to Nikolai Akimov's controversial production of *Hamlet* at the Vakhtangov Theater in 1932. In this volume, see the interludes for this production, and the parody of it.

[9] This and the preceding two-plus lines are crossed out in the manuscript. (From Brighella's "You should laugh in Shakespearian laughter," through Truffaldino's "...through our tears.")

Three Interludes for *Hamlet*

WRITTEN WITH VLADIMIR MASS

1932

1.

CHARACTERS

ROSENCRANTZ
HAMLET

ROSENCRANTZ.[1] …And here they come, to offer you their services!

HAMLET. Actors? I love actors! A hero who pretends to be a king is much more pleasant than a king who pretends to be a hero. Don't you think an intelligent jester playing a small role on stage is better than some stupid jester playing a leading role at court? The leading man in a theater is always the leading man to the end of a play, even if ten years pass between acts. In real life, a woman's leading man often has to play fourth or fifth fiddle even if only ten days pass between the first and second acts.[2] A heroine's feelings always go straight to the heart, straight to the heart. Even if the verses she speaks are as crippled as they come. What players are they?

ROSENCRANTZ. Even those you were wont to take such delight in. 'Tis a local troupe.

HAMLET. How chances it they travel? Their residence, both in reputation and profit, was better both ways.

ROSENCRANTZ. I think their inhibition comes by the means of the late innovation. It used to be that spectators came to the theater. These days, the theater has to come to the spectator.

HAMLET. Do they hold the same estimation they did when I was in the city? Are they so followed?

ROSENCRANTZ. Oh, no, my lord. It is much worse.

HAMLET. How comes it? Has their repertoire changed?

ROSENCRANTZ. No. Their public has changed.

HAMLET. Can it be that the new public has ceased to understand old actors?

ROSENCRANTZ. No. Old actors have ceased to understand the new public.

HAMLET. Are there really no new authors?

---

[1] This interlude replaced a portion of Hamlet's conversation with Rosencrantz in Act II, scene two. A few lines adhere to the original.

[2] This and the preceding sentence are crossed out in the manuscript.

131

ROSENCRANTZ. There are.

HAMLET. Then why don't they write new plays?

ROSENCRANTZ. Because they prefer to redo old ones.

HAMLET. How do you explain that?

ROSENCRANTZ. I believe that many of them are troubled by the glorious literary debate that recently took place here in Denmark.

HAMLET. Literary debate? About what?

ROSENCRANTZ. About what comprises the main road of our literature: the living or the unliving man.

HAMLET. What did the authors conclude?

ROSENCRANTZ. They concluded that, at present, writing about a living man is a dead affair. Consequently, it was necessary to write about an un-living man, that is, a dead man. But it is customary either to speak well about the dead or not to speak at all. And since there was nothing good to say about that dead man about whom they wanted to speak, they decided for the time being to say nothing at all.[3]

HAMLET. But are there no new plays that please the public?

ROSENCRANTZ. There are.

HAMLET. Then, why don't they play them?

ROSENCRANTZ. Because the critics don't like them.

HAMLET. What critics?

ROSENCRANTZ. The ones who play the leading role during intermission.

HAMLET. Tell me, do they play it well?

ROSENCRANTZ. No. They play their role only with the aid of a prompter, while the public already knows their role by heart.

HAMLET. What do the critics say?

ROSENCRANTZ. They always say one and the same thing.

HAMLET. What exactly?[4]

ROSENCRANTZ. When they see a heroic play, they say it is insufficient. And when they see a satiric play they say it is excessive.

HAMLET. But in that case, authors have a simple solution.

ROSENCRANTZ. What is that?

HAMLET. They should do everything in reverse. In satiric plays, they should speak insufficiently, and in heroic plays, they should speak excessively.

ROSENCRANTZ. You are absolutely correct. That's just what many do.

HAMLET. And what do the critics say?

ROSENCRANTZ. They say that is excessively insufficient. However, there are the players.

---

[3] This and the preceding five lines are crossed out in the manuscript. (From Hamlet's "How do you explain that," through Rosencrantz's "...they decided for the time being to say nothing at all.")

[4] This, and all lines through the end of interlude, are crossed out in the manuscript.

2. The Scene of the Gravediggers

(A cemetery. Night. One gravedigger sleeps, covered with a bast mat. The other enters with a bottle)

FIRST CLOWN.[5] Well, so much for that. I finished off the bottle, and now…. *(Tosses back the edge of the bast mat)* What have we here? Feet. When I left, there was a head here. Then it's true what they say: The earth turns. I'll just have to wait for the earth to make another revolution and then the head will be back here again. *(Sits down)* However, in the final analysis I think I can talk with feet, too. In my opinion, you're even better off talking with feet than with a head, because feet are more important. What does a man say in critical moments? He says, "Lord, I pray give me fleet feet." That means feet are more important. Furthermore, where does the soul go in critical moments? It sinks to your feet. That means the soul resides in the feet. Or, take a king of some sort. How does one bow to a king? To his head or to his feet? To his feet. That means the feet are more important. Or, for example, Magdalen didn't wash Christ's head, she washed his feet. Once again, the feet are more important. In a critical moment what does a man lose first? His head. For example, he meets a pretty little shepherdess and loses his head on the spot. But when it comes time, his feet will be itching to go. Therefore, we can conclude that one can chat much more easily with feet than with a stupid head. Gentlemen feet, would you like a drink? No? Well, I would. *(Drinks. Noticing that the second clown has awakened, he hides his bottle and starts staring into the heavens)*

SECOND CLOWN. What are you sitting here for? What are you thinking about? Why aren't you digging?

FIRST CLOWN. To dig or not to dig, that is the question.

SECOND CLOWN. What kind of a question is that? The boss ordered you to dig, so that means you dig.

FIRST CLOWN. Am I refusing to dig? I'll dig. Only I want to doubt a bit first. Who can forbid me to doubt?

SECOND CLOWN. The boss.

---

[5] This interlude was performed as a part of Act V, scene one. Some latter portions adhere closely to the original text.

FIRST CLOWN. Forbid it?

SECOND CLOWN. Forbid it.

FIRST CLOWN. To doubt?

SECOND CLOWN. To doubt.

FIRST CLOWN. I doubt it.

SECOND CLOWN. Well, you'll come to doubt that. All our brethren must work. And the more one doubts, the less one works.

FIRST CLOWN. The more one doubts, the less one works? I doubt it. I, for example, I always work and doubt. Parallel operations. I love to doubt.

SECOND CLOWN. Why?

FIRST CLOWN. That's my character. I'm an enthusiast of doubt.

SECOND CLOWN. And what do you doubt?

FIRST CLOWN. Well, for example, recently I have been doubting whether it's worth doubting or not.

SECOND CLOWN. In my opinion, it's not worth it.

FIRST CLOWN. I doubt it.

SECOND CLOWN. That's enough goofing off from you. Get digging.

FIRST CLOWN. There, you say, "Get digging." But what kind of a life is that, just digging and digging. That is the question.

SECOND CLOWN. I consider that there couldn't be anything more endearing. Judge for yourself. All our brethren toil for others their whole life through. Let's say, a stonemason builds a home. But other people live in it. That's not very nice. But we dig graves and other people are planted in them. That's very nice.

FIRST CLOWN. I doubt it. Nice, but not always. Let's say, you have to dig a grave for one of your bosses. That's very nice. You want to work. You're even seized by a certain inspiration, as if you'd rather do nothing but dig and dig for the rest of your life. But when you have to dig a grave for some poor drifter or a student, your arms just don't seem to want to move. The scoundrel ought to be out living it up. But instead, you're stuck digging his grave. Like now, for example. Who are we digging a grave for? For a suicide by self-drowning. Can you bury someone like that according to the Christian rites? I doubt it.

SECOND CLOWN. I don't doubt, that, on the grounds of all your doubting, you're going to get a knock on the head someday. If the bosses decided hers was a Christian death, that means it was a Christian death.

FIRST CLOWN. I doubt it. If some drunken sailor or inebriated courtier had drowned her, then it would have been a Christian death. But if she drowned herself self-sufficiently, how can that be a Christian death? That is a blatantly anti-government act. You could even call it proper robbery.

SECOND CLOWN. Robbery? Why?

FIRST CLOWN. If a man kills himself, himself, that means nobody else can kill him. Not even the government. In other words, it's a form of robbing the government. After something like that, how can you bury him according to Christian rites in a common cemetery? That is the question.

SECOND CLOWN. The Christian law is written for suicides of common heritage. It doesn't apply to the aristocracy. Dig.

FIRST CLOWN. Dig? I'll dig. But when they start burying her, is that going to be pleasing or unpleasing to God?

SECOND CLOWN. They say nowadays that there is no God.

FIRST CLOWN. There's no who?

SECOND CLOWN. God.

FIRST CLOWN. There's no God?

SECOND CLOWN. That's right.

FIRST CLOWN. I doubt it.

SECOND CLOWN. You know, I also think there's a God.

FIRST CLOWN. There's a what?

SECOND CLOWN. A God.

FIRST CLOWN. There's a God?

SECOND CLOWN. That's right.

FIRST CLOWN. I doubt it.

SECOND CLOWN. How's that?

FIRST CLOWN. Quite simple. God only knows whether God exists or not. And until such time as he appears and says that he doesn't exist, I'll keep doubting

SECOND CLOWN. Keep doubting what?

FIRST CLOWN. That he exists.

SECOND CLOWN. But if you doubt that he exists, that means you think he doesn't exist.

FIRST CLOWN. Obviously not.

SECOND CLOWN. How can that be? Where did he go?

FIRST CLOWN. Where did he go. God is omnipotent. Wherever he wanted to go, that's where he went.

SECOND CLOWN. That's true, of course. In that case, let's drink to the Christian faith.

FIRST CLOWN. With pleasure.

SECOND CLOWN. Why don't you run down to the tavern and buy a bottle.

FIRST CLOWN. With pleasure. (*Doesn't move*)

SECOND CLOWN. What are you just standing there waiting for?

FIRST CLOWN. To drink or not to drink. That is the question.

SECOND CLOWN. What question can there be? Obviously, to drink.

FIRST CLOWN. Who says I refuse to drink? I'll drink. I only want to doubt a bit first.

SECOND CLOWN. If we're talking about drinking, what's there to doubt?

FIRST CLOWN. What? Will one bottle be enough or not? That is the question.

SECOND CLOWN. Of course it's enough.
FIRST CLOWN. It's enough?
SECOND CLOWN. Yes.
FIRST CLOWN. One bottle?
SECOND CLOWN. One bottle.
FIRST CLOWN. I doubt it. (*Exits*)

(*Enter Hamlet and Horatio*)

SECOND CLOWN. (*Sings*)
    I once was young and brave,
    Was of a stronger stature.
    I wanted to marry so bad,
    That I couldn't even tell her…

HAMLET. Has this knight no feeling of his business, that he sings at grave-making?
HORATIO. Custom has turned his line of work into a common affair.
HAMLET. 'Tis e'en so: the hand of little employment hath the daintier sense.

(*The gravedigger tosses out a skull*)

This skull had a tongue in it, and could sing once: how the knave jowls it to the ground, as if it were Cain's jaw-bone, that did the first murder! It might be the pate of a politician, which this ass now o'er-reaches…

(*and so forth, according to Hamlet's actual text*)

I will speak to this peon. Whose grave's this, sirrah?
SECOND CLOWN. Mine, sir.
HAMLET. Are you truly preparing to die?
SECOND CLOWN. On the contrary. I'm preparing to live.
HAMLET. If you are preparing to live, then what do you need with a grave? Graves are for the dead.
SECOND CLOWN. If I were dead, I wouldn't be able to dig it. I'm digging it for myself, but somebody else will lie in it.
HAMLET. If somebody else will lie in it, then you aren't digging it for yourself.
SECOND CLOWN. No, I'm digging it for myself. I am not digging it for the one who will lie in it, but I'm digging it so that someone will pay me for digging it. That means, I'm digging it for myself, not for somebody else.
HAMLET. Who will lie in it?
SECOND CLOWN. Whoever they put in it.
HAMLET. Who is this person?
SECOND CLOWN. It is no person.

HAMLET. Who is it, then?
SECOND CLOWN. A breathless body.
HAMLET. But, in life, this breathless body was a person.
SECOND CLOWN. No, sir…[6]

3.

OSRIC.[7] Your lordship, I beg you accept assurances of my most complete respect as well as my congratulations on account of your return, which, without a doubt, arouses delight in all without exception.[8] I do beg your pardon!

HAMLET. I, too, am delighted by your appearance as well as by the felicity of your congratulations. Although certainly you do exaggerate![9] *(To Horatio)* Do you know this trained dog?

HORATIO. No, my good lord.

HAMLET. So much the better for you. He is a true swine, the only difference being that a swine is filthy and penniless, while this beast is filthy rich. As for filth, they each love it in equal measure.[10] Only the swine luxuriates in the courtyard mud, while the other luxuriates in the mud at court.

OSRIC. If, at the present moment, your lordship were in a suitably well-disposed frame of mind and would deign to suffer himself a few moments of attention to hear me out, I would consider it a most high honor to impart a thing to your honor from His Majesty.

HAMLET. Whatever your honor should desire to impart to my honor, I shall hear it with such attention as you are deserving. Of all the swains who inhabit the court, there is but one swain at whose service I am ever ready. Naturally, you understand which swain I have in mind? You, sir, are more swainish than any.

---

[6] The manuscript breaks off here, perhaps because it segued with the original text.
[7] This interlude is an expansion of a part of Act V, scene two.
[8] The second half of this sentence, from "…which, without a doubt," is crossed out in the manuscript.
[9] Hamlet's first two sentences are crossed out in the manuscript and replaced with the stage direction: "He bows."
[10] This sentence and the second half of the previous sentence, from "…that a swine is filthy," are crossed out in the manuscript.

OSRIC. I thank your lordship.

HAMLET. Only, I beseech you, your honor, put your bonnet to its right use. Please, put on your hat.

OSRIC. I thank your lordship, but it bothers me not.

HAMLET. Your bonnet?

OSRIC. My hat.

HAMLET. Yet it bothers me.

OSRIC. My hat?

HAMLET. Your bonnet. I fear you may catch cold.

OSRIC. Oh no, your lordship, it is very hot.

HAMLET. No, believe me, the wind is northerly; 'tis very cold.

OSRIC. You are absolutely right. Only now do I feel that it is very cold.

HAMLET. But yet methinks it is very sultry and hot, or my complexion —

OSRIC. Exceedingly hot, my lord.

HAMLET. But what is it then? Cold or hot?

OSRIC. You see, your lordship, in the end it is a matter of taste.

HAMLET. And yet?

OSRIC. On the one hand, I can't but agree with you that it is definitely rather hot. On the other hand, I wholeheartedly share your opinion that it is definitely rather cold. But my mission, your lordship, is to inform your lordship that His Majesty has laid a great wager on your lordship. The fact is...

HAMLET. ...that you should put on your hat.

OSRIC. But, honestly, your lordship, I am quite at ease. You need not doubt.

HAMLET. Nevertheless, I beseech you! (*Puts the hat on Osric's head*)

OSRIC. I beg your pardon. My Lord, here is newly come to court Laertes. Believe me, my lord, he is a genuine nobleman—the picture of desecration and taste. His visage and subtle ways bear witness to his true nobility. Indeed, to speak feelingly of him, he is a true self-taught man, in whose good manners you shall find showing of all those qualities which a nobleman would wish to see in a nobleman.

An Evening of Theatrical Parodies
WRITTEN WITH VLADIMIR MASS
1932

1. The Tragedy of Hamlet, Prince of the Danes
A JOKE ON THE ARBAT IN FIVE SCENES
A COMPOSITION OF WILLIAM SHAKESPEARE AND ERASMUS OF ROTTERDAM

CHARACTERS IN ORDER OF APPEARANCE

ASSISTANT DIRECTOR — called Gumozkin
THEATER MANAGER — called Fyodor Semyonovich
DIRECTOR — called Nikolai Pavlovich Akimov [1]
KING — Claudius
LAERTES
POLONIUS
QUEEN — Gertrude
NOVIKOV — the actor playing HAMLET
OPHELIA
GUILDENSTERN
ROSENCRANTZ
A COURTIER
COURTIERS, VENDORS AND VARIOUS OTHERS

PROLOGUE

ASSISTANT DIRECTOR. Much-respected organized spectators and dearest drifters! We will now commence a draft dress rehearsal of the sum of our theater's work. In this manner, we will introduce you, as it were, to the very laboratory of our creative work.

But, before beginning the performance, I should say that Soviet drama has grown colossally. The fact that we are staging Shakespeare is clear

---

[1] Nikolai Akimov (1901-1968) directed the production of *Hamlet* at the Vakhtangov Theater in 1932, of which *The Tragedy of Hamlet, Prince of the Danes* is a parody. This staging was controversial for making several major rearrangements of Shakespeare's text and for presenting Hamlet not as a man of doubt, but as a man of action. Akimov justified his changes by referring to several ideas he found in the works of Erasmus of Rotterdam. In this volume, see three of the interludes that may have been performed during Akimov's production.

proof of that.

For the opening segment of our concluding evening, we will perform for you *The Tragedy of Hamlet, Prince of the Danes.*

There can be no doubt that every one of you knows that in order for the mass spectator to sense the genius of any work, that work of genius must be made accessible to contemporaneity. What needs be done to do that? In order to make a work of genius accessible to contemporaneity, you must discard from a work of genius everything there was in it, and introduce into the work of genius everything it lacked. This meticulous, but inspired task was undertaken by our own respected Nikolai Pavlovich Akimov. In his work on *Hamlet,* Nikolai Pavlovich cast a bridge from Shakespeare to our time. His task was made easier because he espied in Hamlet not an indecisive and doubting individualist, but an experienced and forthright lone wolf who trusts in the masses, a tireless advocate for the emancipation of the flesh, a typical representative of an age obsessed with amassing mercantile capital in the era of its struggle with rotting feudalism.

But that was still not enough.

There can be no doubt that even a drifter knows that, until now, all theaters have seen in Ophelia an ideal model of the loving woman. That happened because until now, no director ever took note of her social origin. But at that moment when Nikolai Pavlovich began reading *Hamlet,* the first thing that struck him was the fact that the much-vaunted Ophelia is, in fact, the daughter of a highly-placed official. Yes, comrades, there's nothing to be done about it. It's an incontrovertible fact. Therefore, Nikolai Pavlovich, with the mastery characteristic of him, humiliated this woman. And our theater expresses to him our sincerest gratitude.

(The Director stands and bows)

MANAGER. Gumozkin.
ASSISTANT DIRECTOR. Yes.
MANAGER. Summon the troupe.

(Enter the troupe of actors)

MANAGER. Comrades, let's thank Nikolai Pavlovich for humiliating Ophelia.

(The actors applaud. The director bows all around)

DIRECTOR. Comrades, I am sincerely touched. But I must say that my work on Ophelia was only a beginning. Alas, comrades, as strange as it may seem, there remain many unhumiliated models throughout the riches of world drama. Therefore, I give you my solemn vow that, in the near future, I plan to humiliate Desdemona, the king's daughter Cordelia, Tatyana

Larina,[2] Anna Karenina, Sofya Borisovna...

MANAGER. Who's that?

DIRECTOR. She's my friend. I may also take on the fairy Rautendelein,[3] as well as the three sisters, the three musketeers and the three Karamazov brothers together with Dostoevsky himself.

(The actors applaud and then leave. The Assistant Director runs up hurriedly)

ASSISTANT DIRECTOR. Nikolai Pavlovich... *(Agitatedly mutters something to the director)*

DIRECTOR. That's impossible. *(Grabs his head)* They've murdered me. Fyodor Semyonovich... *(Agitatedly mutters something to the manager)*

MANAGER. What do we do now? We have to inform the public. My dear Nikolai Pavlovich, there's no one to do it but you. Tell them.

DIRECTOR. Comrades. One final thing. It is lamentable, but I must forewarn you that, due to the illness of our two lead actors, we will not be able to show you *Hamlet* in its full artistic perfection. Tapeworms have deprived us of the two finest representatives of our troupe. These are the horse, who performs the central role of Fortinbras's horse, and the chestnut mare, who performs the role of the queen mother's stallion. Of course, you understand that without these two key figures from Shakespeare's tragedy, our interpretation of *Hamlet* loses its entire philosophical and sociological underpinnings. We are compelled, therefore, to beg your indulgence. We have also had to modify Hamlet's famous lines, "let the stricken deer go weep." This is because, although we were able to find a deer, we are fresh out of anything to strike him with. And so, we begin. *(Takes a seat at his director's table together with the manager)* Curtain!

(Overture. The curtain parts)

SCENE ONE

(A room in a castle. A high staircase covered with a curtain stands upstage center. Queen Gertrude stands downstage right. Before her are a washtub, a bucket and a basket filled with dirty linen. The King, in a white sweater and ballet shoes, sits stage left. Scribes stand to his right. Polonius, Laertes and a group of courtiers are positioned from right to center. As the curtain rises, all remain in their sitting or standing positions, holding their noses)

DIRECTOR. Well, Fyodor Semyonovich, how do you like the beginning?

MANAGER. Vivid! Very vivid! Only, pardon me, Nikolai Pavlovich, I don't

---

[2] Tatyana Larina is the main heroine in Alexander Pushkin's *Eugene Onegin.* She quickly came to be known as the epitome of Russian femininity after the novel's appearance in the 1820s.

[3] Rautendelein is a character in Gerhart Hauptmann's play, *The Sunken Bell.*

quite understand what they are doing.

DIRECTOR. What are they doing? They're holding their noses.

MANAGER. Why?

DIRECTOR. What do you mean? This is a completely innovative interpretation of one of the tragedy's most significant moments.

MANAGER. I don't understand.

DIRECTOR. In Shakespeare's tragedy, the so-called corpse of Hamlet's father has an enormous significance.

MANAGER. Oh. The corpse of Hamlet's father. Yes, I know, I know.

DIRECTOR. Well. The idealist Goethe, tooting on the same flute as everybody else in his 19th century, naturally interpreted this corpse as a specter, that is, as frank mysticism. We, on the other hand, the young Shakespearologists of the revolutionary Arbat, want to cleanse this corpse of the slightest tinge of romantic nonsense. Therefore, we naturally consider it proper to portray the corpse in its primary function. That is, as a concept which is totally material. Our corpse is a real corpse.

MANAGER. But, if you will….

DIRECTOR. Pardon me. In Shakespeare it plainly says that Hamlet's father died, does it not?

MANAGER. Yes.

DIRECTOR. Well, if he died, then it is entirely natural that the spiritual airs rising from him are genuine and powerful. I would even say the stench must be unbearable. This is the nature of our corpse.

MANAGER. Aha, I see. Now I understand. Vivid. Very vivid.

DIRECTOR. However, let's not dally. Let's have the rooster crow.

(Off stage a rooster crows)

The stench disappears together with the corpse. Continue.

(The actors on stage come to life. The courtiers clean the King's crown and scepter with emery. Gertrude washes the dirty linen in the washtub. She wrings it out, throws it in the bucket, takes dirty linen out of the basket and throws it in the washtub)

KING. *(Dictates as he sniffs the air)*
>As fresh as mem'ry's breath
>Of our dear brother's death,
>I joined in hasty matrimony
>With my sister former, now my wife,
>Who helps me guide our country's life.

(Dancing, he approaches the Queen. He embraces her, kisses her a few times and then returns)

Now we must hear out Laertes.
LAERTES. Worthy sovereign, I would that we
Return to France.
KING. Polonius,
What say thou?
POLONIUS. I beg you heed
My offspring's need.
QUEEN. Why not? Thus shall it be.
KING. Thus shall it be.

(The first note sounds in the orchestra. The curtain parts. Hamlet, in a black raincoat and a black top hat, draped with a banner of mourning, slowly descends the staircase. Following him are four girls playing a waltz from Princess Turandot *on combs. Hamlet stops in the center of the forestage. The King races about the stage in agitation)*

DIRECTOR. Hold it, comrade Novikov. Is that what I showed you? Who are you playing?
NOVIKOV. What do you mean? Prince Hamlet, if you don't mind my saying so.
DIRECTOR. I see that it's Hamlet. But what kind of a Hamlet? I told you, we have to discard the ordinary, mistaken interpretation of Hamlet as a weak, neurotic and indecisive man. That's the Hamlet that Goethe thought up. Such a Hamlet is alien to us. Shakespeare's Hamlet was a representative of the burgeoning young class. He was a strong Hamlet. Hamlet the fighter. You have got to play a fighter.
NOVIKOV. Oh, a fighter?
DIRECTOR. Of course. I already explained that to you.
NOVIKOV. I understand.
DIRECTOR. Take it from the top.

(The first note sounds in the orchestra. Hamlet slowly descends the staircase. The entire scene is repeated as before. Hamlet flings off his top hat and raincoat. He is wearing a traditional strongman's costume: a red knit sweater with a wide blue ribbon across his shoulder. On the ribbon are orders, medals, etc. His bare arms are muscular and athletic. Hamlet lies on the ground, raises his knees and arms on which others place a platform. The four girls jump up onto the platform)

HAMLET. Hah!

(The girls jump down from the platform. Hamlet stands and bows to the public)

QUEEN. Dearest Hamlet,
Quit, once for all, your lamenting way.
And be thou not sorrowful.

HAMLET. Eternity swallowed father before he could expire.

> And my mother, sharing love with sundry spies,
> Has not yet worn out a single pair of shoes
> In her short hour of mourning the king's demise.

DIRECTOR. No, no, no. What is that odd intonation you've got? "In her sh-sh-sh-ort hour of mourning the king's demise." What do you mean, "Sh-sh-sh-ort?"

NOVIKOV. I'm interpreting, Nikolai Pavlovich.

DIRECTOR. I don't understand.

NOVIKOV. What's to understand? "Sh-sh-sh-ort hour of mourning." I'm showing that it took place a long time ago.

DIRECTOR. That's just where you're wrong.

NOVIKOV. Wrong? Are you joking? That's just what is needed. Whose shoes are they talking about? They're talking about shoes from Shakespeare's time. It's only in our days that you buy a pair of shoes that falls apart the next day. But in Shakespeare's era any old queen who bought a pair of shoes wore them for three years without ever having to take them to the cobbler. With my intonation, I am trying to underscore the fact that Hamlet is still sorrowful despite the fact that his father died three years ago.

DIRECTOR. And what about the corpse?

NOVIKOV. What about the corpse?

DIRECTOR. Do you mean that the corpse couldn't have aired out in three years time? You are ruining the whole idea of my creation. In general, I ask you not to interpret, but to obey. What you've got to emphasize is the shoes. Repeat your lines, please.

NOVIKOV. Eternity swallowed father before he could expire.

> And my mother, sharing love with sundry spies,
> Has not yet worn out a single pair of shoes
> In her short hour of mourning the king's demise.

(The King faints into the arms of his courtiers. They lift him above their heads)

(Curtain)

MANAGER. That's the whole first act?

DIRECTOR. That's the first act.

MANAGER. Very vivid. Only, tell me, Nikolai Pavlovich, what is your queen up to?

DIRECTOR. She's doing her wash.

MANAGER. What is she washing?

DIRECTOR. The fact is, according to my creative plan, she must wash away the boundaries between the court that existed at that time and the one that exists today. But you surely understand yourself that forcing an actress to wash away a boundary is extremely difficult. On the other hand, I couldn't bear to refuse having her wash at least something. Therefore, I decided that if she couldn't wash boundaries, then let her wash something else. Pants, for example. Or socks. What's the difference?

MANAGER. Ah, so that's it. Very vivid. And I didn't even get it right away. You know, I'm simply amazed at your colossal erudition. I suppose you have read a lot?

DIRECTOR. The fact is, my erudition consists not in how much I have read, but in how much others haven't read.

MANAGER. So that's it. Very vivid, indeed.

DIRECTOR. Curtain.

SCENE TWO

(*A garden at Polonius's home. In the middle is a table covered with hors d'oeuvres and wine. To the right is a washbasin in the form of a large, marble camel. Ophelia stands by the table and pours a glass of wine, downs it in one gulp, exhales heavily and sniffs a slice of black bread. This is repeated several times*)

MANAGER. Nikolai Pavlovich, who is that?

DIRECTOR. That's Ophelia.

MANAGER. Ophelia?

DIRECTOR. Yes.

MANAGER. How come she's drinking here with you?

DIRECTOR. She's not drinking with me, she's drinking by herself. She's at her father's home.

MANAGER. Oh, I see! By herself. Very vivid. But why is she drinking at all?

DIRECTOR. There is plenty of reason for that. The fact is, my thought process went something like this: First, in Shakespeare it never says that she doesn't drink. That alone gave me reason to assume that, perhaps, she drinks. Then, when studying the play further, I came across Hamlet's words which he addresses to Horatio:

> But, what is your affair in Elsinore?
> We'll teach you to drink deep ere you depart.[4]

One can conclude from this that, in Elsinore, everybody drinks, and, in fact, they drink very deeply. In this manner, it only remained to determine who drinks deeply in Elsinore. Shakespeare answers this cardinal question in the third act, when Ophelia says:

> O, what a noble mind is here o'erthrown!
> ….
> And I, of ladies most deject and wretched,

---

[4] *Hamlet*, Act I, scene two.

That sucked the honey of his music vows...[5]
Etc.

Well, "noble mind" doesn't have the slightest significance in the given situation. But Ophelia, by her own admission, often "sucked the honey." In this manner, Shakespeare provides the ultimate answer to our question of who, in fact, drinks deeply in Elsinore. It's Ophelia.

MANAGER. Marvelous!

DIRECTOR. And the main thing is that this ties in beautifully with her social origins. As the daughter of a cobbler, she is a drunk. I think the critics will love it. However, let's move on.

(Enter Hamlet. He embraces and kisses Ophelia. Laertes's steps are heard. Hamlet runs away)

LAERTES. *(Enters holding a blanket tied up with a strap. A large metal teapot is attached to the strap)*
I'm ready for the road. Farewell, sister. And write.
And pay thou no mind to the love coos of the prince.
Know thou well that they are naught but empty caprice.

OPHELIA. Yes, brother dear. I will be careful.

(Enter Polonius, singing a tune from Princess Turandot*)*

POLONIUS. You're here, Calaf?[6] I mean, Laertes?
The ship is ready. Be quick. And by the way,
I want to give you an exhortation:
Hold your tongue. Be servile with
All. And by the way, don't think
Of borrowing money, and don't think
Of lending it either. In lending money
We lose our friends and money both.
But most critical of all, be true to thyself.
Farewell.

(Kisses Laertes)

LAERTES. Farewell, sister.
OPHELIA. Farewell, Laertes.

(Laertes leaves)

---

[5] *Hamlet,* Act III, scene one.

[6] Calaf is a character in *Princess Turandot,* which was still a popular entry in the repertory of the Vakhtangov Theater when *The Tragedy of Hamlet, Prince of the Danes* was written. See one of the interludes to *Princess Turandot* in this volume.

POLONIUS. Well, daughter mine, what have you two
        Been bantering about?
OPHELIA. About Hamlet.
POLONIUS. Marvelous.
        I heard, myself, that recently
        The prince seeks to see you. Tell me true,
        What is between you? Speak.
OPHELIA. Oh, father mine, I sewing sat
        And suddenly entered Hamlet. He entered hatless,
        In nothing but a shirt. His arms were naked
        And he wore no suspenders.
POLONIUS. He is insane
        From loving you.
OPHELIA. I do not know, but fear
        That you speak true.
POLONIUS. Come with me
        Quickly to the King. His brain is touched,
        There is no doubt. And love, thou art the reason.

(Runs off stage, tugging Ophelia by the arm)

(Curtain)

MANAGER. That's the whole second act?
DIRECTOR. That's the second.
MANAGER. Pardon me, Nikolai Pavlovich, but what happened to Hamlet's famous monologue: "To be or not to be?"
DIRECTOR. The fact is, I forgot to warn you that in the given production we are using the famous Sokolovsky translation where the lines "to be or not to be" are translated not as "to be or not to be," but as "to live or not to live." That is much closer to the original and, moreover, illuminates the sense of the following act in finer detail.
MANAGER. Ah, "to live or not to live." But, in that case, then where is the monologue?
DIRECTOR. I moved it to the third act. You will hear it now.
MANAGER. Very interesting.

SCENE THREE

(A hunting scene in the woods. Rabbits, deer and horses, mounted by propmen, scamper in the background. The King, the Queen and Polonius pass through with hunting rifles and dogs of various breeds. Ophelia appears with a bottle. She drinks)

OPHELIA. *(Singing)*
>Then up he rose, and donn'd his clothes,
>And dupp'd the chamber-door.
>Let in the maid, that out a maid,
>Never departed more.[7]

(Gestures to her servants, who carry on stage a canopy bed and place it at center stage. They leave)

MANAGER. I don't quite understand, Nikolai Pavlovich. Why did these people bring a bed into the woods? That seems unnatural to me.

DIRECTOR. Why? They didn't bring it there of their own volition. Ophelia ordered them to do it.

MANAGER. But why did Ophelia order them to bring a bed into the woods?

DIRECTOR. What do you expect of a drunken woman?

MANAGER. Amazing. You know, at first I thought maybe you were drunk, but now I definitely see that it is she. Very vivid.

(The King, Queen and Polonius return)

KING. Gertrude dear, we sent
>Forthwith for Hamlet, to arrange
>A tryst—one might say, quite unplanned—
>With fair Ophelia. Her father and I,
>Lawful spies, will hide right here
>To see and watch, and then discuss,
>All that which we have seen.

POLONIUS. May he show
>His colors true, thereby himself exposing.
>Is it truly love or something else
>Has caused in him his madness?

QUEEN. Fare-thee-well.

(Leaves)

POLONIUS. I hear his sabre. Let us hide.

(The King and Polonius crawl under the bed. Ophelia lies on the bed. Enter Hamlet, who approaches the bed. Ophelia beckons to him with her finger)

HAMLET. To live or not to live. That is the question.
>Ha, ha, ha… I did love you once, Ophelia.[8]

OPHELIA. Indeed, my lord, you made me

---

[7] *Hamlet,* Act IV, scene five.

[8] This small section follows closely the original text of *Hamlet,* Act II, scene one.

Believe so.

HAMLET. You shouldn't have done it.

I loved you not.

OPHELIA. I was the more deceived.

HAMLET. *(Sits on the bed and picks up the bottle. He notes that it is empty. Hands the empty bottle to Ophelia)*

Get thee to a nunnery, Ophelia.

(Ophelia takes the bottle and walks up stage. She knocks at a gate over which hangs a sign: "Benedictine Monastery." A friar with a lantern comes out. He takes Ophelia's empty bottle and gives her two full ones bearing the label: "Benedictine.")

OPHELIA. *(Returns, singing)*

Let in the maid, that out a maid,

Never departed more.

DIRECTOR. Good. Everyone sing the refrain. *(All sing the refrain)*

HAMLET. *(Crawls into the bed. Pulls a flask out from under the pillow. On the label are printed a skull and cross bones)*

Alas, poor Yorick.

(Tosses away the bottle, searches under the bed with his hand for a two-handled tub that he put there upon entering. Seizes Polonius by the beard. Tears off the beard and tosses it in the tub)

Where is your father?

OPHELIA. At home, my lord.

HAMLET. Next time, lock him in so that he'll only go about playing the fool at home. *(Leaves)*

KING. *(From beneath the bed)*

No, that is not love. His

madness

Is not from her.

POLONIUS. I see you may be right.

(Crawls out from under the bed without his beard. In its place he crudely sticks a sponge that Hamlet had left behind)

KING.   He presents a danger. We must quickly

Send him to England. Let us be off.

(The King crawls out from under the bed and follows Polonius off stage. Behind him trails an endlessly long red cape)

SCENE ON THE FORESTAGE

(A door is carted in bearing the sign: "Doctor Guildenstern. Hours: 10 to 4. Doctor Rosencrantz: Hours: 4 to 8." Rosencrantz and Guildenstern come out of the door wearing hospital frocks. From the opposite side appears a pregnant Ophelia accompanied by the King, Polonius and the Queen)

KING. Welcome, dear Guildenstern and Rosenschweig.
    Have you heard? A very strange change
    Has come to Polonius's daughter.[9] We cannot
    Hold our silence more, for all
    Who gaze her, see themselves.
QUEEN. Therefore, you must try,
    Insofar as your talent and means allow,
    To extract the reasons for this secret misfortune.
GUILDENSTERN. *(Falls to his knees)*
    We are prepared to fulfil your every order.
    May the heavens help us in our task.

(Rosencrantz and Guildenstern lead Ophelia through the door. The King and Queen follow)

HAMLET. *(Enters)*
    Forty thousand brothers and a hundred devils.
    The King has ordered me forthwith
    To England. *(Opens a dictionary, repeats)*
    A "Hund" is a "dog." A "dog" is a "Hund."
    "To sleep" would be "schlafen." And "schlafen" is "sleep."
    "Sein" is "to be."
    "Oder" means "or."
    "Nicht sein" is "not to be."
    Then "Sein oder nicht sein" is "to be or not to be."
POLONIUS. What are you reading, my lord?
HAMLET. *(Shows the dictionary)* Words, words, words!

(There is a scream behind the door. After a few moments, the King runs across the stage screaming wildly: "Fire! Fire!" His red cape trails after him. The agitated Queen follows after him. Ophelia runs after the Queen carrying a baby. Guildenstern and Rosencrantz appear carrying surgical instruments)

HAMLET. Aha! Let the stricken deer go weep,
    The hart ungalled play...

(Enter four girls with combs)

GUILDENSTERN. My lord, His Excellency is beside himself.
HAMLET. Ha, ha, ha… What is it has moved him?
ROSENCRANTZ. The Queen, your mother, is quite in despair. Your behavior amazes her. She wishes to talk with you immediately in her room.

---

[9] In the original, it is Hamlet who has undergone a "transformation." The King's line reads: "Sith nor the exterior nor the inward man/ Resembles that it was." See *Hamlet*, Act II, scene two.

HAMLET. I surrender. (Leaves)

SCENE FOUR

(A huge tapestry portrays full-sized portraits of Shakespeare, Molière, Cervantes and others. Several chairs. On stage are Polonius and the Queen)

POLONIUS. He'll now appear. Attempt to be
           Severe with him.[10]
QUEEN.   I'll warrant you; fear me not.
POLONIUS. I'll hide in here. Be skilled
                In all.

(Hides behind the tapestry)

(Hamlet enters with a mousetrap in his hands)

QUEEN.   What is that, Hamlet?
HAMLET. This? A mousetrap. (Puts it on the rug)
           Now, mother, what's the matter?
QUEEN.   Hamlet, thou hast thy father much offended.
HAMLET. Mother, you have my father much offended.
QUEEN.   Why, how now, Hamlet!
HAMLET. What's the matter now?
QUEEN.   Have you forgot me?
HAMLET. No, by the rood, not so:
           I swear upon the holy cross, you are the Queen
           and mother mine. You mother… uh, you mother...
QUEEN.   Impertinence! If so, I call
           to me my people.
HAMLET. Come, come, and sit; you shall not budge.

(Steps on the Queen's train. Her skirt rips off and lies on the floor. The Queen remains in her undergarments)

QUEEN.   What wilt thou do? thou wilt not murder me?
           Help, help, ho!
POLONIUS. What, ho! help, help, help!
           I must come to aid.
HAMLET. How now, a mouse?
 (Plunges his rapier into Shakespeare's portrait)

(The portrait begins waving its arms and legs and then falls still)

---

[10] The scene in the Queen's closet follows closely the original text of Hamlet, Act III, scene four.

POLONIUS. O, I am slain!
QUEEN.   Hamlet! What hast thou done?

(Hamlet removes the mouse trap from behind the tapestry. In it is a dead mouse. The King and courtesans run into the room)

HAMLET. *(Pulling out Polonius's corpse)*
          Farewell, my friend. And, now, let me
          Dispose of you…
ALL. A mouse! A mouse! A mouse!

(They jump up on the chairs. Hamlet sets the mousetrap with the dead mouse on Polonius's chest and runs out)

KING.   A dastardly deed. After him, all!

(All race after Hamlet. An empty stage. Enter Ophelia, tugging behind her a baby carriage with a baby in it)

OPHELIA.*(Sings)*
          Let in the maid, that out a maid,
          Never departed more.

(She stumbles on her father's corpse. Cries, "Father!" and in despair leans over his body. She caresses him. Convinced that Polonius is dead, waves her hand, throws the baby out of the carriage and pulls from there a bottle. She uncorks it. Then she pulls the mouse out of the mousetrap and tosses it in the baby carriage. Removes the cheese from the mousetrap. Drinks straight from the bottle and nibbles the cheese. She leaves, staggering)

MANAGER. It seems to me, Nikolai Pavlovich, you've gone a bit too far. Why does she nibble the cheese out of the mousetrap?
DIRECTOR. She's a drunken woman, Fyodor Semyonovich! What do you expect of her? Maybe she already has the shakes and that's why she's nibbling cheese.

(The King and his courtiers return. Shooting and a terrible ruckus are heard off stage. The King hides behind his courtesans)

KING.   What happened?
COURTIER. Your Excellency, beware.
          Here comes an angered Laertes.
LAERTES. *(Enters at a run)*
          Where is my father?
KING.   He is killed.
LAERTES. Murderer!
KING.   No.

Not I, but Hamlet killed Polonius.
LAERTES. This death I will avenge.
QUEEN. *(Enters at a run)*
One woe doth tread upon another's heel…
Ophelia…
LAERTES. Dead?
QUEEN.   No, drowned.

(Courtiers carry on stage a large barrel bearing the sign: "White burgundy." The drowned Ophelia's feet dangle over the edge of the barrel)

LAERTES. Misfortune. O, Lord. I have a speech of fire
That fain would blaze.[11] Ophelia. Sister.

SCENE ON THE FORESTAGE

(The King and Laertes stand holding candles)

KING.   Prithee summon him to a duel.
You'll cross with swords, and with your killing
Art, shall smite the murderer
And requite him for your father.
LAERTES. Yes, yes. That's what I'll do.
KING.   I'll poison your sword's tip,
That if with lip alone he kisses
Your sword's tip, he'll die.[12]
LAERTES. So shall it be.

SCENE FIVE

(A boxing ring. Up stage, stick dolls portray the crowd. A poster: "Today! There will be a meeting between the Danish champion Hamlet and the lightweight champion Laertes who is appearing for the first time since his return from France!" Off to the side stands a ticket booth. A ticket seller sells tickets. A vendor sells ice cream. Enter the King, the Queen, Laertes, courtiers and Hamlet)

KING.   'Tis time to start the cruel duel.
Courtiers, hand out the swords.

(Enter a courtier with two volleyballs. He gives one to Hamlet, the other to Laertes. Two other courtiers stretch out a volleyball net)

---

[11] This sentence is a direct quote from Hamlet, Act IV, scene seven.

[12] In the original, of course, it is Laertes who suggests poisoning his sword. See *Hamlet*, Act IV, scene seven.

MANAGER. Pardon me, Nikolai Pavlovich. As far as I recall, in Shakespeare the duel scene is played with swords.

DIRECTOR. The fact is—swords, spheroids—what's the difference? It's merely a minor matter of language. We decided that "spheroids" has a more proper resilience, so to speak, which brings us closer to the original.

KING.   I trust the referee will follow carefully
             The course the battle takes.

HAMLET. To arms.

LAERTES. To arms.

HAMLET. Touché.

KING.   Referees, referee!

HAMLET. Hah!

LAERTES. Begin again.

QUEEN.   Our son will win.

KING.   We soon shall see.

HAMLET. Nay, serve again.

(The game continues)

Time out. We've got to inflate the ball.

(Laertes takes the ball and blows it up. All gather around him)

MANAGER. My good Nikolai Pavlovich, as far as I remember, in Shakespeare there aren't any such words as "We've got to inflate" in the duel scene.

DIRECTOR. "Inflate" is from Erasmus of Rotterdam.

MANAGER. Marvelous!

(Having blown up the ball and holding the plug hole, Laertes hands it to Hamlet. He heaves a sigh, hands it to the Queen. Laertes staggers and falls)

LAERTES. I die. Hamlet, hear me: The plug
             Is poisoned. The King, he is to blame.

HAMLET. Evil deed. Poison on the plug. I'm poisoned.

MANAGER. I hope you'll pardon me, Nikolai Pavlovich, but there's no plug in Shakespeare either. Is the plug from Erasmus of Rotterdam, too?

DIRECTOR. Yes.

MANAGER. Marvelous.

QUEEN. *(Falls)* Ah…

HAMLET. Where is the murderer? Scoundrel, blow.

(Forces the King to blow up the ball)

(The King falls and dies)

HAMLET. *(Falls)* I'm dead. Now, too, has come my end. *(Dies)*

HORATIO. *(Enters, looks at all the dead bodies)* How wonderful it is to live!

(Curtain)

(The actors come out onto the forestage and applaud the director. The director bows)

MANAGER. I congratulate you, Nikolai Pavlovich. I congratulate you with all my heart. I consider that you have created a work of worldwide proportions which will send a thundering echo from one end of the Arbat to the other.[13]

(The director bows)

Tell me, Nikolai Pavlovich, do you create alone or with a collective?
DIRECTOR. Alone. I always create alone. I've been like that ever since I was a child. I remember once, when I was a little boy and my parents left me alone, I created such havoc that even the angels wept.
MANAGER. Marvelous. Marvelous. But tell me, how did you happen to stage *Hamlet?*
DIRECTOR. You see, we young people have never seen a production of *Hamlet.* And since it's such a boring play to read, I figured, why not stage it and have a look at it? And so we staged it.
MANAGER. Splendid. It must have been a long and arduous road that brought you to this point in your career.
DIRECTOR. Oh, I don't know. I just kept trudging along and trudging along until I got to where I am now.
MANAGER. You are a genius, Nikolai Pavlovich. A true genius.

---

[13] The Arbat is the famous street in the center of Moscow on which the Vakhtangov Theater is located.

2. The Work Whistle, or the Stomach Incision

CHARACTERS IN ORDER OF APPEARANCE

DIRECTOR — Pyotr Petrovich
AUTHOR — Fyodor Semyonovich Agenofinov [14]
NALIMOV — the Director's assistant
PROSHKA — actor who plays the PIONEER SCOUT
IVANOVA — a medical doctor played by the actress Olga Minishna
EMILIYA — her assistant
KASYAN — a patient played by the actor NAPOIKIN
A GIRL
A NURSE
YAKOV
YURY
PROMPTER
VARIOUS NURSES, PIONEER GIRLS AND BOYS

DIRECTOR. *(In front of the closed curtain)* Dear public and respected spectators. We will now show you one of our productions not of a classic play, but of a completely new contemporary play. The play we have selected for production is called *The Work Whistle, or the Stomach Incision.* It is a play about new people and new machines. It is the product of the inimitable pen of Fyodor Semyonovich Agenofinov. Fyodor Semyonovich is a completely new playwright whom we created by our own hands and produced ahead of schedule.[15] Fyodor Semyonovich is a specialist in positive heroes. Fyodor Semyonovich finds them even where they can't be found. Fyodor Semyonovich writes in a new style only about new topics. Fyodor Semyonovich is a dialectical playwright. But even his dialectics are completely new. If, in Hegel, dialectics were upside down, and, if Marx turned Hegel around and put him on firm footing,[16] then Fyodor Semyonovich can be said to have gone even further. He attacked his theme from the blind side and pinned it on the mat for the eight-count. Therefore, we would not be mistaken were we to say that Fyodor Semyonovich played it fast and loose with dialectics. And he plays it fast and loose with

---

[14] This is a pun on the name of the playwright Alexander Afinogenov. See note 4 to the interlude for *Princess Turandot.*

[15] The phrase, "created by our own hands and produced ahead of schedule," is repeated frequently in various forms throughout this sketch. It refers to the Communist Party policy that was then exhorting workers to over-fulfil their plans as the first Five-Year Plan was nearing an end.

[16] See note 6 to the interlude for *Princess Turandot.*

everything else he does. Generally speaking, Fyodor Semyonovich is a very strong playwright. But he wasn't always that way. Earlier, Fyodor Semyonovich was a rather right-leaning fellow traveller.[17] But in recent times, he has shifted into a new gear and been reborn. And it seemed to happen all of a sudden. Without giving it much thought, Fyodor Semyonovich suddenly shed his old obscurantism, and then, without giving it much more thought, he assimilated an alien, new, world view. Having enriched himself in such a manner, Fyodor Semyonovich began creating. And he amassed a multitude of absolutely unimaginable works. We shall now show you one of them. I'm done. *(He steps off the stage and addresses the Author)* It's all yours.

AUTHOR. Not bad, only you could have done better in a few spots. It seems to me that, when you were characterizing me as a master, you forgot one very important stroke of my oeuvre.

DIRECTOR. What's that?

AUTHOR. I donated two-week's salary to the third collection for the Five-year plan.

DIRECTOR. That's right. I did forget. Oh well, Fyodor Semyonovich, I'll mention that during my conclusion. However, isn't it time we begin? Nalimov!

NALIMOV. Yes.

DIRECTOR. Is everything ready?

NALIMOV. Absolutely everything except for two problems.

DIRECTOR. What's wrong?

NALIMOV. As the critics say, Pyotr Petrovich, the new life has strangled the arts.

DIRECTOR. What new life has strangled the arts? What happened?

NALIMOV. Just imagine, Pyotr Petrovich. Today during the lunch break, our cat Murka had babies in the saboteur's wig.

DIRECTOR. And?

NALIMOV. For now, there are no problems. Everything came off nicely. She had her babies and is lying there in the wig raising her children. However, Ivan Ivanovich is sitting there next to his wig and refuses to put on his makeup.

DIRECTOR. Why?

NALIMOV. He says that, as the theater's leading actor, he refuses to perform in a makeshift orphan's home. Ca-te-gor-i-cal-ly. And that's that.

DIRECTOR. Tell him, my friend, that if he's late for his cue, I'll fine him.

NALIMOV. All right, Pyotr Petrovich. And then...

DIRECTOR. Now what?

---

[17] The term "fellow traveller" was coined by Anatoly Lunacharsky in 1920 to describe writers who were not members of the Communist Party, but who supported the Party's policies. By the late 1920s, the designation had become synonymous with criticism.

NALIMOV. The pioneer scout went on a drinking binge.

DIRECTOR. What pioneer scout?

NALIMOV. The positive pioneer from the first episode.

DIRECTOR. Who plays him?

NALIMOV. Kazun-Tamovsky.

DIRECTOR. Will this never end? Who is going to play the pioneer now? Can't Proshka play the pioneer?

NALIMOV. Proshka, can't you play the pioneer?

PROSHKA. Basically, no. But if the local committee orders me to, I can.

NALIMOV. Can you play him well?

PROSHKA. If the local committee orders me to, I'll play him better than Kachalov.[18]

NALIMOV. He says if the local committee orders him to, he'll play him better than Kachalov.

DIRECTOR. The local committee has nothing to do with it. If he knows the lines, then let him play.

NALIMOV. He says the local committee has nothing to do with it. If you know the lines, then you've got to play.

PROSHKA. Well, I can play without an order from the local committee, of course. But I'll play worse.

NALIMOV. He says, he can play without the local committee, but it'll be worse.

DIRECTOR. Better it be worse than get the local committee mixed up in it.

NALIMOV. Proshka, he says you can play worse. That will be better.

DIRECTOR. Nalimov.

NALIMOV. Yes.

DIRECTOR. Let's begin. Everybody in their places. Curtain.

(The curtain rises)

(An operating room. In the center is an operating table. In the corner is an instrument table. By the wall is a cabinet with all kinds of retorts and instruments. On the wall is a poster: "The Moral Death to Social Traitors Operating Room." Comrade Professor Ivanova and her assistant, comrade Emiliya are in white hospital coats, looking at something in one of the retorts. An orchestra strikes up a march)

IVANOVA. Ugh. I hear music. What is that?

EMILIYA. Those are the recuperating pioneers from ward number fourteen accompanying a patient to the operating room.

---

[18] Vasily Kachalov (1875-1948) was one of the great Russian actors. Already possessing something of a reputation, he joined the Moscow Art Theater in 1900, just two years after it was founded. He remained there to his death. By 1932, when *The Work Whistle* was written, he had long been a living legend.

IVANOVA. With an orchestra?

EMILIYA. Yes, professor. Yesterday at the general assembly of whooping-cough and diphtheria victims, the recuperating pioneers resolved that illness in our age of constructing socialism must be a joyous affair. And so now they are giving the resolution a lively interpretation.

IVANOVA. My dear, sweet youngsters. Now I recognize you. Comrade Emiliya, wash up the instruments. We have to be in top form today.

(A march. To a drum roll, the pioneers lead in the patient Kasyan on a stretcher. Kasyan is groaning)

KASYAN. Oh, oh, oh.

PIONEER. Hut, two, three, four. Hut, two, three, four.

(The music stops)

Comrade professor! We, the young whooping-cough and diphtheria victims of ward number fourteen, congratulate you with the first deathly-ill patient of our new hospital which was built ahead of schedule. Pioneers! A fanfare!

(A fanfare)

KASYAN. Oh, oh, oh.

PIONEER. Dear, deathly-ill comrade. Before they begin cutting you up, allow us to read you the joint resolution issued by the aged asthmatics and young girls stricken with measles from our new hospital which was built ahead of schedule.

KASYAN. Oh, oh, oh.

GIRL. *(Reads)* "We, the aged asthmatics and young girls stricken with measles, unanimously resolved at our 14th joint conference that you should not despair."

KASYAN. Oh, oh, oh.

GIRL. "However, should some idiotic incident suddenly deprive us of your place among our ranks, know that thousands of new deathly-ill patients are standing by, ready to take your post. In the meantime, dear deathly-ill patient, please accept as a gift our own beloved drum, which we built ourselves ahead of schedule." *(Puts a drum on Kasyan's stomach. All applaud)*

KASYAN. Oh, oh, oh.

AUTHOR. You know, Pyotr Petrovich, I'm not very happy with the way this segment has been interpreted. Why is he always groaning?

DIRECTOR. What are you talking about, Fyodor Semyonovich? He is a deathly-ill patient. Patients always groan.

AUTHOR. But Pyotr Petrovich, that was in the old days that patients always groaned. New patients in our inimitable epoch cannot possibly moan.

DIRECTOR. Don't tell me that you think he's supposed to lie on the operating table and laugh his head off?

AUTHOR. Well, perhaps it would be a bit much for him to laugh his head off, but, in my opinion, he could giggle a bit.

DIRECTOR. That's what you think, is it?

AUTHOR. I never think at all. I am convinced of it absolutely officially. As the author of the play.

DIRECTOR. Comrade Napoikin, the author here has suggested a very interesting and quite fresh intonation for your role. You should giggle instead of moan.

NAPOIKIN. Giggle. There's a fine idea. But, I'm ill.

DIRECTOR. You may be ill, but our epoch is healthy and that's worth illuminating. You got that?

NAPOIKIN. Got it.

DIRECTOR. Well, illuminate it.

NAPOIKIN. Hee, hee, hee.

DIRECTOR. Very good. Let's move on.

(Nurses enter the operating room, carrying a banner)

NURSE. Our dear expiring patient! We, the nurses, technical personnel and night watchmen of our hospital, which was built ahead of schedule, are following the progress of your illness with undying interest. And we firmly hope that it will bring you to one or another conclusion.

KASYAN. Hee, hee, hee.

DIRECTOR. Stop. Fyodor Semyonovich, say what you will, but somehow giggling just doesn't fit this scene.

AUTHOR. Why?

DIRECTOR. How can I put it? The nurses are following the progress of his illness with undying interest, and, meanwhile, he's giggling. It's rather awkward.

AUTHOR. You're right. He can groan in this spot.

NAPOIKIN. Come on now. What am I supposed to do? Groan or giggle?

AUTHOR. You must strive for a synthesis, comrade Napoikin. Build your role dialectically. Sometimes your past instincts begin speaking in you and you begin groaning. But as soon as you begin to groan, you are inundated by a vision of our new life, and you begin giggling. You get what I mean? You groan, you giggle, you giggle, you groan. That's called dialectics.

NAPOIKIN. Thank you, kind heart.

DIRECTOR. Take it from the top.

NURSE. And we firmly hope that it will bring you to one or another conclusion.

KASYAN. Oh, oh, oh, hee, hee, hee.

AUTHOR. Fabulous! Very good. That is the true unity of opposites. Go on.

IVANOVA. Will there be any more greetings from any other organizations?

EMILIYA. As far as I know, that's all. Patients from the appendicitis ward planned on coming, but they're all going under the knife themselves today.

IVANOVA. In that case, comrades, I declare the official festivities closed. And now we can get on with the operation.

KASYAN. Oh, oh, oh, hee, hee, hee.

IVANOVA. Comrade Emiliya, slap the chloroform mask on him.

KASYAN. Oh, oh, oh, hee, hee, hee.

IVANOVA. Start counting, you'll soon fall asleep.

KASYAN. One, two, three, four... (*Snores*)

IVANOVA. He's asleep. Expose his stomach.

DIRECTOR. Olga Minishna, I asked you to shudder at this point. As soon as his stomach is exposed, you shudder. Got that? Kasyan's naked stomach is the trampoline from which you must leap into the impending love scene. I implore you, Olga Minishna, start your leap from his stomach.

IVANOVA. Somehow, I don't feel right with this scene, Pyotr Petrovich. Comrade Napoikin has an extremely unexpressive stomach. How could it possibly make me shudder? It's absurd.

NAPOIKIN. Don't worry, Olga Minishna, for the actual performance I'll cover it with so much makeup that you'll shudder for half an hour.

IVANOVA. Braggart.

DIRECTOR. Keep moving.

IVANOVA. Comrade Emiliya, hand me my scalpel, scissors, thread and a thimble.

DIRECTOR. I don't quite get the point of the thimble.

AUTHOR. You see, I use this thimble to sketch an outline of the heroine's biography. The fact is, that in the author's overall plan, Ivanova used to work in a sewing workshop. This thimble allows us to show subtly that, first of all, Ivanova still hasn't been separated from her origins in the production sector, and, second of all, that she is already a fully qualified doctor, whom we have created ourselves ahead of schedule. That is crucial.

DIRECTOR. I see. Olga Minishna, you have two very important tasks in this scene. They are represented by Kasyan's stomach and your thimble. By means of his stomach, you will tip off your future relations with Kasyan, while, by means of the thimble, you will portray your origins in the production sector. Your job is to synthesize these two links into one compact whole. You've got to perform in such a way that the spectators won't be able to figure out where his stomach ends and your thimble begins. Do that for me, won't you, Olga Minishna?

IVANOVA. I'll do that when the show opens, Pyotr Petrovich. Showing my link to the production sector right now isn't so important. After all, there aren't any critics here yet. Comrade assistants! Let's begin the stomach incision! Scalpel. Before I begin cutting, I consider myself bound to direct your insistent attention to the fact that this scalpel is better than anything they make in America, and that we produced it ourselves ahead of schedule at one of our own gigantic factories. I shall now snip off the top sheet. Comrade assistants, fold the ends and pin them back. Good. Now I shall descend into the intestines. Good.

(A work whistle blows)

KASYAN. The work whistle! *(Sits up)* I've got to go! *(Tries getting up from the operating table)*
IVANOVA. Madman! What are you doing? Hold him.
KASYAN. Let me go. Let me go to her.

(The work whistle blows again)

Did you hear that? My beloved communist, red, black metallurgy is beckoning me. *(Breaks free and runs for the door, but Ivanova blocks his path)*
IVANOVA. Do you realize that your stomach is split wide open?
KASYAN. Hee, hee, hee.
DIRECTOR. What are you doing?
KASYAN. I'm illuminating our epoch. Hee, hee, hee. I'm not some petty individualist who thinks of nothing but his own stomach. As long as I have hands, I've got to work. Let me go to my brothers and sister in labor. I can't waste a single man-hour.
IVANOVA. Give us just one day.
KASYAN. Not one single man-hour.
IVANOVA. We'll zip up your stomach today and you'll be back at work by the 28th.
KASYAN. You mean today is the 27th?
IVANOVA. Yes.
KASYAN. In that case, zip me up. The 27th is my day off.
IVANOVA. *(Aside)* Thank goodness for the five-day work week. *(Looks long and hard at Kasyan)* Lie down, sweetie.
KASYAN. How come there are so many of you, sugar?
IVANOVA. You're absolutely right. Comrade assistants, in the name of rationalization and industrialization, please leave us tête-à-tête.

(The assistants leave)

KASYAN. I'm ready. Sew me up.
IVANOVA. So as not to keep you here any longer than necessary, I'll do a loop stitch. It won't be as pretty, but it'll hold you tight.

(Kasyan lies still as Ivanova sews up his stomach. A squeaking sound is heard)

What's your name, comrade?

KASYAN. My name is Kasyan, comrade. But all my old comrade fellow-workers simply call me comrade Kasya.

IVANOVA. Oh, all those old workers are nothing but babies. Tell me Kasyan, what do you think about love?

KASYAN. I consider that a woman who thinks about love during our grand epoch of gigantic social reconstruction is nothing but trash.

IVANOVA. What happiness! You know, Kasyan, in our grand epoch of gigantic social reconstruction, I have constantly been thinking that any man who thinks that love is nothing but trash in our grand epoch of gigantic social reconstruction, is, himself, the dearest, most wonderful man there could possibly be.

KASYAN. What?

IVANOVA. I have constantly been thinking that any man who thinks that love is nothing but trash in our grand epoch of gigantic social reconstruction, is, himself, the dearest, most wonderful man there could possibly be.

KASYAN. I don't understand what you're saying.

IVANOVA. Fyodor Semyonovich, I don't understand anything in this, myself.

AUTHOR. It's called dialectics, Olga Minishna. It can't be explained.

IVANOVA. Oh, it's dialectics. Now I see. Well, let's move on. Kasyan, do I excite you as a woman?

KASYAN. Not in the slightest. Do I excite you as a man?

IVANOVA. Not in the faintest.

KASYAN. What happiness! I'll say even more. Only that woman whom I, as a man, don't excite as a woman, and who doesn't excite me as a man, is capable of exciting me the way a woman excites a man.

IVANOVA. Darling!

KASYAN. My pet!

(They kiss)

IVANOVA. Kasya!

KASYAN. O, bliss! When you call me Kasya, I feel as though it's not you, but one of my old comrade workers who is embracing me. And your embrace becomes so sweet and pleasant. Call me Kasya!

IVANOVA. Kasya! *(Embraces him)*

KASYAN. *(Passionately)* Frolov! Frolov!

(They embrace and kiss)

AUTHOR. You know, Pyotr Petrovich, I don't quite agree with your interpretation here. Why is he embracing her around the waist?

DIRECTOR. What do you mean? Lovers always embrace like that.

AUTHOR. Pyotr Petrovich, lovers under the old regime may have embraced like that, but the new lovers of our inimitable epoch can't possibly embrace like that.

DIRECTOR. Then what is he supposed to grab hold of?

AUTHOR. He should grab her by something new.

DIRECTOR. Comrade Napoikin, the author has suggested a very interesting and quite fresh intonation for your role. Since you are performing new human relations and new people, find something new on her to embrace.

NAPOIKIN. Something new?

DIRECTOR. Yes.

NAPOIKIN. There's a task for you. In that case, Pyotr Petrovich, find yourself a new actress. Everything on this one is old.

DIRECTOR. Napoikin, you are fined.

NAPOIKIN. What do you suggest I embrace?

DIRECTOR. Well, grab her by the... hmm. I see what you mean. Look, grab her by the... grab her by something factory-like. I don't know. Grab her by the corpus.

NAPOIKIN. The corpus. All right. My s-s-s-weetheart! (*Embraces her*)

(*Enter Yakov, followed by Yury. Yakov holds a big daisy and plucks off the petals, one-by-one*)

YAKOV. I believe in socialism, I don't believe in socialism. I believe, I don't believe. I believe, I don't believe. Yes, no. Yes, no. Yes, no. Yes. (*Firmly*) Yes! I don't believe in it.

YURY. What are you muttering about, Yakov.

YAKOV. Nothing, Yury. Nothing. It was just your imagination. Say, Yury, do you believe Kasyan?

YURY. Yes, I do, Yakov. He's an honest worker. Why do you ask?

YAKOV. Nothing, Yury. Nothing. It was just a figment of your imagination. But how about me? Do you believe me?

YURY. Yes, Yakov, I do. Only, from time to time, your eyes give off the kind of glow that our eyes shouldn't.

YAKOV. (*Turns away and covers his eyes with his hand*) It's nothing, Yury. Nothing. That's just a figment of your imagination.

YURY. Open your eyes a bit wider and you'll get a better glimpse of our new life with all its new people.

YAKOV. (*Opens his eyes and sees Kasyan kissing Ivanova*) A-h-h-h!

YURY. What's wrong?

YAKOV. Look at those new people.

YURY. O-o-o-o-h.

YAKOV. Ha, ha, ha.

KASYAN. Yury!

IVANOVA. My husband!

YURY. Don't try making excuses. I saw everything. (*To the prompter*) Well,

my good man, do your stuff. I haven't the vaguest notion what comes next.
PROMPTER. Your eyes, they give birth to love.
YURY. What?
PROMPTER. Your eyes...
YURY. Your eyes...
PROMPTER. ...they give birth...
YURY. ...Hey! Give birth!
IVANOVA. What did you say?
YURY. I said, "Your eyes... Hey! Give birth!"
IVANOVA. Are you nuts? I'm not pregnant.
YURY. You are too.
IVANOVA. I am not.
YURY. If the prompter says you are, then you are. And that's that.
PROMPTER. Not "Give birth!" but "...give birth to love."
YURY. Eyes can't give birth.
PROMPTER. I didn't say they're giving birth, period, I said they give birth
    to...
YURY. What's the difference?
PROMPTER. I didn't say they "give birth," I said, "they give birth to love."
YURY. Whose eyes?
PROMPTER. Her eyes.
YURY. Oh, so that's it. I got it. Your eyes, they give birth to love.
IVANOVA. Listen to me, Yury.
YURY. Shut up, snake.
PROMPTER. Yakov.
YURY. Yakov.
PROMPTER. This woman has always been an enigma for me.
YURY. This woman has always an enigma for me.
PROMPTER. And now she begets new doubts.
YURY. Aha! I was right. If she isn't pregnant, then how can she beget?
PROMPTER. She's not begetting anyone, she's begetting doubts.
YURY. Oh, doubts. I get it. She begets new doubts. I'm deceived.
KASYAN. Yury.
YURY. Shut up, scoundrel. You stand there kissing my wife, when you know
    perfectly well that you're late for your shift at the factory.
IVANOVA. You have no right to humiliate him so, Yury. This is his day off.
YURY. Oh, it's you, Kasya. Forgive my suspicions. And, sweetie, you forgive
    me, too.
IVANOVA. That's my good Yury.
YAKOV. They're deceiving you, Yury. She's been sleeping with him.
YURY. Were you sleeping with him?
IVANOVA. Yes.
YURY. When did you find the time?

IVANOVA. Before the work shift started.

YURY. That's my good Ivanova. Kasyan, I'm no greedy feudal lord. You can have her.

KASYAN. Oh, no, Yury. You keep her.

YURY. Don't be so shy. Take her.

KASYAN. No, no, Yury. I'm not greedy, either. You keep her.

YAKOV. My God! These aren't people, they're monuments to mankind. *(Falls to his knees)* Seize me! Tie me up! I confess!

ALL. What's the matter with you?

YAKOV. I'm a criminal.

YURY. Yakov, are you mixed up in a conspiracy?

YAKOV. Worse, Yury. Worse.

YURY. Yakov, did you kill someone?

YAKOV. Worse, Yury. Worse.

YURY. What crime did you commit?

YAKOV. Back in peaceful times, my daddy... owned a laundry.

ALL. Ah!

YAKOV. Beat me, new people! Beat me! I'm guilty. I confess.

YURY. No, Yakov. You still have a chance to be reborn. Stand.

YAKOV. But, what can I do?

YURY. Sleep with my wife. That will help you be reborn not only mechanically, but organically. Ivanova, do you consent?

IVANOVA. What about Kasyan?

YURY. Sleep with him, too. Basically, you can sleep with anyone you want, except Mitya.

IVANOVA. Why?

YURY. Because he's not one of us.

3. A Meeting About Laughter

CHARACTERS IN ORDER OF APPEARANCE

ORATOR — Comrade Kosupko
CHAIRMAN
FIRST SPEAKER
SECOND SPEAKER — Comrade Vagankov
THIRD SPEAKER — Comrade Gvozdilin
FOURTH SPEAKER
A WOMAN
SIXTH SPEAKER
UPOKOINIKOV
VARIOUS VOICES

ORATOR. Comrades! You probably have all read in the pages of our press that we need joyous, cheerful art and that we must do something to make spectators in theaters laugh. Yes, comrades, the proletariat wants to laugh! That is why I am asking you to discuss this problem jointly and thereby, so to speak, to set it on a practical course.

(A courier approaches the Speaker and whispers something in his ear)

All right, all right. Just a minute! Comrades, begin without me. I'll be right back. *(Leaves)*

CHAIRMAN. Who would like to say something?

FIRST SPEAKER. Me.

CHAIRMAN. Go ahead.

FIRST SPEAKER. Comrades! With the perspicacity characteristic of him, comrade Kosupko dropped a rather eloquent phrase about the fact that the proletariat wants to laugh. But, comrades, we know that if the proletariat wants something, even if it wants to laugh, then what we have, comrades, is no laughing matter. Truly, it would be absurd if individual comrades wanted to make jokes at that very moment in time when the proletariat wants to laugh. I believe I would be immeasurably correct were I to say that laughter in the sixteenth year of the revolution is no joke. Therefore, I request that you relate to laughter with a maximum of seriousness. What do we need, comrades? We need the broad masses laughing as much as possible. We need laughter so badly, it's enough to make you weep. I see that a few of those present are grinning. Shame on you, comrades! There is nothing to grin about when I am speaking to you about such an important sector as laughter! I see nothing funny in it. I repeat once again with all categoricalness: We need laughter. Thoughtful, serious laughter without the slightest grin. I'm done.

CHAIRMAN. Who else would like to say something about laughter?

SECOND SPEAKER. Allow me!

CHAIRMAN. Please.

SECOND SPEAKER. Comrades! The previous orator, speaking about laughter, summoned us to seriousness. But comrades, the previous orator himself was far from serious in his attitude towards laughter. The previous orator said that we need laughter. I consider that such a conclusion is very grim. I consider, comrades, that every person, before laughing, must take into full and clear account who he is laughing at, why he is laughing and what kind of laughter he will laugh. That is what is most important. What kinds of laughters do we have as of today's date? At today's date we have the following laughters: their laughter and our laughter. What is the difference between their laughter and our laughter? The primary determining feature of our laughter is that our laughter must be organized. What does that mean? That means that we must laugh only at that for which our general assembly passes a resolution stating that it is truly funny. The provinces, for instance, must coordinate their laughter with the center. Authors, for instance, must coordinate their laughter with the repertory committee. The Communist Youth League, for instance, must coordinate its laughter with the Society of Old Bolsheviks. As for theaters, well, spectators in theaters must laugh only during intermission after a joint discussion of all those moments which are capable of arousing in them Homeric guffaws.

THIRD SPEAKER. Allow me.

SECOND SPEAKER. I haven't finished yet.

CHAIRMAN. One minute. Let comrade Gvozdilin[19] say a short word about Homeric guffaws.

THIRD SPEAKER. Comrades! Besides our laughter and their laughter there are several laughters which we have inherited from past ages. An enormous place among the above-mentioned laughters is occupied by the so-called "Homeric guffaw." Let us try to understand how our laughter will relate to the given guffaw. What is a Homeric guffaw? The great blind man Homer laughed in Homeric guffaws. Consequently, he laughed at what he couldn't see. Do we need this kind of guffaw?

VOICES. — Yes.

      — No.

THIRD SPEAKER. Comrades, I consider that we do. Because, to laugh at what we do see is, I would say, uh… somewhat ticklish.

VOICES. That's right!

THIRD SPEAKER. Shall we then consider the Homeric guffaw to be our own

---

[19] "Gvozdilin" might be translated as Mr. Nail. See also note 23.

kind of laughter?

VOICES. — No!

    — Not entirely!

    — Yes!

    — Almost!

THIRD SPEAKER. In that case, let's consider it half-way ours.

VOICE. If it's half-way ours, that means it's half-way theirs!

THIRD SPEAKER. No, half-way ours and half-way not theirs!

VOICE. Then you'd be better off saying half-way nobody's!

FOURTH SPEAKER. I have a proposal.

CHAIRMAN. Go ahead.

FOURTH SPEAKER. In light of the unclarity of the Homeric guffaw, I propose replacing it temporarily with Shakespearean laughter.

VOICES. That's right!

THIRD SPEAKER. Comrades, I categorically oppose. We still do not know what laughter Shakespeare laughed in. If he was the son of a Lord, then he laughed the belly laugh of the rotting upper crust. But if he was the son of a salt-of-the-earth merchant, then consequently, he laughed the bold and healthy laugh of a half-starving commoner. For the time being, no one can answer this question because Shakespeare's heritage remains unknown. We might wind up in a tight spot, comrades. What if we start laughing in Shakespearean laughter and William Shakespeare suddenly turns out to be a Lord Rutland? Therefore, I suggest all manner of abstention from Shakespearean laughter.

CHAIRMAN. The floor returns to comrade Vagankov concerning the ongoing topic of laughter.

SECOND SPEAKER. Comrades, I continue. The second determining feature of our laughter is that it must be a mass laughter. I consider that the laughter of two or three people, or, the even more disgraceful laughter of one person alone, is entirely unacceptable. We must wage a decisive battle against loner-laughers, for such laughter cannot be subjected at all to any kind of qualifications. Let's say a man is sitting in a tram car laughing. The devil only knows what he is laughing about! I consider that all laughter must begin with at least fifteen people who are under the surveillance of an experienced leader. Moreover, every instance of laughter, before bursting from the breast, must be given a theoretical basis. There you have it!

CHAIRMAN. Who else would like to say something about laughter?

FOURTH SPEAKER. Me.

CHAIRMAN. Go ahead.

FOURTH SPEAKER. Comrades! The previous orators expressed themselves extremely abstractly. I consider that the question must be posed practically. Therefore, I suggest that those gathered here immediately demonstrate their general preparedness to laugh. Attention, comrades. I will now say something funny. Quiet, I'm beginning. One poor Jew came home and found his wife's lover under her bed. "What are you doing here?" asked the poor Jew. "Waiting for the tram," the lover answered.

(Everybody laughs)

Comrades, don't get ahead of yourselves. That, comrades, is their laughter because this joke ridicules one poor Jew. Now let's turn their laughter onto the road of our laughter. One rich Jew comes home to his rich wife and finds a rich lover under her bed. "What are you doing here?" asked the rich Jew. "I'm waiting for my automobile," answered the rich lover. This, comrades, is our laughter, because the joke does not ridicule one poor Jew, but two rich Jews and one rich Jewess. Now, comrades, let's get to the bottom of whether this is funny and, if so, why. This, comrades, is very funny. Why? Because the lover is waiting for his automobile. And we, comrades, can say in full confidence that if the current crisis continues to deepen, the given lover won't travel far in this automobile of his. Therefore, comrades, we are all bound to laugh at this second variant with all our hearts.

(All but one laugh)

CHAIRMAN. Why aren't you laughing?
SECOND SPEAKER. Why should I laugh?
CHAIRMAN. Because it's funny.
SECOND SPEAKER. Do you have a resolution of the general assembly stating that it's funny?
CHAIRMAN. No!
SECOND SPEAKER. Then who decided that it's funny?
CHAIRMAN. What do you mean? We did.
SECOND SPEAKER. Then you go ahead and laugh yourselves. But without a resolution of the general assembly stating that it's funny, I have no intention of laughing. I might start laughing and then find out the general assembly has resolved that it isn't funny. Where would I be then?
VOICES. That's right!
CHAIRMAN. Comrades, cut the laughter. On the suggestion of comrade Otpevayev,[20] I put to a vote the laughter at two rich Jews and one rich Jewess. Who finds it funny? No one? In that case, I'll pose the question differently. Who finds it very funny, raise your hands.

(One person raises a hand)

CHAIRMAN. You?
WOMAN. No. I request the floor.

---

[20] Earlier, the Second Speaker was called Comrade Vagankov.

CHAIRMAN. Go ahead.

WOMAN. I shall speak in the name of women. I have nothing against rich Jews, but I am opposed to immorality.

CHAIRMAN. What immorality?

WOMAN. I consider that there should be no lovers in our laughter. Therefore, I suggest replacing the lover with a comrade from the Party or his non-Party relative. Let's say, like this: The husband comes home and finds his wife's cousin under her bed. With a correction like that, I will admit it is funny.

CHAIRMAN. Let's vote. Who is for making the rich lover a rich cousin?

(Everybody raises their hand)

Considering the correction, do we vote that it is very funny?

(Everybody raises their hand)

SECOND SPEAKER. Now that's a different story. After the resolution, I agree to laugh. Ha, ha, ha, you're killing me! *(Bends over, holding his stomach from laughter)*

CHAIRMAN. Who else would like to speak? Perhaps you would like to say something? After all, as a peripheral worker, you have come from the periphery, so to speak, straight from the production line. We would be quite interested to hear your opinion.

SIXTH SPEAKER. I have never worked with laughter, comrades. For now, I'm just getting a feel for it.

CHAIRMAN. But the fact is, we are conducting a campaign...

SIXTH SPEAKER. Oh, a campaign? Well then, of course I'll speak. Comrades! Allow me to say a few words about the development of laughter in the industrial regions of the Moscow, Leningrad and Ivanovo-Voznesensk territories. The deployment of laughter must be conducted on the basis of amateurism in various organizations and the maximal employment of local resources.

(Applause)

Comrades! Laughter, being an animal that multiplies very quickly, produces tasty white meat...

VOICES. What meat? What are you talking about?

SIXTH SPEAKER. Pardon me, comrades! To tell the truth, I usually speak about rabbits.[21] Laughter for me is something new! However, comrades, you laugh in vain.

---

[21] In the early years of Soviet power, there was a push to develop new industries, one of which was the raising of rabbits. See the sketch "New People, New Songs" for a spoof of this phenomenon.

CHAIRMAN. Comrades, let's move along to the proposals. Who would like to introduce a proposal?[22]

WOMAN. I would. I propose singling out of our midst the staunchest, most serious comrade to take control of everything concerning the nidus of our laughter.

CHAIRMAN. Let's have the nominations.

VOICES. — Comrade Vagankov.[23]

    — Otpevayev.
    — Comrade Kaldbishchev.
    — U-po-koi-ni-kov.
    — Nadgrobin.
    — U-po-koi-ni-kov.
    — I nominate Sofya Andreyevna Zastup.
    — Nadgrobin.
    — Upokoinikov.
    — Panikhidin, Panikhidin.

CHAIRMAN. Comrades, I think it would be best to appoint comrade Upokoinikov to this position of high responsibility.

VOICES. That's right. Upokoinikov. Where is he?

THIRD SPEAKER. He informed us he would be a little late, comrades. He's burying his wife today.

VOICE. Here he is, now.

(Enter Upokoinikov)

CHAIRMAN. Comrade Upokoinikov. We have just elected you unanimously to take control of everything concerning the nidus of our laughter.

UPOKOINIKOV. I thank you.

CHAIRMAN. I have received the resolution, comrades. Shall I read it?

VOICES. Yes, yes!

CHAIRMAN. Attention, comrades. The resolution reads as follows: The general assembly of the Learned Society of Friends of Soviet Laughter, having heard the report of comrade Kosupko on the theme of laughter, resolves to welcome fervently any kind of laughter excepting the following:

    a) animalistic,
    b) guttural,
    c) tickling,
    d) chewing,

---

[22] This and all subsequent lines through Upokoinikov's "I thank you" were cut from the published versions of this sketch.

[23] All of the names in the following list, to one degree or another, are necrophilic. "Vagankov" is the name of a Moscow cemetery; "Otpevayev" implies a reader at a burial service; "Kaldbishchev" is a distortion of the word for cemetery; "Upokoinikov" might be translated as Mr. Deceased; "Zastup" means a shovel or a spade; "Nadgrobin" suggests a gravestone; "Panikhidin" suggests a requiem.

e) relishing,
f) hysterical,
g) pragmatic,
h) ill-defined,
i) twilight-like,
j) falsely healthy,
k) foot-stomping,
l) premature,
m) premature come slightly late,
n) half-hearted,
o) half half-hearted,
p) completely half-hearted,
q) inscrutable,
r) inscrutable, but only to some,
s) empty,
t) light-hearted,
u) superficial,
v) hormonal,
w) unbalancing,
x) generalizing,
y) lecherous,
z) self-satisfied.

Comrades, there are still several laughters left, but the alphabet has run out. Therefore, such laughters as,

sated,
universal,
malicious,
half-expressed,
arm-pit,
visible through invisible tears,
invisible through visible tears

and also, laughter at anyone, laughter as such and laughter in general shall all remain unlettered temporarily, until such time as the alphabet is expanded. The following laughters are unconditionally recommended:

a) laughter at the Tatar yoke,
b) laughter at serfdom,
c) laughter at our Lord Jesus Christ, and
d) laughter at the People's Commissariat of Post and Telegraph.

SECOND SPEAKER. How come the People's Commissariat?
CHAIRMAN. Comrades, I had in mind telegrams. They're always late.
SECOND SPEAKER. Then you should have said that you mean telegrams.
THIRD SPEAKER. I propose clarifying this point: not telegrams in general, but personal telegrams.

CHAIRMAN. Who opposes? No one? Then here's how it sounds: Laughter at our Lord Jesus Christ and at personal telegrams should not, excluding the following exceptions,
    a) deliver blows to the head,
    b) arouse instincts,
    c)...

(Curtain drops in a timely manner)

4. New People, New Songs

CHARACTERS IN ORDER OF APPEARANCE

DIRECTOR
MAX
A HOTEL ATTENDANT
STESHA — whose full name is Stepanida Spiridonovna Mishkina

DIRECTOR. Comrades. Now we will show you one of our theater's experiments in the so-called small, but resilient forms. We will perform a sketch, the author of which is the unforgettable Ivan Alexandrovich Ditya.[24] He might well be called an industrious author in the fullest sense of the term. His oeuvre is so watered down that he is capable of simultaneously filling two dammed reservoirs at once. On the one hand, he directs his torrents at the unorganized spectator, while, on the other hand, he aims them at the organized spectator. It's difficult to say which of these torrents is the most effective. But it's not difficult to say that, with his aforementioned watered-down works, our respected author has no difficulty in simultaneously serving every category of spectator there possibly could be. The sketch is called *New People, New Songs*.

(A hotel room with a table, a closet, and a bed covered with a bedspread. Max and the Attendant enter in near-darkness. The Attendant carries a briefcase and a suitcase)

MAX. This isn't much of a room. Don't you have anything better?
ATTENDANT. All the rooms are taken, citizen. There's nothing you can do about it.

---

[24] This may refer to the playwright, poet and journalist, Sergei Tretyakov (1892-1939?). Vsevolod Meyerhold worked on his play, "I Want a Child," from 1927-1930, but never completed the production. The name "Ditya" means "child" in Russian. Tretyakov was an active supporter of the bolshevik cause, and he once wrote that the writer is a "Communist verbal functionary." He eventually was executed while in prison.

MAX. Oh, well. So what. Give me the key. Put that over there and hang this over here.

ATTENDANT. Will there be anything else?

MAX. No. On the other hand, maybe so. Listen here, dear heart. Are there any enthusiasts of rabbit farming among the attendants who work as service personnel in your hotel?[25]

ATTENDANT. What?

MAX. I said, are there any enthusiasts of rabbit farming among the attendants who work as service personnel in your hotel?

ATTENDANT. What?

MAX. I said, do you raise rabbits? Do you have any rabbits in this hotel?

ATTENDANT. No. I haven't heard any complaints, anyway. I can say that with a clear conscience. We have no rabbits. Bedbugs, yes. As many as you like. But no rabbits. We wouldn't allow it. We keep on top of these things, you know.

MAX. That's just where you're wrong. Oh, well. You can go.

(The Attendant leaves. Max takes off his jacket and begins undressing)

I can see it's going to take a lot of labor and iron will to awaken the consciousness of the broad working masses insofar as the importance of raising rabbits goes. Finally I got a room in a hotel. How nice it'll be to crawl in bed and fall asleep after a fruitful day of work. Then I can get up tomorrow morning with renewed strength and devote myself once again to my beloved pursuit of raising gigantic bunny-rabbits. *(Sits on the bed)*

STESHA. Ah!

MAX. Ah! *(Staggers away, then runs to the other side of the stage)* What... What are you...

STESHA. I don't have any money.

MAX. I assure you... What money?

STESHA. Take it all. Take all I have. Only don't touch me.

MAX. I assure you... You've mistaken me for someone else.

STESHA. You... You're a thief.

MAX. I am not a thief. I am an honest man.

STESHA. Then why were you trying to crawl under my pillow?

MAX. I just wanted to get in bed.

STESHA. With me? You scoundrel.

MAX. Pardon me, but...

STESHA. I see right through you. Don't come near me or I'll shoot. *(Crawls out from under the bedspread)*

MAX. *(Hides behind the chair in fright)* I implore you. Don't come near me. I'm not dressed.

---

[25] See note 21 above.

STESHA. Who are you? What are you doing here?

MAX. I raise rabbits.

STESHA. In my room? You're crazy.

MAX. Pardon me, citizeness, but this is my room.

STESHA. This isn't your room, it's my room.

MAX. Your room? What do you mean, your room? It's my room. I just registered for it.

STESHA. I registered for it this afternoon.

MAX. Room ten?

STESHA. Room ten.

MAX. That's my room.

STESHA. Would you please relieve me of your presence immediately?

MAX. Calm down, citizeness. I'll call the attendant and we'll clear things up. *(Rings for the attendant)*

ATTENDANT. Did you ring?

MAX. What's going on, here? I have a woman in my bed.

ATTENDANT. Sorry, citizen. She's probably left over from the last tenants.

STESHA. Are you crazy? I demand that you give me another room this instant.

ATTENDANT. I can't promise I can do that. We're all booked up.

STESHA. You have no right. I'll complain. I was sent here to install heatification pipes. Here are my papers. *(Throws her i.d. on the table)*

(Max looks it over)

ATTENDANT. I'll go ask. Only I'm telling you, we're all booked up. *(Leaves)*

STESHA. What the hell is going on here?

MAX. Pardon me, citizeness, are these your papers?

STESHA. Yes.

MAX. Your name is Stepanida Spiridonovna Mishkina?

STESHA. Yes.

MAX. *(Turns on the overhead lamp and stares attentively at her face)* Stesha!

STESHA. *(Gives him a long, hard stare)* Max? Is that really you? Max!

MAX. Stesha! It's you! I can't believe my eyes.

STESHA. It's me—Stesha. Once I was Stesha the Gypsy, and now I'm a member of a research group testing the feasibility of wooden pipes.

MAX. Wooden pipes?

STESHA. Yes. We have to economize on metals since they are crucial in the construction of our gigantic socialist industry. And, anyway, wooden pipes are cheaper.

MAX. Sounds like a fairy tale from the *Arabian Nights*.

STESHA. What about you? What are you doing, now?

MAX. I'm solving the problem of rabbit farming.

STESHA. The problem of rabbit farming?

MAX. That's right. In addition to providing tasty meat, rabbits provide fur. You can make fur coats out of rabbit fur and you can make excellent glue out of their ears and paws.

STESHA. Sounds like a fairy tale from the *Arabian Nights.*

MAX. Doesn't it, though? Just think. Now you're an engineer, and I'm an inspector for one of the most important sectors of animal husbandry. Stesha! Do you remember 1913? The drunken nights at that little Arcadia Tavern? And there you were—a youthful representative of one of the oppressed nationalities—singing Gypsy songs in a Gypsy choir.

STESHA. And what about you? You were a brand new intellectual commoner doing American tap dances to entertain the fatted crowd.

MAX. Yes. What a terrible time it was. Taverns... war... We thought it would never end...

STESHA. And then suddenly the revolution happened and we lost track of each other.

MAX. And after that came the front... studies... struggles... And you lost your head in pipes and I started assimilating rabbits. The past is gone. And here we are—new people standing on the doorstep to a new life. Are you happy?

STESHA. Oh, Max... And what about you?

MAX. Oh, Stesha...

STESHA. It's so strange to recall those far-away, awful times, now. I would sit on stage and sing... (*Motions to the conductor and then sings a romance*)

MAX. What vulgarity. How fortunate that those times are gone forever and we don't have to listen to those disgusting songs anymore.

STESHA. Just think where we'd be if it hadn't been for the revolution. Instead of being a progressive-minded engineer, a social activist—you might even say an intrepid explorer—I would have had to spend my whole life singing horrid songs like this... (*Motions to the conductor and sings a romance*)

MAX. Horrors! Horrors! But tell me, don't memories of the past ever remind you of your former self?

STESHA. Never. Although, you know, there was one time. We were taking inventory of the volume of water that leaks out of our pipes and pipe joints. Our inventory showed that our early models with the thin walls leaked significantly more than the newer models with the thicker walls. And that was even though the early models were totally covered with asphalt, while the newer models were only partially covered with asphalt. Afterwards, we all travelled out to an affiliate collective farm. And as we were lying there in the field, a couple of comrades asked me to sing a Gypsy song. I was so offended, I refused to do it.

MAX. What was the song you didn't sing?

STESHA. This one. (*Motions to the conductor and sings a romance*)

MAX. What a nightmare. How right you were not to sing that song. No doubt they all would have been shocked by its pitiful vulgarity. Nowadays, we have bold new songs that just can't compare to those old romances. Like this one, for instance. Maestro, shall we?

(They sing a duet which ends with a dance number)

STESHA. Thank God such vulgarities are a thing of the past. Yes, now we have splendid, bold, healthy, new Soviet songs. For example...

(Enter the Attendant)

ATTENDANT. It's all taken care of, citizens. I found you a room. Who will be taking it? You?
MAX. No, I'll stay here.
ATTENDANT. Then, you'll be moving.
STESHA. No. I'm staying here, too.
ATTENDANT. I get you. No more questions asked. *(Leaves)*

Private Schultz

WRITTEN WITH MIKHAIL VOLPIN

1942

CHARACTERS

A SOLDIER — Johann Schultz, private third-class
A PLENIPOTENTIARY

SOLDIER. Private third class Johann Schultz reporting on your orders, sir.

PLENIPOTENTIARY. Why didn't junior Lance Corporal Klinger report?

SOLDIER. Junior Lance Corporal Klinger has been arrested, sir.

PLENIPOTENTIARY. Arrested? What for?

SOLDIER. For a riddle, sir.

PLENIPOTENTIARY. What riddle?

SOLDIER. For this riddle, sir. Why are our senior lieutenant and cognac similar and not similar at the same time?

PLENIPOTENTIARY. What nonsense! What similarities can there be between cognac and a lieutenant, to say nothing of a senior lieutenant?

SOLDIER. Both of them bear three stars, sir, and both of them attack the head after one glass. As for the differences, cognac attacks the lieutenant's head after one glass, while the lieutenant, after one glass, attacks anyone's head he can get his hands on.

PLENIPOTENTIARY. That's disgusting.

SOLDIER. It certainly is, sir. I don't understand why he has to attack people's heads, as if there wasn't some place lower he could attack.

PLENIPOTENTIARY. That's not what I'm talking about. I'm talking about the riddle. It's disgusting and immoral. Only an inveterate enemy and diehard conspirator could dream up such a thing. I am certain that any other German soldier… well, take you, for example. You wouldn't be able to compare a lieutenant to cognac, would you?

SOLDIER. Not on your life, sir. First of all, cognac doesn't attack nearly as viciously and second of all…

PLENIPOTENTIARY. What are you, a drunkard or an idiot?

SOLDIER. I don't know, sir.

PLENIPOTENTIARY. All right, come here. Breathe in my face. What's that smell about you?

SOLDIER. Chicory, sir.

PLENIPOTENTIARY. What?

179

SOLDIER. Chicory. I ate two pounds of it today.

PLENIPOTENTIARY. Don't lie, you bum. That's not chicory I smell. It's vodka.

SOLDIER. That's because the chicory these days is very bad, sir. It used to be that whenever you'd drink, one bite of chicory would hide the smell instantly. You could safely breathe in the face of the Commander-in-Chief himself. Nowadays, you can chew a whole wagon-load of chicory but you still smell like vodka. It's not even chicory, it's soy.

PLENIPOTENTIARY. Don't breathe in my direction, you bum! So, you've been drinking vodka after all?

SOLDIER. With the permission of the brass, sir. In preparation for the attack.

PLENIPOTENTIARY. That's a different story. Alcohol before attack is approved by the high command. You may breathe in my direction.

SOLDIER. But maybe you find it unpleasant, sir?

PLENIPOTENTIARY. No, no. I like… chicory. How long did today's assault last, private Schultz?

SOLDIER. Two hours, forty minutes, sir. If you count in both directions.

PLENIPOTENTIARY. Is that so? You mean you attacked in two different directions?

SOLDIER. Yes sir. One there and the other coming back.

PLENIPOTENTIARY. Why coming back?

SOLDIER. The vodka didn't hold out, sir. We drank too little.

PLENIPOTENTIARY. You should have drank more.

SOLDIER. That doesn't always help, either, sir. Yesterday, for example, the 142nd infantry was supposed to attack, so they were given their ration of vodka. They heaved a few heavy sighs and set off. And as soon as they reached the enemy encampment, they realized they were more sober then, than they had been drunk just a short while before. And what kind of soldier is a sober soldier? They gave it a few minutes of thought and then turned on their heels. And then there was the incident that happened with us recently. They gave each of us a glass of vodka and sent us off on assault. But as soon as the enemy appeared out of the forest, we started seeing double and every Red Army soldier looked like four to us.

PLENIPOTENTIARY. How come four? If you were seeing double, then it should have been two.

SOLDIER. Because, even without vodka, every one of them looks like two.

PLENIPOTENTIARY. Private Schultz, from now on, answer only those questions I pose without tacking on anything extra.

SOLDIER. Yes sir.

PLENIPOTENTIARY. How old are you?

SOLDIER. Thirty with a few years tacked on, but considering your order, we can call it thirty even.

PLENIPOTENTIARY. Who are your parents?

SOLDIER. Well, sir, I have no parents.

PLENIPOTENTIARY. No parents?

SOLDIER. No sir.

PLENIPOTENTIARY. Then how were you born?

SOLDIER. By correspondence, sir.

PLENIPOTENTIARY. By correspondence? Don't lie to me.

SOLDIER. I'm not lying, sir. Allow me to explain.

PLENIPOTENTIARY. No.

SOLDIER. Thirty-some years, I mean, exactly thirty years ago, on the estate of the old, but robust, Baron Von Finsternant, there lived and worked a young married couple, Mrs. and Mr. Schultz. One fine day, the old baron summoned Mr. Schultz and sent him on a long trip about Germany. It should be said that Mrs. Schultz passionately loved her husband and Mr. Schultz adored his wife. There wasn't a day went by without their writing to one another. They wrote to one another every day and suddenly, a year into this long and intense correspondence, Mrs. Schultz gave birth to me.

PLENIPOTENTIARY. What nonsense! People aren't born by correspondence.

SOLDIER. Why can't a man be born by correspondence if he can die by correspondence?

PLENIPOTENTIARY. What's that supposed to mean?

SOLDIER. Quite simple. There have been several instances in our company. People corresponded with their family, telling about the situation at the front. And for that they were court-martialed and shot. One wonders: What was the cause of death? Correspondence, naturally.

PLENIPOTENTIARY. I'm very happy you bring that up. I have come to the front as a government plenipotentiary and my job is to put an end, once and for all, to that about which you have spoken.

SOLDIER. Executions, sir?

PLENIPOTENTIARY. No, letters. Letters which give birth…

SOLDIER. Aha, sir! Now you, too, are saying that letters can give birth!

PLENIPOTENTIARY. Silence! …Letters which give birth to unhealthy attitudes, both behind the lines and in the active army. I trust that you don't write such letters?

SOLDIER. I do not, sir.

PLENIPOTENTIARY. I gather that you write cheerful letters, filled with a militaristic spirit?

SOLDIER. Yes, sir!

PLENIPOTENTIARY. Excellent! People such as you should write letters as often as possible. How many letters have you written to your wife this week?

SOLDIER. Not a single one, sir.

PLENIPOTENTIARY. I see. And how about last week?

SOLDIER. Not a single one, sir.

PLENIPOTENTIARY. You mean you have no desire to write to your wife?

SOLDIER. Desire? Yes, sir.

PLENIPOTENTIARY. Then what's the problem?

SOLDIER. I have no wife.

PLENIPOTENTIARY. Well, do you have any family at all?

SOLDIER. Well, sir, a little. I have half an aunt is all.

PLENIPOTENTIARY. What do you mean, half an aunt?

SOLDIER. Quite simple. She writes about it herself.

PLENIPOTENTIARY. How's that?

SOLDIER. Alas, sir, it's true. Allow me to read you her letter. Here. She writes: *(reads the letter)* "Dear Fritz!" Oh, how she loves me! So: "…For God's sake, when will there be an end to this damned war…" Oops, that's not it. Wait a second, I'll find it. Here! "They say there was a rout…" Oops, wrong place again. Ah, here it is! "There's nothing in the stores at all. Everyone is losing weight terribly. I'm only half of what I used to be." There, you see? There's only half of her left.

PLENIPOTENTIARY. I don't like that letter. I don't see any cheerfulness in your aunt. How do you explain that?

SOLDIER. I imagine all her cheerfulness was located in the half of her that she lost, sir.

PLENIPOTENTIARY. Well, do you see? If she's lost her cheerfulness, it's all the more important for you to write her a letter filled with courage and fervent confidence in our lightning-like victory. Sit down, take that pen and write. I will dictate. "Dear Aunt!"

SOLDIER. "Dear Aunt!" *(writes)*

PLENIPOTENTIARY. "Don't believe rumors, believe only me." Did you write that?

SOLDIER. I did.

PLENIPOTENTIARY. "Know that we are undefeatable." Did you write that?

SOLDIER. I did.

PLENIPOTENTIARY. Read it!

SOLDIER. "Dear Aunt! Don't believe rumors. Believe only me. Know that we are in defeat and able…."

PLENIPOTENTIARY. What?

SOLDIER. "Know that we are in defeat and able…."

PLENIPOTENTIARY. Is that what I said? I said, "Know that we are undefeatable."

SOLDIER. That's what I wrote. "We are in defeat and able…."

PLENIPOTENTIARY. You wrote "defeat" and "able" separately. Write "defeat" and "able" together.

SOLDIER. Oh, I see. "We are in defeat, and able together…" Together with whom, sir?

PLENIPOTENTIARY. Not with anyone, you idiot. "Undefeatable" together. Then a period.

SOLDIER. "In defeat and able together." Period.

PLENIPOTENTIARY. Oh, let's move on. "I must admit that although we are near a victorious…" What are you writing there?

SOLDIER. "I must admit that although we are never victorious…"

PLENIPOTENTIARY. Then who is victorious?

SOLDIER. The Russians.

PLENIPOTENTIARY. What do you think we are talking about here?

SOLDIER. What's there to think? You dictated the truth and nothing but the truth, sir. We'll never be victorious.

PLENIPOTENTIARY. All right, cross out everything you've written. Start again. "Dear aunt! Wholeheartedly believe Doctor Goebbels. In abbreviated…"

SOLDIER. *(Writes)* "…inebriated…." So that's it! You mean Goebbels is inebriated!?

PLENIPOTENTIARY. What did you say?

SOLDIER. I always imagined that Goebbels could do what he does only if he were good and inebriated.

PLENIPOTENTIARY. That is a lie spread by our enemies! Doctor Goebbels never drinks. He's too busy for that. He is in charge of propaganda and press. He writes directives that are capable of intoxicating all true Germans with enthusiasm. Understand?

SOLDIER. Yes, sir. You mean he doesn't drink himself, he just intoxicates others.

PLENIPOTENTIARY. Now write: "Dear aunt, be courageous and remember what the poet said.

Of victory be ever assured,
Though our road may not be easy.
And remember, living like a pilgrim
Does not mean living in poverty."

SOLDIER. Aha, I get it. You mean it's better to live like a pilgrim than be a beggar.

PLENIPOTENTIARY. Now write: "Everyone at the front and everyone behind the lines knows Hitler's ways seal victory." That's all. Period. Read it!

SOLDIER. "Hitler's a weasel." What comes next, sir? He's a weasel, period?

PLENIPOTENTIARY. Silence! Arrest this man! About face! One, two, march! If this idiot writes letters like that even under my own dictation, I wonder what soldiers are writing from the front!?

On Laughter

WRITTEN WITH YAKOV ZISKIND

1954

CHARACTERS

HE — an emcee
SHE — an actress

HE. And now an actress will perform for you Russian folk songs…

SHE. That's all?

HE. No, that's not all. Afterwards, an actor will…

SHE. No, I mean, is that all you can say? What kind of emcee announces an act like that? An emcee is supposed to create a gay, happy mood for the audience—to prepare everyone to laugh…

HE. Everyone?

SHE. Everyone.

HE. Almost everyone. Two or three people may not laugh.

SHE. Why?

HE. Because in every auditorium there are always two or three people whom nobody could make laugh.

SHE. Two or three in every auditorium?

HE. Yes.

SHE. Tell me, how many auditoriums are there in Moscow?

HE. Well, if you count clubs, probably several hundred.

SHE. And in every one of them there are two or three people who won't laugh?

HE. Yes. Almost always.

SHE. And who arranges for these two or three people to be distributed throughout each auditorium?

HE. Nobody. They come on their own.

SHE. Listen, then maybe all of them have gathered together tonight in this auditorium?

HE. No! That's impossible!

SHE. Why? I could understand it if the ticket seller didn't just sell tickets at random, but did it selectively. "I can't sell you a ticket, citizen. Our quota is full. Three gloomy people already bought tickets. Try another auditorium,

185

maybe they still have some vacancies…."

HE. You know, it's interesting, I wonder why some people don't laugh.

SHE. In my opinion, there are different reasons. Some people don't laugh because others aren't laughing.

HE. How's that?

SHE. Well, for example, subordinates don't laugh because their bosses aren't laughing.

HE. But what about bosses?

SHE. Bosses don't want to laugh in front of their subordinates. It's demeaning. They might lose their authority. And some people don't laugh because they are doing mathematics during the show.

HE. Mathematics?

SHE. Yes. They're counting. One: Two tickets at eighteen. Two: Two pieces of cake at two-sixty. Three: The metro here, a taxi home. Four: A glass of soda. You think you can make someone like that laugh? And then there are some men who don't laugh because they are trying to figure out what they'll say to their wives when they get home.

HE. But that's foolish. Just say you were at a meeting and you can laugh all you want.

SHE. But what if she doesn't believe you?

HE. Why shouldn't she believe you? Most good wives know that meetings can run overtime.

SHE. True. Most good wives may know that, but they also know their own husbands good and well. Incidentally, you're a man. Do you know why women don't laugh?

HE. Who knows why women don't laugh? Half the time you can't even figure out why they are crying.

SHE. And then there are times when husbands and wives don't laugh in tandem. The wife doesn't laugh because she's wearing a new dress and she's waiting to show it off and stun everybody at intermission.

HE. What about the husband?

SHE. The husband doesn't laugh because his wife just ordered a second new dress. And then there are those who don't laugh professionally.

HE. How's that?

SHE. Well, critics, for instance. You come to a show, laugh, and then you find out later that the show wasn't funny. Why laugh? You might compromise yourself.

HE. True, laughter for critics is no laughing matter…

SHE. And for us actors…

HE. In my opinion, laughter isn't the main thing for us actors. The main thing for an actor is to create a joyous, festive atmosphere for the audience.

SHE. I agree. Personally, I know two kinds of actors. It's enough for one kind merely to appear on stage for the audience's mood to become joyous and festive. The other kind comes out on stage, talks forever, and the audience becomes joyous and festive only when they finally leave the stage. Don't you agree?

HE. I do.

SHE. Then why don't you get off the stage? Announce the next number and get out of here!

Appendix

The Suicide at the Vakhtangov Theater:
A Document

TRANSCRIPT OF A MEETING OF THE
ARTISTIC-POLITICAL COUNCIL OF THE
VAKHTANGOV STATE THEATER, SEPTEMBER 17, 1930[1]

KAZACHENKO[2] — Comrades, I'm not going to focus on several errors of a purely ideological order, a whole series of expressions—clearly unnecessary for us and alien to our ideology—which are put forward in this play. I don't want to say that this was done on purpose, but they are alien to us. For example, take an expression like: "Where else can an unemployed worker shoot himself, except in the bathroom," "Stores are being closed," or, "Public opinion is nothing but a factory of slogans."[3] All of this wouldn't carry so much weight if something would counteract these words and ideas. But since nothing counteracts them, these expressions and thoughts are nothing but food for the bourgeoisie, which will watch this play with pleasure and laugh at it. Let's assume it would be possible to annihilate these things, which are inadmissible in a purely ideological sense. That is, speaking essentially, what does this play consist of? What is its goal, its purpose? What does it give the spectator? It's nothing but a bouquet for the bourgeoisie. Moreover, it is presented exclusively incorrectly, sort of comically. After all, in recent times, the bourgeoisie has been living out its final days and is in no mood for comedy. Therefore, it is presented incorrectly. One wonders, is the bourgeoisie so serious in our age of industrialization that it can make us want to pay attention to it? It doesn't deserve that. We have more valuable and important problems. And, for that reason, such a play which paints a picture of the bourgeoisie is absolutely pointless and unnecessary for us. In it, we can often see the shadow of thoughts about the problem of the intelligentsia's role in the revolution, and it is presented clumsily. Who is presented here as central figures? There isn't any intelligentsia. What we have is a bouquet, a complex, a combination of a

---

[1] This is a raw stenographer's transcript of the remarks made about *The Suicide* shortly after a reading of the play. As such, the language is highly conversational and bears all the convolutions and peculiarities of unguarded speech. Moreover, several of the speakers are clearly uneducated. In this translation, I have attempted to find a balance between providing a coherent text and maintaining the undeniable color of the speakers' often chaotic remarks.

[2] I was unable to identify this speaker.

[3] Throughout the transcript, most quotes from *The Suicide* are paraphrases rather than faithful renditions of the text. The Vakhtangov Theater copy probably differed from those Erdman submitted to the Meyerhold Theater and the Moscow Art Theater, but most of the discrepancies here are certainly due to the speakers' carelessness.

priest, a kulak,[4] a merchant[5] and a petty bourgeois. They have to be differentiated. We have to understand that they are class enemies. Do you really think that class enemies are waging their battle by assuring the public that, as they say, "we are dying"? No. They find other methods for their struggle—elements of arson and sabotage. That is their direct method of struggle. But here, they are presented as some sort of comedians who want to do something but don't do anything. For that reason, the play does not hit its mark.

I recently compared this play to *The Warrant.* In that play the basic idea was clear. In that play the bourgeoisie sensed that it had to assimilate itself into society somehow and, in the course of the whole play, it conducted a policy of assimilation, which, in the end, is exposed. In that play you could see the basic thread. But here in this play there is no such thread. Of course, you can't deny that the play is written wittily and that we all laughed. But, I also laughed when I used to read Averchenko.[6] But whenever I read his stories—two days later I can't remember them anymore. And it seems to me that, if we were to toss such a major play out into the masses, it would be hasty and incorrect.

One has to regret that comrade Erdman, a talented author, did not direct his energy at a whole series of more timely questions which need to be illuminated for the public.

LEMBERG[7] — We are so lacking, so poor in talented plays that it seems to us that we have found an author who has a brilliant command of the pen. And it would seem that we should be happy to have found such a talented play. But, at least as it concerns me, I don't experience any such joy. The author constantly walks the sharp edge of a knife, drawing his spectator along after him. And the double-entendres, of which this play is full, invariably fall off the knife's edge—not in the direction of ridiculing the bourgeoisie—but in the direction of ridiculing the Soviet public. A demarcation line like that is very risky. It causes us to stand on guard and listen more thoughtfully and sensitively to the wisecracks of which this author has such a command. I don't think that these wisecracks are in the interests of the spectator. The working spectator will laugh at first, and then, towards the

---

[4] Properly speaking, the Russian word, "kulak," designates a wealthy peasant farmer, against whom the Soviet government waged a bitter battle in the late 1920s and early 1930s. In common usage it also referred to any well-off petty businessman. The speaker may have in mind Alexander Kalabushkin, the director of the shooting gallery.

[5] In some versions of *The Suicide,* the butcher Pugachyov is identified as a merchant.

[6] Arkady Averchenko (1881-1925) was a popular author of humorous stories and plays in the first two decades of the 20th century. He left the Soviet Union in 1920, after which his works were labeled as unfit for publication or staging.

[7] This was probably K. F. Lemberg, a member of the factory committee at the Moscow Regional Electric Plant, who often participated in Artistic-Political Councils at various theaters.

end, he will get bored of this author's wisecracks and then go home, without taking with him that significant and profound content which we would like to see in this play.

I suppose, that—without going into a discussion of individual details of this play—I should say that this play is inadmissible for the Vakhtangov Theater, or for any other Soviet theater for that matter.

ARTAMONOV[8] — Whoever speaks out against this play cannot pass over its talent in silence. Therefore, before saying anything else about it, I must bow down before a talented play. The play is written with great talent, although I must admit, it's not for us. If a play like this were to be presented on stage for the spectator, it would cause a reaction that would be extremely disadvantageous for us. Whom does this play mobilize and for whom would such a production be intended? Obviously, neither the working spectator nor the Soviet intelligentsia. I would suggest the play will find resonance in those very segments of society, against whom an all-out attack of the class war has been declared in our country. So, what good would such a call to our clear enemies do the Vakhtangov Theater—when our path leads in the exact opposite direction? That is all the more true in this time of an intensified class war—a moment, when it wasn't so long ago that the Kondratyev, Groman and Sukhanov group was arrested.[9] After all, no one is so naive as to think that the arrest of this group and the liquidation of a series of seditious organizations has exhausted the class war. Imagine for a minute that you don't know the name of the play's author, and you would think that it was written by someone in emigration.

That is the situation Erdman has fallen into with this play, knowingly or not (one wants to think and believe—unknowingly). Because, in a subtly veiled form, this play contains a hidden protest of the "intelligentsia," which, in places, is invested with dual meanings. In other words: "Understand it as you will."

Every single character in the play speaks in a language which cannot be called anything other than reactionary. And this philosophy of theirs—the philosophy of an offended, dissatisfied, intellectual philistine—is the play's essential leitmotif. Listen carefully to the philosophy of a couple of the play's characters:

1st character — Podsekalnikov

"The unemployed aren't allowed to work." "I read Marx and I didn't like him." "Public opinion is a factory of slogans." "When war is declared, a man

---

[8] Georgy Adamovich Artamonov was deputy director of the Vakhtangov Theater in 1930.

[9] Nikolai Kondratyev, Vladimir Groman and Nikolai Sukhanov were prominent economists accused of belonging to the so-called Working Peasants Party, the falsified case against which entailed 100,000 arrests. The case went to "court" September 2, 1930 amidst a vitriolic publicity campaign mounted by the OGPU, i.e., the secret police.

asks what age group is being drafted. He doesn't ask why the war is being fought." "I gave my right hand to the revolution and now it votes against me." "Keep your revolution to yourself and just give me a decent salary and a peaceful life." "When we say life is hard, it makes life easier." "I've got the truth, but there's no paper to write it on." "People and members of the Party." His address, "Is that really an international situation? *(Reads a newspaper)* It's written here in the chronicle of events that an eighteen year-old girl poisoned herself to death—now there's a real international incident." And, finally, you can assume that the story about the chicken with its head cut off is about the intelligentsia, which continues to walk and live, although it's lost its head.

Second character — Aristarkh Dominikovich

What kind of thoughts and views does he have?

"The intelligentsia is a slave in the harem of the proletariat." "Those without ideas want to die, while those who have ideas don't want to die. These days we need ideological corpses more than ever." "Our government would be better off turning up its toes than extending a hand." "Shoot yourself as a social activist, you are not alone." "The intelligentsia is silent because it is forced to be silent." "It is impossible to speak, but you can speak, citizen Podsekalnikov. You're going to die, anyway." "Protect the intelligentsia." And finally, the story about the chicken and its baby ducks, which, according to the nature of the story, should have had another fate in store for her. But here, she is forced to do what she shouldn't.

Characters of a secondary importance.

Margarita Ivanovna—"Why is he shooting himself in the bathroom?" Margarita[10] Lukyanovna—"Where else can an unemployed worker go?"

Semyon Semyonovich—"I have the desire, an estimate and an instruction booklet. I don't have a horn." Alexander Petrovich—"You're not the only one, citizen Podsekalnikov."

Alexander Petrovich[11]—finishes his speech, "O, Russia! Where are you racing to? Give me your answer."

Serafima Ilinishna—"There's so much to be done in Russia that there aren't enough connections to go around."

And then we hear various discussions of art. This question is of particular interest to us.

"Art is a red slave in the harem of the proletariat." "Have your inspirations within the bounds of the law." "Art is an endless game of fanfares on all kinds of topics at the table of the proletariat." "I'm not a critic, I'm a butcher."

Let's assume that these are negative characters and that they should be expected to express such nonsense. (We must keep in mind that the lines I

---

[10] The speaker or the stenographer confused the two characters, Margarita Ivanovna and Mariya Lukyanovna.

[11] In the play, these lines, which are quoted from the end of Nikolai Gogol's novel, *Dead Souls,* are actually spoken by the writer, Viktor Viktorovich.

have quoted are only a tenth of their kind in the play. We might even say that the entire text consists of nothing else.) But now let's look at the play's so-called "positive" character, Yegorka.[12] One might say that, among all these characters, he represents the people, the workers, the proletariat.

When you look carefully at this "positive" character, you will discover such ridicule in this "representation of the working class," that you won't believe your ears. Moreover, this ridicule aims its arrows at something larger still.

"I am a courier, and I want to read about couriers." This is a coercive comment about the limitations of taste and conceptions about literature. Erdman's Yegorushka is an extremely politically literate man. He already looks at life from a Marxist point of view. But, he races around philistine apartments like a worker correspondent,[13] seeking advice about a comma for his senseless articles, and he signs them with the pseudonym of "35 thousand couriers."

Yegorushka possesses such unique manners of thought as: There won't be any people under socialism and he can't drink right now because, "what if you get used to drinking and there's no wine under socialism? Let's see you get out of that one." Or, how do you like this idea: "I'll just climb up on the Eiffel Tower in Paris and look at it from a Marxist point of view. And it will become so disgusting...." Is that supposed to mean that if you don't look at it from a Marxist point of view that it will look good? Is that what you had in mind, comrade Erdman?

But let's return to the first character, Podsekalnikov. In reading the play very well, Boris Yevgenyevich Zakhava[14] presented Podsekalnikov in the same plan and tone as if he were Gulyachkin from *The Warrant*. But Podsekalnikov doesn't resemble Gulyachkin at all, Boris Yevgenyevich. Gulyachkin is nothing like Podsekalnikov. Podsekalnikov is a very intelligent person and the things he says are far from stupid. He propagates the kind of reactionary philosophy which is deserving of close scrutiny if for no other reason than it coincides with the philosophy of a certain segment of our public. Podsekalnikov appears to be a bourgeois, a philistine. He pretends to be. But, in fact, that is only a unique device intended to curse

---

[12] Note that the speaker automatically assumes that the Marxist courier, Yegor Timofey-evich, is a positive character.

[13] In the 1920s and early 1930s, factory workers were often enlisted to write articles for cultural and other publications. The purpose was to expand the influence of the working class on general social developments. Several of the speakers at this meeting were worker correspondents themselves. See, also, notes 7 and 21 to this document, and note 2 to *Moscow From a Point of View*.

[14] The actor and director Boris Zakhava (1896-1976) began an illustrious career in 1918 with Yevgeny Vakhtangov's theatrical circle. He was a founding member of the Vakhtangov Theater (1922) and remained with the theater to the end of his life. His remarks about *The Suicide* are contained later in this transcript.

Soviet power through the lips of a burned-out bourgeois and philistine. In his own time, Smirnov-Sokolsky[15] used the same device when he recited his feuilletons. And when he shouted—"I want to grumble, Mikhail Ivanych, I want to grumble"—it came out simpler and less offensive. It didn't arouse doubts. But Erdman's bourgeois philistines don't only grumble offensively—very offensively—they hiss, they ridicule and even use threats. Now, that is just too much.

This is not the time for the theater to provide an outlet for all these petty reactionary conversations and ideas.

"I don't want to shoot myself for the sake of my class, for the sake of science or for the sake of social ideals. I want to live. Let me live. We don't need much. Only to live and talk and speak in a whisper, a whisper, a whisper."

Basically, this is the point of the whole play: to prove that there exist such pitiful, "harmless," whining people who do nothing but busy themselves with their own bourgeois affairs and dream of the impossible. They won't bother you. Leave them alone. Their life is so hard that you can give them the right to grumble. As if to say, "Why shouldn't they grumble? After all, we truly do have a lot of problems." We can assume that Fedya Petunin's suicide and his suicide note bear witness that we really are living badly and that they are right to do what they do.

Translating this notion into political language, we can call this nothing more than a crime against the class war. And if that is so, consequently, the notion is seditious and deserving of severe criticism in the name of the public.

Our life is not so peaceful that we can make room for these kinds of ideas—all the more so in artistic form. Life is tense and filled with the struggle for socialist construction. The theme alone—to say nothing of the content—is seditious, and such a theme will not rouse the workers to the struggle for a new life. It will weaken the energy and will of the working class.

The play's talent forces me to ask the question: Can it be corrected and staged with artistic and theatrical means in the spirit of a true Soviet comedy? I think not. More to the point is that it should be rewritten from scratch.

AIZENSHTADT[16] — If we were to accept everything that has been said here, we would have to do away with the entire genre of drama. It would be absurd to put into the mouths of these characters words about the necessity

---

[15] See note 2 to "The Qualification Exams."

[16] I was unable to identify this speaker's first name. He may have been the same person who was the secretary of the Artistic-Political Council at the Bolshoi Theater in 1930, and whose name was spelled in Bolshoi documents as "Aizenshtat."

of industrializing the country, about the shortcomings we have, and words which would exhort them to struggle. The play's basic flaw is that its people are too petty and insignificant to waste a whole full-length play on doing battle with them. They are not drawn with sufficient clarity. Their own harmfulness is too insufficient. They have no place in our life. This is all something out of the past and, in my opinion, there just isn't any reason to struggle with it. That's the main thing.

ZAKHAVA — Georgy Adamovich concluded his remarks by asserting that a production could not possibly have the necessary resonance no matter what approach a director might take. I would like to call this assertion into doubt. It seems to me, that some of those who have spoken up to now have not analyzed the play ideologically. They have not yet discovered its social meaning. The most fallacious method of evaluating any work negatively is merely to list phrases without taking into account who is saying them and what the function of a given image is. It's obviously impossible to discern the play's meaning and its social significance if you go about selecting random phrases from various voices which have a counterrevolutionary, anti-Soviet tone, etc. For that reason, it's quite possible to miss the forest for all these trees. But it seems to me that there is a forest here. There is a thread in this forest which we can latch onto, and it is both necessary and timely. I will try to justify what I mean.

If we exclude the hero himself—Podsekalnikov—from the list of characters, we see that all the rest of the characters can be given an extremely satirical theatrical interpretation. This is quite easy and simple. It is possible to portray all these people in a way that—no matter what they say, no matter what they express—the result will be extremely vivid satirical characters who will discredit anything they say on their own. (The most daring phrases can be cleaned up.) The spectator will not believe anything that such a being might say. For me, this is not a world of living people—it is a dead world. (I exclude for now the main characters, Fedya Petunin and Podsekalnikov.) If we portray them by scenic means, then it seems to me that we can present them as a museum of oddities or wax figures.[17] This is an extremely interesting theatrical device. This would create splendid satirical masks in the spirit of Saltykov-Shchedrin or Sukhovo-Kobylin.[18] I am talking about Aristarkh

---

[17] Erdman may have used Zakhava's idea of a museum of oddities when writing the second variant of *The Hypnotist*. It includes a character who is the wife of a curator of such an institution. Furthermore, Zakhava's references to a "living" and "dead" world may have provided Erdman a basis for his references to "the living and the unliving" in the first music hall sketch and the first interlude for *Hamlet*.

[18] Mikhail Saltykov-Shchedrin (1826-1889) wrote some of the most bitterly satirical stories, novels and plays in Russian literature. Alexander Sukhovo-Kobylin (1817-1903) wrote the dramatic trilogy consisting of *Krechinsky's Wedding*, *The Case* and *Tarelkin's Death*. Their black humor and grotesque satire had a major influence on *The Suicide*.

Dominikovich, the butcher, the priest and other characters in the play. The case of the main character, Podsekalnikov, is different, in my opinion. And I believe that the play's fundamental meaning is expressed through this very character. Everything else is an absolutely dead, lifeless world, against the background of which this being, called Semyon Semyonovich Podsekalnikov, somehow manages to live. Who is he?

He is a philistine, a nonentity. No matter what he says about life or death—he is a total nonentity. What is a philistine? He is a representative of the petty-bourgeois psychology. Some comrades here have asked: "Who cares about philistine psychology? Who cares about philistinism? It is dying out. Its time has passed. We have more important matters to worry about. All the more so since these enemies of the working class have better methods of disorganizational work than suicide. They are struggling with the proletariat by means of sabotage, murder, conspiracies, etc. These are their real methods." It seems to me that those who have expressed such ideas underestimate several manifestations of our life and that they enter into contradiction with the declarations, thoughts and ideas which we have often heard in recent times in the name of the Party.

We know the following term: "Philistinism in the party ranks." We are familiar with such things as deviations in the Party. We know that the petty-bourgeois psychology and petty bourgeois elements are undermining workers and party members alike, right up to the top echelons of the Party. For that reason, I think that the comrades here have either expressed themselves improperly, or they have not thought things through completely.

Now. Of course sabotage and counterrevolutionary conspiracies are terrible things, but I would say that they are not what is most dangerous. For all of these things we have the GPU,[19] which is doing a pretty good job and which is coping pretty well with all of these dangers. It seems to me, that there are more dangerous things. For example: the coercive effect on the psychology of the builders of socialism and on those who are struggling for socialism. We know that such coercion exists. Otherwise, there would be no deviations. But no one has yet been able to show convincingly through artistic methods how this coercion functions, what is its chemical, molecular process, how this coercion works. And it seems to me that this is the play's very theme. This is an exceptional artistic work, both in its artistic nature, as well as in the content of its fundamental message. If the comrade considers that philistinism is a thing of the past—that it is not dangerous—then I would suggest that he go stand in a line sometime. There he will find this very philistinism, the representative of which, in my point of view, is this person, Semyon Semyonovich, who is deprived of any ideology whatsoever. His ideology is a "peaceful life." He's turned a deaf ear to everything else. His

---

[19] See note 11 to "The Qualification Exams."

ideology is to speak in a whisper while marching under the banner of "Life is hard." It seems to me that the comrade underestimates the importance for social life which is contained in this "Life is hard," and which sounds like the rustling of cockroaches.

And so I think that this circumstance forms the fundamental theme of this play. For that reason, in my point of view, Fedya Petunin is far and away the most necessary character. Without him, there is no play. Otherwise, it is nothing but an ill-aimed satire. The play's content arises at that moment when Fedya Petunin's name first appears. He possesses the kind of psychology which can easily be infested by a worm.[20] This circumstance is extremely vital, and the play, of course, achieves its thematic resolution in the finale. And, it seems to me that this has simply gone unnoticed. What is the point of the very end? I exclude Podsekalnikov from the wax museum of the other characters. In his final monologue—and this isn't bad, it's good—he is capable of winning—even if it is with a certain measure of disgust—at least some semblance of *pity* from the spectators. This is necessary in order for the finale to abruptly turn the spectator backwards. This is necessary in order for the spectator to sense all the more clearly the force of this play's blow. Fedya Petunin's suicide is a prosecutor's concluding speech in regards to Podsekalnikov. It is an extremely cruel speech. It is the blow, carried out on stage, which strikes at that very philistinism which seemed so harmless and capable of arousing the semblance of pity in the beginning. We have our share of problems and, for that reason, I don't think it would be such a bad idea to strike a painful blow at that philistinism which is capable of wielding powerful political influence. And in this sense, Podsekalnikov is a symbolical figure who epitomizes the quintessence of the petty bourgeois psychology, characterized as it is by the absolute lack of interest in anything whatsoever other than the desire to live a "quiet life." I consider that this is a good, strong blow. And I consider that we possess the theatrical means to carry it out and that the play gives us the grounds to use those theatrical means. First of all, if the play itself doesn't contain the necessary contrasts, that doesn't mean that we can't provide the necessary contrasts theatrically. We can create contrast. When Podsekalnikov is reading the paper about "the international situation," he thinks that the international situation is nonsense in comparison to the fact that a "tram car ran over some person." These words express the typical philistine psychology. We can find an absolutely topical contrast to this. Do you really think there aren't theatrical means for that? There are. Take, for example, Podsekalnikov's last monologue, where he talks about war and what age group is being drafted. We can also find the means for contrast here.

---

[20] In Act II, scene twenty-two and Act III, scene two of *The Suicide*, the writer Viktor Viktorovich speaks of Podsekalnikov's potential suicide as a worm that will gnaw at Fedya Petunin.

Georgy Adamovich uttered the phrase that Podsekalnikov appears to be a philistine and tells reactionary stories. What kind of stories does a philistine tell, other than reactionary ones? If we take that approach, then we are shut off from every possibility of portraying a negative character on stage. Because it's only natural that he is incapable of saying anything other than filth. Are we really not interested in what our enemies are saying? And if our enemies speak well, intelligently and with force, then there's nothing wrong with portraying that.

SHVARTSMAN[21] — Basically, I agree with comrade Artamonov, and when Boris Yevgenyevich says that his is an improper method of phrase-listing, I have to say that this is just a little untrue. The fact is that words like this flow throughout the entire play. It's not just one phrase. It's the whole play. All of its characters speak in this language. And those expressions which comrade Artamonov quoted—naturally, such phrases will definitely mobilize the spectator. Naturally, not the working spectator, but the philistine spectator who goes to the theater merely in order to squeak and exclaim in delight. Them, they will definitely mobilize. And I don't care how many of those phrases you cross out, you can't cross them all out, because the whole play is made up of them. Boris Yevgenyevich says that since a negative character is talking, that means you can't put some other words in his mouth. But what is contrasted to them in this play? Nothing. Yegor—a worker correspondent, a courier—is contrasted to them. But who is this worker correspondent who runs to his neighbors to get them to tell him where to put a comma? We don't have any such worker correspondents in our masses. They have all become politically and technically literate and they don't write articles like that. That isn't a realistic character, and giving a worker correspondent with a signature of 35 thousand couriers is a political error. This Yegorka—how does he imagine a socialism where, unfortunately, there won't be any vodka, there won't be any women, there won't be any people and there will only be masses? Contrasting all that together, what you get is sheer counterrevolution.

What is Boris Yevgenyevich saying? He thinks he can imagine them as wax figures in a museum. But he contradicts himself. If philistinism is still alive, then, at least, it can't be a wax museum. We have class enemies and we have to struggle with them, instead of mounting a struggle with windmills.

And then, Podsekalnikov, of course, is not a nonentity and his philosophy—it can probably infect more than just Fedya Petunin.

I think that there is absolutely no way we can give permission to this play. The author of all these characters mobilizes around this anecdotal incident of Podsekalnikov's suicide. But we know that there were attempts to capitalize

---

[21] I was unable to identify this speaker's first name. He was a worker correspondent who took part in Artistic-Political Councils at various Moscow theaters.

on Mayakovsky's death.[22] True, one of the heroes[23] says, "if only some leader would commit suicide. But all we have is some Podsekalnikov." And they want to capitalize on that. That's not realistic. I consider that this play is an absolutely seditious play, thanks primarily to its talent. Because it is written wittily, because the spectator will understand everything and all these lines are capable of unnoticeably feeding the philistines. If a worker went to see it, then, in any case, he doesn't need it. It doesn't mobilize any tasks or problems of our reality at all.

KHRUSTALYOV[24] — Comrades, in all the time our Artistic-Political Council has been active, we have given the stamp of "ideologically unfounded" to many of the plays we have heard. But this play, in my opinion, doesn't even deserve that. In my opinion, it can't be called anything but counterrevolutionary. And the sociological analysis which comrade Zakhava tried to give us—without providing any proofs, in my opinion—it ended up being insubstantial. In his defense speech, comrade Zakhava wanted to prove and object to those comrades who have said that there are no philistines left, that the philistine is an empty hole and that there's no point in struggling with him. I agree with him about that part. He says that there still are philistines, that we have to struggle with them, that it's a pretty significant force which we can't afford to overlook. And comrade Zakhava's entire talk boiled down to the idea that this play is a powerful blow against philistinism. And here, one has to ask: What is this play's goal? What is its basis? In my view, Erdman has two slogans here which express both the social tendency of this play and that right which he wants to win with this play. It is: "The worm will eat all." And this entire play screams about that. And the second slogan belongs to the philistine: "I love my stomach." This formula—to live in order to eat—it overshadows everything and is the starting point of all this play's conclusions. In other words, it will find resonance among these philistines. It does not strike a blow against philistines, but, on the contrary, forces the philistine to mobilize. All of those places with dual meanings about how the "intelligentsia is a slave in the harem of the proletariat"—all that won't sound the way we are told it will by comrade Zakhava, who says that we have theatrical devices which are capable of localizing the places which smell of counterrevolutionary tirades. Why, then, for, at least, *Zoya's Apartment*,[25]

---

[22] The speaker's reference to Mayakovsky's "death" rather than "suicide" (just five months earlier), indicates the extreme care with which people already touched on this subject. After Stalin canonized Mayakovsky as the "best and most talented" Soviet poet in 1935, there was no official recognition of his suicide for decades.

[23] Aristarkh Dominikovich says something similar to this in Act IV, scene sixteen.

[24] I was unable to identify this speaker.

[25] *Zoya's Apartment*, by Mikhail Bulgakov (1891-1940), premiered at the Vakhtangov Theater in 1926. After it was attacked ferociously in the press, Bulgakov and the Vakhtangov revised it substantially. It remained in repertory until 1929, when it was banned.

couldn't the Vakhtangov Theater find counterweights and make that play speak out in our Soviet language? After all, the theater had the necessary theatrical devices and means. Even so, *Zoya's Apartment* didn't speak in our language. And *The Suicide* will definitely speak out the same way. No matter what the theater tries, it will not speak out in our language. Comrade Artamonov here gave an absolutely correct analysis, that this play intersects not with the thoughts and hopes of the Soviet intelligentsia, but with those who are hanging out in the courtyards of Parisian cafés. It will give them just what they are looking for. In my opinion, this is no protest of the intelligentsia. This kind of intelligentsia has become extinct. The fundamental mass of the intelligentsia has joined in lock step with the working class, while the other intelligentsia—the white guard—it protests. Podsekalnikov wants to give it the right to whisper. But Erdman wants to give it a trumpet of Jericho, so that it can bellow out from the stage at the Vakhtangov Theater. In my opinion, we cannot give this white-guardism an opportunity to speak through a Soviet theater. I propose rejecting this play for production at the theater.

KISELYOV[26] — If there is a protest here of the intelligentsia against our government and working class, then it is that the play plainly states that a summons to, and organization of, protest, is being prepared for the future. Of course, Zakhava portrayed it as not being so terrible. But there is plenty in this play that speaks about this summons which is trying to crush the might of our country. I not only consider that it can't possibly be produced in the Vakhtangov Theater, but that it can't be produced anywhere in the entire Soviet Union. I think it's necessary to place a definitive ban on this play.

SHUBIN[27] — It's not difficult to prove that this play is seditious in general, and, in particular for the Vakhtangov Theater. What's interesting is to get to the bottom of this work from an ideological point of view. There is no doubt that the play is funny. But the truth of its laughter is unintelligible and two-edged. It seems to me that working on this play right now, in 1930, would be the same thing as rehashing what Meyerhold did in 1924—a rehashing of *The Warrant*.[28] What is my understanding of this work? Six or seven years ago, the play, *The Warrant*, painted a detailed picture of petty bourgeois philistines at a time when they had just been liberated from the fear instilled in them by War Communism.[29] True, the petty bourgeoisie was

---

[26] I was unable to identify this speaker.

[27] I was unable to identify this speaker.

[28] Meyerhold's production of *The Warrant* actually premiered April 20, 1925.

[29] War Communism is the term used to define the fundamental policies of the Soviet government during the Russian Civil War (1918-1921). It included the nationalization of industry, services and land, and the introduction of compulsory labor.

still hesitating a little, but Erdman seized on a moment in his play when the petty bourgeoisie was still laughing at itself. Now, these six or seven years don't exist for Erdman. All of these groupings....[30] And now there is no point in interpreting or ridiculing the question of philistinism. We have to underscore the fundamental thing: that the philistine, under the influence of the period of reconstruction, often races back and forth, organizes underground organizations and political blocks. This is the theme we have to attack. Neither the author nor the play give us any of this in any form. They are still existing in 1924. And if the mask of the intensified class war is lurking under this, then, or course, from that point of view, the play is seditious. And I consider that, for the Vakhtangov Theater, the choice of a play standing on a point of view from 1924 is unsuccessful, to say the least.

KUZA[31] — It is my responsibility to speak in the name of the theater's directorate, which accepted this play in the absence of Georgy Adamovich Artamonov. First of all, what was it in the given play that so interested the theater, and why did we approach it so warmly? I won't try to hide that we made no attempts at a detailed analysis of this play. All of us—as artists— were primarily attracted by the splendid form of this brilliant theatrical work. We have not had a good theatrical work in a long time. We are starved and we stand shouting on every street corner: "We want a talented theatrical work." We haven't seen such a contemporary play since *A Conspiracy of Feelings.*[32] Therefore, this play primarily attracted us as a brilliant example of dramatic literature that provides the opportunity of creating a splendid production that is near and dear in its form to our theater. That is the main idea which ruled the Vakhtangov Theater. I want to emphasize that.

I have listened carefully to all the comrades here and I must admit that I have yet to hear an exhaustive Marxist analysis. In their remarks, comrades Shubin and Artamonov attempted to give analyses, but, unfortunately, I have yet to hear in all of the remarks a coherent and ideologically exhaustive analysis. For that reason, those hesitations which I have—they remain in force.

What is the problem here, after all? Why such panic? I assure you that the Artistic-Political Council has approached the given play in a rather panicky fashion. If the Artistic-Political Council is right, then we must expose the counterrevolutionary essence of this play to the very end, moreover, since it is not exhausted by a mere series of phrases which are put in the mouths of

---

[30] The sentence is unfinished in the transcript.

[31] Vasily Kuza (1902-1941) was an actor and director at the Vakhtangov Theater. At the time of this discussion, he was also the director's assistant on repertory. His potentially brilliant career was cut short when he was killed in a bombing raid on Moscow during WWII.

[32] *A Conspiracy of Feelings,* by Yury Olesha (1899-1960), was a stage adaptation of the author's own novella, *Envy.* It premiered at the Vakhtangov Theater in 1929.

our enemies—the characters of the play. It's another thing to ask whether it can be allowed for the theater or not. When one comrade here said that philistinism is such an insignificant element that there's no point in talking about it, I have to allow myself to say that this comrade commits a serious political error. Philistinism in our country supports itself on a series of class strata. Philistinism seeps even into the ranks of the working class. So, tell me comrades, why do you think that the self-seekers, liars and idlers, who are hindering us from fulfilling the industrial and financial plans in many factories, don't march under Podsekalnikov's slogan? Why are you so convinced that those who march under Podsekalnikov's slogan are not philistines?

It is my opinion that the workers who are abandoning the collective farms—after all, aren't we being summoned to liquidate sabotage?—all of them are marching under the slogan of the hero of this play, Podsekalnikov. One comrade here said that the author is constantly balancing on the sharp edge of a knife. That is correct. He seized on an extremely sensitive topic. A production can have the resonance of a Parisian production in a Parisian émigré café, or it can be a powerful production here. It all depends on the devices which are used to do it, and on the position from which the theater and author aim their fire. If we aren't convinced that Yegorushka is a negative character—that he is one of those figures we can find in our present life, such as all kinds of false shock workers and false worker correspondents—then we can remove this character entirely. Because he may be able to mobilize the spectator against the working class. It is not our intention to create some sort of false proletarian or pasquinade on the proletariat out of a single character. In fact, he is not a proletarian. In my opinion, he has infiltrated the proletariat from the petty bourgeoisie. There is only one positive character here. That is Fedya Petunin. And truly, in such condensed satirical plays...[33]

---

[33] The text of the transcript breaks off unfinished.

Two Fragments from *The Hypnotist*

Late 1930s

Variant One[1]

CHARACTERS IN ORDER OF APPEARANCE

ANTONINA GAVRILOVNA
PORFIRY FILIPPOVICH
GRIGORY ANTONOVICH
MAVRA YEGOROVNA
VLADIMIR IVANOVICH GOLOSHCHAPOV — her son

ACT ONE
SCENE ONE

(A room in the home of Vladimir Ivanovich Goloshchapov. Antonina Gavrilovna, Porfiry Filippovich and Grigory Antonovich sit silently. Mavra Yegorovna sits on a trunk off to the side reading a book. All is quiet. Snow is visible through the window)

SCENE TWO

(Enter Vladimir Ivanovich. All except Mavra Yegorovna stand and bow)

VLADIMIR IVANOVICH. *(Looks everyone over)* It seems that everyone here is family, excepting my mother?
GRIGORY ANTONOVICH. Everyone that you summoned is here, Vladimir Ivanovich.
VLADIMIR IVANOVICH. Good. Mama, please go into the next room for now. I would like to remain among family. *(Exit Mavra Yegorovna)*

SCENE THREE

(The same except Mavra Yegorovna)

PORFIRY FILIPPOVICH. What's wrong, Vladimir Ivanovich?
VLADIMIR IVANOVICH. I have summoned you all, comrades, with the

---

[1] Erdman worked on *The Hypnotist* between 1934 and 1941. It is uncertain when these two fragments were written.

intent of informing you of a very unpleasant piece of news. A hypnotist has come to town.[2]

PORFIRY FILIPPOVICH. What? A hypnotist?

ANTONINA GAVRILOVNA. What hypnotist?

VLADIMIR IVANOVICH. That famous pupil of professor Bekhterev, and student of Indian thought, Alphonse Daudet.[3]

GRIGORY ANTONOVICH. I have the feeling I've heard that name somewhere before.

ANTONINA GAVRILOVNA. You're always getting feelings of some kind.

PORFIRY FILIPPOVICH. Why did he come, Vladimir Ivanovich?

VLADIMIR IVANOVICH. He came to hypnotize.

PORFIRY FILIPPOVICH. Here?

ANTONINA GAVRILOVNA. Who?

VLADIMIR IVANOVICH. The answer is obvious: those who want to be hypnotized.

PORFIRY FILIPPOVICH. Aha, those who want to be hypnotized. Where is he going to find fools like that, Vladimir Ivanovich?

VLADIMIR IVANOVICH. We have been advised to select them out of our own habitat.

GRIGORY ANTONOVICH. Who suggested that?

VLADIMIR IVANOVICH. Pochekutov. Pochekutov told me firmly and concisely. "Life," he said, "demands insistently that you, as workers in this club, come out shooting on the front lines on this score."

ANTONINA GAVRILOVNA. Oh, my Lord!

VLADIMIR IVANOVICH. Would anyone like to say anything?

PORFIRY FILIPPOVICH. Vladimir Ivanovich, wouldn't we be better off consulting someone about this first?

VLADIMIR IVANOVICH. Consult? Aren't you romantic, Porfiry Filippovich. Whom are you going to consult? These days, everyone soaks everyone in spittle, and everyone undermines everyone like a mole. I can't even trust my own mother and you want to consult some unknown person?

GRIGORY ANTONOVICH. You're absolutely right, Vladimir Ivanovich. Man, these days, is a beast.

VLADIMIR IVANOVICH. I don't agree with you, Grigory Antonovich. Let's say man is a lynx. Lynxes don't defile their young. No. A lynx adores its offspring. On the other hand, Mavra Yegorovna defiled me. And who is she? My mother. And whom did she defile? Her own natural son.

ANTONINA GAVRILOVNA. Isn't that interesting, Volodya. Did she defile

---

[2] This line is a play on the opening of Nikolai Gogol's *The Inspector General*.

[3] Vladimir Bekhterev (1857-1927) was a prominent Russian neurologist and psychologist. Alphonse Daudet was a popular 19th century French writer.

you terribly?

VLADIMIR IVANOVICH. I'll say she did. And how do you think it all started, Antonina Gavrilovna? It was pure nonsense. A few thespians came to see me recently. They hemmed and hawed a bit and then said, "Vladimir Ivanovich, for a play we're working on, we need someone to consult us on what life used to be like. We have some doubts," they said, "about the figure of the merchant, what kind of clothes the village constable wore, and the governor's two governesses. Vladimir Ivanovich," they said, "we want to avoid getting hung up in historical veracity." "All right thespians," I said, "if you can keep your language clean at your meetings, I'll send you my mother this evening. She's a woman," I told them, "an elderly one and she's been around. And while she was never a governor's governess, she knows what a village constable looks like. She's just what you need, thespians." So I primped and primed my mother and sent her off to rehearsals that very day. The old woman moaned and groaned a bit and then set off. She came home at eleven-thirty and before she even got through the door she said, "How come people in your club have steam coming out their mouths, Volodya?" I told her it's a law of physics. She said, "We don't live by the laws of physics anymore, Volodya. We live by the laws of the Soviet state and they ought to keep the temperature at 60° and not 48°." "Mama," I told her, "they invited you to consult on what life used to be like. Can't you talk about anything besides the new life?"

GRIGORY ANTONOVICH. I'll bet that was Fedka Pankratov who was agitating her.

PORFIRY FILIPPOVICH. No doubt. Him and Zoika Shaternikova.

ANTONINA GAVRILOVNA. How base. Working over somebody's mother to get at somebody else.

VLADIMIR IVANOVICH. That mother hasn't been born yet, Antonina Gavrilovna, who could have any effect on me. I just tell her, "Mama, I've always been a hothead and I'll always be a hothead."

Variant Two

CHARACTERS IN ORDER OF APPEARANCE

ANTONINA GAVRILOVNA — wife of the museum curator Konstantin Sergeyevich Timofeyev
PORFIRY FILIPPOVICH
VIKTOR VIKTOROVICH
MAVRA YEGOROVNA
VLADIMIR IVANOVICH ZATRAVKIN — her son

ACT ONE

(A room in the home of Vladimir Ivanovich Zatravkin)

SCENE ONE

(Antonina Gavrilovna, Porfiry Filippovich and Viktor Viktorovich sit in total silence at a table. In a corner, Mavra Yegorovna sits on a trunk reading a book)

SCENE TWO

(Enter Zatravkin in a half-length fur coat and a fur hat. All those sitting at table rise, bow and take their seats again)

ZATRAVKIN. *(Looks everyone over)* It seems that everyone here is family, excepting my mother?
VIKTOR VIKTOROVICH. Everyone that you summoned is here, Vladimir Ivanovich.
ZATRAVKIN. Good! *(Takes off his hat and coat)* Mama, please go into the next room for now. I would like to remain among family. *(Exit Mavra Yegorovna)*

SCENE THREE

(The same except Mavra Yegorovna)

PORFIRY FILIPPOVICH. What's wrong, Vladimir Ivanovich?
ZATRAVKIN. I have summoned you all, comrades, with the intent of informing you of a very unpleasant piece of news. A hypnotist has come to town.
PORFIRY FILIPPOVICH. What? A hypnotist?
ANTONINA GAVRILOVNA. What hypnotist?
ZATRAVKIN. That famous pupil of professor Bekhterev, and student of Indian thought, Alphonse Daudet.
GRIGORY ANTONOVICH. I have the feeling I've heard that name

somewhere before.

ANTONINA GAVRILOVNA. You're always getting feelings of some kind. Why did he come, Vladimir Ivanovich?

ZATRAVKIN. He came to hypnotize.

PORFIRY FILIPPOVICH. Here?

ANTONINA GAVRILOVNA. Who?

ZATRAVKIN. The answer is obvious: those who want to be hypnotized.

PORFIRY FILIPPOVICH. Aha, those who want to be hypnotized. Where is he going to find fools like that, Vladimir Ivanovich?

VLADIMIR IVANOVICH. We have been advised to select them out of our own habitat.

VIKTOR VIKTOROVICH. Who suggested that?

ZATRAVKIN. Pochekutov. Pochekutov told me firmly and concisely. "Life," he said, "demands insistently that we, as workers in this club, come out shooting on the front lines on this score. Only," he says, "be on the constant lookout and, in addition, keep in mind your experience with hobgoblins."

PORFIRY FILIPPOVICH. With who?

ZATRAVKIN. Hobgoblins.

PORFIRY FILIPPOVICH. What are they, Vladimir Ivanovich?

ZATRAVKIN. You mean you don't know, Porfiry Filippovich?

ANTONINA GAVRILOVNA. He couldn't know anything about that, Volodya, he was sent here after the hobgoblins.

ZATRAVKIN. Well, since that's the case, I can inform him in two words. It goes like this. Last year, we organized an anti-religious museum at the club. The curator was Konstantin Sergeyevich Timofeyev, Antonina Gavrilov-na's husband, Porfiry Filippovich. And so, right before the Easter campaign, he succeeded in obtaining for the museum two unique exhibits, a real hobgoblin and an ancient pistol. Then, it was suddenly discovered that the hobgoblin wasn't real at all and that there is no such thing as an ancient pistol.

PORFIRY FILIPPOVICH. How did they find that out?

ZATRAVKIN. From the newspapers. They delivered our newspapers and we started reading them. In one of the central papers we read an account of a congress of museum workers where a certain authoritarian comrade began working over our hobgoblin as a clear example of uncritical attitudes towards unique exhibits. True, he said we have made colossal progress, but then he added that some people are lagging behind. That's when he lit into us. And every time the article mentioned the word hobgoblin, it was followed by the word "laughter" in parentheses. Well, the participants of the congress may have laughed in parentheses, but we all burst out into tears. It was obvious we wouldn't be able to hush up the Moscow newspaper, so we ran off to our unique exhibits in the museum instead. We were all as pale as could be and nobody knew what to do.

PORFIRY FILIPPOVICH. What did you do?

ZATRAVKIN. We removed him.

PORFIRY FILIPPOVICH. The hobgoblin?

ZATRAVKIN. The curator.

ANTONINA GAVRILOVNA. Only that wasn't the end of it. Ever since, parentheses have been suffocating Konstantin Sergeyevich.

PORFIRY FILIPPOVICH. Suffocating him? How?

ANTONINA GAVRILOVNA. At night. Oh, Porfiry Filippovich, it became so terrifying to sleep with him, that I kept wanting to invite somebody else to sleep with us. As soon as he'd close his eyes, he'd start shouting, "Parentheses! Parentheses! Open up! I'm suffocating. Comrades, they're suffocating me, they're suffocating me!" Naturally, I'd start shaking him and then he would grab me by the throat with his hands, look me in the eyes and shout, "Hobgoblin!" And what was most killing of all, comrades, was that his eyes were always wide open when he would say that. Well, obviously, I would say, "Punkin…"

ZATRAVKIN. You mean you call him "Punkin?"

ANTONINA GAVRILOVNA. At night I do. And so I would ask him, "How come you don't sleep at night, Punkin?" "Don't you hear?" he would ask me. "What?" I would ask. "They're laughing," he would say. "Where?" I would ask. "In Moscow," he would say. "Punkin," I would say, "do you really mean that when people laugh in Moscow 9,000 kilometers away, that's enough to wake you up? You have to be joking. Why don't you go back to sleep?" And he would say, "I can't sleep under such conditions any more." Well, naturally, as a woman, I was offended. I said to him, "You and I have slept together under the same conditions for years and suddenly you can't sleep?" And he would say, "From now on, I will only sleep to the accompaniment of the audience's sustained applause and, until they start printing that in parentheses after my name, I categorically refuse to sleep with you." We lived miserably for a whole month and then he bought himself some woolen long underwear and disappeared into the wilderness.

PORFIRY FILIPPOVICH. What does a museum curator do in the wilderness?

ANTONINA GAVRILOVNA. Mine steers the center pole of a cart. And I must say, he does it marvelously. He earned two bonuses in half a year.

PORFIRY FILIPPOVICH. Are they good?

ANTONINA GAVRILOVNA. Well, I thought the first one was quite nice, but the second wasn't so good, Porfiry Filippovich.

PORFIRY FILIPPOVICH. What are they?

ANTONINA GAVRILOVNA. The first one was a gramophone and the second was a gramophone.

ZATRAVKIN. We don't have time for bonuses, Antonina Gavrilovna. Because of this Alphonse Daudet, we may wake up one day and find that we have no income at all.

ANTONINA GAVRILOVNA. How's that?

ZATRAVKIN. Because we haven't been informed exactly how we should relate to him. If he's a fraud, Antonina Gavrilovna, we must exhibit bolshevik vigilance and expose his true face. If he's a real scientist, comrades, we'll have to create the proper conditions for the public to take an interest.

ANTONINA GAVRILOVNA. Then that's what we'll do, Vladimir Ivanovich.

ZATRAVKIN. Don't be so hasty. What are you going to do if you start creating conditions for him and then find out that he's a fraud? Even worse, what if he is a real scientist, comrades, and we reveal his true face? Imagine how it could all end. For something like that, they'd stick us with such a hobgoblin that we'd all end up on a fast track to hell, dear comrades.

ANTONINA GAVRILOVNA.[4] Then, what are we going to do?

ZATRAVKIN. First of all, I want to clarify the following. Do you know, comrades, what our view on hypnosis is?

ANTONINA GAVRILOVNA. You mean we have a view on hypnosis, Vladimir Ivanovich?

ZATRAVKIN. Absolutely. We have to keep a watchful eye on everything. Antonina Gavrilovna, why are you afraid of speaking?

ANTONINA GAVRILOVNA. I am not afraid of speaking, I am remaining silent.

ZATRAVKIN. In moments like this, he is afraid of speaking who remains silent.

---

[4] From here to the end of the fragment, Erdman did not designate who is speaking. I inserted the names based on the context.